Shades of Grace

Shades of Grace

BARBARA DELINSKY

AVON

An Imprint of HarperCollinsPublishers

A hardcover edition of this book was published in January 1996 by HarperCollins. A rack-size edition of this book was published in February 1997 by Harper paperbacks and in November 2005 by HarperTorch.

HarperCollins books may be purchased for educational, business, or sales promotional use. For information please write: Special Markets Department, HarperCollins Publishers, 10 East 53rd Street, New York, NY 10022.

First Avon paperback edition published 2009.

Designed by Rhea Braunstein

Library of Congress Cataloging-in-Publication Data available upon request.

ISBN 978-0-06-171352-1

09 10 11 12 [WBC/RRD] 10 9 8 7 6 5 4 3 2 1

Acknowledgments

As a rule, the first ones ever to see a manuscript of mine are my agent and my editor. *Shades of Grace*, by virtue of its subject matter, begged exception. Book research gave me facts, but for insight into the emotions involved, I relied on discussions with any number of people who have lived with Alzheimer's disease in those closest to them. Two of those people generously and graciously agreed to read my manuscript to assure its authenticity.

The first was Anna-Mae Barney, who spent twelve years as a caregiver for her mother. We met quite by accident when my book was nearly done. When I learned that her mother's name was Grace, I knew she had to read my book.

The second was Margaret Mullen, who, as program director at the Newton & Wellesley Alzheimer Center, works on a daily basis with patients and their families. For me, Peggy was both resource and reader. For those patients and their families, she is a daily source of support and comfort.

So, my thanks to Anna-Mae and Peggy. My thanks also to Karen Solem, who loved this book from the start, and to Steve and the boys—Eric, Andrew, and Jeremy—for bearing with me yet again.

A more poignant thanks to my aunt Sadie. When I was in sixth grade, I was given a homework assignment for which I had to write a descriptive essay on the sun. After struggling for hours, I was close to tears. Taking me calmly in hand, she had me speak my thoughts aloud while she wrote them down. All I had to do then was to reorganize and polish my own words.

To this day, when I am struggling through a particularly thorny patch of writing, I remember the calm she projected, the deep breath she had me take, the satisfaction she shared with me.

I wish she could share with me now, for the satisfactions of my life are deeper and more stunning than either of us ever imagined. But she lives in her own diminished world and doesn't recognize me anymore.

Shades of Grace

One

Character is a commodity best set off by tasteful clothes, refined speech, and dignified carriage. Any good merchandiser knows that the wrapping is a preview of the gift inside.

—GRACE DORIAN, from an interview with Barbara Walters

Grace Dorian stared in bewilderment at the papers on her desk. She had no idea how they had gotten there, had no idea what they were for.

She riffled the stack, searching for hints. Not papers. Letters. Some were handwritten, some typed, some on white letterhead, colored stationery, torn notebook paper.

"Dear Grace . . ."

"Dear Grace . . ."

"Dear Grace . . ."

Think, she cried, fighting panic. People were writing her letters, lots of people, judging from the courier pack that stood open on the chair. It brimmed with more of what she had on her desk. They were there for a reason.

She put a hand to her chest and willed herself to stay calm. The heel of her hand pressed her thudding heart. Her fingertips touched beads.

Rosary beads? No. Not rosary beads. *Pearls*, Grace. *Pearls*.

Frightened eyes cast about for the familiar, lighting on the mahogany credenza, the velvet drapes, the brocade settee, the burnished brass lamps. The lamps were off now. It was morning. Sun spilled across the Aubusson.

Shakily she fitted her reading glasses to her nose, praying that if she studied the letters long enough, hard enough, something would click. She noted return addresses—Morgan Hill, California, Burley, Alabama, Little River, South Carolina, Parma, Ohio. People were writing her from across the country. And she was in . . . here was . . . she lived in . . . Connecticut. There, over the rim of her glasses, scripted elegantly on an antique map on the wall. Setting the glasses aside, she crossed to the map, touched the gilded frame, took comfort in its solidness and, yes, its familiarity.

She lived in western Connecticut, on the sprawling estate left her by John. The original house had been in his family for nearly as many generations as the old sawmill had. The sawmill was silent now, craggy with vines and as bent as John in his final years, but what time had taken from the mill, it had given to the house. Initially a single stone homestead facing west, it had grown a north wing, then a south wing. A garage had sprouted and multiplied. The back of the house had swollen to include a suite of offices, the largest of which she stood in now, and the solarium. Beyond the solarium was the patio she adored, flagstoned and April-bare, but promising. It opened to a rolling lawn beyond which, framed by firs, lay the Housatonic. In late summer it meandered along the eastern edge of her property. This time of year it rushed. She could hear it even now, through the mullioned panes.

These things were familiar. And the other? She glanced anxiously at the door before reaching again for her glasses.

"Dear Grace, I've been reading your column for almost twenty years, but this is the first time I've written. My daughter is getting married next fall, but my ex-husband says that if she wants him to give her away, the children from his second marriage have to be in the wedding party. There are five of them. They are all under ten and unruly, and they've been awful to my daughter . . ."

"Dear Grace, You have to settle an argument between my boyfriend and me. He says that the first guy a girl sleeps with shapes her insides to him, so it's never as good with another guy . . ."

"Dear Grace, Some of the letters you print are too far-fetched to be real . . ."

"Dear Grace, Thanks for the advice you gave that poor woman whose gifts to her grandchildren are never acknowledged. She has a right to a thank-you, family or no. I clipped your column and posted it where my children could see . . ."

Grace held the last letter in her hand for another minute, trembling with relief now, before gently setting it down.

Grace Dorian. *The Confidante.* Of course.

If she needed proof, there were plaques on the far wall marking addresses she had given to professional organizations and, beneath those, scrapbooks filled with articles praising her nationally syndicated column. The courier pack on the chair was the latest shipment of readers' mail from New York. By the week's end she would have read most, selected a cross section, and written five columns.

She hoped.

But she would. She had to.

What did Davis Marcoux know? By his own admission, he had simply ruled out a few alternatives. But he was wrong. Her spells were momentary lapses, tiny strokes perhaps, causing no permanent damage. She knew what the letters were now. She knew what her job was. She was in control.

The phone buzzed. She jumped, then stared at the instrument for a confused minute before snatching up the receiver. "Yes?" she said to a dial tone. Her finger hovered unsurely over a panel of buttons. She punched one and nothing happened, then another and got a busy signal. She was debating which to push next when the buzzing stopped. She was standing with the receiver in her hand and an irate look on her face when the door swung open.

"I can't use this phone, Francine!" she snapped. "It's too confusing. I've had trouble with it since the day they put it in. What was *so awful* about the old phones?"

Francine bore her a cup of tea and a smile. "The old phones could only carry two lines, and we need five." Setting the tea on the desk, she gave Grace a squeeze. "Morning, Mom. Bad night?"

Grace's irritation eased. Francine would never be a dynamo, but she was constant—a devoted daughter, a loyal friend, an able assistant. In these things, Grace was blessed, as she was blessed in so much else. Yes, indeed, Davis Marcoux was wrong. She hadn't come this far only to be stopped short. Momentary lapses, that was all, and there didn't have to be a physical cause. All things considered, she had earned the right to a spell now and again.

"I don't sleep the way I used to," she told Francine. "Two hours here, two hours there. They say old people don't need as much sleep. I need it. I just can't get it."

"Sixty-one is not old," Francine said.

Grace welcomed the reassurance. "My mind isn't what it was."

Francine denied this, too. "Your mind is perfect, which is why you're in such demand. That's what I was buzzing you about. Annie Diehl just called to ask if you'd be interested in doing a talk show in Houston."

Annie Diehl was the publicist the newspaper paid to coordinate Grace's appearances. Grace remembered that very well. She also remembered the panic she had experienced the last time she'd been on a plane. Mid flight she had drawn a total blank about where she was headed and why. The disorientation hadn't lasted long and was no doubt caused by the altitude, but Grace wasn't asking for trouble if she didn't absolutely, positively, have to.

"I've already done a dozen talk shows in Houston."

"Four, and none for several years."

"Is my Houston readership slipping?"

"No."

"Then I'd rather not fly there. I have too much to do here." She glanced at the desk. "On top of all this, there's my book. I'm already late starting it, and Lord knows when I can, what with six speaking engagements between now and June." She used to be able to whip up a week's columns in two days, leaving three days for what she called *The Confidante*'s fringe. Things took her longer to do now. "Why *did* we accept all those commencement invitations?"

Francine grinned. "Because you love getting honorary degrees."

"Well, wouldn't you, if you didn't have one of your own?" Grace returned without remorse. "It's sickening to be constantly sitting on panels with people who have more letters *after* their names than in them. Besides, college seniors, even high school seniors, are such vulnerable creatures." Picturing her granddaughter, she corrected herself. "Except for Sophie. Sophie isn't vulnerable. She is one bold child."

"No child. She's twenty-three."

"And personally responsible for these phones and everything else around here that I can't understand." Grace shot a despairing glance at the computer on a sidearm of her desk. She pined for her old Olivetti.

"Yes, these are an improvement," Francine said just as Grace was about to ask it. "They simplify my work. They simplify Sophie's work. And they make an important statement about The Confidante."

"That she's *computerized*?" Grace asked in dismay. The Confidante was gentle and personable. She was informative but compassionate, and entirely human. She was definitely not a machine.

"That she's au courant. Really, Mom. When someone writes asking about condom use, you give a different answer today than you did when pregnancy was the only issue. Your advice changes with the times. Shouldn't your technology?"

The businesswoman in Grace knew it had to. Still, advanced technology intimidated her. She wasn't ruling out the possibility that the complexity of the world was directly responsible for her bouts of disorientation. A mind could only juggle so much.

She smiled when a redheaded finch and its mate settled at the feeder beyond her window. "Thank goodness, some things don't change. Spring is on its way. I love this time of year. Once everything is in bloom, my guests start arriving. Does Margaret know to start cleaning the guest rooms?"

"Yes."

"Did you order new carpet for the attic suite?"

"Uh-huh."

"What about the invitations for my May party? Have they arrived?" She had ordered cards with stunning hand-painted borders that no computer could duplicate in a million years, thank you.

"Not yet."

"Have you called about them?"

"No."

"You have to keep on *top* of things, Francine. How *many* times have I told you that?"

All the worse, Francine didn't look bothered. "The invitations were promised by the end of the week. That gives us more than enough time to get them to the calligrapher. Did you finish the guest list?"

The guest list. Grace drew a blank. "Don't you have it?"

"Not me. You were working on it yesterday afternoon when I left. You said it would be on my desk this morning."

"Then it's there. You must have put something on top of it."

"I just got here. I haven't touched my desk."

"Just got here?" Grace cried. Tardiness was a fair digression. "It's after ten. Must you wander in so late?" She gave Francine a pleading once-over. "And must you wear sweat suits to work?"

"Sweat suits are comfortable."

"They aren't appropriate for an office setting. Neither is—" She looked pointedly at Francine's hair, which was caught up at the crown of her head in a way that let tendrils fall every which way. The color was soft brown, the look sexy and decidedly wrong. Shorter was neater, shorter was more *professional* every time.

Francine cleared her throat. "We're not talking the financial district here."

"Still, how we look makes a statement to the world. Like our being computerized."

"Ahh, but the world knows if we're computerized. It doesn't know what I wear."

"Thank goodness for *that*," Grace muttered, "and that goes for your daughter, too." She was appalled by most of what Sophie wore. Such a beautiful child. Such a waste. "Don't you have any control over that girl?"

"No girl," Francine sang softly, absently, as she pulled a paper from the tray on the credenza. "Here's your guest list." She frowned. "But it's not done."

Grace reached for the list, then her glasses. She saw plenty of names. "It looks fine to me." She handed it back.

"You only have the paper people here. What about publishing people? What about reviewers? And the media? I thought the point of this party was to start hyping the book. What about your agent? What about *Annie*, for goodness sake?"

"Well, there you have it," Grace declared. "You know exactly who has to be invited. You can do the list yourself. Don't forget the neighbors. And Robert."

"Robert who?"

Grace gave her a long look in lieu of launching into a diatribe about the pathetic state of Francine's social life.

"All right," Francine yielded, "I'll invite Robert, but only as a friend. He is not the love of my life."

"Give him half a chance and he might be," Grace advised. "I like the man." She paused. "Yes. I know. I liked Lee, too. And it's none of my business. But this party is. So, do the guest list, like a good girl? I also need the latest figures on domestic abuse, and on the long-term effects of liposuction. Be an angel and get them for me?" She nodded toward the desk. "I'm swamped."

"So am I," Francine protested, though weakly. "Fine. But don't yell if I inadvertently leave someone off that list."

"I never yell."

"No. But you do get your point across."

"Well, someone has to keep the business running smoothly. I really do need a secretary."

"You have one. Marny Puck. She sits right down the hall and sends lovely thank-yous to all the people who write you, but she isn't involved in your personal life. She doesn't do guest lists."

Grace was shaken. Marny. Of course. "Why don't I have a *personal* secretary?"

Francine smiled and strode toward the door. "Because you have me." She raised the hand with the list. "I'll be back."

The minute the door closed, Grace sat at the desk and drew a small spiral-bound book from the top drawer. She flipped past earlier jottings to a blank page. "Marny Puck," she wrote in capital letters and, beneath it, "Secretary. Sits down the hall. Answers readers' mail." Fondly, she added, "One of Father Jim's people. Cleans up nicely. Follows direction well." Wryly, she tacked on, "Sister of Gus, my chauffeur. As reputable as Gus is not."

On the next page, she made notes about the use of the telephone. Francine and Sophie had each tutored her countless times. She knew how to use it. She just got rattled sometimes.

So she wrote out simple instructions, just in case.

On a third page, unthinkable five years before, she listed her chores for the day, just in case.

When the list looked too sketchy to do much good, she elaborated on each one, just in case.

Marginally reassured then, she slipped the notebook into

the top drawer of her desk and reached, while the reaching was good, for the letters that defined her life.

Francine had been barely eight when *The Confidante* was born. She had sat in on the debates, though there had never been any doubt in her mind. Of course, Grace should write an advice column for the local newspaper. Didn't she give advice all the time? Wasn't that what her friends rushed over for? Didn't they pour out their deepest, darkest secrets to Grace? Didn't Francine do it herself?

There was something about Grace—a directness, a warmth—that begged the trust of even the newest acquaintance. How could you not confide in someone who regarded you with such compassion, listened with such patience, seemed so *rapt* with what you said, and always had sensible advice? Francine had considered herself luckier than any of her friends, having a mother in whom she could confide. Nor was the relationship one-sided. As *The Confidante* broadened its scope, Francine became a resource. She was a teenager, experiencing the same problems about which many of Grace's readers wrote. She was late in developing, and then she shot up well before she shot out. She hated her hair, hated her nose, hated her hands. She got pimples. She suffered unrequited crushes. She agonized over New Year's Eve months in advance.

Oh, yes, she was a resource. She knew the heartbreak of losing the election for sophomore class president by a handful of votes, knew the humiliation of elimination in the first round of a tennis tournament that her own family sponsored, knew the disappointment of being rejected by her top college choices. She also knew what it was to have a mother whose fame rose in seeming counterpoint to her own mediocrity.

Francine was to Grace as earth tones were to pastels, brown eyes were to blue ones, attractive was to beautiful, terrestrial was to divine.

Simply put, Francine was flawed. In being flawed, she experienced things Grace never had. Grace had never been divorced. Grace had never felt guilty about Sophie's diabetes, or about letting her come home after college rather than insisting that she stay in the city with friends. Grace didn't understand Francine's need to excel, or how Grace's sky-high standards made that impossible. She didn't understand Francine's craving for grandparents, aunts, uncles, and cousins.

Francine counted herself fortunate in many, many respects; still, she had dreams that left her torn. Grace didn't understand what it meant to be torn because she never was. She saw the world in absolutes. One took control of one's life by making choices and seeing them through.

Yet, for all these differences, Grace had always been there when Francine needed her most. So she returned to her desk and went at the guest list. With regard to domestic abuse and liposuction, Sophie was their statistics person, but Francine hated to wake her. The figures could wait.

Francine wasn't so sure about the party invitations, so she called the stationery store where they had been ordered. The owner promised to call the artist painting the borders, and call Francine back. In the meantime, cradling the phone between shoulder and jaw as she added names to the guest list, Francine called Annie Diehl. "Grace would rather not do Houston at this point," she explained as kindly as she could, but even then, Annie was miffed.

"It's a good show."

"I know. But the timing's wrong. It's graduation season. The next few weeks will be mad."

"This is television, Francine. The exposure is ten times greater than any one of those graduations."

"Tell that to Grace and she'll lecture you on the importance of quality over quantity. Promise Houston another time?"

"They'll be disappointed. I told them she was free. Does this mean she won't want to do anything until July? I can't guarantee any bookings then. Things are dead after the Fourth."

"That's fine," Francine said as lightly as she could, though she hated ultimatums. They put her between a rock and a hard place. She ended up the bad guy more often than not. "We have plenty to do here. My apologies to Houston."

Annie made a not-so-gracious sound that Grace would have objected to even more than Francine—and Francine would have smarted from herself, had not the owner of the stationery store called then to say that the invitations would be done by the first of the week.

Francine was appalled. "*Next* week? They were supposed to be done by the first of *this* week." And Grace was right. She should have called sooner to check.

"Artists can be temperamental."

"So can advice columnists," Francine remarked. She didn't relish having to tell Grace that the invitations would be late.

"Why don't I have the artist ship them directly to your calligrapher?"

And if the artwork wasn't just so? Francine relished that scenario even less. "Grace has to see them first. Have your artist ship them directly to us."

Frustrated, she hung up the phone. Grace liked things done on schedule. She saw The Confidante as an elegant woman donning her gloves, each movement measured and poised. Francine's job was to preserve that image. Unfortunately, the rest of the world didn't run as efficiently as Grace Dorian did.

Or used to, Francine thought with a glance at the unfinished guest list, but before she could return to it, her phone rang again.

It was Tony Colletti, Grace's editor at the paper. "What's wrong with this column, Francine?"

"What column?"

"Next Wednesday's, about guests who are allergic to their hosts' cats. It doesn't make sense."

It hadn't made sense to Francine, either, when she had first read it. Poor Grace had screwed up something or other on the computer. Rather than making her usual nominal edits, Francine had rewritten the column and had Sophie send it off with the rest.

No. Sophie hadn't sent it off. Sophie had been out. So Francine had sent it off. She must have screwed up, herself.

Not about to tell Tony that, she said, "Oh dear. You must have the stuff that was supposed to have been left on the cutting-room floor."

"That's my fate in life, around you."

"Tony."

"I have Knicks tickets for Sunday afternoon."

Francine sighed.

"Okay. Forget the Knicks. How about brunch? That's practical. You have to eat."

She didn't make a sound.

"Okay. Forget brunch. How soon can you get the damn column on my screen?"

"Two minutes if I can do it myself, a little more if I need help. I'll call you in either case, okay?"

She hung up the phone, turned on her computer, and pulled up the file in question. Grace's convoluted original appeared on her screen. She scrolled forward, then back, then returned to the file directory, searched it, and scanned other files into which she might have inadvertently unloaded the rewritten piece.

The phone rang. "I haven't received it," Tony bleated.

"Of course not. I haven't sent it. We're having technical difficulty. I said I'd call you back." She hung up the phone.

Desperate, she set off for the south wing of the house. She needed Sophie. Buzzing her would have been faster, but Francine liked the quiet intimacy of waking her daughter. She always had.

Assuming Sophie was alone.

Francine faltered, decided to risk it, went on. Yes, there was the guest list to complete. Yes, she had a courier pack as thick as Grace's to wade through. Yes, Tony was waiting in all his macho glory for a column to appear on his screen.

But there was always time for Sophie, who, despite Grace's little jabs, was Francine's crowning achievement. Sophie was a genius. She was beautiful, and spunky, and vulnerable, yes, she was. Mothers knew those things.

Time with Sophie was always time well spent, and if it meant that Francine was behind when she returned to her desk, that was fine, too. The busier she was, the less she dwelled on things she couldn't change.

Sophie was different from her mother in that respect. She couldn't help but dwell on things she couldn't change. They dictated her behavior. She took delight in thwarting them whenever she could.

That was one of the reasons she was still in bed. Her alarm had rung an hour before. Since it was a workday, she had turned it off and gone back to sleep.

"Sophie? Wake up, sweetie."

Her mother's soft whisper might have been a memory from the past, had not the urgent shake of her shoulder been so real. She cracked open an eye to Francine's earnest plea.

"I lost a day's column in the computer. Tony's champing at the bit for it, and I've searched everywhere. Will you come look?"

Sophie closed her eye. She felt the mattress shift, then the press of Francine's hip.

"Come on, babe. I wouldn't wake you if it weren't an emergency. I rewrote the whole column, but transmitted the original. Typical, huh? So Tony's gloating. He loves it when I slip up."

"He's annoyed because you won't date him."

"Well, do you blame me? He has the emotional drive of a two-year-old and the arrogance of ten men. One hour, and we'd be at each other's throats, and not in passion, my dear."

"Too bad," Sophie said through a yawn. "Passion is a great outlet."

There was a pause, then a tentative, "Did you have fun last night?"

"Uh-huh."

"With Gus."

"Uh-huh." She stretched.

"I worry about you, babe."

Sophie knew that, and hated it. But Gus excited her. He filled the perverse need she had to tempt the devil and thumb her nose at social constraint. Her relationship with Gus drove Grace nuts. That was reason in itself to go on.

But she did feel for her mother. So, mustering a burst of energy, she climbed out of bed. "Not to worry. I'm fine." She rummaged through the dresser drawers.

"Cool pajamas," Francine remarked.

Sophie was nude. "They're comfortable." She pulled on panties, black leggings, and a black bustier.

Francine sighed. "Ahh. Grace's favorite outfit."

Sophie grinned. "I know."

"You're bad."

"But you do love me."

"Don't forget your shot."

Sophie ignored the reminder. She ran a brush through her hair and pushed a comb in at just the right angle to create asymmetry, then loaded her ear with the row of earrings that Grace *really* loved. After a brief stop in the bathroom to rinse away the taste of last night's scampi—and, yes, address her diabetes—she waved Francine toward the hall.

"Insulin?" Francine prompted.

Sophie gave an affirmative grunt.

"Did you take a reading first?"

"Yes, yes," she grumbled. "How did I ever make it through college without your monitoring my health?"

"I've often wondered."

Sophie vented her frustration in a long-legged pace. Francine's concern didn't bother her half as much as the illness itself. She had felt like a freak at the age of nine, when it had first been diagnosed. She still did, sometimes.

So she didn't mind being woken by her mother to go looking for lost files, because handling computers wasn't freakish. It gave her a semblance of control. Being expert at something—particularly something Grace couldn't master if her life depended on it—was empowering.

"I rewrote the whole thing," Francine muttered under her breath. "If I have to do it again, I'll scream."

Sophie sat down at Francine's computer. "Maybe it's time to hire another person. This isn't the first column you've had to rewrite in the last few months."

"It's the first one I've lost."

"Not lost. Misplaced. It's here."

"Unless I erased it by mistake."

But Sophie had minimized the chance of that when she had set up the system. She brought up the trash file and began sifting through it.

"Cat allergies," Francine prompted.

"About which," Sophie mused as she worked, "neither of us knows a thing, never having owned a cat. And do we care? No."

"Of course we do."

"Says Grace. I sometimes wonder about all this."

"The work? It isn't so bad. Your friends envy you. You said it yourself."

"They envy me my work. I envy them their freedom."

"Doesn't it help, living in your own end of the house?"

"Yes. No. I don't know." She had a little home within a home, replete with kitchen and gym, perfect when friends came to visit. But it wasn't like living in an apartment with those friends—and then there was the matter of insulin shots and blood-sugar tests and the kind of constant vigilance that made her a social queer.

Francine's hand was gentle on her hair. "You didn't have to come back."

"I *did*." Totally aside from her health, which was easier to monitor at home, there was Grace. Love-hate, love-hate. "The business is part of me, too. It's the Dorian thing, the Dorian *women's* thing. I can't explain it. Ahh. Here we go." She sat back in the chair. "Cat allergies. About which Grace doesn't know anything either. So how did she write the column?"

"She didn't," Francine reminded her. "I did, with the help of my favorite vet."

"Whom you will date, but won't marry. Tom is the nicest guy in the world. Not quite pedigreed enough for Grace, is that it?"

"In part."

"What's the rest?" She had no trouble interpreting her mother's dry look. "Ahhh. He's too tame. You'd like Gus, you know."

Francine arched a brow. "Send this to Tony for me, babe? Oh, and Grace needs new stats on domestic abuse and liposuction. But have breakfast first, please?"

Sophie sent the column along to Tony and was about to delay breakfast on principle when Grace emerged from her office. "Sophie. You promised me material on incest." She waved a letter. "Victims keep asking me what to do. It's time I address the issue again."

"You just did," Sophie said. "It was in the paper last week."

"No, it wasn't."

"She's right, Grace," Francine put in from her desk across the room. "That mail must be in response to it."

"It has been *months* since I've done anything on incest," Grace insisted.

"I'll show you," Sophie offered, delighted to be able to prove Grace wrong. "I clipped it yesterday."

"Goodness, Sophie, you look like you just rolled out of bed. Francine?" Grace begged.

Francine guided Grace back to her office. "She'll change later."

"Appearing in this office in that getup is as bad as blowing her nose in her dinner napkin. *Please*, Francine. *Talk* to her."

The conversation receded. Sophie propped a hip on the desk and waited, prepared to do battle if Grace reappeared. But Francine emerged alone.

She dropped her arms on Sophie's shoulders. "That was predictable."

Sophie was unrepentant. "I like getting a rise out of her."

"Well, you do that. She keeps asking me what happened to the sweet little girl she used to hold on her lap. She says she doesn't know you anymore."

The feeling was mutual. Sophie had wonderful memories of warm times with her grandmother, just the two of them taking trips, reading books, exploring the woods, laughing. Her grandfather had played a peripheral role; Grammie had been the star from the start. She had doted, and Sophie had eaten it up, right along with the idea that the Dorians were invincible. Then Grammie had become Grace and the doting had ended. Expectations had grown. Reality had closed in.

Still, some things, like the power of the Dorian name, hadn't changed. "I'm not that different," Sophie sighed. "If I were, I wouldn't be here."

"I'm glad you are."

That was some solace, Sophie thought. Francine needed a champion. Sophie was the only one she had.

"Cold?" Francine asked, rubbing Sophie's bare arms.

Sophie gave a little headshake no. "How could Grace have forgotten the column on incest? We discussed it for days."

"She's written so many columns. One runs into the other."

"But it was just last week. She's losing it, Mom. She isn't as sharp as she used to be."

"Oh, she's sharp. She just asked me whether you've pulled out the old speeches she asked for last week. She hasn't forgotten."

Sophie drew away. Over her shoulder on her way to the door, she said, "Digging through files is *the* worst part of this job. It's mindless and boring, *not* the best use of a degree from Columbia."

"I'll do it, if you'd rather."

"No, no," Sophie said. Better her than Francine.

"Do it now, and get it over with," Francine suggested. "But have breakfast first."

Sophie did head down the hall for breakfast, but not because her mother wanted her to, and *not* because the doctors told her to. She would have breakfast—and dawdle over it—because anything was better than drudging through files.

Under Margaret's watchful eye, she ate a boiled egg, a piece of toast, and a banana. Her third cup of coffee had grown cold by the time she had read the newspaper cover to cover, and then she sat staring out the window, wondering as she wondered nearly every morning what in the world she was doing back home. Her friends were in New York, Washington, Atlanta, Dallas, working frivolous first jobs, partying to their hearts' delight. She could have been with them. Instead, she was back with her mother and grandmother in the house where she'd grown up. Worse, she was there of her own choosing.

By way of punishment for that, she retreated to the file room, dug up Grace's old commencement addresses, and entered them on the computer by date and content. By then, for warmth—certainly not because Grace was scandalized by a bustier—she had put on a sweater. She had also done a computer search for the latest figures on domestic abuse.

She paused for lunch not because she was hungry, but because lunch was a ritual with Grace. It was always a three-course meal—salad, entree, and fruit. Sophie didn't have to think twice about waiting for Grace to start first, or using her utensils from the outside in, or blotting—not wiping—her mouth with her napkin. Those things were second nature by now.

She did think twice about absolutes. She resented it when, out of the blue, Grace announced that she had canceled their reservations for a Martha's Vineyard Fourth of July. Not that Sophie had wanted to go, what with her own friends meeting in Easthampton, but Francine had had her heart set on the trip.

She resented it when, moments later, Grace raised the issue of *Architectural Digest* photographing the house. "My part of the house," she specified before ticking off necessary preparations. Not that Sophie wanted her own rooms included. She lived in them, and they looked it. The same with Francine's. Grace's part of the house, like Grace, was perfect. Sophie resented *that*.

There was some satisfaction when Legs burst into the kitchen, ugly as sin but sweet, as greyhounds were, and eager for a little love from Francine. Grace jumped up and started sputtering, as though the dog were a stray who'd wandered in off the street. Her tizzy lasted only until Francine led Legs out, but it was gratifying.

Still, Sophie was primed for spite when, rising to return to work, Grace looked her in the eye and said, "I wanted to go for a drive last night, but when I went looking for Gus, he was gone."

"We went dancing."

"He dances?"

"Does he ever. You know—" She raised her arms and undulated, shoulders to knees.

Grace turned to Francine. "Doesn't this bother you?"

Francine smiled. "I'm envious. I could never move that way."

Grace spared them a disparaging glance and left, but not before she said, "I want him around tonight if I call."

The words echoed in Sophie's head for one long, frustrating hour. Then, leaving behind nothing that couldn't be done as well the next morning, she put on head-to-toe leather and set off for the garage.

Grace took tea, as always, at four. Father Jim O'Neill joined her, as he did whenever his commitments allowed. Francine dropped in for a short time, before returning to work.

Grace didn't feel like returning to work. She had put in several good hours, but the strain of concentrating, of forcing her mind back from the ragged edge of the fear that had seized her that morning, had taken its toll. She had a nagging headache. Neither the tea nor the time with Jim had helped.

After waving him off at the door, she wandered through the house, but the fear followed her there, too, as nagging as the headache and more daunting.

She wanted to talk, but she couldn't.

She wanted to work, but she couldn't.

She wanted to *sleep*, but she couldn't.

So she took her wool coat from the closet, put on a beret and fur-lined gloves, and went looking for Gus.

He wasn't in the garage. Nor was he in the main house, or

the greenhouse, or the cottage he shared with his sister. He wasn't answering his beeper at all.

But Grace wanted to go out. Reasoning that she had done her best to find a driver and had failed, she returned to the garage, slipped into the Mercedes, and, feeling the exhilaration of being alone and in momentary command of her wits, headed off down the drive.

Two

Denial is the innocent's way of putting off for tomorrow what hurts too much to admit today.
—GRACE DORIAN, from *The Confidante*

"Grace? Are you with us, Grace?"

Grace awoke to the handsome face of Davis Marcoux. She frowned and looked around. Her eyes widened on white sheets, a white curtain, white ceilings. She wasn't at home, she knew that much. *Her* house wasn't this sterile. Nor, to the best of her recollection, was Davis's office.

"Where am I?" she asked, perturbed.

"At the hospital, still in the ER. That was quite a bang you gave your head."

At its mention, she identified a throbbing. Cautious fingers found a wad of gauze high on her forehead. "What happened?"

"You were in a car crash."

"Me?" She tried to remember, but the throbbing in her

head discouraged it. "I've never been in an accident in my life."

"Then this was a first. You ran a red light."

"I don't run red lights. How did I bump my head?"

"It hit the steering wheel when you hit another car."

When *she* hit another car? She tried to remember, but all that came to her were threads of scary thoughts—the sense of being lost, of losing control, of panicking. "What happened to the other car?"

"It's a mess, from what I hear, but the driver walked away without a scratch."

"Thank God," she breathed. A mess? "Was I going *that* fast?"

"You don't remember?"

Well, she did, now that he mentioned it. She remembered being *frightened* by how fast she was going and trying to slow down.

"What happened?" Davis asked, more softly now. His voice held an intimacy reminiscent of other discussions they'd had.

Grace was quickly defensive. She still didn't buy into those other discussions. "I don't remember seeing a red light. It must have been obscured by the trees."

"You were at the intersection of South Webster and Elm. It's wide open."

But she persisted. "It was dusk. We both know how tricky the light can be then."

"It can be. Was that what happened?"

"Well, it *had* to have been. I certainly wouldn't have run a red light if I'd seen it."

"What if you saw it, but didn't know what it meant?"

She glared at him. "I know what a red light means, thank you."

"Right now, yes. But if you were disoriented."

"I wasn't. I was just confused. For a minute I couldn't get my bearings. I must have been trying to see the street sign when the light changed. The other car must have jumped the green."

"The other car was the third one into the intersection, the light had been green that long."

"Well, then it was just an accident." She refused to make a mountain out of a molehill. "Everyone is entitled to one now and again."

"What if someone had been hurt? How would you have felt?"

"Terrible," she replied honestly.

"I warned you against driving."

"I don't do it often. But my chauffeur wasn't around, and I wanted to go out. So I drove."

"And here you are."

"An accident, Dr. Marcoux. A simple accident."

"I'm concerned with its cause." He paused. "Have you talked with your family?"

Grace's eyes widened. Her family would want an explanation. "Do they know I'm here?"

"Your daughter is outside. She arrived with the ambulance. One of your neighbors witnessed the accident. He phoned her from his car."

Grace might have known it. The curse of the caring. Nothing stayed a secret for long.

She squeezed her eyes shut against her head's throbbing, which was exacerbated, no doubt, by the hammer of her heart. Taking a slow breath, she looked at the doctor again, cautious now. "What have you told them?"

"Only that you aren't seriously hurt. That doesn't mean the situation isn't serious."

She held his gaze. "It isn't."

"Grace."

"You didn't prove a thing with your tests," she argued in a rush. "You said it yourself. You simply ruled out a few alternatives."

"More than a few. Your symptoms are classic."

She waved a hand. "Forgetfulness is inevitable at my age."

"Not repeated spells of disorientation. That was what brought you to me in the first place. What happened to you in the car is typical of Alzheimer's sufferers."

"I do not have Alzheimer's disease."

"What if the occupants of the other car had been maimed or, worse, killed? What if *you* had been killed?"

"My estate is in order."

"That's not the point. The point is that your family should be aware of what's happening."

Grace shook her head. "I won't have them panicking over a diagnosis as inconclusive as yours."

He gave her a chiding look. She looked away.

"Have you told Father Jim?" he asked quietly.

Her eyes flew back. "Definitely not."

"He would want to know. He may be able to help."

"Help with what?" Grace cried. "Help feed me when I can't do it myself? Lead me around by the hand when I don't know where I'm going? Tell me who he is when I can't remember his name?" She thumbed her chest. "I've read about this disease. *I* don't *have* it."

Davis slid his hands in his pockets and frowned down at the floor. Grace was trying to guess his thoughts when he turned and sat on the edge of the bed. His head was bent, his back to her. "Does your family know about the spells you have?"

"No."

"Then they don't know you had tests?"

"I told them I was visiting friends in the city."

Over his shoulder, his eyes found hers. "Let me tell them. I'll explain my conclusions. They can agree or not."

"And if they agree?" Grace asked, voicing her greatest fear. "If they agree, they start looking at me strangely. They start suspecting everything I do. They label every little lapse, whether it has to do with the disease or not. It becomes self-perpetuating."

"You can't leave them in the dark. Haven't they noticed any changes in your behavior?"

"They indulge me. I'm sixty-one."

"Sixty-one is not old."

Grace didn't find that anywhere near as pleasing to hear coming from Davis Marcoux as from Francine.

"They'll have to know sooner or later," he said.

"Not if your diagnosis is wrong," she insisted.

"Suppose, just for a minute, that it isn't. Shouldn't your family be prepared? From what you've told me, you and your daughter are very close. Wouldn't she want to know about this?"

"About a death sentence? She'll be devastated."

"She isn't a child."

"She'll be *devastated*," Grace repeated. "I speak from personal experience."

She had been fighting devastation since the very first time she had thought to associate her symptoms with Alzheimer's disease, and that had been months and months before she had ever seen Davis Marcoux. She read the papers. She read news magazines. She was receiving an increasing number of letters from readers of her column on the subject. She knew about the anguish the disease caused cognizant victims and the way it ravaged their families. Devastation didn't cover the half of it.

"You don't understand, Doctor. My family revolves around me. My career is what the Dorian family is about. How can I tell them that might end? You said it yourself. I could go for years with nothing more than the occasional bout of confusion."

"What about the accident you just had? What if your daughter or granddaughter had been in the car?"

"Then they would have been driving. I never drive unless I have no one to do it for me."

"That doesn't excuse it," he scolded, but his manner remained gentle, making his words increasingly harder for Grace to deny. Yes, her family revolved around her, but they were also precious to her. If she were ever responsible for their being hurt, she would never forgive herself.

She closed her eyes and pressed her fingertips to the throbbing in her head. "I can't deal with this right now."

"Your daughter is waiting outside to hear how you are. Wouldn't this be as good a time as any to tell her?"

"No."

"She'll be asking how you could have run a red light."

"No. I've taught her to prioritize. Running a red light isn't as important as the fact that I'm fine."

"But you're not."

He was wearing her down. She could feel it. She wanted to refute his arguments, but the same old answers weren't working. Yes, she was confused sometimes, and disoriented, and forgetful, and yes, she had a right to be all those things at her age. But it was happening more often. She couldn't deny it, or the terror it caused.

She put her fingertips to her lips to still their quivering.

"Let me tell her, Grace," he urged in a voice that was

deep and persuasive. "If she at least knows of the possibility, she'll be in a better position to help if need be. Same with Father Jim."

No one can help, Grace cried inside. If you're right, I'm lost. "Father Jim knows about the spells."

"But not about their cause. He'll be upset that you didn't tell him sooner. He's waiting outside now, too."

Grace turned her head away. She didn't want Jim to know. She would rather die than let him see her as a mindless fool.

"How about it, Grace?" Davis persisted. "No one was hurt this time, but what about next time? Accidents can be prevented, but only if the parties involved know the score."

"We don't know it ourselves, for sure," she argued, but weakly now. Blame it on the shock of the accident, or on her relentlessly throbbing head, or on a recollection of wanting to stop that car and not knowing how, or Davis's sheer persistence, but she felt suddenly tired.

Then she had a thought. If Davis shared his suspicions with her family, they might be as vehement as she that he was wrong. It would be nice to have an ally or two after fighting alone for so long.

Francine had been in the waiting room for a frightened eternity when a man emerged from the ER's innards and purposefully strode her way. He was tall, long-legged and limber, with thick amber hair that was windblown, a square, beard-shadowed jaw, and such outdoorsy good looks that, lab coat notwithstanding, she would never have pegged him for a doctor had not Father Jim said, "Ah, here's Dr. Marcoux."

Heart pounding, she rose.

The doctor extended his hand. "Francine? Davis Marcoux."

"How's my mother?"

"She has a bump on her head, a few stitches, and a mild concussion. I'd like to keep her overnight for observation. She should be able to go home in the morning."

"Thank goodness," Francine breathed in relief. She had no experience with an ailing Grace. Mothers didn't get sick.

"I wonder," Davis asked, "if we could talk for a few minutes?"

She was quickly wary. "About what?"

"There's a private lounge down the hall."

Her heart beat faster. Private lounges were for serious discussions. "Something's wrong, isn't it?"

He hitched his chin toward the end of the hall.

She didn't want to go to any private lounge. "Wouldn't it be better if I sat with Grace?"

Father Jim touched her arm. "Let me do that."

She turned on him. "Do you know something I don't?"

"No, but you're Grace's daughter. It's natural that the doctor would want to discuss the accident with you. You can join us after you talk with him."

"I don't want to talk with him," she cried, then, hearing her own foolishness, relented. "All right. Tell Grace I'll be right there." She was halfway down the hall, keeping pace with the doctor, when it occurred to her to call Father Jim back. Even before her father's death, he had been a steady presence in the Dorian home, and he was all the more so now. He was more friend than spiritual adviser, remarkably liberal, consistently supportive. She might have liked to have him with her in Davis Marcoux's private lounge.

But they had arrived. The lounge was small, with a sofa, several chairs, and a coffeemaker. Davis gestured toward the latter. "Would you like a cup?"

"Will I need one?" she asked.

His smile was dry. "Not a hospital person, I take it?"

"Births are fine. Anything else . . ." She waved a hand in distaste and slipped into a chair. "My daughter is a diabetic. When they involve people I love, hospitals give me the willies." What the hell, she couldn't pretend. "*Doctors* give me the willies."

"Well," he said, "that's good to know."

"I don't like beating around the bush. What's wrong with my mother?"

"This isn't the first time I've seen her."

Francine's unease grew. "When was?"

"Several months ago. Her internist referred her to me. She was suffering spells of disorientation. I'm a neurologist. I deal with symptoms like that."

"She didn't mention them to me."

"She didn't want you to worry. She thought she was having small strokes."

Francine hugged her middle. "Was she?"

"No. We ruled that out."

Something told her not to be relieved. "How?" she asked.

"Blood analyses, EEGs, CAT scans, MRIs. You name it, we did it."

Francine was confused. "But *when?* Those tests take time. How could I not know about them? Grace and I *work* together. I'd know if she was taking day after day off to have tests."

"Hasn't she taken any time off in the last few months?"

"Yes, but not for tests. She goes into the city to visit friends, or to go to matinees or rehearsals of the Philharmonic. She goes to the beauty shop." Francine didn't have to be a genius to read the look on his face. "She lied to me? No. Grace doesn't lie."

He lowered himself to the sofa and sat with elbows on splayed knees. "She lied this time, albeit with the best of intentions. She did have those tests. I have files filled with the results."

"What do they say?" Francine asked. She braced herself, all the more so when Davis's expression softened.

"They say that the most logical explanation for the spells she's been having is senile dementia—"

Francine cut him off. "Not Grace."

"—Alzheimer's type."

She gasped. Then she shook her head. "Not Grace. She's too sane."

"Sanity has nothing to do with it."

"But Grace's mind *is* Grace. It's what sets her apart from everyone else on this earth."

"I could say the same about every other Alzheimer's patient I've known."

Francine wasn't talking about every other Alzheimer's patient. She was talking about her mother. "Do you know how many millions of people are touched by her mind every week? Do you know how many hang on her every word?"

"How is that relevant here?"

"Her columns mean the *world* to people."

"So someone else should have this disease in her place?"

"Of course not. But you don't *understand*," she pressed. "Grace's mind is her stock-in-trade."

"I understand," he said, still gentle, but somehow more intense, "that something is happening to that mind. The brain is an organ. Grace's is deteriorating."

"Isn't some deterioration inevitable with age?"

"Some is. What Grace is experiencing isn't. There are times when she doesn't know where she is or what she's supposed to be doing. My guess is that's what happened in the car today. She was on the road and forgot how to drive."

"That's absurd," Francine argued. "Grace is in greater control of herself and her life than any other woman I know."

"She forgets things."

"Don't we all?"

"Not important things, like the name of a friend."

Francine nearly laughed. "Grace wouldn't forget the name of a friend. She would consider that the height of rudeness."

"It isn't voluntary."

"I have never heard her forget anyone's name."

"Have you seen her confused?"

"Many times, over anything and everything of a technical nature. She's always been that way. If it's worse now, it's only because we have more machines in the office than ever before."

"What about her work? Any lapses?"

"None," Francine vowed, then felt a twinge recalling the column on cat allergies that hadn't made sense.

"Has she been more moody than usual? More demanding? Does she get frustrated over little things?"

"No. Grace is Grace, the same as ever. She does not have Alzheimer's disease. There must be another cause for whatever symptoms she has."

"I can't find it."

"Then maybe you're not the right doctor for Grace."

He considered that for a minute, still with his elbows on his knees. Finally, in a voice as level as his look, he said, "I'll give you the name of another doctor. You're entitled to all the second opinions you want. But my diagnosis wasn't made in a vacuum. I didn't do those tests myself. They were done by some of the best medical minds in New York. Grace insisted on that."

"See? She does know what she's doing."

"I never said she didn't. One of the most consistent things about Alzheimer's disease is its inconsistency. In its early stages, symptoms come and go. Patients may be fine for long stretches around brief bursts of total confusion."

"I have *never* seen total confusion in Grace," Francine declared.

"She may be compensating. Alzheimer's patients get quite good at that, until the time comes when something either very public or very serious happens—like running a red light and hitting another car. Then it becomes harder to hide."

Francine's stomach was knotting. She didn't like Davis Marcoux, didn't like the steadiness of his eyes or the deepness of his voice—or his beard's shadow, or the small scar over his eyebrow, or the sheer size of him. He was too brawny to be a doctor, too raw and unadorned, too good-looking, too certain.

Grace couldn't possibly be sick. She was the cornerstone of Francine's life, of Sophie's now, too. She was the rug they stood on. No one was going to yank it out from under them, least of all an arrogant male.

Defiantly, Francine asked, "Have you told Grace what you think?"

"Yes. Two months ago."

"And she didn't say a word to me? How could that be, when she preaches open communication within families?"

Davis sat back. "She's denying it as vehemently as you are."

"Aha. So it's two against one."

"Not if you count the other doctors whose opinions helped shape my diagnosis."

"But you said it yourself. All you've done is rule out other things."

"The CAT scan showed signs of possible neural decay."

"Possible."

"Neural decay is indicative of Alzheimer's disease."

"Possible. Can't you do better than that?" She knew she was being bitchy, but she resented his giving as gruesome a diagnosis as this without concrete proof.

"Medicine is an inexact science."

"It certainly is."

"I stand behind my diagnosis."

"Well, of course, you would." She hadn't met a doctor yet who could say he was wrong. "When my father was forty, he was told that he had a liver disease and would be dead within five years. He lived to his mid-seventies."

"Grace may, too. But suppose," Davis came forward again, compelling, as Francine wished he wasn't, "just suppose I'm right. Suppose today's accident was caused by impaired functioning on her part. Can you blithely let her go out driving again?"

"I certainly can't confine her to the house."

"What if it's worse the next time? What if someone in another car is hurt?" He held up a hand. "Okay, forget human tragedy. Forget *morality*. From a legal standpoint alone, can you imagine the kind of lawsuit you'll be hit with once the family of an innocent victim discovers that a diagnosis was made months earlier, *and* that Grace was driving against her doctor's advice?"

"You've documented that, I take it."

"I have to."

"To cover your tail? Is that what this is all about? Defensive medicine?" Francine rose. "That's contemptible. If modern medicine comes down to throwing a patient's life in turmoil for the sake of the doctor's malpractice premiums, I don't want any part of it." She felt a dire need to flee. "Thank you for your time, Doctor. I'd like to see Grace now."

She started to open the door. His flat hand closed it again.

"Dr. Marcoux," she warned, but his hand stayed in place.

"Davis. I hate ceremony. I also hate being made out to be the bad guy in a situation that I don't like any more than you. Believe me, there's no joy in diagnosing Alzheimer's disease. I'd be thrilled if Grace's symptoms disappeared, but they aren't doing that. So please. Get a second opinion. Get a third. And if none of the others tells you what you want to hear, come back to me so we can talk. There's a lot you need to know."

Mustering the kind of indignation Grace found so simple, but which had never come as easily to Francine, she looked up at him. "I already know a lot. I know that *The Confidante* is a multimillion-dollar enterprise that supports seven of us at the house, and God knows how many more in New York, and it all revolves around Grace. So do I. I don't have much by way of family. With my father gone, there's Grace, my daughter, Sophie, and me. I *treasure* my mother and my daughter." She raised two fingers, pressed close. "Grace and I are like this. I can't just . . . just chalk her out of my life."

"I'm not asking you to. Grace is still a fully functioning human being. The last thing you should do is to treat her any differently than you always have. All I'm saying is that you should be aware of what might come. She could go on for another five, six, seven years like she is now, with just the occasional lapse. Or she could go downhill faster. In any case, she isn't immortal. She will die sometime."

"Sometime can just wait a while," Francine said, and gave a tug at the door. It didn't budge.

In his own sweet time, Davis raised his hand and took a step back.

She gave a new tug, a harder one, meant to punctuate her departure with flair. But she was positioned wrong, and the door opened faster than she expected. It rammed her shoulder, throwing her off balance. She staggered.

Davis caught her arm.

She freed it and held up a warning hand. With extemporized dignity, she stepped around the open door and escaped.

At least she thought she had, but his diagnosis followed her down the hall. It was only when she entered the cubicle in which Grace lay, looking pale and unsettled but otherwise so much like Grace, that Francine felt vindicated.

She broke into a smile. "Well, Grace, you did it this time. Right through a red light. That's some bump on your head."

"It's mostly bandage," Grace said, and shook the hand that held Father Jim's. "My friend here says it becomes me. Adds character. The doctor assures me there won't be much of a scar."

Francine forgave her the vanity. If she appeared on even a handful of the stages Grace did, she would worry about her looks, too. Not that Grace had to worry. Her skin was as smooth as that of a woman far younger, and while she had been coloring her hair for years, it remained thick and obedient.

But then, what hair would dare defy as competent a mistress as Grace?

Alzheimer's disease? Fat chance.

That decided, Francine asked, "How do you feel?"

"Homesick. Have you come to spring me?"

"I can't. Not 'til morning. Doctor's orders." She would go along with that one, she supposed. "He wants you monitored overnight for the concussion."

"Why can't I be monitored at home?"

"Because," Father Jim said, "you need to be checked every few hours, and if Francine does that she won't sleep a wink."

"I'd be more comfortable in my own bed."

He squeezed her hand. "Be a good girl and do what the doctor wants. Just for one night. He has your best interests at heart."

Francine couldn't have said it quite as convincingly. She sent him a grateful look.

He glanced toward the hall. "Is Davis still out there?"

"I imagine that he's busily writing up all his thoughts," Francine drawled.

"I want to catch him before he leaves. Behave, Grace?"

"Well, what choice do I have?" Grace asked, then added a bit unsurely, "Will you be back?"

"As soon as they put you in a room."

She seemed satisfied with that answer, for which Francine was grateful to the priest yet again. James O'Neill was a friend. Yes, the sizable sum Grace gave his church each year guaranteed a certain amount of attentiveness, but Father Jim went above and beyond.

As he disappeared, Grace took her hand. "Jim said you were talking with Davis. What did he say?"

Francine felt a catch inside. She hated to repeat the words, but Grace had always preached honesty. Okay, so she hadn't followed her own teachings this time. Perhaps, given the circumstances, it was excusable.

"He told me about the tests you had. If you'd told me you

were having them, I'd have gone with you. They can't have been pleasant."

"Did he tell you his diagnosis?"

"Yes."

"I don't believe it for a minute."

"Neither do I."

"Am I erratic? Unpredictable? Moody?"

"No."

"That's what I told him."

"You also told him that you've been disoriented," Francine accused, because it seemed almost like a betrayal, Grace giving fodder to Davis Marcoux's claims.

"Once," Grace argued in her own defense, "maybe twice, and I know what those bouts are. They're panic attacks. I don't like aging."

"You aren't aging."

"Well, thank you, darling, but the fact is that I am. I don't have the strength, speed, or stamina I had twenty years ago, so I begin imagining all kinds of things wrong, and before I know it, I've whipped myself into a stir. *That's* what the confusion is about."

Francine sighed. Psychosomatic ailments could be dealt with. They weren't degenerative. They weren't fatal. "Well, *don't* whip yourself up. I need you in one piece. And *don't* go driving alone, when we have a chauffeur on the staff to drive you."

"I searched for Gus," Grace charged, "and he wasn't there."

"Where was he?"

"I thought you might know that." Her meaning was clear.

"You think he's with Sophie. She didn't say anything about going out with him."

"Does that surprise you?"

"Yes," Francine decided after a moment's thought. "If she dates him to rebel, what good does it do if no one knows?"

"You should make it your business to know, particularly where Gus Clyde is concerned. You've lost control of her, Francine."

"Of course I have," Francine conceded. "She's twenty-three. It's been years since I've kept track of every little thing she does. It wouldn't be healthy if I did. At least, that's what you always tell your readers."

Grace waved an impatient hand. "Gus may be a fine chauffeur, an able mechanic, even a passable handyman, but grandson-in-law material he isn't. Sophie has special needs. Whoever she marries is buying into those needs. He has to be caring and giving. Gus is neither."

"You hired him," Francine reminded her.

Grace scowled. "Yes, I did, at James O'Neill's behest. I should tell *him* what his precious young man is doing." Her gaze went past Francine. The scowl melted into a saintly expression. "Ahh, here's Dr. Marcoux, come to say that he's changed his mind and is going to let me go home tonight."

"Actually," said the man himself, "Dr. Marcoux has come to say that your room is ready. We're giving you the penthouse suite." He pushed the curtain aside, and moved toward the head of the bed. Given the confines of the cubicle, the trip took him within a hairbreadth of Francine. Along with the heat of his body came his hand on her arm and his voice by her ear. "There's a woman at the front desk asking to speak with one of the Dorians."

"Who is she?" Francine asked, barely breathing.

"She's with the press. You handle her. I'll handle your mom." He moved past her and raised his voice. "Ready to go, Grace?"

Press? What press? How did the *press* know Grace was here? Francine turned to him to ask, but he was gesturing an orderly to the foot of the bed, and before she could gather herself, the bed was heading for the hall.

She followed, half expecting to encounter a lurking photographer, and breathed a sigh of relief when Grace made it onto the elevator without incident. So there wouldn't be a front-page picture of a wounded Grace. But a story?

She retraced her steps past the waiting room to the ER desk and was about to identify herself when a familiar face joined her there.

"Hi, Francine. Robin Duffy, from the *Telegram*. How's Grace?"

Robin Duffy. Ahh, yes. She had interviewed Grace the summer before, and while Grace had been pleased enough with the piece, Francine had thought it snippy. The same for the handful of blurbs on Grace that Robin had written since.

Francine would have liked to give a "no comment" and leave, but she knew that Robin would write her story anyway. Unchallenged, it might be absurd. Better to give it a Dorian slant.

So she said, "Grace is fine."

"I understand there was an automobile accident. What happened?"

"There was an automobile accident," Francine echoed politely.

"I understand she ran a red light."

"Did the police tell you that?"

"No. They wouldn't say anything. But I talked with the driver of the other car. When I arrived at the scene, he was waiting for a tow truck. His car is totaled."

"Is that a professional estimate?"

"It's a quote from the other driver. He said that Grace had to have been going at least fifty."

Francine smiled. "I doubt that. Grace rarely hits *forty*. She has never had a warning, much less a speeding ticket."

"So why didn't she see the red?"

"We don't know that she didn't. My major concern has been making sure she's all right. The doctors assure us that she is."

"Was she drunk?"

"Grace?" The idea was absurd. Trust a reporter to suggest it. "Grace doesn't drink."

"I saw her with a glass of wine in a restaurant a month ago."

"If it was there, it was for show. Grace *doesn't* drink."

"Does she take drugs?"

Francine struggled to stay cool. "If she did, she would never be able to accomplish all she does. She's a remarkable woman."

"Then that's a no?"

"Emphatically."

"Not even a sedative? Or a sleeping pill? Was she taking a cold medicine that might have knocked her out?"

"Grace wasn't taking so much as an Excedrin."

"She suffers from headaches, then?"

"No."

"Does she have a heart condition?"

"What makes you ask that?"

"The nurses won't give me an answer."

Francine couldn't help herself. "That's because it's none of your business."

"Grace Dorian is a public figure. Her readers would like to know if her health is failing. Has she had blackouts before?"

"No, and she didn't have one now." Francine put a light hand on Robin's arm. In a voice that was remarkably sympathetic, given the seething inside, she said, "Grace was in a simple accident. It's an open-and-shut case. I know that doesn't make for very exciting press, but there's no story here, Robin."

"She ran a red light."

"For all we know, the light malfunctioned. Like I said, Grace has a clean driving record." Francine smiled. "I'm running upstairs now. I'll tell Grace you were here."

Three

Lies are like rabbits. Put one with another and they multiply fast.

—GRACE DORIAN, from *The Confidante*

ADVICE COLUMNIST HURT IN ACCIDENT

by Robin Duffy, *Telegram* Staff

Nationally syndicated advice columnist Grace Dorian was involved in a two-car accident yesterday on a road near her home. Dorian was rushed by ambulance to a local hospital, where she was treated for injuries and admitted. The driver of the other car, Douglas Gladiron, was unhurt.

The accident occurred at 5:15 P.M. Dorian, 61, was traveling north on South Webster when she ran a red light at Elm. Her car barreled into the cross traffic, broad-siding the one driven by Gladiron, 38. Witnesses at the scene estimated that Dorian was going 50 mph. There were no skid marks to show an attempt to stop.

The hospital declined to comment on speculation that Dorian had suffered a heart attack.

Police on the scene had no comment, other than to say that Dorian had been cited for a moving violation, and that further investigation was under way. While a family spokesman denied that either alcohol or drugs were involved, those are two of the factors the police will consider.

"Well, of course, the police will consider them," Francine cried, tossing the paper aside in disgust. "*Any* investigation considers them, and when they don't apply, they're crossed off the list. She makes Grace sound sick. She makes Grace sound *guilty*. Why couldn't she have simply left it that an investigation was under way?" But Francine knew the answer, as did Sophie, who was reading the paper over her shoulder.

"She was spicing up the piece."

"At Grace's expense! Why do they do that to celebrities? Why do they imply something that isn't the case at all? What happened to 'innocent until proven guilty'?"

Sophie was subdued. Quietly, she said, "At least she didn't mention Alzheimer's disease."

Francine looked at her sharply. "She had no reason to."

"She didn't have a reason to mention a heart attack. Or alcohol or drugs. When none of those pan out, will she go looking for more? Grace's fans will believe Alzheimer's disease before they'll buy drugs or booze."

"Grace doesn't *have* Alzheimer's disease."

"I *know*."

"Then why do you keep mentioning it?" The words alone made Francine nervous.

"Because you did last night."

"That's right, because you and I swore to always tell each other the truth. I never lied to you about what your doctors said, and I won't lie to you about what Grace's says. But you can see as clearly as me that he's wrong. Grace does just fine for a woman her age. Nothing would have happened last night if Gus had been where he was supposed to be."

To her credit, Sophie looked remorseful. "I've apologized for that ten times, Mom. How many more times should I do it?"

Francine sighed. She had been tense from the minute she'd woken up—and that from a sleep barely two hours long. A vigorous run with Legs had helped, but only until she had come back inside. The newspaper brought reality back in spades.

But Sophie wasn't responsible for either Robin Duffy's annoying piece or Davis Marcoux's misguided diagnosis. Wrapping an arm around her daughter's slim waist, she said, "No more. I know you're sorry."

"It's beside the point, anyway. You're right. Nothing would have happened if Gus had been driving. But Grace was driving, and something *did* happen. What if the police question her doctor?"

Francine had been asking herself the same thing for much of the night. "The police didn't smell liquor on her breath. They didn't ask her to walk a straight line. If they suspected something, they would have asked, and they didn't. They let it go, knowing that the evidence would be gone by morning, which tells me that they weren't suspecting alcohol or drugs. The only one doing that is Robin Duffy. Davis Marcoux can truthfully deny that Grace was high. And he won't volunteer information. That would be a violation of doctor-patient confidentiality."

The phone rang. Francine had already called the hospital and learned that Grace was fine. Still, she felt a pang of anxiety. "Hello?"

"Have you seen the paper, Francine?" The voice was accusatory, but reassuringly aware.

"I wouldn't pay it any heed."

"Well, that's fine for you to say, but do you know how many other people will see it? I don't understand. I never did anything to Robin Duffy. Were *you* the one who talked with her last night?"

"Yes, and I told her that neither alcohol, nor drugs, nor ill health was involved."

"Were you *vehement* about it?"

"As vehement as I could be without sounding defensive."

"She must have thought it anyway. Well, it's done," Grace said, sounding resigned. "Can you handle damage control? No doubt the calls are on their way."

"I can handle it," Francine said. It was the least she could do to redeem herself. She *should* have been more vehement.

"But if you're doing that, who'll pick me up? The doctor just gave me permission to leave."

"How do you feel?"

"Fine. My head is harder than people give me credit for. I'd like to have breakfast at home. And then I'd like to work."

"It wouldn't hurt to relax for one day."

"There's too much to do. So who's coming for me?"

Francine caught Sophie's eye. "Your granddaughter."

"When?"

"Fifteen minutes." When Sophie gestured wildly, Francine said, "Make that thirty."

"She's still sleeping?" Grace asked disapprovingly.

Francine was relieved to be able to say, "No. She's right here in the kitchen with me. But she has to shower and dress and have breakfast first. Or should I send her along without breakfast?"

"Goodness, no. She needs breakfast more than I do. Send her when she's done, but don't let her dawdle, Francine. And, please," this, in a long-suffering way, "do what you can to stop the rumors. I can't afford to have idle speculation about my health. Not at this point. There's too much at stake."

Francine had just enough time for a fast breakfast with Sophie when the phone rang. It was Mary Wickley, an old family friend, deeply concerned about Grace.

Francine assured her that Grace was fine and, indeed, on her way home from the hospital as they spoke. Yes, Mary knew that neither alcohol nor drugs were involved. Yes, she knew how misleading the press could be. Francine stressed that Grace hadn't suffered a heart attack, but a simple concussion, hence the standard precaution of the hospital stay. She suggested Mary spread the word.

She had barely hung up when the phone rang again. It was George, Grace's newspaper publisher, also a close friend, wondering, first, why the *Telegram* had gotten the story over the *Transcript*, and, second, whether Grace was all right.

"Grace is fine," Francine said, reprioritizing the questions, "and the *Telegram* got the story because a reporter there has a fixation on Grace. Story? No story. Grace had an ordinary little accident. She bumped her head, so the hospital kept her overnight. It was more to protect themselves than her."

The next call was from a film critic who lived one town over and was in Grace's social circle. Mary Wickley had called him with the news. "I've seen this happen dozens of times, Francine, no-name reporters trying to make a splash. Don't think *twice* about what she wrote. It'll be forgotten by nightfall. And so *what* if Grace had a little nip with tea?"

Francine denied that, and Robin Duffy's other insinuations. She had barely finished when Tony called. He was stinging from a balling out by George for not getting the story and passed his venom on to Francine. "Okay, so I don't pass muster as Mr. Right, but the *least* you could have done was call me from the hospital."

"Tony, my mother was injured. I was seeing to her needs. The last thing I was thinking about was the paper."

"You talked with the *Telegram*."

"She was there. She asked stupid questions. I denied them. There was no story. I told her that."

"She got the scoop."

"There *was* no scoop."

"Well, I want the next one. Was it her heart?"

"No, it was not her heart. Her heart is fine."

"Then she's depressed."

"*Grace?* She *isn't*. And anyway, how would being depressed relate to having an automobile accident?"

"She could have been so distracted she wasn't paying attention."

"Has Grace ever seemed distracted to you? No. Not once, and *don't* say this was a cry for help—as in attempted suicide—because I'll scream. This is pathetic. It isn't nine o'clock yet, and yours is the fourth call I've gotten." The other line rang. "There's the fifth."

The fifth was from another friend, who then called Francine's vet, making him the sixth. The seventh was from Grace's book publisher, who had received a call from George and proceeded, despite Francine's vehement reassurances, to call Grace's agent, who became the eighth.

By this time, Francine was fit to be tied. "It was a stupid little accident. I don't understand what the uproar is about."

"Idle speculation," was Amanda Burnham's opinion. "People don't have enough else to think about. We can't whisper about Russia because the Cold War is over. We can't badmouth Congress because it's all been said before, and besides, we elected the bums. We need another flood."

Francine let out a breath. "No. We just need a little respect for the privacy of others. I'm going to have Grace write her next column on that."

"Has someone written in about it?"

"Someone will, if I have to be that someone myself." She had a new thought. "Oh, Lord, are we going to be swamped with get-well cards?"

"Probably. But don't worry. I'll call Tony. He'll have someone handle them." The phone rang again. "Let it ring," Amanda advised.

But Francine couldn't. "Grace asked me to do damage control. An unanswered phone may do more harm than good."

"Where's Marny?"

"Not in until nine." She checked her watch. "Okay. It's nine. She'll be here any minute. In the meantime, I'd better get this. It may be Grace."

It was Annie Diehl. "What's this I hear about Grace breaking a hip?"

"Breaking a hip? Where did you hear that?"

"There was talk down the hall. Something about an accident."

"An *automobile* accident."

To Francine's astonishment, Annie sounded relieved. "Thank God. Old-age things make me nervous. Last year alone, between my mother and three aunts, there were two broken hips, one cancer, one pair of cataracts, and two sets of dentures. Grace is approaching the age when those things start to happen."

"She's only sixty-one!"

"So how is she?"

"Fine. No broken hip, no cancer, no cataracts, no dentures. She banged her head. There may be three stitches in all, and they'll fade into her hairline."

"That's good, because she's been invited to be part of a panel on adolescence in Chicago in July. It's a full month after her last graduation speech. Unless she really isn't up to it." The gauntlet was thrown down.

"She'll do it," Francine said quickly. Grace had wanted damage control—this was the strongest kind. "Fax us a confirmation, and we'll put it on her calendar. And, Annie? If anyone asks about a broken hip, set them straight?"

Grace left the hospital in a cloud of the perfume that one of the nurses, a fan, had given her. It was more fruity than her normal, but she hadn't wanted to appear ungrateful. Nurses were powerful people. They had access to the kinds of private information that could ruin someone like her—which made them dangerous people.

So she had thanked each one by name, giving each hand a squeeze. "People need to know that they're appreciated," she told Sophie on the way to the car. Accordingly, she thanked Sophie for picking her up, without criticizing her driving, and told her how pretty she looked, without gloating over the unusually sedate way she was dressed.

She didn't say a word about Sophie's making Gus unavailable the day before, because that would mean mentioning the accident, which might lead to a discussion of its cause, and Grace didn't want to talk about that. She suspected Francine had told Sophie of Davis Marcoux's diagnosis, suspected that was behind Sophie's docility. Then again, it might have been guilt at absconding with Gus.

In any case, Grace let her off the hook. She was feeling benevolent. She had had a brush with something or other, and had escaped.

But there was more, an advisory on family solidarity. Yes, Francine was loyal. Sophie, too, or she wouldn't have come back after college. But solidarity could be tried past its limits. If Grace behaved erratically or grew difficult, her own family might choose to believe she was sick. She couldn't have that. She needed their wholehearted backing if the image of The Confidante was to remain intact.

The thought of losing their backing, the thought of the world viewing a lesser Grace Dorian, the thought of what just might have caused the accident set her to shaking. But the shaking was self-defeating. It distracted her. It sent her into mini-panics that jumbled her world.

She had to remain calm and lucid, had to project total control.

So, after giving Sophie a hug and a kiss, she went to her bedroom to shower away the accident, the hospital, and the fruity perfume. Once she was properly repaired, she went to the kitchen.

Francine was on the phone, looking as if she had just come in from a run, and while Grace had always asked her to shower after exercising, she didn't say a word now, neither about the sweat nor about the dog that sat by her feet looking up at her with pure adoration. Crankiness was characteristic of Alzheimer's patients. Grace refused to display it.

Francine hung up the phone. "How do you feel?"

"Much better. There's no place like home."

"Does your head hurt?"

It did. But Grace wasn't complaining. "My head is fine. There was no need for me to stay at the hospital overnight. They kept waking me to see if I was all right. I didn't sleep a wink."

"That explains it, then," Francine said with a smile, and began working at the buttons of Grace's blouse. "You're done up wrong."

Grace batted her hands away and flattened her palms on the buttons. "I certainly am not. I know how to button a blouse."

"When you're feeling one hundred percent," Francine agreed, "but you had a concussion. I'm amazed that you don't want to lie around in bed all day."

"Why would I want to do *that*, if I'm fine? I'm *fine*, Francine," she argued, keeping her arm aligned with the buttons of her blouse, "and I won't be treated like a patient! I am not sick," she said in a huff. "I wish you wouldn't keep saying that I am! Honestly. If I didn't know better, I'd wonder if you weren't looking to usurp me." She found some satisfaction in the drop of Francine's jaw. "Now. I'm going to work. Margaret, I'll have my usual breakfast. Bring it to the office." She marched from the room with her head held high. Only when she reached the refuge of the hall did she duck into the powder room and, with unsteady hands, rebutton her blouse. While she was at it, she rechecked herself in the mirror. Face, hair, clothes—all were fine. She checked a second time, then a third, and was finally assured. It was another minute yet before she felt calm enough to return to the hall.

Another hour passed before Francine appeared in the office herself, and then it was to find a bespectacled Grace working intently at her desk, looking so productive that Francine felt uplifted.

She leaned against the doorjamb. "What's the subject?"

"Mother's Day protocol for children with multiple steps."

"Need any help?"

"Thanks, sweetheart, but this is an easy one."

"Your flowers are gorgeous." One vase was filled with daffodils, another with tulips, a third positively stuffed with roses. "If this is what comes from cracking up the car, I've been driving safely for too long."

Grace shot her a look so droll, so human, so *right* coming from Grace at that moment, that Francine laughed aloud.

"The tulips are from Amanda," Grace informed her, "the roses from George, and the daffodils from Jim. They were delivered to the hospital first." She spied Francine over her glasses. "You are telling people that I'm home, aren't you?"

"Of course. You just beat us all to the punch." She glanced at the telephone. The panel was lit. "Calls are still coming in?"

"Sophie and Marny are juggling them. As for me," Grace held up both hands, "I'm not *touching* the phone."

"Good. There's no need. The calls will quiet down once word spreads that you're home and well. Did Margaret bring your muffin?"

"Yes."

"Can I get you a fresh cup of tea?"

"No, dear."

"Well, I'll go to work then," she said, because that was what getting back to normal meant. It didn't mean waiting hand and foot on Grace, or offering to do her work for her, or standing at her elbow looking for mistakes. It meant walking out and pulling the door shut as she always did when Grace was at work.

Sophie was just hanging up the phone as she passed. "That was our Minneapolis affiliate. He heard that Grace was thrown from her car. *Thrown* from her car. There's an irony here, y'know. Grace prides herself on having control. Well, she doesn't have it now. Rumor is running rampant."

"It's temporary. The truth will prevail."

"Yeah, but what is the truth?"

"She had an accident, and she's fine. Back to work the next morning. How was she during the drive home?"

"An absolute peach. Didn't utter a single sweet, back-handed barb. The contrast was marked. She's usually more sly. But then, she had our attention this morning. She does love to be the center of things. Maybe she ran that red light on purpose."

"For the *attention*?"

"Either that, or she did it to punish me for going out with her chauffeur."

"No, Sophie. She wouldn't do that. The accident was a simple mistake. She has a lot on her mind."

"*She* does? Try *we* do. We're the ones who grease the wheels of this machine. We make arrangements and coordinate things. We take the guff when things go wrong. All *she* has to do is sit there and spew out her thoughts. She has a pretty nice life. We're the ones who jump when she calls. Look at you." She ran an eye down Francine. "Tailored slacks and a silk blouse. That's Grace's style, not yours. I'd forgotten you owned clothes that were so—" spoken with distaste— "staid."

"Actually," Francine confessed, because Sophie would have seen through anything but the truth in a minute, "it took me ten minutes to find these. They were buried in the back of my closet. But I didn't put them on for Grace. I did it for me. The accident shook me, too. I'm feeling edgy." She smiled, then breathed a sheepish, "So why risk a confrontation with Grace?"

Phone calls continued to come, as did flowers, but the day was otherwise uneventful, to Francine's relief. Grace wasn't quite as productive as she looked, but Francine couldn't begrudge her that, after what she'd been through. She was trying, at least. She was sitting at her computer, entering thoughts. If some of them were too vague to be useful, that was fine. Francine was good at fleshing things out.

Grace drew the lines, Francine colored them in. They had been doing that to one extent or another for forty-some-odd years. This was normal.

Father Jim came for tea and stayed through dinner, and this, too, was normal. He did it several times a week, and Francine never minded. Jim was like family. He was an easy conversationalist, comfortable discussing any subject, knowledgeable in most. Francine loved talking with him.

So did Grace. She was at her best when Jim was around, less expectant, gentler. Father Jim had that effect on people. His manner was serene, his words kind. Francine wasn't ardently religious, but when she was with Jim, she felt soothed. Never once had she seen him ruffled. Never once had she seen Grace pull rank with him around.

They had finished dinner and were in the den, Sophie reading a book, Grace perched on the arm of Jim's chair while he played chess with Francine, when the doorbell rang. Francine glanced first at Grace, who was the picture of innocence, then at Sophie, who shrugged.

It was too late for flowers. It was also too late for Margaret, who had retired to her quarters.

Francine had a vision of Robin Duffy, after single-handedly

wreaking havoc for the Dorians that day, dropping by unannounced in the hope of catching someone off guard.

Gearing for battle, she dragged Sophie over to hold her position against Jim, and strode from the den, down the long hall and through the front foyer to the door. She boldly swung it open. Robin Duffy wasn't there. Davis Marcoux was.

He came right behind Robin on Francine's list of people she didn't want to see.

Inherent manners—and his foot, which had stolen slyly over the threshold—kept her from closing the door in his face. "Dr. Marcoux."

"Davis. How are you, Francine?"

"Relaxing. It's been a long workday." She meant it as a hint. The sooner he was gone, the better. He made her nervous.

"How's Grace?"

"Excellent. She wouldn't hear of taking the day off. She worked right along with us."

"Did she have any trouble?"

"Confusion? Disorientation? Lunacy? Sorry, but no."

"I'd like to say hello."

"She really is fine."

"Then you won't mind showing me in."

Put that way, Francine had no choice. If she refused him, he would think she was hiding something. So she stood aside for his entry, then recrossed the foyer at a confident pace and strode back down the hall toward the den. He matched her step for step.

"Beautiful home."

"Thanks."

She wasn't giving him a tour. Nor was she encouraging

friendly chitchat. It took concentration to remain confident when all she could think of was the diagnosis he'd made.

Actually, he looked even less like a doctor than he had the day before. He still wore slacks and an oxford-cloth shirt, but where the knot of a tie had been there was now a deep vee of bare throat. A leather bomber jacket had replaced the lab coat, and beneath the slacks were boots. Not new boots, but worn ones, loved ones. They went with his shadowed jaw and his mussed hair, and made him seem taller and more the rogue than ever.

She concentrated on not tripping on the rug.

He followed her into the den, where Grace promptly produced the smoothest of smiles. "Dr. Marcoux. What a surprise. It's a rare breed of doctor that makes house calls nowadays."

Davis smirked. "I didn't have much choice. It was either stop by to see how you were, or face my nurses' wrath in the morning."

Francine didn't believe that for a minute. She figured he had come here on his own and for a very specific purpose, and that annoyed her. She hated phonies. She wanted him gone.

But he was shaking hands with Jim, who introduced him to Sophie—which gave Francine a moment's pride, in spite of it all. Then he was turning to Grace.

"You look well."

"I feel well."

"Headache?"

"Gone."

"Soreness around that gash?"

"Barely."

"Well, that's good, then."

Francine stayed by the door, poised to show the good doctor out.

"Are you just coming home from the hospital?" asked Father Jim.

"'Fraid so."

Grace asked, "Do you live nearby?"

"Several miles up the road. I bought a corner of the Glendenning estate."

Grace arched a brow. "That's prime land. I'm impressed."

"Don't be. My corner's the one without the house."

"If there's no house, where do you live?" Sophie asked.

"In a trailer."

There was an elitist silence.

Then Father Jim chuckled. "Shame on you, Davis."

"I *do* live in a trailer."

"True," Jim chided, "but that only tells half the story." To the others, he said, "The trailer is hidden in the woods about fifty feet from where his house will be. The foundation was poured last fall. Last time I was there, the frame was going up." He returned to Davis. "Have you done much inside?"

"Nah. The winter was too cold. I will now."

"A trailer," Sophie said. She was clearly intrigued by the thought of something so lowbrow on land so highbrow. "That's cool."

Francine didn't care if he lived in a tent, as long as he went back there before he stirred things up here.

"I'm the general contractor," he explained, "hence the trailer. I'm not sure the town realizes I'm living in it, but this way I'm right there and can get more work done."

"A regular jack of all trades," Francine remarked, thinking master of none, which would explain his misdiagnosis of Grace. "Being a doctor and a building contractor are two big jobs. How can you do either justice?"

His eyes held hers. "Medicine comes first. But I'd crack up if that was all I did with my life. Everyone needs an outlet. Mine is carpentry. I've always been good with my hands, and I have plenty of local advice. Besides, it's my own house, so I'm in no rush. I'm enjoying the process of building it."

As far as Francine was concerned, building his own house could be as much a reflection of egotism or stupidity as skill. Stupidity would explain his misdiagnosis, egotism his refusal to admit it. And yes, there was a chance that she was being unduly rough on him. But she didn't know why he was here, other than to drive home his point.

"Do you play chess?" Father Jim asked.

Francine could have killed him. She was relieved when Davis slipped his hands in his pockets and said, "Nope. Gotta run, anyway. I just thought I'd drop by, since it's on my way. I'll see you in five days, Grace?"

"Five days?" Francine asked in alarm. "What for?"

"My *stitches*," Grace answered. "Francine, show the doctor out now, like a good girl."

Francine managed a smile, but it faded the instant she started down the hall. She felt Davis beside her—impossible *not* to feel him—and tried to think of something to say, but her mind wouldn't work along sensible lines. She kept imagining that he was an actor playing a doctor. He had the bad-boy looks, the self-confidence, the gall.

"Do I make you nervous?" he asked.

He was too close, too cocky. She lengthened her stride. "Of course not. What makes you think that?"

"You're walking hard. Do you run?"

"Regularly. Do you?"

"No. I lift."

"Weights?"

"Wood."

She refused to picture it. The important thing was getting him out of the house. Her heart was hammering again. Davis Marcoux did that to her.

"Here we go." She swung the front door open. "Thanks for dropping by, Dr. Marcoux."

"Davis."

"As you can see, Grace is fine. I appreciate your concern for her."

"My concern is for you," he said, facing her across the threshold.

She laughed, so nonchalant Grace would have been proud. "Then you really *do* need an outlet from work. You're getting carried away. I assure you, I'm fine."

"You're uncomfortable with what I said last night."

"Well, wouldn't you be, if you were in my shoes?"

"Definitely. But I wouldn't be trying to deny it."

"What would you be doing? Making arrangements to have Grace committed?"

"I'd be thinking about the spells she has. I'd be worrying that if she continues to drive, she may have another accident. I'd be wondering how much she compensates for other failings and how long she can keep it up. I'd be assuring her that you'll love her whether she's perfect or not."

Francine waved a hand to erase what he'd said. "Doctors are alarmists. I've learned that from experience, and it's our fault," she said, "a reaction against paternalism, against years of doctors telling patients only as much as *they* decided we needed to hear. So we scream for patients' rights. Now doctors share everything, even half-baked diagnoses."

"It's not *my* fault she's having those symptoms."

"No, but you're turning our lives upside down by labeling them something they aren't. I'm with Grace for the better part of every day, and I haven't seen any sign of disability."

"Well, you may. And if you do, and if you want to talk with someone, I'm here."

"Thank you," she said, because that seemed the best way of getting him to leave. "You've been very kind."

"Not yet. But I can be. Right now, I'm the bad guy. You don't want me here because I remind you of something you don't want to know. But there may come a time when you need to know more. Dealing with AD can be a nightmare. I can help."

"I'll remember that," she said, but her voice was clipped, her message clear.

"And you want me to leave."

"My daughter is in charge of my chess pieces. If I stand here much longer, the game will be lost."

"Wouldn't want that." He started across the porch.

"Well, that's *my* escape," she defended herself, because he made her sound shallow. "If I thought for a minute that hovering over Grace would make things better, I'd do it. I *love* my mother."

He paused on the top step, seemed about to say something, then went on into the night.

Francine bit her tongue to keep from calling him back.

Four

Family is the only earthly enterprise in which the job description is written in blood.
   —GRACE DORIAN, in an address to the American
   Association of Family Therapists

Grace returned to routine so smoothly that she decided the accident had been a fluke. If she spent longer writing the next few weeks' columns, she attributed it to quality control.

"My readership expects the best," she told Francine. "I'm appalled at the way I used to rattle off bits of advice, right off the top of my head. I should be taking more care. Saying foolish things in my columns will tarnish The Confidante's image—not to mention lower the worth of my book. I owe it to my audience to spend longer on every response."

It sounded good to her.

Besides, taking more time meant catching some pretty

goofy things. On the rereading, some paragraphs made no sense at all. It was a problem with typing. She still hadn't mastered the computer. One sentence was merging with another midway. So she had to work harder on what she did, but the finished product was fine, regardless of what Francine said.

Not that Francine was brash about it. She either joked, or was meek, or pretended to be totally befuddled. "This doesn't make sense, Grace," she would say. Or, "We'll really shock the readers with *this* one." Or, "I am *totally* ignorant on this subject. Tell me more."

But Grace stood behind her work. She proofread what she wrote. She saw no problem at all.

Nor were there any bouts of major disorientation, significant periods of oblivion, or monumental catastrophes. Each day without an incident buoyed her more. Grace 9, Davis 0. Grace 10, Davis 0. Grace 11, Davis 0.

She didn't go out driving alone, because there was always someone to drive her.

She didn't leave her bedroom suite without double-checking on her appearance, because good looks came harder with age.

She made little notes to herself on all sorts of things, even personal things like grooming, because notes helped. Unfortunately, she sometimes didn't remember them until after the fact, or wrote a second set when she couldn't find the first, but they gave her a needed comfort, what with all she had to do. It was a frighteningly busy time. Francine could certainly help with the daily columns and Sophie with the graduation speeches. But no one could help with the book, which was the most important thing of all.

"Don't worry so," Francine urged after finding her fretting before a blank screen. "There's no rush."

"There *is* a rush," Grace cried. "The pub date is less than a year away."

"You have until October. Katia said so."

"Katia didn't tell *me* that." Grace had an awful thought. "Did you tell her that I was having trouble?" She wouldn't stand for that. It was a betrayal of the first order. Naturally, Francine denied it, but Grace remained skeptical. "How did the subject come up?"

"She was working on scheduling and wanted a rough guess as to when we'd have something for her to see. I threw the question right back and asked when she needed it. She said October."

"But that's just a *first* draft."

"You rarely do more."

"Is that a complaint? Are you saying my work is shoddy? If you feel overburdened picking up the pieces, just tell me, and we'll hire someone else to help. Honestly, Francine, I don't know what gets into you sometimes." She looked despairingly at the screen, then at the pile of notes and outlines and other thoughts upon which the book contract had been based. But getting a contract was one thing, writing a book something else. She didn't know where to begin.

Of course, if she admitted that, Francine would think she was confused, or disoriented, or unable to function. So she simply said, "October is optimistic."

"If we need an extension, we'll get one," Francine said, seeming undaunted in a way that only annoyed Grace more.

Optimism was one thing, reality another. She had a disconcerting flash of one extension after another all the way to oblivion. "If we do that, they may postpone the publishing date, and that's the *last* thing I want. This is the most important project I've ever done. It's my *autobiography*, my stamp on the world."

"Your columns are that."

"But this *cements* it. This is *proof* of what my columns have done." How to explain the urgency she felt? "This is a statement that I've truly *become* someone, Francine. Yes, yes, I know. My columns go onto microfiche, but this is different. Only important people are approached about writing their autobiographies—and we're being paid a good sum, which means that someone is hoping for big things, which means that my autobiography will be in bookstores, department stores, hotels, supermarkets, airports. And libraries. Books put on library shelves stay there forever. Sophie's children, Sophie's *grand*children will see my autobiography on those shelves. If you'd been born a nobody, you'd understand."

And that was the crux of it. Because Grace had been born a nobody, writing this book was a milestone. Likewise, because she had been born a nobody, its writing was a nightmare.

Where was she from? Who were her parents? What was her home like? Who were her friends? What events had shaped her life? Why had she never, ever, returned to the town where she was born?

She had made her name writing nonfiction. Her autobiography was something else. She could clean up the truth—or twist it some—or chuck it and offer all-out lies. She had read *plenty* of autobiographies that had been fabricated. It was done all the time.

What to do? She couldn't decide. But she had the feeling that if she didn't hurry, she would run out of time.

Francine typed as fast as the thoughts came. The Confidante was behind again, and Tony was braying for copy.

"She's getting worse," Sophie said, scrutinizing Francine's screen. "You've rewritten every column this week."

"Not every one," Francine argued, but absently. She was wallowing in unrequited love, feeling the angst of a teenager whose friend had captured the man she adored. Man? Boy. The distinction was germane. "'You and your friend are only fifteen,'" she read aloud. "'That's too young to be focused on love. You should be enjoying your friends and dating different boys. That's the only way you'll learn what you truly want. Have you ever heard the saying about clouds and silver linings? Let your friend date this boy. He may not be such a catch, after all. You may find someone even better.' Sound okay?" she asked Sophie.

"Sounds very Grace."

"Surprise, surprise. I've only read a million of her columns."

"Good thing, since you're writing them now."

But Francine couldn't imagine writing Grace's columns on a long-term basis. Grace was the one who had a way with words, a way with thoughts, a way with advice. Francine mimicked her. That was all.

"I'm just cleaning up," she told Sophie. "Grace does the basics."

"Barely."

"That's temporary. She's preoccupied with the autobiography."

"Have you seen any of that yet? No. Face it, Mom. She has a problem. Know what she did before? She asked for the latest information on CPR certification, so I put a printout on her desk. When she asked for the information again, I pointed to the printout. She laughed at herself and said something about not seeing the trees for the forest, but then a little while later she asked for the same stuff *again*."

"So she's forgetful sometimes. But she was totally coherent when I asked about this column. She remembered reading this little fifteen-year-old's letter, and she quoted two other letters on the same subject. Her mind is sharp."

"Not always, lately."

"Show a little compassion, Sophie."

"I do. But people always tell *me* to face facts. 'Accept your illness, Sophie.' Well, what about Grace? What if she does have Alzheimer's? I've done a computer check on treatments. New medicines keep cropping up, but nothing works consistently. If she has it, she'll only get worse. And then what?"

With a resigned sigh, Francine draped an arm over the back of her chair. She didn't want to discuss this, but Sophie clearly needed to talk. "Yes?"

"She could hurt herself, say, burn herself in the kitchen."

"She never cooks."

"She makes tea in the middle of the night."

"She uses the microwave."

"What if she forgets how?"

"She won't have the tea."

"What if she turns on the gas?"

"Why would she remember that and not the microwave?"

"Because one is recently learned, one not. She'll remember the older one."

Francine felt a headache coming on. It wasn't the first she'd had that week. "This is not what I need to hear right now."

"Maybe she should retire."

"Grace? She's an institution. She isn't retiring."

"Everyone has to at some point. Grampa did."

"Only because the sawmill closed, and his money was invested in operations about which he knew nothing. He was smart enough to let people who *did* know something run them. His job became dealing with his investment banker, which he could do from the den."

"Doesn't Grace deserve a rest?"

"She doesn't want one. Suggest it, and she'll have your head. Some professions are retirement-proof. This is one."

"And why is that?" Sophie asked, then answered herself, "Those retirement-proof professions use the mind, not the body. Those people can keep going from wheelchairs, if need be, or *beds*, if need be, because the tool of their trade— the mind—is intact. But what if Grace's isn't?"

"If Grace's isn't," Francine allowed a moment's pessimism, "then we're all in trouble. *The Confidante* is us. It's what we do, who we are. I can't imagine a world without it. Can you?"

Sophie couldn't, and that was the bitch of it. Grace Dorian had been the focal point of the family from the time of Sophie's earliest thoughts. She was the linchpin around which the others revolved. It was one thing for Sophie to play the skeptic with Francine, quite another for her to imagine the reality of a debilitated Grace.

What would Sophie do if *The Confidante* ceased to exist? She would move to the city and live in anonymity with her friends. She would find a job as frivolous as theirs and focus on having fun.

But without The Confidante? Without the knowledge that *The Confidante* was waiting for her at home? Without that heritage? Without that *rock*?

Grace had all the answers. There were times when that made Sophie sick. Other times, it helped.

Like when she was fourteen. Her hormones had been all

over the place, wreaking havoc with her blood-sugar levels. She spent entire days testing herself, giving herself shots, and seeing doctors, or so it seemed. Her *whole life* was taken up with these things, or so it seemed.

Then one day she'd had it. She sat down on her bed and vowed that she was done. She despised living in a strait-jacket. She didn't care if her diabetes *did* get out of control. So what if the blood vessels in her retina leaked and she went blind? So what if her circulatory system rotted and her feet fell off? She didn't care if she *died*.

When Francine's pleas had fallen on deaf ears, Grace had taken her hand and led her out through the woods to the abandoned sawmill. Carefully, they climbed the stone steps behind the waterwheel. At the top, they slid along the ledge to the corner and sat. Beneath them, the river swirled around tree roots, rocks, and the weather-worn wood of the wheel.

Grace didn't speak. So Sophie fumed silently. She didn't like Grace just then, any more than she liked her mother, her grandfather, her doctor, or her illness. She hated her father for having his own life. She *detested* her friends for being healthy.

She kept waiting for Grace to tell her all the things she had heard a zillion times before. But Grace was silent, and the flow of the river was soothing. Sophie hugged her knees to her chin and watched the downstream dance of a leaf. In time it disappeared around the bend, along with the worst of her anger.

That was when Grace said, "This is my favorite spot in the world. Don't tell your grandfather, he's so proud of the house, but this spot is better. One season is more beautiful than the next here. More peaceful. Look. On the far bank. Goldfinches. Shhh."

"They're just yellow birds," Sophie grumbled.

"They're mated. The bright one is the male. See how he sits off to the side while she pecks around for food?"

"Why doesn't he do it?"

"Probably because she's better at it. Females are more versatile. Some would say they're stronger."

"Do you?"

"Women certainly endure more in their lives, since we're the ones who give birth. We have a capacity for stretching. We adapt to change more easily than men. God gave us that gift."

"Gift? Or curse?" Sophie asked, because she knew where Grace was headed and she wasn't going without a fight.

Grace had grown silent again. Sophie remembered sitting there for a full five minutes, before the current had lulled her and she'd lost track of the time, and then Grace had pointed to the slick head of a beaver that was swimming downstream, dodging rocks in its way.

"No life flows smoothly," she said once the beaver was gone from sight. "We all have ins and outs, ups and downs."

"You don't."

"I most certainly do. You just don't know about the bad things because I don't choose to dwell on them."

"*You* don't have diabetes." *No* one else in her family did. She didn't know why *she'd* gotten it. It wasn't *fair*.

"Some women have worse things," Grace said.

"Like what?"

"Some women can't see. Some can't walk. Some can't hear. Some can't have babies. You can do all those things. Okay, so there's a little official business you have to see to several times a day. But how much time does that take? Out of sixteen hours, waking hours, diabetes may take—

what—twenty minutes? Is twenty minutes a day too much to pay to have all those other good things in life?"

Sophie had started to cry then, had wept in frustration and surrender with her face to her knees because she knew that Grace was right, which meant that she was going to have to live with diabetes for the rest of her life.

Grace had simply held her until the sobs slowed. Then, softly, she had said, "I know it's hard now, muffin, but just think of all you have. You have a marvelous brain and a beautiful face and a wonderful home. You have this river to look at from one season to the next. Yes, you have an unfortunate condition, but aren't you glad there's a treatment for it? You can lead a perfectly normal life, a perfectly *long* life. Aren't you *glad*?"

Put that way, Sophie had been glad. To this day, when she was down, she had only to remember Grace's words to feel that gratitude, and to believe. *You can lead a perfectly normal life, a perfectly long life.* Grace was the embodiment of optimism.

Only now, with Grace possibly ill, did Sophie realize how much she relied on her. One part of her wanted a life of her own in the very worst way. The other part was terrified of loosening the ties.

Francine tried not to think about the possibility of Alzheimer's disease, but it kept popping up when she least expected it, when she was relaxed and feeling safe and most resented its intrusion. It was like a piece of lint that wouldn't be flicked away. She cursed Davis Marcoux for having put the bug in her ear.

Then, one evening in late May, she was playing chess

with Jim O'Neill in the den. Dinner was done and a fire lit—unnecessarily, since the days were warm, but Francine loved a fire. It warmed her beyond the physical, inspiring the romantic notion that when a fire danced in the hearth, all was right with the world.

At this particular moment, all should have been. Sophie was spending the night in the city with friends Francine knew, liked, and trusted. Grace was in an easy chair by the fire, reading a book, looking perfectly normal and as relaxed as Francine felt.

After a time, Grace left the room to soak in the Jacuzzi. Moments later, Legs stole in and curled up at Francine's feet.

Without taking his eyes from the chessboard, Jim asked, "Does Grace seem all right to you?"

Francine had been dreading the question, though it came as no surprise. Father Jim knew Grace better than most anyone else outside the immediate family. "She has aches and pains. You're her age. Don't you?"

"It's not the aches and pains I worry about."

She paused. She stroked Legs's head. She forced herself to ask, "What is?"

"Forgetfulness. Distraction. A while back she said she was having spells. She told me they were better, but she's lost in her thoughts a lot. It happened the other day. I don't think she recognized me when I came."

"Of course she did," Francine chided, but she was shaken. Father Jim wouldn't say anything unless he was legitimately concerned.

So she tried to rationalize. "She tunes out sometimes, and who's to blame her? She has a lot on her mind. I wish we could cancel some of these graduations. When we booked them, we had no idea how busy she'd be. But Grace won't hear of canceling. So she's cutting back on social engagements instead."

"She told me she's getting too old to speak. That she gets rattled."

"Grace, rattled?" Francine asked in an attempt at humor that fell flat. In the ensuing silence, she debated changing the subject. But she needed to talk with Jim. She needed him to deny the worst. Not knowing how much he knew, she asked, "Have you spoken with Davis Marcoux?"

"Yes. He told me everything he told you." Jim smiled gently. "It was something of a confession. He fears he hasn't done a very good job of explaining himself to you, and that Grace will be hurt as a result."

"Be hurt?"

"Hurt herself."

Francine sat back in her chair. "Do you think she will?"

"You're asking if I believe the diagnosis."

She waited for him to go on, and while the waiting should have been painful, it wasn't. Jim O'Neill was a man of gentle thought, even divine inspiration. Francine fancied that he had a hot line to heaven, which was quite an admission for a woman of dubious faith.

He was also devilishly handsome. She imagined that he had broken more than one heart by entering the priesthood. She often thought it a waste of fine genes—and not only with regard to virility. There was sincerity, compassion, dedication. And intelligence.

He looked troubled. "Davis can't find another cause for her symptoms."

"Do you trust his judgment?"

"He comes well-recommended."

"From where?"

"Chicago. Big city, big-city hospital, national reputation."

"Davis?" She didn't want to believe it. Better to think him a fraud. "So why did he leave?"

"He wasn't a big-city person. He saw burnout on the horizon if he didn't make a change."

"How do you know him? Did he just show up in church one day?"

"Not quite. Davis doesn't buy into organized religion."

Francine pictured a stubbled jaw, dare-the-devil eyes, and worn leather boots. She grinned in spite of herself. "Surprise, surprise."

"I'm working on him," Jim vowed.

"When? Where? What's the connection?"

"Tyne Valley."

Tyne Valley. It was a name that had been in the wings of her life for more years than she could count. "He's another one of your people. Well, why not? Our maid is from the Valley, our chauffeur, our gardener, our secretary, and that's only mentioning the ones *currently* in our employ. Now a doctor. I'm impressed."

"You would be if you'd known his family. They've had their problems. Davis started at rock bottom. I helped him when I could, but he's done most of it alone. That's why the house he's building means so much to him. It's his first." He paused. "He's a good man, Frannie. He trained with the best. He's also consulted with the best on this case. I'm not sure we can ignore his theory."

Her heart twitched. "His theory stinks!"

Legs's head came up. Francine soothed it back down.

Quietly, Jim said, "Many things in life do."

"And still you believe," she marveled. "How can you, if this is true? Grace Dorian is her mind. What kind of God would take that from her, leaving the rest of her in perfect working order?"

"One who gives us tests. These tests build character."

"A lot of good character will do if you're dead," Francine remarked.

He looked straight at her. "You won't be dead."

"The test is for *me*?"

"And for me. And for Sophie. And for all of the others who've been touched by Grace. We have a choice. We can deny the diagnosis, or accept it. The latter may be the more compassionate course."

"But what if the diagnosis is wrong? What if accepting it means throwing our lives into a panic?"

"We can be calm."

"Maybe you can. I don't know if I can."

"That's the test," he said with such a small, kind, understanding smile that she couldn't argue more. What she would have liked was to fall into his arms and hold tight to his faith. But he was a priest. Physical displays were inappropriate.

So she contented herself with finishing the chess game and, in the process, absorbing as much of his inner peace as she could. She envied him. She wished she was devout, as he was. It might help to think that things would be all right even if the worst came to pass.

Grace was a nervous wreck on the eve of the Memorial Day weekend, and that compounded her worries. Being a nervous wreck was out of character. She had given many parties before, and bigger ones than this. But some things didn't come as easily to her as they had when she was younger.

The problem was, that after years of experience, she knew too much. Either the rental company would send the wrong linens, or the florist would send the wrong flowers, or the caterer would send the wrong food. So she called them, and they were *rude*. To listen to them, you'd have thought she called them *five times* a day!

So she asked Francine to call them, but Francine was busy supervising Margaret, who didn't know the first thing about getting the guest bedrooms ready.

"Francine, why are we doing this?" she finally asked. "Why do these people have to spend the night?"

"Because you invited them."

"I did no such thing. *You* must have. I don't like having people overnight. The party will be exhausting enough—just like graduations, everyone talking, everyone knowing *me* and my not knowing them, and the worst of it is that they expect me to! Can you imagine? Maybe we should have name tags."

"Uh, I'm not sure we should."

"Why not?"

"It's tacky."

"But I can't remember who everyone is. There are just too many people."

"I'll be right beside you, calling people by name. All you'll have to do is listen to me."

"That's what you said last weekend."

"Last weekend?"

"At the Hornway School."

"I wasn't at Hornway."

"Francine! You were right there beside me! You were holding my speech, but your hands were shaking so I kept getting lost. How could you have forgotten? It was a nightmare!"

Grace cringed just thinking of it. If her party was as bad, she would *die*.

She didn't understand it. Once upon a time, everything flowed. Now she couldn't do much of anything right.

But she was in a bind. To suddenly withdraw from public life would irreparably damage *The Confidante*. So she would go through with the party, the remaining graduations, and the panel discussion in Chicago in July.

And through it all she would pray.

Five

We prize our distractions, not as an escape from what is, but as a dream of what will be.
—GRACE DORIAN, from *The Confidante*

Francine ran through the darkness with Legs by her side. She was sweating freely, purging herself of festering thoughts. Her stride was steady, measured by the slap of her sneakers on the shoulder of the road and the rhythmic sough of her breath. Legs, a runner by trade, made nary a sound.

The trees flanking the road were lush, the grass thick. The lilacs were in bloom, filling the air with June's scents. It was ten at night. The sun had set barely an hour before. It was the eve of the summer solstice.

The day had been endless for Francine, so exhausting and tension-filled that even if she had run earlier, she would have done it again. Lately she ran faster and longer. It took faster and longer to relax.

The drone of a vehicle came from behind, rising steadily along with the beam of its headlights. It was a truck, not a car—she could tell from the sound—a smallish truck, its motor rougher than a sedan, smoother than a semi.

She was on the left shoulder, running against the traffic. The road wasn't wide by any means, but there was still plenty of room and then some for one smallish truck, one slimmish woman, and one skinny dog.

She tightened the leash on Legs. The dog was loping over the ground, but Francine wasn't risking her dashing into the road toward the truck. She loved Legs. In a world growing more complex by the day, Legs was the embodiment of simplicity.

She waited for the truck to pass, but it didn't. To the contrary. It sounded to have slowed. She sliced a look over her shoulder. It had slowed indeed.

She grew uneasy. Rednecks in pickup trucks weren't run-of-the-mill in these parts. If they wanted directions, fine. Anything else and she would launch into her my-dog-loves-raw-meat speech.

She kept running, kept sweating. The truck drew alongside and matched her pace. She darted the open window a warning look and came away picturing a muscled arm bare to the shoulder and an unkempt head of hair. Neither reassured her. Her breathing quickened.

The driver appeared to be alone. She was trying to decide if that was good or bad when he asked, "How's it goin'?"

The voice rang a bell. She slid him another look, a longer one this time. Then her blood began to boil. "What a *dumb* thing to do, Davis Marcoux! Do you have any idea how *frightening* it is to be accosted on a dark road in the middle of the night?"

He had the gall to sound amused. "Accosted? I'm not touching you. And it isn't the middle of the night. It's just ten."

"I nearly sicced my dog on you. It would not have been pretty."

"*That's* a killer dog?"

Francine ignored the slight. She continued to run, doing her best to steady her pounding heart. She wondered how he had recognized her. Forget darkness. Her hair was half-in, half-out of a scrunchy, her tank top was askew, and she was sweating like a pig. She didn't look like anything related to Grace.

"What are you doing here?" she asked, annoyed.

"Driving home."

"From the hospital? In *that*?" She couldn't resist after what he had said about Legs.

"I'll have you know that this is the Cadillac of pickups."

"It must raise brows in the hospital parking lot."

"Sure does," he said with what sounded like pride. "But I'm not coming from the hospital. I got thirsty and went out for a six-pack. Hop in and have a drink?"

She shook her head. "I never drink while I run."

"Stop running. I'll pull over."

"No thanks." She picked up her pace in an attempt to get her message across.

He didn't say anything, just cruised alongside. She shot him a look. "Don't you have anything better to do?"

"Not really. You look cute."

"I'm running."

"That's what I mean."

"Davis, please." Her breath was coming in shorter bursts. "I'm doing this to relax, and you're making the opposite happen."

"I make you nervous?"

"Yes."

"Why?"

"For starters, you make me remember the very things I came out here to forget."

She fully expected him to start talking about Grace, start *harping* on Grace. All he said was, "What else?"

"I'm not used to being paced by a truck." Her legs were starting to feel the strain. She slowed a fraction. So did the truck.

"How far will you run?"

"Home."

"That's another two miles."

She wasn't sure she would make it. "I'll make it."

"You sound winded."

"Only because I'm trying to talk." She decided not to.

"Slow down. Take a rest."

She ran on.

"Doesn't the dog get tired?"

She shot Legs a look. The dog's gait was steadier than hers.

"What do you do? Starve the thing to get it to run?"

That, she couldn't let pass. "I saved Legs's life."

"Legs?"

"Legsamillion."

"That's some name."

"Tried to change it. She ignored Peaches."

"Legs. Does she still race?"

"No. Not fast enough. They'd've killed her. Without me."

"Does she appreciate that?"

"Yes."

"Funny, I'd have pictured Grace with a fuzzy little dog, not something as scrawny as that."

"Legs isn't scrawny. Not for a greyhound. Shows how much you know. Keep it up. She hates men anyway. And she's mine. Not Grace's." Her defense of Legs left her totally winded and distracted enough to miss a tear in the pavement. She landed unevenly and quickly caught herself, but the damage was done.

"Oh, for heaven's sake," she gasped, favoring her ankle as she slowed to a halt. She bent over, hands on knees. Her heart was slamming against her ribs.

She heard the truck stop and the door open. Footsteps followed, then a vaguely concerned, "Are you all right?"

She kept her eyes down. "Fine. Just catching my breath."

"Did you hurt your foot?"

She might have known he would see. He didn't miss much. "No."

"Why were you limping?"

"Old injury."

"Maybe you should sit down." He took her arm.

She took it back. "No need. Just give me room." She saw Legs by her knee. "For your sake. My dog might attack."

He didn't answer. Nor did he move away. Her eyes lifted from the road only enough to make out battered work boots, scrunched socks, and fuzzy legs.

She looked down at the road again, closed her eyes for a minute, then straightened. Taking a deeper breath, she opened her eyes. They touched on his armless, collarless sweatshirt and a pair of similarly gray, similarly ragged, slimmer-fitting shorts.

"That's some outfit," she remarked.

"I was shingling the roof."

"You don't have doctors' legs."

"What are doctors' legs like?"

"Pale and skinny."

"You've seen many?"

"Enough." The town had its share of doctors. They occasionally showed up at Grace's parties. Not a one was drop-dead handsome.

She mopped her face on the inside of her elbow.

"Want a beer?"

She did, actually. Her throat was dry. "Well, why not. You've spoiled my run anyway." Doing her best not to limp, she followed him across the road to the far shoulder. He fished two cans of beer from the truck, popped the tab on one and handed it to her, then popped the tab on his own.

"Sorry," he said. "No glasses."

She gave him a wry look, tipped her head back, and took a long, satisfying drink. Nothing quenched thirst like a cold beer. She had learned that and more traveling through Europe with friends. Those were the years before she had settled in with Grace, the years when she had been nearly as adventuresome as Sophie.

She still had rebellious urges. One of them was driving her now. There was something dangerous about having a beer on the side of the road with the enemy.

She walked—carefully—to the front of the truck and sank down on the grass. After another long swallow, she rested the chilled can on her ankle. Legs settled by her side.

Davis knelt and reached for her ankle. She moved it away.

"Let me see," he said.

"No. It's fine."

"If it's fine, let me see."

She guessed he wouldn't give up until he'd had his way. So, okay, she decided. He would look silly, and she would be right.

She moved her foot into his range. "It's not broken. I can walk on it."

His fingers explored. "I saw that limp."

"It's not broken. Look, I've done this before. I know what broken feels like. This is sprained. Not even. It's barely turned. That's all. See? I'm not flinching when you do that. I'm not writhing on the ground, gasping in pain."

"What do you mean, you've done this before?"

"I trip all the time."

His hand remained on her skin, fingers still while his eyes rose. "Have you seen a doctor about that?"

She laughed—at him, because he was so serious, and at herself, because she knew from experience that it was the best way to deal with embarrassment. "I'm *clumsy*, Davis. Sorry to disappoint you, but I am simply not physically coordinated."

"You run great."

"Period. If there's a snag in the carpet, my foot finds it. If something protrudes, my knee hits it. If there's a hole in the road, bingo. I recall running into a door the first time I met you."

"You were upset."

"Well, this time I was distracted. If I'd been concentrating on the road, I might have seen that little dent."

He grasped the bottom of her sneaker and worked her foot back and forth. "Hurt?"

"No."

Legs growled.

Davis slowly raised his hands and, standing, backed off. "Good dog. No harm meant."

Francine sighed. She folded up her legs and took another drink. Beyond quenching her thirst, the beer was making her mellow. That was the only reason she could think of for why her anger had faded. Then again, it could have been sheer exhaustion.

Davis looked long and rangy with his butt against the hood of the truck and his head tipped back for a drink. When it righted, he said, "I suppose it makes sense, a greyhound having the run of all that land."

"Legs is a house dog. She spends most of the day in my den."

"No. Cooped up?"

Slowly, pedantically, Francine said, "She can go wherever she wants. She just chooses to stay in the den." She draped an arm around Legs and scratched her throat. "She was raised in a cage. She still feels safest in small spaces. She'll go out with me, and with Sophie if need be, but she's wary of strangers."

"Of men, you said."

Francine noticed that he wasn't budging from the truck. She grinned. "Legs isn't wary of men. She *hates* them. You're wise to stay there."

"It figures she's female. All the Dorians seem to be."

"Clearly not all, or I wouldn't be here."

"What was your father like?"

"Charming. Devoted. He died three years ago."

"So Grace said. She said that he was much older than she was."

"Eighteen years, which was how old she was when I was born. He was twice her age then. She was new to the city. They met within a week of her arrival and married within the month. He just—"she gestured—"swept her off her feet."

"That's a nice story."

Francine had always thought so. She had always suspected that John had been even more taken than Grace. Right up until his death, his eyes would light up when she entered the room.

"What did he think of her career?"

"He got a kick out of it. He was proud of her. Since he was successful himself, she wasn't a threat." Francine reflected on her own short-lived marriage. "Not all men are as confident."

"Your husband."

She inhaled. "Yeah, there's one. We divorced when Sophie was seven. He felt superfluous, and he was. No vital role, no driving need. We weren't terribly well-suited to each other. It was a shotgun wedding."

Davis choked on his beer. He came forward fast and wiped his dripping mouth with the back of his hand.

"Was it something I said?" Francine asked sweetly. She loved shocking people. Not that she shared that particular bit of information with many, or that she understood why she was sharing it with Davis, but his response was worth it.

He started to laugh. "A shotgun wedding. With Grace the epitome of propriety. That's great. Did you do it on purpose?"

"Not that I know of. Then again, maybe I did. I've always loved babies. I wanted one of my own. Maybe subconsciously . . ." She paused, shook her head. "Nah. I was only twenty. I would have waited. But Grace adored Lee. I figured she could have him and I could have the baby, only it didn't work out that way. She was very annoyed when we divorced. I tried to explain that a relationship couldn't survive on sex alone, but she couldn't deal with that."

"Why not?"

"Grace is uncomfortable talking about sex."

"She talks about it in her columns all the time."

"That's different. Her columns are technical, intellectualized. One on one, she's prudish. She has an easier time writing words to faceless strangers than explaining them to her daughter."

"Words like?"

"Orgasm."

"That's a fun one."

"Uh-huh. Unless you're prudish, one on one."

"Which Grace is."

"Uh-huh. She is also good, with a capital G. She takes vows seriously. She sees marriage as forever. She thought I should have stayed with Lee for Sophie's sake. But I'm no good at playacting. I couldn't pretend to love the man. Sophie would have seen that in a minute."

"Do you miss it?"

"Having a husband?"

"Having sex."

She had set herself up for the question, she supposed, and it held a wealth of curiosity. Was she sexual? Was she sexually active? Was she actively looking for sex? Men were curious that way, and Davis was very definitely a man. Not that she was answering.

She finished her beer and tried to ignore the hum she felt. Hard to remember that he was Grace's doctor when he stood propped against his truck, looking more than a little earthy.

He was staring at her. On principle, she stared right back. Finally, he said, "So. Things are rough at home?"

She didn't follow. "Who told you that?"

"You. You said you came running to forget. What's to forget?"

With that little bit of coaxing, it came back in a rush. "Work. Deadlines. The media."

"Is there a problem?"

"There's always a problem. All businesses have them."

"I'll rephrase that. Is there a new problem?"

Looking straight at his shadowed face, she said, "Grace's

doctor says she has a fatal disease. The diagnosis—however wrong—has caused a turmoil that simulates the symptoms of the disease. Normal things that any sixty-one-year-old experiences look sinister. Grace gets herself so worked up thinking she'll forget something, that she *does* forget it."

"Maybe she should see a psychiatrist."

"She doesn't have time for that."

"Then ship her files elsewhere and get a second opinion. You never did."

With any other diagnosis, they would have. But there was no treatment for Alzheimer's. There was no conclusive diagnostic test except time.

Davis was quiet, leaning against the fender with his long legs extended and his work boots crossed. He took a drink, moved the can against the side of his neck for a minute, lowered it to the hood. Gently, he said, "You're afraid a second doctor will agree with the first one's diagnosis."

"Well, wouldn't you be?" Francine cried. She wasn't afraid to admit it. "We're not dealing with a strep infection here. We're dealing with a fatal disease."

"You're *not* dealing with it. You're denying it, or trying to, but it's not so easy. She's getting worse, isn't she?"

"It's a hectic season. She's feeling pressure from lots of sides, so she isn't quite herself."

"How was her party?"

Francine wasn't being tricked. Divide and be conquered, Grace always warned. "She's seen you since. What did she say?"

"She said she had the best time in the world. She gave me a rundown on who was there, and told me about the flowers and the food and the music. She thought the harpist was neat." He paused. "I heard it was a string quartet."

Francine shrugged off the slip. "Harpist last year, string quartet this. It's an understandable mix-up."

Davis turned his beer one-handed, then tipped back his head and took a swallow. When he didn't speak, she said, "I'm right."

"If you were, things'd be calmer at home. You say the diagnosis is causing the upset, but it doesn't work that way. Not to such a degree. Not for such a prolonged time. If Grace was well, she'd have put my diagnosis behind her by now."

"That's easier said than done, what with the power of suggestion," Francine reasoned. "You've made her terrified of doing things. She doesn't want to travel, doesn't want to visit friends, doesn't want to speak before groups. She's supposed to be on a panel in Chicago next month, and she's saying I have to come with her. You've made her an invalid."

"Those are all symptoms, Francine. When Alzheimer's patients realize the unpredictability of their actions, they withdraw. They're afraid people will see them doing things wrong. They fear they'll embarrass or betray themselves, so they grow reclusive. They stick to the most familiar people and places."

Francine tugged one blade of grass, then another, from the ground. She didn't know why her family was facing this now. Grace had earned her success. They should be enjoying it.

Davis hunkered down beside her. "You'll do fine, Francine."

She snorted. "You sound like Father Jim."

"I'm not. I wish I were, but I'm not. He gets his faith from a higher being. I wish I could."

"So where's yours from?"

"People. They rise to the occasion."

"Well, I'm not," she said, pushing herself to her feet. "Thanks for the beer." She handed him the can, gave Legs's leash a flick, and started off.

"Let me drive you," he called.

"No need," she called back.

"You shouldn't be pounding that foot."

"It's survived worse."

"Don't be a *mule*, Francine."

She didn't answer. If she wanted to be a mule, that was exactly what she would be. Mules got where they were going. Slowly, perhaps. But surely.

And where was she going? Home. To weekly deadlines that were getting harder to meet. To a spiteful editor and an impatient publisher. To a telephone that kept ringing, a fax machine that kept spewing, and a mother whose needs kept growing.

Take me away from all this, she wanted to cry, but there was no one to hear. So, telling herself that it had to get better simply because it couldn't get worse, she ran on.

She had been home for ten minutes when the phone rang. "Hello?"

"It's Davis. I wanted to make sure you got there all right."

She felt an inexplicable well of tears. "I did. Thank you."

"I also wanted to tell you that I'm here. If you need. Just to talk."

"I'll remember."

"As a friend. Unprofessionally."

She put the heel of her hand to her eye. "Nonprofessionally."

"Nonprofessionally. My number's listed."

"Okay. Thanks." She took a shaky breath. "I'm going to take a shower now. I'm beat."

"I'm envious. My shower stinks. It's minuscule. The one in my house is going to be double-sized and surrounded by glass."

She couldn't resist saying, "Mine is."

"Really?"

"Uh-huh."

He sighed. "While you're taking yours, think of me playing mummy in mine."

She could almost imagine it. "Poor thing."

"Have a nice one."

"You, too." She was smiling when she hung up the phone. It was a soft smile, a gentle one that lingered through her shower, through a play period with Legs, even through several acrosses and downs on the puzzle from the Sunday *Times*. It was fading when she turned out the lights, and when the room went dark, when her feet hit the cold part of the bed and the silence of the night crowded in, it was gone.

Six

The best of intentions are only as good as the circumstances surrounding them.
—GRACE DORIAN, speaking to Parents
of Alcoholic Children, Inc.

Grace sat on the plane to Chicago with her legs crossed at the ankles, her hands clutched in her lap, and her eyes shaded by dark, you-don't-know-me glasses. She wasn't inviting chitchat.

Francine leaned across the armrest. "You look nervous. Is it the plane?"

"It's the whole trip. I'm getting too old for this." She had been days in preparing, what with confusing their departure date, packing, and repacking. She kept changing her mind about what clothes to bring, then checking and rechecking her list so that she wouldn't forget something vital, and even now she was sure she had. She turned to Francine in alarm. "I left my makeup case on the dressing table."

"No you didn't. I saw you pack it."

"You did?" She sat back. "You watched me pack?"

"Helped you pack."

Grace smiled. If Francine had helped, she couldn't have forgotten anything too important, and if she had, there was someone else to blame.

Reassured, she tried to relax, but it was hard. This trip was crucial to her. She had to be as poised as The Confidante was fabled to be.

Something nagged at her, though. They were making their final descent into O'Hare when she realized what it was. "We'll have to stop at Neiman Marcus," she told Francine. "I forgot my makeup case."

"Mom, I saw you put it in your bag."

"Are you sure?"

Francine shot a look skyward. "Yes. I'm sure."

"Well, there's no need to be curt. It was just a thought."

Francine paused, then sighed sadly. "I know."

The sadness bothered Grace, but she didn't have time to dwell on it, what with the flurry of leaving the plane and finding their driver in the crowd. Mercifully, the limousine was dark and quiet. Grace would have been content to sit there for far longer than the ride to the hotel had not Francine ushered her out, because from the very first she didn't like the hotel. It was large and unfamiliar. Her suite was nice enough, and there was the solace of having the conference right there, so that she could slip down for her panel and disappear as soon as the discussion was done—but Annie had committed them to dinner with the organizers of the conference, then breakfast the next morning with the three others on her panel. Grace was nervous.

Dinner turned out to be lovely. She was at her charming best, talking about her career, bemoaning the downside of celebrity status, engaging the others in discussion like the skilled hostess of lore. She was so completely herself, so *relieved* to be that way and hopeful about the success of the trip after such an auspicious start, that she was shaken when she returned to the suite and couldn't find her glasses. Without those, she couldn't read her notes.

"But you don't need to read anything," Francine insisted as she searched. "It's an open discussion. Questions will be put to you from people in the audience."

"I have notes. I have to be able to see them. Where did you put my glasses?"

They were under her purse. She put them on, only to find that her notes didn't make sense. She read them again and again, or tried to. "When did I write these?" she asked, bewildered. "They have nothing to do with adolescence."

Francine held out a hand. "Let me see."

Grace tore them up rather than suffer the embarrassment of sharing them. "They aren't about adolescence at all." She tossed the fragments aside. "What am I going to do?"

"What you always do," Francine said with confidence. "You'll sit on that panel and answer questions, and you'll keep telling yourself that this time tomorrow we'll be home."

Grace liked that thought far more than the thought of what could happen between now and then. There were so many times lately when she couldn't collect her thoughts, when the idea she wanted eluded her and the words stayed just beyond her reach. "What if I don't have an answer?"

"You will. And if not, you'll pass the question on to someone else. You're good at this, Mom. You'll do fine."

She didn't. For starters, she couldn't remember the names of the others on the panel, inordinately embarrassing in a small breakfast group. Then the conversation turned academic, and she could only smile and nod, which increased her discomfort. Adding insult to injury, the waiter brought eggs Benedict after she had ordered a muffin, and *then* he moved her glasses to a spot under a fern frond. She found them only after the entire table launched a search.

She was not in the best frame of mind to take part in any panel discussion, much less one on adolescence, because adolescence was the last thing on her mind when the panel convened. She was thinking that the sea of faces before her was off-putting, the eyes too serious, the mouths too straight, the pens too busy. Conjuring up a happier crowd brought to mind her first New Year's Eve with John, spent at a party at the Waldorf-Astoria in a room not unlike this. After the party, she and John had walked the streets of Manhattan in a light, falling snow. It had been terribly romantic—unreal even, given the changes to her life. She remembered looking down at her satin ball gown, touching the fur collar of her coat, thinking that the New Year's Eve before, she had been bundled up in her big sister's hand-me-downs and an old navy pea jacket, warming her hands at the fire that the group of them had lit out of sheer defiance in Harry Lechter's barn.

She had felt an incredible sadness thinking back.

"Ms. Dorian?"

She took a quick breath and found the source of the voice, a tall man at the podium who looked expectant. "Yes?"

"The question was whether—and, if so, in what ways—the basic concerns of adolescents have shifted in the last decade."

Basic concerns of adolescents. Basic concerns. Grace tried to muster her thoughts, but she couldn't think of what he meant. So she said, "No. I don't believe there have been any shifts. Basic concerns are—" She searched for the word. There was one that she wanted, one that was just right, but it wasn't coming to her. Inevitable? No. Identical? No. Universal? *No.* "Timeless," she finally said with a smile, and sat back. Her smile grew stiff through the short silence that ensued. She was infinitely relieved when the man at the podium turned back to the crowd.

Someone asked about the AIDS epidemic as it affected adolescence. AIDS hadn't been around when she had been growing up. All they'd had to worry about back then was pregnancy and the clap, and there was a cure for the clap. There wasn't any cure for pregnancy, save abortion or childbirth, and abortion was only for those without faith. Her friend Denise had had one and had nearly bled to death. That had been a lesson for the others. Not that Grace would have considered abortion. She could never have aborted Johnny's child.

Grace singled out Francine's face from the front row lineup. She looked alarmed, and rightly so, Grace supposed. Francine had been a lonely only, despite Grace's efforts to fill the void. Perhaps if there had been other children, things would have been different. But then, Francine had something no other child of hers could possibly have. Grace hadn't wanted to share her.

"Ms. Dorian?"

Her eyes flew to the podium again. She glanced at the audience, but had no idea who had spoken. So she cupped her ear. "I'm sorry. I'm not sure I heard the question."

"Dr. Keeble raised the argument that most teenagers find the contraints of political correctness to be so stifling as to cause a backlash against them. Perhaps you would comment on that."

Grace considered it, trying to look pensive when her heart was pounding and her palms were damp. Think, Grace. Think.

She took a breath. "If by backlash, you mean that they are rebelling against political correctness, that's right." She paused. They were waiting for her to say more. "I don't know as I blame them," she managed. "I don't think *I* would be able to remember all the steps outlined for certain behaviors." A chuckle rippled through the audience. Buoyed, Grace went on. "Teenagers are struggling to find their own voices. Anyone who tries to put words in their mouths is destined to failure. The concept of constraint is anathema to the teenager, unless that constraint is self-imposed."

"You are quoting Dr. Keeble now."

Grace hadn't been aware of it. "Well, the thought bears repeating. The mistake is in calling it—calling it—" The term slipped her mind. She searched and frowned and finally said, "Is this any different from politeness? Or respect for others? Or common sense. Teenagers are struggling to find their own voices. I can understand why they rebel. *I* wouldn't be able to remember all the steps outlined for certain behaviors."

The other woman on the panel began to talk. She was wearing a dress with an exotic-looking print that reminded Grace of a piece of art she had seen once. She wasn't sure if it had been in Tahiti. Or New Guinea. It might have been in Borneo. For that matter, it might have been at the Metropolitan Museum of Art.

She tried to remember. The print had a primitive feel to it. Where had she seen it?

John loved traveling. He had the money for it, and the time. Grace had the time, too, before *The Confidante* was syndicated, but she hated leaving Francine. So John hired a live-in nanny, to set her mind at ease. Not that it did. No nanny could take the place of a mother. But Grace knew that

John had a need, and she owed him much. So she traveled with him, called Francine daily, and always came home bearing gifts. Perhaps one of those gifts had been a piece of art.

She wished she could remember, but the only things she could remember bringing home were the large conch shells that she had found on a Caribbean beach. To this day, they served as planters in the powder room.

Intent on visiting that room, Grace whispered a short, "Excuse me for a minute," to the panelist beside her and slipped out of her chair and off the podium.

Francine caught up with her just outside the door. "What are you *doing?*" she whispered with an urgency that smacked of disapproval.

"Going to the ladies' room," Grace said without missing a step.

"You're one of the panelists. You can't just walk out."

"I have to use the bathroom."

"You used it less than an hour ago."

Grace didn't recall that. The fact that Francine seemed so sure gave her pause. "I did?"

"Yes, Mom. I was with you." She softened. "Is it really an emergency?"

Grace thought about it for a minute and decided that it wasn't. So she turned and headed back. "Tell me honestly," she said, because it mattered so much, "am I doing all right?" When no answer came, she glanced sideways.

Francine looked pale. "I don't think you're into this."

"I'm making sense, though, aren't I?"

"You have to listen to the moderator, listen to the other panelists, listen to the audience. Focus in on the subject." She had her hand on the door. "Do you know what I'm saying?"

"Well, I'm not deaf."

"Will you concentrate?"

"Of course."

"Do you promise?"

Grace didn't know why Francine was so worried. She had talked to so many groups that she could do it with her eyes closed, and this wasn't much of a group. Of course, the topic was a strange one for her. Interpreting dreams was a Freudian thing. She had no training in that.

"Francine?" she began, thinking that it still wasn't too late to return to her suite. But Francine had the door open and was ushering her back into the room. What with every eye in the place turning her way, she could do little more than slip quietly into her seat.

Francine had a splitting headache. She pressed the spot that throbbed and cornered herself more deeply in the limousine's backseat. From the opposite corner came Grace's tremulous, "I was terrible, wasn't I?"

Yes, she was terrible. She hadn't said more than two coherent sentences, had repeated herself and been generally out in left field. Terrible was a mild word for the way she had been. Reflecting on it, Francine tried not to panic.

"They were laughing at me," Grace said.

"Well, you were saying some pretty funny things."

"They were laughing *at* me."

They were. And Francine had had to watch, as agonizing for her as for Grace. "You were wandering," she said, trying to be kind, but so sick at heart that she was ready to burst. "It was a discussion of adolescence. Not sleep patterns, violent personalities, or menopause."

Grace looked devastated. She studied her lap, shook her head, and said nothing more, for which Francine was grateful.

She didn't know what to say, herself, and simply worked at staying composed. Once in the first-class lounge at the airport, she took several aspirin, sank deep into a comfortable chair, and closed her eyes. She heard Grace sigh, heard the occasional rustle of magazine pages, heard the plop of it being set aside, then a quiet, "I'll be in the ladies' room."

Francine watched her go, thinking that she looked suddenly older and frailer. It was frightening. Grace had always been dynamic, the orchestrator of the Dorians' lives even when John was alive, with her instinctive feel for people's needs and desires. She knew how to put things in motion and keep them running. She always made the right choices.

Francine didn't want to think of Davis Marcoux's diagnosis, but it wouldn't leave her alone.

Tears sprang to her eyes. She closed them and rested her head against the chair back, then concentrated on swallowing away the lump in her throat.

She sat like that for a while, struggling for composure at first, then simply trying to stay calm. Her mind drifted back to the days when the lines were clearly drawn, when she was the child and Grace the mother, when there was no question about who was in charge. Grace had taught her how to swim, to ride a bicycle, to braid her hair. Grace had even taught her how to sew—remarkable, since Grace didn't sew, herself, but there had been a last-minute prom purchase with the seamstress out of town. Predictably, Grace's half of the hem was perfect, while Francine's had to be done twice. Then, within minutes of arriving at the pre-prom party, Francine had spilled fruit punch on the dress. Red fruit punch. Actually, red fruit punch spiked with champagne. She had proceeded to down two glasses of it and forget about the stain.

Grace had noticed it right off and been heartsick. If she

had known about the champagne, there would have been hell to pay.

Smiling, Francine turned her head and opened her eyes to share the memory with Grace, but Grace wasn't beside her. Nor was she in the immediate area of the lounge. With a nervous glance at the wall clock, Francine went looking for her, but she wasn't in the ladies' room, at the bar, or in front of the television.

"I think I've misplaced my mother," she told the desk attendant, and gave a brief description.

"I believe she left," the attendant said.

Francine was quickly alarmed. "When?"

"Not long ago. Five, maybe ten minutes."

"Did she say where she was going?"

The attendant smiled apologetically and shrugged.

"Oh, God," Francine said. With a tired breath, she looked helplessly around. "I'll be right back."

She dashed out of the lounge. People were passing in droves, but there was no sign of Grace. She ran in one direction, searching, then the other. Frightened, she returned to the lounge.

"I can't find her," she gasped. "Can you page her?"

"Yes. But your plane is boarding now."

Francine put her palm to her temple and tried to think. "She doesn't have her ticket, *or* her coat, or her carry-on." She did have her purse, which meant that she had money, identification, and credit cards, which would please a thief no end, Francine realized. Not that Grace would hand them over without a fight, which frightened Francine all the more. "Will you phone someone at the gate and see if she's there?"

The attendant did everything Francine asked, but Grace was neither waiting at the gate nor answering her page. Francine grew desperate. Reluctant to pull weight, but hoping it might help, she told the attendant exactly who Grace was. Within minutes, the airline had a security team in the lounge. Within minutes of that, one of them had loaded Francine and their belongings on a motorized cart for a fast ride to the gate while the others fanned out on foot.

Faces went by in a blur. Francine scoured the crowd for the one she wanted while the public address system repeated its page. She stood at the door of the Jetway, frightened and fidgety, while the last of the passengers boarded the plane. Only then did the call come that Grace had been found.

"Thank *God*," she cried. She raced their things onto the plane and returned for Grace, who arrived minutes later with her airline entourage, looking none the worse. She was thanking each of the people who had delivered her to the gate, smiling, shaking hands, positively triumphant in her return. She even autographed a ticket stub for one of the guards.

Francine hurried her along the Jetway. "Why did you wander off like that?" she asked, angry now that the fright had passed. "We looked everywhere. I was beginning to imagine horrible things."

Grace beamed at the flight attendant who was waiting at the aircraft's door. "I'm so sorry to keep you waiting. I was stretching my legs and lost track of the time. I hadn't realized how far I'd gone. This is the largest airport in the world, I think, certainly the busiest. I hope I haven't inconvenienced anyone."

"You're here just in time, Ms. Dorian," the man said, beaming right back.

Francine found their smiles infuriating, given the brief hell she had been through, but she didn't say a thing until they were settled in their seats, and the plane pushed back from the gate. Only then did she turn pleading eyes on Grace. "*Please* don't do things like that to me, Mother."

Grace patted her hand. "All's well that ends well."

"I was *terrified*."

"Now you know how I felt when you were six and wandered away from me at the circus."

"That was an innocent mistake. I was a child. I let go of your hand for a minute and suddenly there were dozens of people between us. I didn't know where you were." As clear as day she remembered the panic she had felt. The thought of a future without Grace now, though very different, was as upsetting. "Promise me you won't wander off again."

"Francine, I'm not a child. I don't have to make promises to you or anyone else."

But Francine was desperate. She wanted to believe willfulness was behind what Grace had done—wanted to cry, to scream, to do *anything* to halt the awful sinking feeling she had.

"And don't pout," Grace snapped. "It's childish."

At her wits' end, Francine let loose. "Well, we both know that I've never grown up. So call it a personality defect and be grateful that at least *you* don't have to call out the troops and make a fool of yourself."

"Is that what this is about? You were *embarrassed*?"

"No, *you* were embarrassed, Mother. That's what *all* this is about. We agreed that The Confidante needed this trip to shore up her image. I came along to make sure that happened, and I did my best, but it wasn't enough. Should I have stood at your elbow whispering names in your ear, or made hand signals from the audience telling you what to say when the right words wouldn't come?" The horror of it flooded back. Smooth, knowing, always-in-charge Grace had stumbled badly, and, in so doing, had shaken Francine to the core.

Grace was her idol. She had won her success through sheer persistence, writing *The Confidante* year after year after year, and the success was all the sweeter, given what had come before. Not that Francine knew much about those earliest years. Grace refused to discuss them. But between that refusal, and the few small things that had inadvertently slipped out, Francine knew that Grace's beginnings had been hard.

She deserved her day in the sun. She deserved *many* days in the sun. It was too soon for clouds, too soon.

But there they were, it seemed.

The pilot announced their imminent departure. Moments later, the plane turned into position, picked up speed, and lifted off the ground. Habit would have had Francine gripping the arms of her seat and silently counting through the crucial first minutes, but she felt oddly immune. If Grace had Alzheimer's disease, the plane wouldn't crash. Tragedies rarely overlapped.

Her head was throbbing again, the kind of dull, insidious throb that experience told her would knot itself into a migraine by morning. She rubbed her temple.

"I was uneasy about this trip from the first," Grace murmured.

Francine knew that all too well. She wished she had listened. But she had been thinking of *The Confidante*. She still was. "I need your help, Mom. I'm trying the best I can, but I'm not as good—was *never* as good as you. I couldn't make this trip work. I'm not sure I can make *The Confidante* work." The frustration of three months' worry and work poured out. "Researching and writing and *re*writing columns, running interference with the newspaper, the publisher, the *Telegram*. *You're* The Confidante. Not me."

"You're my assistant."

"But you haven't been the boss in weeks. I'm supposed to follow your lead, only you aren't leading. You're here, but you're not. You're obsessed with this book to the exclusion of all else."

"The book is crucial."

"The book is nothing without the rest. That's what this trip was about. The Confidante was asked to write the book, but the book is pointless if The Confidante falls apart."

"Your job is to make sure she doesn't."

"Which brings us full circle," Francine said, but in a murmur, as the flight attendant was approaching. "Maybe I'm not up to the job. Did that thought ever occur to you?"

"More than once," Grace said under her breath. She looked up pleasantly, smiled, and ordered mineral water with a twist of lime.

Francine ordered something stronger and ignored the censorious look Grace leveled her way.

It wasn't until the drink was gone and dinner on its way that Grace made a remark about weak people needing alcoholic props.

Francine bit her tongue.

"I don't understand why you're so angry," Grace grumbled a short time later.

Angry was the wrong word. Heartsick was more like it. Grace was the one who could have made the difference in Chicago, but she hadn't, and now she was sitting there, garnishing her veal cordon bleu with pat little digs like, "You're making a mountain out of a molehill." Or, "I should have had the life *you* had as a child." Or, "You haven't eaten enough."

"I'm fine," Francine said after the last, and again when Grace told her to take something for her headache, and again when Grace told her to freshen up in the lavatory, and all the while she wanted to scream in frustration at the irony of Grace being lucid when it came to such petty, meaningless, positively mundane things.

The lucidity held up through their descent into La Guardia. "Does Gus know to come?" Grace asked.

"Yes," Francine answered, counting to ten not for the sake of the landing, but for patience. "He has our itinerary. He knows the flight number."

"Did you tell him to call for flight information first? Did you tell him to allow for traffic getting to the airport? He's been late more than once when the bridge was backed up. We're landing at the worst possible hour. Did you tell him that?"

Francine wished Grace would just do things herself rather than grilling her this way.

"Did you remind him, Francine?"

"I *did*. He'll *be* here."

He wasn't, just Francine's luck. She was tired and upset, and her head ached, and Grace, who was equally tired and cranky, launched into a barrage of unanswerable questions. Francine looked around for a pay phone.

"Call him," Grace instructed, as though she wouldn't have come up with the thought on her own.

She left Grace at the door with their luggage while she rounded a corner and made the call.

Gus didn't answer the car phone. He didn't answer the garage phone, which forwarded to his private quarters, until Francine was about to hang up in despair, and then Sophie's voice was the one she heard, Sophie's *groggy* voice.

"Omigod, Mom. I'm sorry. We fell asleep."

"Fell asleep? *We?* At five in the afternoon?"

"There was a party in Newport last night. We didn't get back until dawn."

"Sophie, how could you *do* this to me?" Francine pleaded, suddenly tired of carrying the burden alone. "Chicago was a nightmare! We need to get *home*!" She was desperate for familiar turf, familiar people, familiar boundaries.

Sophie said a hurried something to Gus, then to Francine, in a voice now fully awake and jostled by what Francine imagined to be the search for clothes, "We'll be there—we're getting dressed now—give us—"

"An hour and a half? Two hours? No good. We'll grab a cab." Francine hung up the phone in a fit of pique and ran back around the corner, half expecting Grace to be gone. That she was there with the luggage brought only a fleeting solace. She was irate at Francine's news, even when the version she heard made no mention of Sophie.

Francine cut her off in mid tirade, told her to stay put, and went looking for a cab. Ten agonizing minutes and one hefty tip later, she had a driver.

"There," she said with a sigh when they were finally on their way. "This isn't bad at all."

"It's dirty and it's hot," was Grace's retort. "I've had it. Gus is *out*."

Francine would believe that when she saw it. Gus was one of Father Jim's people, and Grace rarely fired one of those. She might complain, and complain at length, but Father Jim's people always received immunity. Not so Francine.

"Was it so *difficult* to see that Gus got here?" Grace asked when she had finished denigrating the innards of the cab. "If you had called him before we took off from O'Hare, he wouldn't have had time to fall asleep."

"Before we took off from O'Hare," Francine reminded her with what she thought was commendable gentleness, given that she was flat out of patience, "I was frantically looking for you."

"And I showed up, didn't I? But not Gus."

"Why didn't *you* call him?"

"Because *I* wasn't near a *phone*."

And so it went, back and forth. Francine had never been this way with Grace before, with *anyone* before, but she couldn't help herself. Something had happened back at O'Hare that had left her desolate and desperate. Her mind flashed "Alzheimer's disease" at every turn.

She wasn't angry at Grace. She was angry at the situation. It struck her that Grace might be, too. Still, they argued the whole way, arriving home at opposite ends of the cab's backseat, and the arguing didn't end when they entered the house. It simply broadened to include Sophie, which made things even harder for Francine. Her head ached, her body ached, her heart ached. When she couldn't take another minute of it, she threw her hands in the air and walked out.

She took a shower and several aspirin. She went running with Legs, then took another shower. She lay down in bed with a cold pack on her head and tried to sleep, but between her headache and her thoughts, she was queasy. By dawn she was a bundle of raw nerves.

Feeling chilled despite the rising July sun, she threw a sweatshirt on over shorts and steeped a pot of hot, fresh tea. Then, holding a mug in each hand, she went looking for Grace. She wanted to apologize. She wanted to cry. She wanted to hold her mother and be held, and know that Grace knew what she felt for that little while longer at least.

Grace wasn't in the bedroom, the bathroom, or the sitting room. She wasn't in the kitchen. She wasn't in her office.

But she had been there. The chair was pulled out from the desk in the way she left it when she was interrupted while working.

Francine approached the desk. On its top was a thick folder, open wide. She stared at it for an eternity without seeing a thing. Then she forced herself to focus. The folder wasn't labeled. Closed, no one would suspect what was inside. But Francine knew even before she looked. There were newspaper and magazine clippings, and health organization newsletters. There were information booklets. There were handwritten notes.

If Grace was nothing, she was meticulous. When she did something, she was thorough. Apparently she had wanted to know about Alzheimer's disease. Postmarks on some of the material said that she had been gathering information for more than a year.

More than a year. Reading anything and everything about the disease. Wondering if she had it. Analyzing her every move in light of what she read.

Francine pushed a hand through her hair and held on. There was this little last bit of hope. Davis might be wrong after all. Just when she thought she was drained of fight, she found some. She looked frantically around for corroborative evidence.

That was when her gaze penetrated the window and landed on Grace, wearing her nightgown and shawl, sitting in a patio chair halfway out across the rolling lawn.

Seven

It isn't so much that family fights are louder or longer, just that the stakes are higher.
—GRACE DORIAN, from *The Confidante*

Grace stared blindly at the river, only peripherally aware of the lushness of the green grass and lavish hardwoods before it and the tall pines guarding its banks. Her mind was a thousand miles and a lifetime away, back with a dirt-poor family in the tin-roofed shed they called home. The place smelled of sweat, of rabbit and frying-pan grease, of liquor, always liquor because that was a staple. She heard her little brother cry, gag, and throw up the medicine that would never stay down, and her oldest sister try to comfort him, and her mother scream at them both.

"*Mother.*"

The voice was so similar, the impatience. But this was Francine approaching, plaintive now. "What are you doing out here?"

Grace didn't turn. She was bone tired, soul tired. She had been fighting for too long a time.

Francine materialized before her. Squatting, she clutched the arms of the chair. "I found the folder on your desk," she said excitedly. "Do you know what you've done?"

Grace smiled sadly. "Research?"

Francine shook her head. "Self-diagnosis. You read and read until the symptoms seemed so familiar that they fit. Classic power of suggestion," she crowed. "You've written about it dozens of times."

Grace studied her daughter's face. It wasn't a beautiful face, certainly pleasant enough, but interesting in the way that Grace's mother's had been before the strain of a harsh life had taken its toll. Francine knew nothing about Grace's mother or the harsh life, and Grace wasn't sorry. Yes, adversity often spawned dynamism, but she hadn't wanted trauma for Francine. She had wanted only the best, which was why the pain she was causing now was doubly tragic.

A gentle soul with her father's capacity for warmth, Francine had always been spirited. But not once, amid disagreements aplenty in the growing years, had Grace seen the zeal she saw now.

"I'm not sure I know you this way," she said with a soft smile, but the words were a poor choice.

Francine beamed. "See? That's what I'm saying. You know how an Alzheimer's patient typically behaves, so you're behaving that way." She sobered. "What I can't figure out is why. Are you bored? Thinking of retirement? Really, Mom. If you're tired of working, say so. There are a lot easier ways to slow down than by making a fool of yourself."

Grace gasped at the image, at the tone. Just then Francine was every inch her own mother, fighting a reality she didn't want to accept. Grace had felt the sting of Sara McQuillan's venom more than once. She still felt it at times. But Francine's hurt more.

"You don't know anything about it," she murmured, feeling beaten down and weak.

"Then *tell* me."

"It's terrifying," Grace said, so relieved by the invitation that the words poured out in a rush. "I think about it night and day. I doubt myself, I doubt others. I tremble doing even old, familiar tasks because I'm afraid I'll do them wrong. I wonder what will be in a month, in three, in ten, in two years. I—I . . ." She lost her train of thought.

"You what?"

The words had vanished. She looked questioningly at Francine.

"A month, three, ten, two years," Francine prompted. "You what?"

Grace had no idea.

Francine stood, took a step back, half turned away. Grace braced herself for a lashing, but Francine simply turned back, puzzled. "This all started soon after Daddy died. He doted on you, right up to the end. Is it the doting you want?"

"I don't want doting."

"You've written columns on mourning. I remember one. A man wrote saying that he'd been all locked up inside since his wife died. You suggested that he hadn't mourned her properly. Maybe that's what's happening here."

"No, Frannie."

"You were so strong after his death. Stoic, almost."

"I'd had months to prepare. He wasn't young. And he was ill, all knotted up and in pain every time he moved. His death wasn't a shock. It was a—was a—a—bliss."

"A blessing? That's what you said at the time, and the

words sounded right, but maybe the heart works differently. Maybe his death shook you more than you want to believe. Maybe that's what this is about."

Grace didn't know whether to laugh or cry. Poor Francine was still searching for excuses. She ached for her, even more than she ached for herself. Oh, yes, as the victim, she would suffer the indignity of the disease, but only to a point. After that, she wouldn't be cognizant of who and what she was. Then the suffering would be borne by those around her. She would do most anything to spare them that.

With the reminder, she drew herself straight. Time was in short supply, and the clock was ticking. "We have plans to make."

Francine didn't budge. "You don't think you might have worked yourself up to this?"

"Before this weekend, yes. Now, no."

Bless her, still Francine fought. "There is nothing wrong with you. I won't *let* there be."

Grace was amused. "Oh? And how are you going to manage that?"

"I'll stay on your back. I won't let you slack off. Isn't that what you did for me? For all of the six years I took violin lessons, you were on me to practice, do my finger exercises, rosin my bow. I never would have made it to the state competition if you hadn't pushed me along."

"But you lost in the semifinals," Grace reminded her.

"Because I had no sense of rhythm, but the point is that I got that far."

"No. The point is that it was a losing cause, just like this one is." Saying it was killing her, but it had to be said. "Don't you see, *I can't win.*" She'd had enough of denial. She needed Francine to accept what was happening and give her support.

"Listen to me, sweetheart. You're looking at the symptoms, not the underlying problem, but my problem isn't going away any more than your tin ear did. You can keep after me all you want, but it won't change the outcome. I can't be cured. I'll only get worse. Oh, I've tried to deny it. I've learned to compensate. I'm quite good at hiding my failings." She had a thought, a funny one that made her smile. "That was one of the first things I learned when I left home. I arrived in Manhattan knowing no one and nothing. Right off, I bought three nice dresses. I used nearly all my money doing it, but the plan was to look like a lady. Of course, I had no idea how to act like one. So I watched. At the Plaza. Did I ever tell you that? I used to stand there, right near the Palm Court, as though I was waiting for someone, but I'd be watching the ladies—how they walked, smiled, ate. When I went looking for work, I imitated them. The manager of the club bought the charade and hired me, but then I had to follow through. So I learned to ask questions, or be silent until others acted so that I could take my cue from them."

She smiled, first at the memory, then at Francine. But Francine looked miserable. "What's wrong?" she asked, alarmed.

"What are you saying, Mom?"

Grace tried to remember.

"You're talking about New York," Francine said. "I'm talking about Chicago. If I'd been on you more—"

"It wouldn't have mattered. I was *awful*. You couldn't have helped." Her thoughts were crystal clear, her mood impatient. "Read that file, Francine. Talk to Davis. Talk to others with this disease. When I lose it, I lose it. My mind skips, like a broken record, just passes right over certain events. I don't remember what happened in Chicago. Not the details. I just know I was an embarrassment to me and to you."

"You weren't," Francine said, but there were tears in her eyes.

Grace grabbed her wrists. "I *was*. You said it last night, and you were right. If you think you're helping me by denying it, you're being native." She frowned, corrected herself. "Naive. I can't do the work I used to do. The things I write make no sense. Don't tell me you haven't noticed."

Francine snatched her hands free and tucked them under her arms. "I thought you had avoided the celebrity trap. The arrogance, the melodrama, the self-absorption."

"*Self-absorption?*" Grace cried. "*What* self-absorption? The last thing I ever wanted was to saddle you with this, so I denied it all. But I'm tired of beating my head against a brick wall. The wall isn't going away, and the beating doesn't help. We have to face the truth and figure out where to go from here."

Francine covered her ears. "I'm not listening."

Grace raised her voice, angry now. "Then you're a *fool*."

"No, *you're* the fool if you refuse to fight. Look at you, sitting out here like this. I never thought you were a prima donna."

"I never thought you were a *spoiled brat*, but look at *you*, yelling at me because you think I'm deliberately upsetting the balance of your cushy little life. Don't be selfish, Francine. Think of someone else for a change."

Francine made a small, gasping sound and ran back toward the house.

Grace didn't try to stop her. She put a hand to her chest to ease the pain there, and glared at the river until her anger grew manageable. Then she looked skyward and, stiff-lipped, said, "I have spent the last forty-three years of my life trying to make up for what happened. I've been generous. I've been good. What do You want?"

The skies were silent.

Francine didn't return.

Grace felt an overwhelming sense of defeat.

Sophie found her mother at the kitchen table, staring at the polished oak. The not-quite-forward, not-quite-back slant of her body suggested that she didn't know whether to come, go, or stay.

Sophie slid into the opposite chair and waited for her to look up. When she didn't, she grew uneasy. "Mom?"

Francine pressed her fingertips to her temple.

"Are you all right?" Sophie asked.

"No."

"What's wrong?"

Francine didn't lift her eyes from the wood. Sophie could see wet crescents under her lids. They magnified the shadows that had been there first.

"Tell me," Sophie ordered because she knew she was at fault and needed it out in the open and done with. "It's last night, isn't it? I am so sorry. We should have been there to pick you guys up. We should have set an alarm or something, but I never imagined we'd sleep half that long."

She waited for her mother to smile, to reach for her hand, to forgive her like always.

Francine simply rubbed her temple and said, "She's giving up."

"Who?"

"Grace. She's throwing in the towel."

"What towel?"

Francine did look up then. Her face held raw fear. "She made it through menopause without the slightest emotional blip. Same with your grandfather's death. Now suddenly she's crumbling."

Sophie let out a breath. "She has Alzheimer's disease." She slid her elbows over the table and touched Francine's arm. "Accept it, Mom. The doctor does, and the others he consulted with, and now Grace. You've been great to fight it, but maybe it's time to stop. She has Alzheimer's disease. Well, she isn't alone. Others have it, too."

"I don't care about others. I don't live with others. I don't work with others. I don't *love* others."

Sophie wasn't sure what to do. She wanted to make things easier for Francine, but simply saying what she wanted to hear wouldn't do that. "Grace has had a good life. She's been healthy up until now. But she isn't immune to misfortune any more than the rest of us are."

"She's a good person."

Sophie recoiled. "And I'm not? Is that why I got diabetes? When I was *nine*? What did *I* do wrong?"

Francine did reach for her hand then. "Nothing, babe. You didn't do anything wrong. You were genetically predisposed to the disease. Someone way back when, someone we don't even know about, must have had it."

"Same with Grace and Alzheimer's, unless the environment is screwing us up, in which case we're all doomed," Sophie declared, because that possibility had occurred to her more than once. When she ordered bottled water, it wasn't an affectation. She didn't trust what came from the tap.

Not that Grace had to worry about that, or Francine, either. Sophie's generation, and those that followed, would have to clean up the mess their parents had made.

Hardened by the thought, she said, "Grace is sixty-one.

She's lived well. So she'll have to slow down. Most people her age do."

"Slow down," Francine agreed, "not zone out. Grace will be here but she won't be. We'll be able to talk at her, not with her. We'll lose her strength. We'll lose her knowledge, her guidance."

"You and I aren't helpless."

Francine rubbed her temple again. "What is that supposed to mean?"

"Do you have a migraine?"

"Explain yourself, Sophie."

"We will survive. We don't need Grace telling us what to do, when, and where."

"She doesn't."

"She *does*. Oh, she's subtle about it, but she calls and you come. You don't have to. You're strong. You can function just fine. Life won't end just because Grace is sick. She isn't the only one with smarts."

Francine's chair scraped the wood floor when she stood. "So you'd just put her out to pasture and let her die eating weeds."

Sophie snorted. "Really."

"I'm serious, Sophie. What are you saying?"

Sophie knew she wasn't expressing herself well, but she had a point to make. So she tried again. "I'm saying that you idolize her, and that's fine and good. She's your mother. And she's a winner. But she isn't as perfect as you think she is. She isn't as perfect as the world thinks she is. She's human. She makes mistakes like the rest of us. She gets sick like the rest of us. It's terrible that she has Alzheimer's. It's *tragic* that she has it. But life goes on."

Francine gaped. "I knew you resented her. I never realized how much."

. "*Listen* to me. Listen to *you*. This isn't about resentment. It's about common sense, and I wouldn't have said a thing if you'd been reasonable, but you're blowing this out of proportion."

"A fatal disease? Out of proportion?"

Sophie thumped her chest. "I have diabetes. It's a life-threatening disease—"

"Totally treatable."

"Oh, yeah. With shots and blood tests every time I blink. That's fun, and I'm only twenty-three. Just imagine what's in store for me when I'm your age. But when I'm Grace's—if I am ever Grace's—I'll be so grateful to have *reached* that point—"

She broke off and palmed tears from her eyes. It wasn't often that she allowed herself to think of dying, because it frightened her so. She preferred to think about cheating death. Francine had taught her that, in practical, no-nonsense terms. "You accepted my diabetes just fine. But now you're paralyzed. We will survive, Mom."

"But she won't, and she's our lives!" Francine cried.

Sophie gritted her teeth. "She's your life. She isn't mine."

"Oh, yes, she is. She's the authority you love to defy. That's what Gus is about. That's what partying in Newport until six in the morning is about. That's what missing two doctor's appointments in a row is about—see, I knew about those."

Sophie was out of her chair and at the door in a flash, anger overriding any desire to protect Francine. "Fine. I'm getting a new doctor, one who'll respect my privacy. I'm twenty-three, Mother. Whether or not I keep appointments is my business, not yours—and don't tell me it's rude to stand the guy up, because we both know he's so overbooked he wouldn't have noticed I missed if I hadn't been a Dorian. Look at it this way. I did his other patients a favor. Without me, they didn't have to wait so long for their turn." She took off.

"Sophie!"

"I'm going out!" Sophie yelled from the hall.

"I need you *here*," came the echo.

But Sophie didn't know why she couldn't get through to Francine. She was making things worse, not better. So maybe Francine was right. Maybe Grace was the only one with the gift. Good Grace. Precious Grace.

"*Sophie!*"

She might have been six years old, blurting out what she did, but the feelings had been building for too long. "You don't need me!" she bellowed with her hand on the door. "You need Grace! She's the perfect one! She's the one you can't live without! So go talk with her! I—can't—help!" She slammed out.

Francine started driving at ten in the morning. She didn't have a plan, didn't have a destination, only knew that she needed to escape everything that was wrong in her life.

So she went north on roads that were new because Grace didn't like going north. When the glare of the overcast hurt, she lowered the sun visor and directed the air-conditioning full force at the throbbing spot on her temple. All the while words echoed in her mind—Sophie's, her own, those spoken in anger to Grace.

She stopped for a cold drink and sat for a time with her eyes closed, in the far corner of a dirt lot behind a small general store. But the drink didn't help her queasiness, and the rest didn't dull her headache. She couldn't stop thinking, couldn't stop aching.

So she stopped running and headed home. Only the closer she got, the harder it was. She had never been quite so wrong before. She had never felt quite so miserable, quite so inadequate, quite so alone.

She thought to stop at the parish house and talk with Father Jim. But her car passed it by, then passed by the road that would have led to Grace, and instead delivered her to the low brick doctors' building abutting the hospital.

She sat in the parking lot for the longest time, feeling sick to her stomach and thoroughly torn. Then, reluctant but irresistibly drawn, she left the car.

His office was on the third and top floor. She took the stairs, turned in at the door with his name, and said to the receptionist in a shaky voice, "I'd like to see the doctor. I don't have an appointment. My mother is a patient of his. It's important."

The receptionist was young, with wild hair, crooked teeth, and a kind smile. "What's your name?"

"Francine Dorian."

The girl's eyes widened. "I lo-ove your mother's column," she cooed, then caught herself and straightened. "I'll speak to the doctor. He's running late, but I'm sure he can fit you in."

There were four people in the small waiting room. Francine sank into one of two empty chairs. She wrapped an arm around her middle and propped her elbow on that. Head bowed, eyes closed, she pressed the pads of her fingers to her temple and tried to will away the pain, but her will was as weak as her stomach. She needed darkness and warmth. If she had a hole, she'd have climbed right in.

"Francine?"

His voice was gentle. She remembered the last time they

had talked, that night after sharing a beer, when he had called to make sure she had gotten home safely. Tears had come to her eyes then. They did again now.

He was squatting before her. She raised her eyes only enough to meet his, but she didn't speak. Her throat was too tight.

He swore softly, gentle in that, too. Then he took her arm and helped her up. He led her into his office and settled her on the sofa. "I'm just finishing up with a patient. Give me a minute?"

She nodded.

He left through a side door. Francine thought to look around at the office, but her head hurt too much. So she slid into the corner, curled her legs under her, and, propping an elbow on the sofa's generous arm, pressed the heel of her hand to the spot that hurt most.

She didn't open her eyes when the door reopened. She heard his footsteps, felt the give of the leather beside her. It was the moment of truth—the moment when she had to tell him he had been right all along. He would be pleased.

"You don't look like you feel very well," he said with a surprising lack of smugness.

She gave a tiny head shake of agreement.

"Has something happened at home?"

She nodded. "I behaved badly—" Her voice broke. She moved the heel of her hand against her temple and drew her legs in tighter. She might have even moaned. She wasn't sure.

He slipped a hand under her hair and curved it to her nape. "Look at me, Francine."

She managed a squint.

"Head hurts?" he asked.

"Awful," she breathed.

"Migraine?"

She nodded.

"Have you taken anything?"

"Nothing works."

"I have something that may. Don't move."

When he left this time, she put her head down on the sofa arm—butter-soft leather—curled up, and hugged her middle.

Minutes later, large hands shifted her over, and an ice pack was put on the pain. He asked several questions of the general-health-and-allergy type, then swabbed a spot on her thigh and gave her a shot.

Francine was miserable enough not to ask any questions. She lay curled up, facing the sofa back, with the ice pack's weight on her temple and Davis's thigh bracing her spine.

He stayed with her for several minutes, rubbing her shoulder. Then, in that same gentle voice, he said, "Rest here. I'll be back." He closed the blinds to darken the office and left.

Francine actually slept. She awoke disoriented, and turned over to find Davis sitting close in the dimness. His elbows were on his knees, his fingers loosely laced. She couldn't make out the look on his face.

"How do you feel?" he asked.

She shifted the ice pack. The throbbing in her head had faded to a dull ache. "Better." Much, actually. The ache was negligible and the nausea was gone. "This is embarrassing. I'm not the patient."

"Don't apologize. If I can't treat a friend, what's the point? Do you get migraines often?"

"Mild ones. I've never had one like this before."

"What brought it on?"

It didn't seem right that such an innocent question should have such a condemning answer. She threw an arm over her head.

He allowed her that for several minutes, then, softly, said, "Tell me."

"You know," she blurted out meekly. "You've known all along. You warned me, but I wouldn't listen. So I made things worse."

"Worse, how?"

"I wasn't prepared. I didn't help."

"That's not so bad."

"But it was!" she cried, not thinking so much of Chicago as of the backyard that morning. "Grace was sitting there looking so vulnerable, and I hated her for it. So I said spiteful things. I said *cruel* things." She curled into a tighter ball. "I'm so ashamed."

He said nothing for a minute. Then he reached over and tucked her hair behind her ear. "This isn't a happy time for your family. You have a right to be upset."

"But I'm not a mean person. I didn't intend to say any of it. I don't know where those things came from."

"Desperation makes us do things, sometimes."

He was right about that. She had certainly been desperate. She had latched onto a last-ditch hope without considering the hurt she was inflicting. Now she felt lower than low.

Setting the ice pack aside, she pushed herself to a sitting position. It was a minute before she could get the words out, and then they were weak. "What am I facing, Davis?"

"I can't say for sure."

"But we're headed downhill."

"That's the gist of it. She may hit plateaus, but the prognosis isn't good." His voice was held down by the weight of truth.

Francine swallowed. "How long does she have?"

"Three—seven—ten years. I wish I could be more exact."

She whispered a pained, "Of lucidity? Or life?"

"Life. She's had the disease for a while."

Francine made a sound that must have been gut-wrenching, because he reached out and took her hand.

"I'm sorry, Francine. It isn't fair. If you want to kick and scream, be my guest."

But she shook her head. "Been there, done that." She curved her fingers around his and held on tightly. There were questions she needed to ask. But she wasn't ready for the answers yet.

"Your hands are freezing," he said.

"My heater's functioning about as well as the rest of me."

"Want to take a ride? Fresh air might help."

If it was possible for her to like anything just then, she liked that idea. It beat going home. "Don't you have patients to see?"

"I shifted appointments. I'm free for a while."

She was touched. Then she had a sour thought. "Amazing thing, the Dorian name. It parts waters."

She couldn't see his expression with the blinds drawn, but she knew when he shook his head. "This has nothing to do with your name."

"Then with what?"

"We're friends. Aren't we?"

For no reason at all, she started to cry. Mortified, she freed her hand and covered her face to the tune of soft, gulping sobs. She tried to mute them, but they had a mind of their own.

Davis stroked her hair and let her cry. He left only to get tissues. When she finally quieted, he muttered, "I hate this."

She pressed a tissue to her nose. "Hate what?"

"Having to sit here while you cry."

She blotted her cheeks. "I'll bet people cry here all the time."

"Not people I want to hold."

Her eyes filled again. "Oh, God," she wailed, "don't *say* things like that." His kindness opened floodgates, allowing her to be weak and frightened. She hadn't leaned on a man in years. No. That was wrong. She hadn't ever leaned on a man in her life. Which didn't mean that it was wrong. Just strange.

He went to the window and snapped open the blinds, then stood there with his back to her and his hands on his hips while she gathered herself. By the time he turned, she was on her feet, looking anywhere but at him.

His office was thoroughly conventional—neat desk, filled bookshelves, framed diplomas, diagrams of the brain and the nervous system. His only indulgences were the sinfully soft leather of the sofa and chairs. They reminded her of his boots.

A pair of sunglasses lay on the desk. She slipped them on. They were aviator-style and absurdly large, but she didn't care. She had to hide behind something, given how exposed she felt.

Davis hung his lab coat and his tie on a hook behind the door. Then he rolled back his cuffs and opened the door for her.

Eight

In life's darkest moments, even the tiniest spark can light the way.

—GRACE DORIAN, from *The Confidante*

Sitting in the cab of his truck, parked in a wooded spot at the edge of a meadow on the outskirts of town, with the windows down, the doors open, and the late-day summer haze softening the harshest of words, Davis told Francine what she needed to hear. For the most part she listened quietly. He anticipated her questions. He had clearly been through this before.

So had she—at least, some of it, she realized. Many of the behaviors he mentioned were familiar to her. Oh, Grace had been wily. Francine had been in total sympathy when she had thrown up her hands several months back, claimed utter boredom, and relegated the task of paying household bills to Francine, and when it came to questions repeated too often, Francine had actually blamed herself. If she were more on top of things, her reasoning went, Grace would ask only once and leave it at that.

She surprised herself by staying composed, even when the picture Davis painted was bleak. Either he had a calming effect on her, or the shot of whatever it was that he'd given her was tranquilizing. Then again, talking about the problem after an eon of silent torment was a relief.

"What's the worst-case scenario?" she finally asked, feeling numb enough to hear.

"In time, she may not recognize anyone or anything. She may not be able to walk or talk. She may be totally dependent on someone doing even the most intimate custodial tasks."

"Before that. You mentioned misbehavior. What's the worst?"

"Yelling and screaming. Inappropriate behavior, like removing her clothes when she shouldn't. Accusing people of stealing her possessions. Throwing things. Putting herself in harm's way. She'll require constant supervision."

"Like a child."

"Yes, like a child in the need to be watched, but no, not childlike at all. Children grow. They learn. They respond to reason and discipline. Grace won't. In those late stages, yelling will only upset her. She won't be capable of understanding what she did wrong, or remembering not to do it again. She'll feel the brunt of your anger without understanding its cause, and she'll react irrationally. She won't be able to control what she does."

Francine stared out the window. "Grace *is* control. She'll be mortified to lose it like that."

"She won't know, at that point. And there is medication that will sedate her, if she gets unmanageable. Taking care of an AD victim is a labor of love."

Her eyes flew to his. "I do love her."

"I know. But you'll need help."

"Sophie will help. Margaret will help."

"You may need more than that."

"I can hire more. I'll hire round-the-clock nursing care if I have to."

She looked sadly out at the tall grasses. Their sweep wasn't unlike that of the Dorians' back lawn. Grace loved that lawn, loved the garden, the patio, the river. Hard to imagine the day when she wouldn't know enough to love those things. Hard to imagine the day when she wouldn't direct the goings-on around her, or the day when she wouldn't have any advice to give. Hard to imagine the day when she wouldn't *speak*.

Francine felt desolate all over again. "What am I going to do?" she cried, not quite realizing she had said the words aloud until the sound hit the air. She chased them with a quick, "I'm sorry. That's not your worry."

"Of course it is. I want to help. That's why I'm here."

"You can't help Grace."

"I can help you. I did before." He gave her his crooked smile. "Head feels better, doesn't it?"

She nodded. The lethargy she felt could have as much to do with the weight of the discussion as with the lingering effects of her migraine, but at least the pain and the nausea were gone.

"What worries you most?" he asked.

She didn't have to give it much thought. "Losing Grace. She's been the single strongest force in my life. I can't begin to list all that she's shaped."

"Try," he urged softly.

She shot a plaintive glance skyward and breathed an overwhelmed, "Where to begin? Start with breakfast, which, by order of Grace, is always homemade muffins, then go on to lunch and tea and dinner, all Grace's little rituals. Add holidays, birthdays, parties, again orchestrated by Grace, and Grace in the middle of it all with an open ear and time, always time, for the people around her. There are the standards she sets. And the house, the grounds, the staff. And *The Confidante*." She turned sad eyes on Davis. "*The Confidante* is a member of the family. What'll happen to it?"

He studied her face. "You'll have to be thinking about that. Grace may have suggestions. Ask her."

While you can. He didn't say it, but she heard it. She also heard Grace's, *We have to make plans*, just that morning. Grace had been faster on the uptake than Francine, but that was nothing new.

Why us? she wanted to cry. Why this? Why now?

Davis's expression was gentle, but there were those other things—the beard shadow, the scar above the eyebrow, the hair that was not only tousled but now streaked by the summer sun, not to mention what Father Jim had said—that suggested a rougher heritage and gave Francine a pang of guilt. Grace had called her spoiled. She wondered if Davis thought so, too.

She studied her hands. "I shouldn't complain. At least I don't have to worry about money. Many of your patients probably do."

"They have things you don't—like huge extended families living with them and able to help, careers that they can take or leave, lower expectations. Don't minimize the sense of loss you feel, Francine. It's as valid for you as it is for them. Everything is relative. Like age. My mother died when I was very young, so I barely knew her. You've had Grace all these years. Your lives are tightly linked. Which is the greater tragedy? I don't know."

Nor did Francine. She thought about it as silence settled into the cab of the truck. She tried to imagine what she would be feeling now if she and Grace weren't so close. Yes, she would be heartsick. But would she feel this sense of imminent upheaval if she had a career independent of Grace, a *life* independent of Grace?

They sat for a while longer, listening to the meadow sounds, before Davis drove her back to the hospital. He pulled up at her car, caught her hand, and climbed out. She had no choice but to slide under the steering wheel to the ground by his side.

She looked at her car, then at Davis. Backlit, he was a haloed rogue, a paradoxical image if ever there was one. She smiled. But the smile faded. Maybe not such a paradoxical image. He had come through for her today.

She had a sudden wild urge to be held.

His voice barely broke a whisper. "Same bind as before. I can't take the initiative."

Still, his arm opened just that tiniest bit, all the invitation Francine needed. She slid her own around his waist, buried her face against his throat, and felt a great, enveloping calm. She didn't care about the ethical considerations that had given him pause. He was the perfect size and shape for leaning against.

He must have agreed, at least about the ethical considerations, because his arms closed around her. His breath touched her temple. "Don't hate me anymore?"

She snickered against his throat. "That was dumb of me."

"You were upset."

"I was shortsighted. Grace says I'm that, and she's right."

"You feel things passionately. It's a sign of strength. You'll do fine, Frannie."

Feel things passionately. She supposed she did. She certainly had when she'd been younger. But time had muted all that. Time, and Grace. "Why did you call me Frannie?"

"I don't know. It just seems to fit."

"I've always hated it."

"Why?"

"It sounds silly."

"Not silly. Soft."

"Stupid."

"But you aren't stupid. You're very smart. You will do fine."

She breathed him in. He smelled of earth and man and daring. "How can you say that? You barely know me."

"Hey. I've seen you walk into a door. Any woman who can do that, and right herself and walk off with the kind of dignity you showed, will do just fine."

She smiled. "I suppose that image is permanently etched in your mind."

"You bet."

She sighed. Reluctantly, she drew back. "Along the same humbling vein, I need to see Grace."

"Let me know how it goes?"

She nodded, mouthed, "Thanks," and slid into her car before he could see that behind his absurdly large aviator glasses, her eyes were wet again.

Grace was a solitary figure in the parlor, drinking tea. From the door, Francine found the image heart-wrenching. The woman loved by millions was alone.

In that instant, she felt for Grace as she never had—as her mother, yes, but as a friend and fellow human being, as someone who was vulnerable, as someone who suffered.

Then Grace looked up and saw her—and there was another rush of new feeling. Francine saw fear. She couldn't bear it.

Crossing the floor, she wrapped her arms around her. "I'm sorry, Mom. I've been shortsighted and selfish and all the other things you called me. You were right. You always are."

She imagined Grace sighed. One graceful hand closed on her arm.

"I'll be here," Francine went on. "I'll do whatever has to be done. Just tell me, and I'll do it." She drew back. Her heart caught when she saw Grace's eyes. Tears were another something new.

"I'm afraid," Grace whispered.

Francine nodded and whispered back, "So am I."

"I don't want to be laughed at."

"You won't be."

"I don't want to—to . . ." She stopped, frowned, seemed to be searching. When she couldn't find the word she wanted, she looked at Francine in frustration.

Francine was trying to come up with a suitable one to offer, when Grace's expression changed. It became hopeful, almost innocent, and her voice lighter. "Well, one word or another doesn't matter, and anyway, you're just in time for tea. Father Jim couldn't come today. I'm afraid the tea may have cooled. Margaret? *Margaret?*"

"Mom?" Sophie was at the door, looking pale and unsure.

Francine gave Grace's shoulder a soft touch, then went to her daughter and took her face in her hands. "Don't ever," she said in an urgent whisper, "ever suggest that I don't need you. I always have, far more than you know. And I do now, more than ever."

"Where were you? I was scared. I started imagining life without *both* of you—"

Francine stoppered the words with a hand. She slowly shook her head. Grace's affliction might be a lesson in mortality, but mortality couldn't rule their lives. She slipped her arms around Sophie's neck and was holding her tightly, savoring the preciousness of her, when she saw Father Jim.

She wasn't surprised. He was always there when the Dorians were in need.

She held out a hand and drew him in. "Grace said you couldn't come."

He looked concerned. "I couldn't. But I had a nagging feeling." He looked beyond them to Grace, who was looking right at him with yet another new expression. Raw need. That was the only way Francine could describe it. Raw need. Directed at Father Jim.

He went to her, knelt by her chair, and took her in his arms.

Francine was trying to adjust to that sight when she heard sounds that tore through her. Muffled, they suggested uncertainty and fear, and signified even more forcefully than the rest of the day's events that life had changed.

Grace was crying.

"I made a list," Grace said the next morning. "We need to go through it."

Francine was at her desk, nursing a cup of coffee and a sense of displacement. Everything around her looked the same. Grace certainly did. She sounded as self-assured as ever. The vulnerability of the day before might never have been.

How easy it would be to pretend, just a little longer. But harmful. She knew that now. Not that she was ready for Grace's list. Accepting the truth was one thing, acting on it another.

"Will you call Sophie?" Grace asked. "I want her here. She's part of this, too."

Sophie was still asleep, with good cause this time. She and Francine had talked into the wee hours. Francine would have let her sleep if it hadn't been for Grace. But Grace was priority one. Her thoughts were an endangered species.

Sophie seemed to agree, because she joined them soon after, wearing a distinctly conventional sundress and sandals, and a single pair of earrings. She kept her thumb tucked into her fist, forefinger rubbing cuticle. The gesture was a relic of childhood. Francine hadn't seen it in years.

She hoped Grace wouldn't see. It was the kind of thing Grace hated.

But Grace was obsessed with her list. She put it flat on the desk, facing Francine. "Everything's here. Read it aloud, please. If I start going on about something else, get me back."

Francine read, " 'Number one. Francine becomes The Confidante. ' " She looked up, startled. "Forever?"

"Well, until you're too old or infirm. Did you think it would end with me?"

No. She hadn't. She just hadn't given the details much thought. Grace had always been too young, too energetic and able to allow for anything but the assumption that she had years and years ahead.

"You're already doing it," Grace said, "and I can't anymore."

"Do the column in an advisory capacity," Francine urged.

Grace *was* The Confidante. A period of transition was better than nothing.

Grace shook her head. "I work too slowly. My thoughts are scattered. Besides, I need to do my book. So I want—I want . . ." She frowned, waved a hand, stopped talking.

Unsettled by the faltering, Francine returned to the list. "'Number two. My book gets done.' We've already covered that. 'Number three. No one tells. The Dorian image stays intact.'" Francine saw problems. She set down the list. "That could be hard. The columns are one thing. No one knows whether you write them or not. But what about the rest—speeches, talk shows, panels?"

At the expectant look Grace slid her, she felt the rush of a chilly frisson. She arched both brows, wavered, pointed to herself.

Grace nodded.

"But I *can't*," Francine protested. "You know that. I can't speak before groups." She appealed to Sophie. "I throw up. That's how nervous I get. There are only three bookings so far for the fall. It's not too late to pull out."

"No," Grace said.

"Why not?"

"Because—because that won't—help."

"Help what?"

Grace thought for a minute, then said, "My book."

"But I'm not you. My making appearances won't help your book." The mere thought of it made her stomach bottom out. "Besides, if you don't show up as The Confidante, people will speculate, anyway."

Grace tapped the list.

Francine saved further arguments for later. She waited only until she had steadied herself, then read, "'Number four. Burial instructions are with Father Jim.' For *heaven's* sake, Mother." It was a gruesome thought, raised too soon.

"It's important," Grace said.

"I thought everything was decided when Daddy died." There had been a new area cleared in the Dorian family plot, a new headstone carved.

"There are some changes." Grace glanced at the door, seeming uneasy. In a quiet voice, she said, "I heard them last night."

"Heard who?"

"My family."

Francine felt another chill. Davis had mentioned the possibility of hallucinations, but she wasn't ready for those, either. So she arched a brow. "Well, *that's* something. Not everyone hears the dead."

Grace didn't blink. "They were in my parlor, yelling at me. They always yelled. I never listened."

"To your parents?" Sophie asked, sounding intrigued.

"They're still angry at me for leaving. I went into my bedroom, but I could hear them out there."

"That may have been your imagination," Francine suggested. When Grace didn't argue, she returned to the list. Two items remained. The first was "Robert." "Robert?"

"Robert Taft. I want you to marry him. He's a nice man. I'll feel better about what's happening to me if I know you're married."

It was an antiquated thought if ever there was one. Francine didn't believe for a minute that she needed a man for security, health, happiness, or anything else, but she wasn't eager to argue, so she simply said, "Things like that can't be orchestrated. You tried once before, remember?"

"I wanted to say it while I could."

"Okay. You have."

"And Sophie." Grace gestured toward the list.

Francine read, " 'Sophie.' " That was it. She raised uneasy eyes to Grace.

"I want her married, too. I want you married, too, Sophie."

Sophie laughed. "That's nice."

"I want someone taking care of you."

"I don't need someone taking care of me."

"You need someone responsible."

"I'm not looking to get married."

"Well, you should be."

Francine could see Sophie's color rising. As ominous signs went, it had nothing to do with diabetes, and everything to do with temper, and Francine didn't blame her. Men were far from a panacea. Marriage didn't guarantee a thing. Still, arguing just then was futile.

Sophie tried. "What about your columns, Gram, the ones telling parents to let grown kids make their own decisions?"

"I'm not your parent. I'm your grandparent. There's a difference. I want you married to a good man. And not Gus."

Sophie gaped pleadingly at Francine, who was doing her very best to convey the idea that she should just shut up, but Sophie wasn't the type to do that. "I don't believe this," she said. "Does she give a name there? Does she list the time and place? Is there a dowry?"

Francine forced the smile Sophie would have produced if she'd had twenty more years of practice. "She's concerned, babe. That's all. About both of us. That's sweet, Mother."

Grace scowled. "Don't patronize me, Francine. I don't like to be patronized. I'm trying my best to get everything done while I can. I won't be laughed at."

"I'm not laughing."

"You certainly aren't taking me seriously. But I'm *dead* serious."

"I know."

"No, you don't. Every mother wants her daughter settled before she dies. If you were in my shoes, you'd be saying the same thing to Sophie. My goodness, I'm only trying to help." She got up in a huff and stalked off.

"She isn't trying to help," Sophie said a short time later, incredulous still. "She's trying to rule our lives from the grave."

"Not from the grave," Francine warned. "She isn't dead yet."

"But it's more of the same. She's programming our lives for years to come with all of the things that *she* deems important. Well, what about what *we* deem important?" She thought of the rules and regulations that dominated her life. "Maybe we don't want to keep *The Confidante* going. Maybe we don't want to lie about her health. I mean, that one's *really* funny. *She* was the one who told me to tell people I had diabetes. Be confident, she said. Be up front, she said. Talk about not practicing what you preach. Really. What you do with your marital status is your business, not hers. Robert is a bore, by the way. He may be great on paper, but if you ever married him I'd be totally disappointed in you."

"Now you know how I feel about Gus," was Francine's quiet reply.

"I'm not marrying Gus."

"Does he know that?"

"He should. I've never suggested anything else."

"Men tend to jump to conclusions, particularly where wealthy women are involved. Clue him in, babe."

"And spoil a good thing?" Sophie asked. Gus was a toy, enamored enough of her to let her call the shots. Except in bed. There he was macho all the way. His gear was first-rate, and he knew how to use it. She wasn't dumping him yet. "Do *you* want to see me married?"

"For marriage's sake alone? No. You don't need it. If you want it, that's something else." She sighed. "Look, I'm not telling you to do what Grace says, just not to fight her on it. Fighting is pointless. She can't win. She insisted we go over that list today because she knows that next week or next month or next year she may not know what it means."

Sophie was trying to grasp the reality of that. She might hate the imperious Grace, but she didn't like the thought of Gram being reduced to a whimpering mass of nothingness, either.

Francine touched her cheek. "We aren't in disagreement, you and I. We both know Grace likes to run things. The issue is how we deal with her requests."

"Her requests are absurd," Sophie said. When Francine didn't respond, she cried, "You'd go along with them? Make public appearances? Marry *Robert* . . ." She gargled the name, then rushed on, because the matter of the business was something else. It directly affected her life. "Do you want to keep *The Confidante* going?"

"Grace is The Confidante," Francine said, looking lost. "I never imagined that changing."

"Wouldn't you like to be The Confidante?"

"God, no. I pale beside Grace."

Sophie was tired of hearing that. "You do not. You have things Grace couldn't *begin* to have."

"Well, it's the things she has that *I* couldn't begin to have that make *The Confidante* work."

"Like what?"

"Tact. She takes every letter seriously. She can give patient answers to even the dumbest questions. I avoid the dumb ones. But they aren't dumb to the people who ask them. I don't have Grace's generosity."

"Maybe it's a subconscious attempt on your part to up-grade *The Confidante.*"

Francine didn't look impressed by that theory. "Maybe I'm missing relevant issues. Grace gets them all. She anticipates what's important and what isn't. She'll write about some-thing, then, boom, within days that something crops up on the evening news. It's like a sixth sense. I don't have it."

"So what will you do with *The Confidante?*"

"Grace wants it continued."

Sophie wanted to shake her mother. "What do *you* want?"

Francine answered cautiously. "I love *The Confidante.* It's part of me. And it's Grace's legacy."

Which was about as ambivalent an affirmative answer as Sophie's reaction to it.

Francine was sitting on the floor that night, stroking the silky spot between Legs's ears, when the phone rang. Her eyes flew to the clock. It was ten-thirty. Any number of friends called this late. Her private line rang only here.

She remembered another night, another call, and dared to hope.

"Hello?"

"Hi."

She felt something warm bloom inside. "Hi, Davis."

"How's it going?"

"Okay."

"Well?"

"We talked. Grace and I, Grace, Sophie, and I, Sophie and I."

"Did it help?"

"I think so. I don't know. I'm kind of numb. Shell-shocked."

"That's a protective mechanism. It's hard, accepting the reality of something like this."

"I always thought I was a realist."

"Grace is your mother. If there's one relationship that people are typically unrealistic about, it's that one. Emotions run high, and no wonder. Think about it. Nine months in utero, years of early childhood and mutual dependence—"

"Mutual?"

"Sure. Babies, because they're totally helpless. Mothers, because they need to satisfy maternal instincts."

"Grace was never dependent on me."

"She kept you close all her life."

"I *stayed* close. It was my doing."

"Are you sure?"

"Sure I'm sure."

"What would Grace have done if you'd gone away to college and never returned home?"

"It's a moot point. I wouldn't have left. I was too involved with *The Confidante*. Grace gave me a role early on—" She caught herself, then argued around his point. "But she didn't do it because she needed to have me around. She wanted to have me around. There's a difference."

"Why didn't she have any other children?"

"They just didn't come."

"Did she want them?"

"She must have. She adored me. She adores Sophie."

"What about you? Did you want more children?"

"I might have, if the marriage had lasted. Then again, I had my hands full with Sophie. I often wonder what it would have been like to have more."

"What's your conclusion?"

"I think I'd have liked it. It might have freed Sophie up. She feels pressure, being the only grandchild."

"Pressure to stay close to Grace?"

"To the business. She has a love-hate relationship with it. And, yes, with Grace. She's great with her one minute and horrid the next. Even now. She accepts Grace's illness on one level, rejects it on another. She's torn. There are times when I think that the *worst* thing for her is to be here with us."

"What does she think?"

"As we speak? I'm sure she thinks she can't *possibly* leave now, what with things so topsy-turvy."

"They won't always be. They'll settle down."

"Lord, I hope so. I feel jittery all the time."

"How's the head?"

"Fine. How's the house?"

"Hot as hell, actually. I rigged up the hose and made an outdoor shower. It was great."

Francine conjured a picture that was vaguely erotic. "Where are you now?"

"On the trailer steps. It's a nice night. Did you run?"

"Sure did. I think I wore Legs out. She's right here, half asleep with her chin on my knee."

"Lucky Legs."

Francine remembered the way he had held her in the hospital parking lot the afternoon before. Just thinking about it brought a measure of calm. So she kept thinking about it, feeling the connection over the telephone wire, wishing just for an instant that he would hold her again.

He was like a nightcap—relaxing, possibly addictive, def-initely not something she would tell Grace about.

"Why the sigh?" he asked.

"Just tired. You're sweet to call, Davis. Thanks."

"Remember. I'm here."

She wasn't about to forget.

Nine

As salt measures worth and sage speaks the mind, so sugar wins hearts.

—GRACE DORIAN, from an interview in *FoodFest* magazine

In Chicago's wake, the official story was that Grace was taking the summer off from the public eye. Her agent bought it, as did her book editor, her newspaper editor, and her publicist. Her friends weren't as malleable. Accustomed to her involvement in the season's festivities, they dropped by unannounced to protest that she was becoming a hermit. Francine, who sat in on these impromptu visits, got quite good at covering lapses and filling voids. She refused to stand by and see Grace embarrassed.

So she felt a pang of unease when the doorbell rang one afternoon in August. Grace had awoken in a foul mood—had accused Margaret of stealing her pearls and Francine of stealing her glasses and Sophie of stealing her address book, though Sophie was in Easthampton with friends—and the day hadn't improved. She was subdued now, brooding at her desk.

But the fight had taken its toll on Francine. She hadn't written a word all day. When Tony called, she put him off. Then the air conditioner broke and she couldn't reach the repairman, and Marny got sick and had to leave, and the mail brought a summons for jury duty.

She felt hot, distracted, and pressured, definitely not in the mood to risk Grace with her friends.

It wasn't a friend at the door, but Robin Duffy.

Francine might have figured it, what with everything else going wrong.

"I thought I'd stop by and say hello," Robin said brightly.

"Hello," was Francine's dutiful response.

"Actually, I wanted to talk with you."

"About?" As if she didn't know.

"Grace."

Francine remembered all too well the last time they had talked about Grace, remembered the article that had followed and the chaos following that. She felt a surge of resentment. "If you're wondering whatever happened after the accident last April, the answer is nothing. The police couldn't find a thing to charge Grace with."

"I know."

"You do? Huh. I hadn't realized that. There was no follow-up in the paper. I guess being cleared of charges isn't news." Her voice hardened. "Of course, there never were any charges, only the ones you made, and they were half-baked from the start." She wasn't handling Robin as Grace would, but it had been that kind of day.

Robin stood straighter. "I didn't do anything that any good reporter wouldn't do. I reported the news. An investigation was part of that news."

"You didn't report the news," Francine charged. "You *made* the news. The police weren't looking into drugs or alcohol. They never mentioned those things. You did. All they said was that an investigation was under way, which is standard for any automobile accident, I might add. You made the inference."

"I'm not here about the accident."

Francine stood silently, waiting.

"May I come in? It's as hot as hell out here."

"It's as hot as hell in here, too. The air-conditioning isn't working." She stepped onto the porch, closing the door behind her. "I'll walk you to your car."

"I was hoping to see Grace."

Francine was without sympathy. "We don't take drop-in reporters."

"Is she inside?"

"Working hard and not to be disturbed."

"Writing her autobiography."

"Correct."

They approached Robin's car. It was a spiffy little Honda with a side full of dents. Francine arched a brow. "And you wanted to know about Grace's accident?"

Robin studied the car with what looked to be genuine wistfulness. "I have a seventeen-year-old son. He lacks judgment sometimes. I've reached the point where I'd rather he dent the dents than dent a pricey repair job." There was a second's pause. "I heard Grace was sick."

Francine might have actually commiserated with Robin—Sophie had been hell on wheels at seventeen—if Robin hadn't tacked on the last. "Where did you hear that?"

Robin shrugged. "I have contacts. By this time last summer she'd been to a dozen parties. This year, aside from her own, she hasn't been to a one."

Contacts? Francine wondered who. "She's taking the summer off."

"Will she be back on the scene come fall?"

"If she chooses to be."

"Will she choose to be?"

"I don't know. I'm not Grace."

"You seem to be, sometimes. When I call people asking about Grace, all they can say is that they've talked with you."

"That's my job. Grace can't be talking with everyone."

"Not even Katia Sloane?"

Francine felt a qualm. "Katia hasn't called with anything worth bothering Grace about. Why are you calling Katia?"

"Because I'm interested in Grace. She was on a panel at a conference in Chicago last month. I heard she was awful."

"You heard wrong. I was there."

"She was incoherent."

"I didn't think so," Francine said. Not incoherent, exactly. "If your snitch was looking for academic jibberish, he was barking up the wrong tree. Grace doesn't pretend to be an academic."

"I've heard her on panels where she's held her own, where she's actually been good, in her way."

"'In her way'?" The phrase was Francine's undoing. "Tell me, what *do* you have against Grace?"

"Nothing. I barely know her. If you'd let me in so that I could talk with her—"

"You had four hours last year, four hours of baiting her, then you wrote a piece with a definite anti-Grace slant." Sugar wins hearts, Grace always said, but Francine had been sour from the instant Robin had shown up. The damage was done. She saw no point in making amends. "Another part of my job is to shield Grace from hostile reporters. I don't know what your problem is, but I don't want you coming here again. You won't get past me to see Grace. There's nothing in it for us." She turned and set off for the house.

"You're hiding something," Robin called.

"Don't you wish," Francine called back.

"I'll find out what it is. Grace is public property."

Francine whirled, in a fury. "Grace is *my* mother, and you are on private property. Trespass again, and I'll call the police. They weren't thrilled with your last piece either. They don't like troublemakers." She whirled front and was off again, covering the drive, then the stone steps, in long strides. It wasn't until she was inside, with the door shut tight, that she stopped. Her temper took a while longer to settle.

But settle it did, leaving her with the guilt of having done something—a whole conversation of somethings—that Grace wouldn't have approved of at all.

Francine left the house at ten with Legs by her side. She had run hard through the darkness for twenty minutes, reached her turning point, and started back, when a truck approached from behind. It was a smallish truck, its motor rougher than a sedan, smoother than a semi. When it had come abreast and slowed to her pace, the driver gave a wolf whistle.

She grinned. "Thank you, Davis."

"I tried calling, but you weren't home. Figured you were running. How's it going?"

She had been wound tight before leaving the house. The run had worked out most of the kinks. Davis's arrival took care of the rest. There was something about that deep voice of his. "It's going okay."

"How's Grace?"

"Moody. It wasn't one of her good days."

"Want to talk about it?"

It wasn't only his voice. It was the truck, the muscled arm, the darkness. There was a suggestiveness here. Did she want to talk about Grace? "Not particularly."

"Want to stop for a drink?"

"Last time I did that, I got stomach cramps running home."

"Only because you wouldn't let me drive you. This time I will. You'll see. You'll be fine."

Francine ran on for a minute longer, thinking that Davis wasn't Robert, that he wasn't a purebred or necessarily a gentleman, that there was something unconventional about him, and that that excited her. After the day she'd had, she was feeling reckless.

Tapering slowly to a walk, she ran her wristband over the sweat on her cheeks and neck, and took her time catching her breath. By then Davis had pulled onto the shoulder of the road and climbed out.

"All I have is root beer."

"Is it wet?" she asked, then took the can his thumb opened and found that it was cold, too. "Mmmm. Feels good. It's a hot night." She followed him to the back of the truck. When he lowered the tailgate, she hopped on. Legs sat on the ground, close by. "Working on the house?" she asked.

"How'd you guess?"

She eyed his boots. "They're a dead giveaway." Paired with shorts and a T-shirt, they were cool. "How's it going?"

"Great. I think I can be in by winter."

"Hey. That's terrific."

"It won't be finished, exactly. There'll still be detail work to do. But I'll be able to get my furniture out of storage and ditch the trailer. It's getting claustrophobic."

"The shower."

"Shower, kitchen, living area, sleeping area—just about everything. I keep waiting for you to come see it."

"I've never been inside a live-in one before. I've led a cloistered existence."

"Come see the trailer, and I'll show you the house, too."

She sliced him a glance. "Is that an invitation?"

He held her gaze. "No pressure, of course. I wouldn't want to take advantage of you."

She gave him a last look, then took another drink. "So. You're from Tyne Valley. When did you meet Father Jim?"

"He and my dad were friends growing up. They ran with the same pack for a short while. It was a wild one."

"Father Jim, wild?" She didn't believe that.

"He was. My dad swears it. For what it's worth." He looked off into the night. "My old man isn't the best of authorities."

"Does he still live there?"

"In his way."

"What way's that?"

"Drunk."

"Oh." Francine didn't know what else to say.

Davis grinned crookedly at the night. "Right. Oh. He isn't a pretty sight. Never really was."

"Did he always drink?"

"Pretty much."

"Do you have other family there?"

"Two sisters. Both are married to dead-end guys—doing nothing, going nowhere. I've tried to get them to move, but they refuse. Same with my dad."

"Because the Valley is home?"

"Because the outside world isn't. They cling to the familiar, even if it's stagnant."

"Is Tyne Valley that bad?"

"In a word, yes."

"Describe it."

He shot her a look. "You've never been?"

"No. Grace has no desire to go north. East, south, or west. Not north."

"That's funny. I thought she was from the Valley herself."

Francine laughed. "God, no—though I can understand that you'd make the connection, what with Father Jim and all. Grace is from a town in northern Maine that was flooded when a dam was built to generate hydroelectric power."

"That's funny," Davis repeated. After a minute, sounding puzzled, he said, "Are you sure?"

"Of course I'm sure. I'd know where my own mother came from." She paused. "Tell me more about you. Have you ever been married?"

"No."

"Why not?"

"I'm drawn to the wrong women."

"What women?"

"Smart, classy, career types."

"What makes them wrong?"

"They have aspirations I don't."

"Like what?"

"Making millions."

"What about making babies?"

"Exactly."

"Do you want them?"

"You bet. Gotta finish my house first, though."

"Sophie is the best thing I ever did," Francine mused. She took a drink, set the cold can on her thigh, crossed her ankles. "She is my legacy to the world."

"Are you Grace's legacy?"

"*The Confidante* is Grace's legacy."

"Does Grace see it that way?"

Francine nodded. "*The Confidante* is a bona fide success story. She takes great pride in it."

"She's proud of you."

"Not like she's proud of *The Confidante*."

"Has she ever said that?"

"Not in as many words."

"In any words?"

"No. I guess not."

"Ask her sometime. You may be surprised."

"I doubt that. Besides, do I want to risk her choosing *The Confidante* over me?"

"Sounds like you've already assumed the worst, so what've you got to lose?"

Francine supposed he had a point. He usually did, logic-wise. But the issue wasn't one of logic for her. It was one of sheer emotion. "Where'd you get the scar?"

"Which one?"

"There's another?" she asked with a look at his eyebrow.

He tugged up his T-shirt and pointed to a spot near where his shorts rode low. Francine couldn't see any scar in the dark. All she could see was a beautifully shaped torso. "I got this in a knife fight when I was fifteen," he said, and, to her disappointment, dropped the shirt and touched his eyebrow. "This one is from hockey."

"A knife fight." She wanted to see that scar again.

"I ran with a rough crowd. There was a rival crowd—"

"Gang?"

"Crowd, group, gang—we were always plotting against each other. Had nothing better to do with our lives." He touched his shirt where the scar was. "I nearly died from this. I was in the hospital for a week. It was the worst week of my whole life. Forget the pain, which was incredible. They didn't medicate me so much that I couldn't hear their constant lecturing. The high school principal, the police chief, half his department—they all knew me from past encounters—the local probation officer, a social worker— every damn one of them got on my case, telling me what would happen if I didn't wise up. Then Father Jim came along. To this day, I don't know who called him. Probably my old man, but if I'd known it then, I might have tuned out."

"What did he say?"

"He said he wasn't going to repeat what the others said, because they were right, and if I didn't know that already, then his saying it again wouldn't make much difference. He promised that if I got my act together, he'd help me get out."

"Is that when the hockey started?"

"No. I'd been playing hockey on the town pond for years. That comes with the territory, growing up up north. Not that the kind of hockey I'd been playing was civilized. We made our own rules, the more vicious, the better. I didn't know anything about traditional hockey playing—but I could sure as hell skate. It took a little taming before I was fit to play on a team, but it worked. Father Jim pointed the scouts in my direction, then lobbied for the kind of scholarships I needed."

"Why medicine?"

He looked straight at her. "Because it seemed the single most unlikely career for me to succeed in. If I failed, I could look at the do-gooders and say, see, you were wrong. If I succeeded, I'd have something great. I never had anything great when I was a kid."

"Do you ever go back?"

"Once or twice a year."

"To see your family?"

"Yeah. I send money. I don't think it's well spent. Maybe I should do what Grace does and let the church dole it out." He paused. "You're *sure* she isn't from Tyne Valley?"

"Positive."

"Boy, I misunderstood someone. A little town in Maine, huh? Tell me about her childhood."

Francine shook her head. "I don't want to talk about Grace."

"Tell me about your childhood."

"I don't want to talk about Grace."

"That entwined?"

"That entwined."

"Even during your marriage?"

Francine nodded. "Lee decided he couldn't take it at about the same time I decided I couldn't take him, hence the mutual parting of ways."

"You don't use his name. Does Sophie?"

"No. She changed her name legally to Dorian."

"How did Lee feel about that?"

"He saw it as a formalization of what already was. He wasn't a fighter." She thought about that. "Maybe if he had been, we'd still be married. He's a nice guy."

"Does Sophie see him much?"

"Actually, yes. He lives in Manhattan. He manages the family business." She sent Davis a wry look. "They're in disposable diapers."

"Lovely," Davis said.

"They've made a killing. First there was one kind for babies. Then two kinds. Then six kinds. Then training pants. Then diapers for adults. That's where the growth is now, with so many people living longer and losing control." She stopped talking, thinking of those adults for whom Lee's products were designed. Late-stage Alzheimer's patients were among them.

She must have made a sound, because Davis put a hand on her arm and said gently, "Francine—"

"I don't want to talk about Grace." She had to live day to day, couldn't agonize over what would happen down the road.

"Okay." His voice found a different depth. "Let's talk about orgasms, since Grace won't."

"Orgasms." She grinned. Davis wasn't shy with words. It remained to be seen whether he was all talk. He had the body for action. He had the *attitude* for action. She guessed that he was phenomenal in bed. Her insides shimmied at the thought.

"Do you like them?"

"What's—"she cleared her throat—"what's not to like?"

"Losing control. Some women hate that."

"But it's what orgasms are about."

"Do you like to watch?"

She knew she was blushing, could feel the heat of it. "Until I lose control. Then sensation takes over."

"Are you a multiple person?"

"Can be. It depends on the man. And you? Are you the slam, bam type?"

"Nope. I like it slow and long and deep."

For an instant she had no breath. Then she found some, laughed it out, covered her face with a hand. "This is too much."

"You asked."

She shook her head, muttering, "Slow and long and deep." Then, wondering if it *was* all talk, she said, "Is that the way you kiss?"

"Can be. It depends on the woman."

She stared through the night at his shadowed face and waited. When he simply stared right back, she taunted, "You'll never do it."

The air hummed around them in the ensuing silence. Then, in a gritty voice, he said, "Is that a dare?"

She kept staring at him. Oh, yes, it was a dare. He had broached the topic; she wanted him to see it through. There was a fire inside that she hadn't felt in way too long. It was nice.

"What about the dog?"

"She won't be traumatized."

"Will she bite me?"

"No. She knows your scent." It was earthy, healthy, male. He set down his soda and sat there for another minute.

"Ethical considerations?" she whispered, goading again.

She barely had time for another breath when he took her face in one large hand. His mouth covered hers completely, lips firmly stroking, teeth nipping until she opened to him, and then his tongue began the slow, long, and deep that said she was the kind of woman who took it—and take it she did, with delight. Francine had guessed that Davis would kiss like a guy from the wrong side of the tracks. What she hadn't guessed was how exciting it was. Something electric sparked inside her, something wild and wanting, to match the wild and wanting in him. He was the goader now, but she rose to the occasion, giving as good as she got, unable to get enough. She touched his stubbled cheek, his neck, his chest, suddenly hungry, suddenly *starved* for this kind of heart-pounding, body-heating bliss.

He took his mouth from hers only while he slipped off the tailgate. Then he was lodged between her legs, giving her another mind-blowing, belly-curling kiss that had her

stretching straight up on either side of his neck, then, needing more, skimming his chest and clutching his hips. Her
knees hugged his flanks. Hands on her backside, he pressed
her closer.

He whispered something sexy into her mouth that fired
her more, and then he was kneading her breasts, lifting them
as he might to his mouth, if it were free. When his fingers
scraped her nipples, she felt a searing all the way to her belly.
She cried out at the pleasure of it.

As suddenly as it had started, it was done. His mouth was
against her forehead, his breath ragged. "We'd better stop."

She didn't have to ask why. His arousal was impressive,
no doubt painful. One part of her would have quite happily
slipped off her shorts and given him relief. She needed it
herself.

The other part knew it wasn't wise. "This was how I got
Sophie."

"Against a truck?"

"In a movie theater." When he made a disbelieving sound,
she said, "We were alone in the balcony. I didn't like the
show."

"You said he was a wimp."

"I also said the sex was great, but he never kissed me like
you just did." She swore softly and raised her mouth for another one.

This time his kiss was even slower, longer, and deeper,
and held something she could only call tenderness. Incredibly, it was more powerful than the last.

She slid her hands down between them, to the point
where their bodies strained.

He caught them and drew them back up. "I don't have
anything with me," he whispered against her mouth.

"Would you do it, if you did?" she whispered back.

"Right here, right now."

Which was where and when she wanted it. "Maybe I'm too old to worry."

He made a sound that said what he thought of that theory.

She wondered if she would conceive as easily as she had conceived Sophie, if a pregnancy would be a nightmare at her age, if she would have the patience for a baby.

She would.

Only she wasn't having one.

She took a shuddering breath, returned her legs to the tailgate, and rested her forehead on Davis's chest. "Just as well. This would only be another complication in an already complicated life."

"Maybe you need the outlet."

"I haven't so far." Yes, she was lonely at night. Yes, she missed good sex. But she had never gone in for affairs. Not with Sophie around. Not with *Grace* around. Grace had been marginally scandalized when she had gotten pregnant with Sophie. Grace would *die* if anything happened now, particularly with someone from Tyne Valley.

Francine thought of what Davis had once been and who he had become. She looked up at him. Even in the dark, his eyes were hot. Tamed? Fat chance. "You're a dangerous man."

"Only when goaded. So. When are you coming over to see my house?"

"When do you want me to?"

"Now."

She snickered. "That would be asking for trouble. Besides, I need my beauty sleep."

"Then tomorrow."

"Gotta work."

"Tomorrow night."

"Is there a reason for the sudden rush?" she asked, knowing just what it was.

"That isn't true," he protested. "I don't even have a bed there."

"That won't stop us."

"I promise I won't do anything you don't want."

"I don't know what I want. I want, but I don't."

"No sex, then. How's that for blunt?"

She sighed. "I don't know, Davis. Something happens when we're together." Legs nudged her knee. She touched the dog's head. "We have to go."

Davis stepped back. "I promised I'd take you home."

Francine didn't argue with him. He dropped her at the end of the drive with the lightest touch to her chin. While Legs dashed ahead, she walked slowly back to the house, then sat on the front steps for a while, then sat in the dark on her bed for another while.

It was a long time before she fell asleep. The last thing on her mind before she did was Davis. The first thing on her mind when she woke up was Davis.

That was why, when the hour turned reasonable, she put in a call to Robert Taft.

Two days later Francine received a letter. It was handwritten, in the kind of neat script, on the kind of fine vellum that Grace loved. The return address wasn't a newspaper office, but a town halfway between the Dorians and Manhattan. Curious, Francine turned to the second sheet to see who it was from. When she saw Robin Duffy's name, she nearly threw the letter, unread, in the trash. But the presentation was classy, more so than Francine had thought Robin to be. She was intrigued.

Dear Francine,

I imagine that your first impulse will be to throw this letter away without reading it, and I don't blame you. I've handled things wrong. I apologize. I did consider calling before I showed up at your door the other day, but I was afraid you wouldn't see me. So I took the chance, and it seems to have backfired.

I imagine that your second impulse on receiving this letter is to wonder why one particular reporter is obsessed with your mother.

Francine smiled dryly. She had been wondering that, indeed.

Obsessed may be too strong a word, but I do have a greater interest in Grace than another reporter might have. My mother adored her. She opened the newspaper each morning to The Confidante. Rarely did a day pass when she didn't mention that column to my brother and me. Rarely did a week pass without one of those columns being posted on the refrigerator door. My mother thought the sun rose and set on Grace. She saw Grace each time she was on television. She even wrote to her once, and got a lovely note in return. I can't tell you how many times she read and reread that note. I don't know where Grace found the time to write it, but it brought my mother much happiness.

Francine figured that either Robin was being deliberately polite, or she was an innocent if she didn't realize that Grace hadn't written that note. Grace couldn't possibly personally answer all the mail she received.

My mother died last year. She was reading The Confidante right up to the end. The column made her

think about everyday things. Even when she couldn't re-
late to them herself, she felt she was getting a glimpse of
what was going on in the country. She swore that Grace's
column told her more about the mood of the people than
any news item might.

Francine had never thought of *The Confidante* in quite
those terms, but she liked them. Robin wrote nicely.

I disagreed with my mother on many things. Despite
her belief that Grace wrote gospel, she didn't always follow
those teachings. At times she had a double standard—a
rigid one, based on Grace's thoughts, that she applied to
my brother and me, and a more lenient one that she ap-
plied to herself. She seemed able to interpret Grace's ad-
vice in ways that suited her own needs.

Hearing a familiar ring, Francine felt a sudden, unexpected affinity with Robin.

A while back, for instance, my brother announced
that he was gay. Grace had addressed the issue many
times, advising acceptance and love. As many times as I
reminded her of that, my mother couldn't manage it. As
far as she was concerned, the acceptance and love was to
come from us, as in our accepting her aversion to what
she considered abnormal, and loving her in spite of it.
She and my brother were estranged for the last few years
of her life. He still lives with the guilt of having disap-
pointed her.

Had Grace been as manipulative? No. She would never
behave as cruelly as Robin's mother had. Was telling her

forty-three-year-old daughter whom to marry manipulative? No. The circumstances were extenuating.

Francine thought of Robert, with whom she was having dinner on Saturday night, and of Davis, with whom she wasn't placing herself alone in a room. When both thoughts seemed wrong, she returned to Robin's letter.

> *So my interest in Grace has deep roots. She is as much a part of my life as she is a part of the lives of millions of readers. I am fortunate in that my profession allows me to tell those readers more about Grace than they would otherwise know.*
>
> *A final apology. If I offended you with my coverage of Grace's auto accident last April, I'm sorry. I thought I was reporting the news. If it's any consolation, the paper received a rash of phone calls in protest of that article. My editor wasn't any more pleased with me than you were.*
>
> *I understand that you don't want me at your home. I would truly like to meet you elsewhere, perhaps for lunch, on neutral ground. Grace preaches communication. We should talk.*
>
> *My dream is to be the one most informed reporter on matters to do with Grace. I'm not sure whether I want this for my mother, or for myself, but in any case my history with The Confidante makes me the perfect candidate. Please consider this. I may be able to help.*
>
> *I have printed my home address, and telephone and fax numbers, below. I hope to hear from you.*
>
> *Sincerely,*
Robin
Duffy

Francine felt as torn about the letter as she felt about most everything else in her life. Coming as it did from an intelligent woman, it was one of the most flattering letters she had read. Coming from a woman with the power to make or break Grace, it was frightening.

The only thing Francine knew for sure was that, as things stood now, she didn't dare take Robin up on her offer.

Ten

No matter how modern the world may become, tradition will always be the scaffolding of family life.
—GRACE DORIAN, from *The Confidante*

Over the next few months, Francine was on a treadmill, running fast, getting nowhere. She kept tripping—grouping columns in ways that had Tony asking if Grace was ill, getting caught in lies about why Grace couldn't make this talk show or that seminar, asking Grace questions that set her off in a rage.

After spending Labor Day in atypical Dorian solitude, the curiosity mushroomed. Reporters crawled out of the nation's woodwork wanting interviews. Annie Diehl was besieged with booking requests. Friends begged to do lunch. There were calls from Tony, from Katia, from Amanda, from George, from editors of more of the papers *The Confidante* appeared in than Francine cared to count, all concerned about

Grace. On top of that, work was a nightmare. What used to take Grace two days was taking Francine five, which meant that one unproductive day set her back, which meant that Tony was on the horn blaring his impatience too often for comfort.

Likewise, too often for comfort, were arguments with Sophie. Exasperated at one point, Francine threw up her hands. "What is going on here? We should be giving each other support, not grief. Why are we *bickering*?"

"We're bickering because you're behaving ridiculously," Sophie declared. "There is *nothing wrong* with easing away from etiquette questions. They bore you to tears. They bore me to tears."

One part of Francine agreed with Sophie. The other part said, "Grace always answered them."

"Well, we aren't Grace. Okay. I can see certain kinds of etiquette—general manners, politically correct stuff. But what to do with your dirty knife when the waitress hands it back to you to use later in the meal? Really."

"Grace would address that," Francine insisted.

"So address it."

"But I *hate* addressing it."

"I *know*. This is what we bicker about, Mom. I say that if you hate something, you shouldn't do it. You say that even if you hate something, you should do it for Grace. But you aren't Grace, and I'm not Grace, and at some point, since she pretty much washed her hands of *The Confidante*, we have to take the helm. Grace can't give you practical feedback. She doesn't remember what subjects we deal with from one week to the next. She doesn't remember *us*."

"She certainly does."

"Our faces, yes, but she's totally preoccupied with herself and her work. When was the last time she asked how you were feeling or how *your* work was going?" Her tone moved from petulant to hurt. "I should be grateful, right? I always hated it when she asked about my health, because she always knew what I was supposed to be doing, and I wasn't doing it. But she doesn't think about that anymore. It's like she doesn't care. I don't think she'll remember my birthday."

The last came fearfully, and touched Francine in a spot that sometimes took Sophie's maturity for granted. Looking at her now, so pretty and fresh and apprehensive, Francine saw how young she still was.

"Grace will remember your birthday," she said, and vowed to make sure she did.

"She won't want to go out. But we always go out. Lunch at the Pierre is as much a tradition as Thanksgiving or Christmas. We've been celebrating my birthday there since I was three."

Tradition was the scaffolding of family life, Grace always said. Francine wished she had said something about what to do when elements within the scaffolding changed.

"I really want to go," Sophie pleaded. "It would be so good for Grace."

Francine wasn't sure about that. Grace wanted privacy. She wanted the familiar. As familiar as the Pierre was after all these years, Manhattan was an ever-changing beast.

But Sophie had needs, too, and this one was strong. So Francine swore to try. "If she's uncomfortable with the idea, we can do something else. Or you and I can go ourselves."

"Can't Grace manage one day, just for me? I mean, we've

been busting our butts working for her. We constantly do
things we don't want to. Why can't she, once in a while?"

"Because her problem isn't rational," Francine said, and
felt like a traitor of the first order under Sophie's stare.

Then the vulnerable child hardened. "This doesn't have
to do with her problem. It's how she's always been. Grace
comes first. Period. And *that*," she announced with a flour-
ish, "is what we bicker about. Grace is either with us or she
isn't. You say she is—I say she isn't. You say we have to be
sympathetic—I say she's playing on our sympathies. You say
she's vital to everything we do—I say we can do fine on our
own."

It continued to amaze Francine that, after being the first
to accept Grace's illness, Sophie showed such a lack of sympathy for her plight. "I can't just cut her out, Sophie," she
argued. "I can't just pretend she isn't an authority on the
kinds of things that you and I can't begin to master. She is an
incredible resource."

"Was. She's slowing you down. You agonize over every-
thing, Mom. You used to be able to whip off columns for
Grace, just sat down and did it. Now it takes you forever,
because you're so consciously trying to write the column
Grace would write. You're second-guessing style and content.
You're revising a million times to make your columns hers.
You're wearing slacks and blouses. And *pearls*. For God's
sake, Mom. *Pearls?*"

They had been a gift from Grace many years before, the
obligatory grown-up string of pearls. Grace was always
pleased when Francine wore them, which was why she wore
them now.

"Well, maybe *they're* slowing you down," Sophie said.
"Maybe you work better in a sweat suit. You don't look like

Grace, Mom. You never will. And then—" a pregnant pause—"and then—"more slowly—"there's Robert."

Francine should have known it would come. Sophie had been grousing about Robert for weeks. Grace, on the other hand, smiled every time Francine said she was seeing him. Just seeing that smile—so rare, so fleeting, so numbered—made dating Robert worth Francine's while. "Do you have something new to say about him?" she asked Sophie now.

"You two have certainly done some interesting things."

Francine ignored the sarcasm. "We go out to dinner."

"One—restaurant—after—another," Sophie droned. "Are you wildly in love? Of course not. Robert is a bore. What have you told Tom, by the way?"

"Nothing. Tom just petered out."

"Which tells you how dynamic old Tom was. The only difference between Tom and Robert is that Grace likes Robert. Which brings us back to where we started. How much obedience do we owe Grace?"

The question was just the type Francine would have talked over with Grace, but she couldn't this time. The subject matter was too delicate, for one thing. For another, Grace was failing.

Whatever plateau she had been at during the summer had been left behind. She was more forgetful than ever and more annoyed when she forgot, more distracted than ever and more frightened when it happened. She had trouble remembering what day of the week it was, sometimes even what time of day it was. Francine would as often find her fully dressed, staring at a blank computer screen at two in the morning, as in her nightgown in bed.

There were still lucid stretches when she was the Grace

Francine knew. But those times were shadowed by the knowledge that the other would return.

When September became October and Katia Sloane started calling about the book that hadn't been written, Francine knew they had a problem. Grace disagreed. "They'll just wait," she declared, and stared at her screen.

Francine saw words there. She tried to read them, but they didn't make sense. "What part is that?" she asked innocently.

"Part? Part of what?"

"Your book. Isn't that what you're working on?"

Grace thought for a minute. "Well, I'd like that, but it isn't easy. I keep doing my research—" she touched the papers strewn all over the desk—"and then I don't know what to put down. They're not happy with me, Francine."

Francine didn't have to ask who she meant. The hallucinations were coming more often. "We've been through this before, Mom. They aren't there."

Grace couldn't quite meet her eyes. "Yes, but I do hear them. They're in my sitting room every night. My father sits, half drunk, in my wing chair. My brother and sisters are on the loveseat."

"You only had one sibling," Francine reminded her. "Your brother, Hal. He died of whooping cough when he was five."

"Well, that's *another* bone of contention. They blame me for that, too. My mother paces the floor waiting for me to come out."

Opting to try to keep Grace rooted in reality, Francine said, "Your family is gone. You're just imagining that they're here. Trust me. You can put what you want in your book. They won't know."

"They will."

"Are you thinking that they're looking down at you from heaven?"

"Not down," Grace sputtered. "They're *in my sitting room*."

"Well, then," Francine offered, trying to deal with that as best she could, "we'll just have to make sure that they don't see what it is that you're writing. We can hide it from them. How does that sound? We'll lock everything in the credenza and hide the key."

Grace hesitated. Cautiously she said, "I suppose we could."

"Show me the pages you've finished, and I'll lock them right up."

Grace gazed at Francine. Her expression went from cautious to resigned to embarrassed, none of which boded well for what she had to show. Francine hadn't seen a single page yet. Grace was vehement that no one look until she was ready to show. Each time Francine was tempted to sneak a peek, she chickened out.

Grace looked at the desk. She hesitated, then moved several papers around until a bright yellow folder appeared. She passed it to Francine without quite meeting her eyes. "I haven't done as much as I'd hoped to."

It was an understatement. The folder contained bits and snatches of elaborations on Grace's original outline. There wasn't any order to things. There wasn't a single completed chapter. There wasn't enough to fill a novella, much less cheer Katia.

Francine was stunned. Sophie had warned her, but still she had hoped.

She pushed a hand through her hair. "I'll have to call Katia. May publication is out." She thought aloud. "Maybe September. Or Christmas. That's better. They can market it as a Christmas gift rather than a Mother's Day gift. So if it comes out in December, we should have it to them by March." She shook her head in dismay. "That's pushing it, too."

"We'll have to try," Grace said. "The longer we wait, the more difficult it will be."

It took a minute for the words to sink in—the total lucidity of them, and their sadness. Francine reached for Grace's hand and held it until the knot in her throat eased. "You're the only one with the information."

Grace touched her head. "It's here. I just have trouble getting it out." Her expression grew hopeful. "You can write, sweetheart. You can write it for me."

"Me?" Francine was appalled. "Uh. Uh. *When?*"

Grace waved the question aside and pleaded, "Help me, darling. Please? It may be the last thing I'll ever ask you to do. You know how much this means to me. Will you help?"

Francine felt raw panic. The book was a full-time project, and she was already stretched to the limit. Besides, she knew nothing about writing a book. Books weren't simple three-paragraph replies to readers' mail. They had beginnings, middles, and ends. They ran several hundred pages at the least. They took strategic planning.

Grace had prepared her to take over *The Confidante*. She hadn't taught her a thing about writing a book.

Francine wanted to refuse in the very worst way. But the book meant the world to Grace, and Grace meant the world to Francine. She took the equation to its natural solution, and would have started to cry if Grace hadn't looked so unabashedly pleased.

Sophie's birthday was the first week in November and often coincided with Election Day. She had vivid memories of sitting in the backseat of the town car between her mother and her grandmother, passing campaign signs and banners en route to the city. She had actually turned eighteen on an Election Day. Grace and Francine had made a big thing of escorting her into Town Hall to vote for the very first time.

Of course, Grace had gone over the ballot with her in advance, had outlined her choices, had told her who *she* was voting for and why. In the spirit of the fight, Sophie had proceeded to vote for everyone Grace hadn't. Naturally, she told Grace what she had done the instant she left the voting booth.

Grace had looked at her, then looked at the sky, then, in all her goodness, had shaken her head and smiled. "It's your birthday, muffin. You can do whatever your little heart desires."

That was the way it had always been. An elegant luncheon at the Pierre was the centerpiece around which were arranged an assortment of little joys. In the early years there were the Rockettes, the observation platform at the Empire State Building, and buggy rides through the park, in later years Barney's, Tiffany's, and Broadway. Always, it was Sophie's choice, and Sophie never had trouble deciding.

This year she wanted seaweed body wraps, followed by lunch, followed by the purchase of a single small ruby stud for her ear.

"I don't know, sweetie," Francine said with some hesitance when Sophie ran the list past her. "Grace isn't into seaweed wraps."

"She's never had one. She doesn't know what she's missing. Remember the ones you and I had at the spa? They were awesome."

"I don't think she'll be able to stay still that long."

But Sophie held firm. "She will be *so* relaxed, she won't even *think* of moving. Besides, it's my day, my choice, remember?"

She knew that Francine wasn't pleased. She even knew that she was taking a chance, because Grace was increasingly unpredictable. But she wanted her birthday to be the fun it had always been, wanted it so badly that she was willing to take that chance.

The day started with bright sun. Sophie wore an Armani pantsuit. Gus wore the dark suit and cap that Grace deemed his uniform. Sophie teased him about it while they waited by the car. She told him that he did something naughty to the uniform, what with his brooding darkness and smoldering eyes. Elaborating on that theme, she leaned against him, whispering dirty nothings in his ear until the results of her provocation were quite visible. He swore to get even.

Francine and Grace were late, but as a pair, striking. Francine wore a pantsuit differing from Sophie's only in a subtle upgrading of elegance and sophistication. Grace's pantsuit was less subtle in both. But she was distracted. She slid into the middle of the backseat, leaving Sophie outside, waiting for the annual big birthday hug and smiley wish.

"She got off to a bad start," Francine whispered, making up for the oversight with a doubly long hug of her own. "She had her dates mixed up. She thought tomorrow was the day."

"Does she know where we're going?"

"I know where we're going," Grace barked from inside the car. "Can we leave? It's cold."

Francine climbed in beside Grace. Gus closed the door and escorted Sophie to the other side.

Grace didn't say much. She kept her eyes on the road and

her hands in her lap. They talked around her, until Sophie finally said, "Wish me happy birthday, Gram."

Grace looked at her in surprise. "Another birthday?" She let out a breath. "Can you imagine it. Where have the years gone?"

"Somewhere," Sophie said. "I'm twenty-four."

"Twenty-four." Grace squeezed Sophie's knee. "That is old." She said a sweet, "You look beautiful. Have I told you that?"

"No," Sophie answered with a smile. This was the Grammie she had known as a child. "You can say it again if you want."

Grace obliged, just as she had back then. "You look beautiful."

They laughed.

Grace took her hand. "I remember when you were born. Do you remember that day, Francine? You thought you had indigestion. We barely got you to the hospital on time. You were such a beautiful baby, muffin. I spent hours at the nursery window." Still holding Sophie's hand, she sank deeper into the seat and, smiling, returned her eyes to the windshield.

Sophie had a flash of herself in that middle seat, smiling, gazing out the windshield at a glittery birthday world. With Grace in the middle now, she had the disconcerting sense of roles reversing, and glanced at Francine. Francine was staring out the side window. From what little Sophie could see of her face, it looked tired. It always looked tired lately. She was working too hard.

"We really have to do this kind of thing more often," Sophie decided. "We should take off and go somewhere at least once a week."

Francine made a wistful sound.

"We should," Sophie insisted. "We don't *have* to work five days a week."

"Driver?" Grace called. "Driver?"

"Ma'am?" Gus called from the front.

"Why are we passing all these cars?"

"They're taking the turnoff," he said.

"I think you're going too fast. Please slow down."

Sophie knew he was trying to make up the time that had been lost when Grace had been late. If they hoped to have leisurely treatments before lunch, they had to be at the spa by eleven. She told Grace as much, when again Grace complained about Gus's driving.

"But he's making me nervous," she cried with such fervor that Francine told Gus to slow down.

Sophie bit her tongue. This was *her* day. She resented Grace controlling it. But control it Grace did, complaining about the speed a third time, then switching to, "I shouldn't have come," and repeating that every few minutes. Francine tried to mollify her. Sophie tried to mollify her. Grace wasn't being mollified.

They arrived at the spa fifteen minutes late, but if the Dorian name was worth anything, this was it. Though Sophie usually preferred anonymity, she shamelessly used the name as Grace always had.

Incredibly, Grace shushed her. "Don't do that," she whispered, hanging on Sophie's elbow. "I don't want people to know it's us."

"Why not?" Sophie asked.

"Because it's better that way." To Francine, she said, "I'm uneasy about this."

"It'll be just fine, Mother."

"Better than fine," Sophie put in. "You'll *love* it."

And she might have, if she'd given it half a chance. But she didn't like the room, didn't like the smells, didn't like the fact that she had to remove her clothes. She didn't like the technician. She didn't like the attempts at calming her that Francine and Sophie made from their adjacent tubs. She climbed early from hers and had the technician running after her to lead her back and wash her off, and then refused any of the follow-up treatments.

Sophie mightn't have minded if Grace had waited patiently for them to finish. But Grace wanted Francine with her. Then she wanted to leave. Francine offered to drive Grace around the city while Sophie finished, but as far as Sophie was concerned, the adventure was spoiled.

It got worse still. Since they were too early for lunch, they headed for Tiffany's. Its manager had been personally responsible for selling them every piece of fine jewelry that Sophie owned, including numerous prior birthday gifts. He showed them the best of the rubies. When Grace's eye caught on a simple solitaire diamond ring in a nearby case, he quickly removed it and slipped it on her finger. She oooed and ahhhhed for a while, holding her hand up as though she had never seen it bearing a diamond before—which would have been fine if she didn't already own several far more elaborate than the one on her hand, which made her gushing admiration of it seem mocking.

Sophie tried to guide her back to the earrings, but Grace just glanced at them and walked away. Francine, clearly feeling bad for Sophie, slipped an arm around her and focused on the rubies—during which time Grace walked right out of the store and down the street with the solitaire on her finger. Neither Francine nor Sophie realized this until a cadre of guards returned her to them.

Sophie was mortified. Moments later, after Francine had

taken the ring from Grace and returned it to the manager, who was trying to cover the awkwardness by insisting that she take it on loan, Sophie's embarrassment gave way to something sadder. She knew that Francine was trying, could see the struggle written all over her face, but it was the same old same old. Grace dominated everything.

They left the store without a purchase and drove around for a bit while Francine did her best to get Grace to relax. In a last-ditch attempt to salvage the day, they went on to the Pierre, and Grace was fine at first. She stayed glued to Francine's side, taking her lead from Francine when it came to greeting people she was supposed to know. She let the maître d' seat her and flashed him a brilliant smile. But things went downhill from there. She couldn't read the menu and was incensed. She got angry when Francine ordered for her, and didn't like the food when it arrived. She claimed that a man at a nearby table was staring at her. She went to the rest room and returned convinced that the waiter had given her someone else's picked-at lunch. She went to the rest room a second time, and didn't return, at which point, after an agonizing five minutes of looking at their watches and wondering if they should panic, Francine finally went after her and found that she had locked herself into a stall and didn't know how to unlock it. She was so flustered when she was finally freed that Francine quickly asked the waiter for the bill.

Sophie stewed during the long drive home. It didn't help that Grace was suddenly sweet, suddenly apologetic, suddenly solicitous. "I feel just awful, muffin. We were always able to count on the Pierre for a fine meal. I never would have suggested going there for your birthday if I'd known they'd deteriorated. But I want to buy you something special. What would you like? Something pretty? Maybe a piece of jewelry?"

Sophie would have had an easier time if Grace had been as irrational then as earlier. But the unpredictability—the swings from Grace to not Grace—infuriated Sophie. If Grace had wanted to, she reasoned, really wanted to, she would have been herself for those few short hours when it mattered. She would have done it for Sophie, if she'd really wanted to. But she hadn't—hadn't wanted to, hadn't done it—and a tradition was shattered.

Feeling angry and frustrated and sad, Sophie went straight to her end of the house. She waited for Francine to come to suggest an alternate celebration, just the two of them, but she didn't. So Sophie called her friends in New York. Within the hour, she was headed back to the city. This time she made the trip in the front seat, plastered to Gus.

Francine had had every intention of settling Grace in, then doing something with Sophie. But Grace was in rare high spirits, wanting to talk about her book.

"I was thinking about the birth of *The Confidante*," she said. "Do you remember how it started? Your father and I were talking with Peter and Joanna Daltrey one day about ways to spice up Peter's paper—he published the local one, *so* provincial, *so* boring—of course, we weren't as blunt as that in front of Peter, but it was *awful*. So we suggested he run an advice column, then he turned around and suggested *I* write it."

Francine was pulled in two directions at once. "I can't stay, Mom," she pleaded. "I have to spend time with Sophie. She's upset."

"Well, I don't know why she should be," Grace remarked. "She has a very lovely life."

"It's her birthday. She's feeling melancholy." Which was putting it mildly, but Francine didn't think Grace was up to hearing about what Sophie was really feeling. "I thought she and I might go out for a bit."

"We were out before. Now it's time to work." She smiled brightly. "Do you remember how we sat around trying to find a name for my column? Do you remember the first names we tried?"

"Please, Mom," Francine begged, wanting one last little bit of understanding from the woman who had once cornered the market.

But Grace wasn't hearing her. "You wanted it to be called 'Go Tell Grace.' Your father wanted 'Graceful Advice.'"

"Mom. Mom. Can't this hold?"

"Well, it can," Grace warned, "but I may lose the thought."

Francine wanted to scream. Put that way, with the threat of a blank future looming, she couldn't refuse. Sophie would have her forever, Grace for a far shorter time. Sophie would just have to understand.

So she jotted down Grace's thoughts as they came. It wasn't long before Grace lost interest, but by then it was teatime anyway. When Father Jim was delayed, Grace became agitated and blamed Francine. Calm came only with his arrival.

He had a present for Sophie. Francine rushed off to get her, only to find that she had gone out.

Feeling defeated as a mother, very much alone, and on the verge of tears, she left Father Jim with Grace and took Legs for a walk. Her tears stayed put, along with a keen sense of loss, until she returned. Then she sat on the floor of her den, hugged Legs close, and let them flow.

In time, they yielded to a migraine. Lying in the dark

with a cold cloth pressed to her head, she knew that something had to give.

Something did. At ten that night she was woken from a sleep two miles thick by the peal of the phone.

It was a frantic Gus. "Sophie's sick. We're at the hospital. You'd better come."

Francine was abruptly awake and terrified. "Sick how?"

"Insulin shock. We were in the city. She didn't feel good, so we started back. She passed out halfway home."

Francine's heart thundered. "Is she conscious now?"

"I don't know. They won't let me in."

Grateful that she had been too upset to undress earlier, she raced to the garage and committed any number of moving violations on her way to the hospital, but getting a ticket was the least of her worries.

Father Jim was arriving just as she did. "Gus called me," he explained as he ran in beside her. "They were at a dance club in the city. She gave herself a shot when they got there, but they never got around to eating. She had a couple of drinks. Between those and the dancing, her blood-sugar level fell way down."

"I'll die if I lose her," Francine whispered.

"You won't lose her," Father Jim said. Then, "Ah, there's Gus."

With his black hair and the total lack of color in his face, Gus looked ghostly. "She's conscious now." He led them down the hall.

Francine wasn't prepared for the sight of Sophie lying on another gurney. She had blotted out the rash of emergencies that had occurred during Sophie's volatile teenage years, because living with that fear had been no way to live, but the fear rushed back now. It hit her on top of everything she had felt earlier, on top of the tears and the headache and the sense of loss and confusion and failure.

But strength is the show that must go on, Grace always said, so Francine was strong. She took Sophie's hand.

"I'm sorry, Mom," Sophie whispered. "I blew it."

"Shhhh." She tucked Sophie's hand to her throat, then asked the doctor, "How is she?"

He was finishing another blood-sugar check. "Better now. Her fellow was smart to get her here fast."

Sophie insisted on talking, though her voice was slower than usual and the slightest bit slurred. "I kept thinking my birthday had been a bust, so what the hell, nothing I did could be any worse. Then I felt it coming. When I started shaking and sweating, I asked Gus to take me home. I should have had glucacon with me, but I was angry and left in a rush. Boy, did I mess up. I passed right out in the car. I'm sorry, Mom."

"Don't be. Not on your birthday."

"What a *disgusting* birthday."

"All's well that ends well."

Sophie's eyes went wide. "Grace isn't here, is she?"

"No, no. She's home."

Sophie closed her eyes.

Francine smoothed silky blond hair back from her daughter's face. She meant what she had told Father Jim. She would die if she lost Sophie. The question was how to prevent it. She was doing something very wrong if Sophie ended up angry, defiant, and, ultimately, in insulin shock on the day that should have been a family affair.

Sophie opened her eyes. "I keep thinking about how she took that ring, just walked right out of the store and down the street without a word to anyone. She didn't know she was doing anything wrong." Tears welled in her eyes. "I want to hate her. She created an incredible machine and got us involved, and now the gears don't mesh. I want to chuck the whole thing, only I can't. I want to hate her for letting her mind rot, like she had something to do with it." She laughed at herself. "What a joke, how she can determine everything else in her life and not this. Only the joke's on us. On you. We can't keep on like we are, Mom. What are we going to do?"

Eleven

The human spirit is irrepressible, rather like the birthday candle that, when blown out, relights itself time and again.
—GRACE DORIAN, addressing the graduates of
Smith College

Francine stayed with Sophie in the emergency room until the wee hours of the morning, then took her home, put her to bed, curled up beside her, and watched her sleep. If she dozed herself, it wasn't for long. Her peace came from the steady rise and fall of her daughter's chest.

Come morning, Sophie was feeling spent, but otherwise no worse for wear from her ordeal.

Francine was the shakier of the two. She knew that the time for kidding herself had passed. She had to face the future.

She spent the morning alternately sitting with Sophie, trying to write, trying to handle Grace, trying to think ahead. By early afternoon she abandoned writing and Grace, and focused on Sophie and the future. By mid-afternoon she was a bundle of nerves. By late afternoon her mind was in grid-lock.

Sophie was reading in bed. Francine sat with her for a time, wanting to talk about what had happened the day before, but feeling all bottled up. Sophie was the one to say an exasperated, "Go out, Mom. Please? Go to dinner or a movie. Take a run. Do *something*."

Francine didn't want to go out to dinner. She wasn't in the mood for a movie. So she went running with Legs, but the fresh air helped only until she returned to the house. Then the turmoil was back. So she deposited Legs, climbed into her car, and set off.

She didn't have any trouble finding the road to Davis's house. She had been by it dozens of times since August, had driven right on, knowing it was the smartest thing to do. But she didn't care about smart anymore. She was past that point.

It was nearly five. She doubted he was home from work. But this was the only place she wanted to be.

Her headlights picked out the newly paved drive that cut through the woods, then fell on a house nestled there. More sprawling than tall, more curved than formal, it gave the impression of something Victorian but not. She cut her headlights, left the car by the garage, and, swathed in Gortex, parked herself on his front steps.

By the time the lights of his pickup lit the drive, two hours had passed. She had shifted in stages from the steps to the porch to the door, and now sat huddled against it.

"Francine?" he called from the truck. He slammed the door and took the flagstone walk and the steps in a handful of long strides that left him squatting before her. "What's wrong?"

She had spent the better part of the two hours wondering how to explain why she hadn't come by before, why she had discouraged all but the occasional phone call and had limited those few to discussions of Grace, why the only glimpses she'd had of him had been professional.

There was nothing professional about her presence here now. She needed out of the morass of her life. Davis was her escape.

But words eluded her. She felt suddenly, starkly emotional.

He chafed her shoulders. "You're cold. Come on inside." He pulled her up and kept her close while he unlocked the door, drew her in, and flipped on a light. Then he led her through the entry to the kitchen, put her in a chair, and set about making a hot drink.

Francine didn't take her eyes from him for a minute. The mere sight of him was a diversion.

He turned to look at her from time to time. She didn't say anything, just looked right back and let his presence and the warmth of the house chip away at her chill.

At one point he said, "Sorry this is so raw. It's functional for now. Beauty will come."

Only then did she realize that though she was sitting in an oak Windsor chair at a matching oak table, most everything else, save the appliances, was Sheetrock and unfinished wood. Not that she cared. She hadn't come for a Ladies' Club Kitchen Tour—and told Davis as much with her eyes.

He set a mug of hot chocolate before her and sat facing her with his own. They drank in silence. When she finished hers, he asked, "Better?"

She nodded and swallowed. Then she released the kind of panicky moan that had been just waiting inside for a sympathetic ear.

"What is it?" Davis asked softly.

"Everything."

"Care to narrow that down a bit?"

She shook her head. She didn't want to talk about it. She didn't want to *think* about it. There was only one thing she did want to do at that moment. It was a totally selfish something that had to do with chemistry, the thud of her heart, and an ache deep inside.

He said her name in a low, roughened voice.

She studied her mug. "I kept wanting to come. After last time. I kept thinking about it. I didn't have the guts."

A silence followed, do or die, love or leave, run or stay. Then his hand came her way. She reached for it and held on while he drew her from the chair.

His bedroom was on the far side of the living room. She was aware of peripheral things—a cathedral ceiling, lots of glass, the smell of new wood—but the way he looked at her took her breath, and when he kissed her, time stopped. Ceiling, glass, wood—forgotten. Worry, heartache, fear—all gone. There was an explosiveness when they came together that obliterated the rest of the world. She had experienced it on his tailgate in August, had come for it now, and she wasn't let down. His mouth was even more exciting than she remembered it, all avid slantings and hungry bites, a heated progression of kisses sparked as much by the elemental attraction between them as by the knowledge of what they were about to do.

Francine had had it with facing facts. She didn't want to *think* of the future.

So she abandoned herself to his mouth and the escape it brought. She wove restless fingers into his hair and moved against him while his large hands molded her close. When close was too far, he shoved clothing aside only enough and tumbled her down on the bed, but when he started to penetrate her, he froze.

He muttered an oath, then a guttural, "I need a condom."

But she was frantic to have him inside. "No, do it *now*."

He drove into her with a force that took her breath, and added to the madness with each successive stroke. She didn't have to tell him what she wanted. He knew it, and did it, and when she hovered on the edge of orgasm, he held her there, held her there for such a piercing eternity that she cried aloud, more than once, in the free fall that followed.

When it ended, he drew her up to straddle his lap, wrapped her in his arms, and rocked her. "So much for long, slow, and deep," he said in a ragged breath. He rocked on. "Did we just do something dumb?"

If they had, Francine couldn't think of it. "That was," she whispered against his throat, "the best time I've had in months." Surely since Grace's accident had changed her life. "No. More. In *years*," which was how long it had been since she'd been with a man.

"I won't make you sick, Frannie."

"Me neither."

"How about pregnant?"

"I don't think so."

His lips were against her forehead, warming what few thoughts she had, while she floated in blissful irresponsibility. After a bit, she said, "Can we get naked?" It seemed the best way to stay mindless.

She felt his grin seconds before he began removing her things. If serious thoughts hovered on the sidelines, they were pushed back by the heat of his eyes on her nakedness, then farther back by the heat she felt when she removed his shirt. He had a stunning chest, all firm skin and sinew. Its breadth was accentuated by a tee of tawny hair that narrowed toward his navel before flaring beyond.

"Don't move," he whispered. He tossed their clothes off the bed and went into the bathroom. Moments later he dumped a handful of condoms on the nightstand. Then he slipped his legs around her again and touched her face. "You're very quiet."

"I'm stunned," she breathed. He was dynamic clothed. Unclothed, he was breathtaking. His posture, his walk, the natural grace of his sex. Breathtaking. There was no better word.

He kissed her with a hand cupping her cheek, then with his fingers in her hair. He opened his mouth and teased her, whispering kisses, pulling back to admire her with his eyes alone. Gently he stroked her breasts, stroked her shoulders, stroked her arms. Pausing only to protect her, he slipped inside. And she loved it. She moved against him, feeling happy and free. Something was working. She knew it with the rise of his heat and the rasp of his breath. She was good at doing this with Davis. Everything about him told her so—the way he sounded, the way he moved, the way he smelled. The thickness of him inside her was the crowning glory.

When it was over this time, they lay facing each other on the bed. She brushed sweat from his nose and left her hand on his neck. "So much for *your* promises."

"That promise expired two months ago. What took you so long?"

Since she wasn't ready to think of the havoc at home, she said, "I decided I'd wait until you moved in. I love your house."

"You haven't seen much of it."

"I did. While I was waiting for you to get here, I kept

walking around. If you see a trail where the rhododendrons will be, that was me. I made the circle five times. I looked in every window. Saw this bed first thing."

He smiled his crooked smile. "You did, huh?"

She nodded again. "And the kitchen. What else y'got?"

"Living room, dining room, den on the first floor, and space enough for a couple of bedrooms upstairs. It's not a big house."

"It's perfect. Do you really work on it every night?"

"When I can. I gave in last month and hired some guys to work days. Good thing. We'd'a been cold tonight without heat."

She was plenty warm just then, and startlingly calm. It was a far cry from how she had been such a short time before.

"Want to tell me about it?" he asked in that soft, coaxing way that made her want to cry.

She closed her eyes against his chest. Then she told him about the fiasco of Sophie's birthday.

"Why didn't you *call* me?" he asked. "I'd have been at the hospital in a minute."

"Oh, Davis, it wasn't your worry. She isn't your patient. I couldn't drag you back there for us."

"You sure as hell could have. Sure as hell should have."

She curled closer, burying her face against his throat. "Well, I wasn't thinking straight," she finally said. "I was in a panic about Sophie, and once she was stabilized, things seemed all right. Only they aren't. They're *lousy*. It's all coming apart, Davis, the nice, neat little life I've had, and I'm standing here watching, not knowing what in the hell to do."

He lay quietly, stroking her hair.

The silent caring was her undoing. She let loose. "Grace

can't work, can't write the book she's supposed to write, so she asked me to do it. That's her solution for everything. Ask Francine. I do *The Confidante*. Now she wants me to write her book. She asks me to call so-and-so about such and such because she's afraid to do it herself, then she asks over and over if I've made the call, asks me five times in thirty minutes. She wants me to pick out her clothes, which would be fine and dandy once, but she changes clothes three or four times a day. She wants me to do her makeup. She wants me to cut her hair. I can't cut her hair. I don't know the first thing about cutting hair, or giving a proper manicure. But she won't leave the house."

"Get people to come in."

"I did finally, but Grace nearly drove me mad until it was arranged. I've never been so busy before, not even when Sophie was little. Some women are cut out for eighteen-hour days. I'm not. I used to love going into the city to see friends, but I don't have the time anymore. I used to love buying a new book and spending the weekend reading it, but I don't have the time for that, either. And look at what I did to my own daughter. On her *birthday*. Grace is a seven-day-a-week job. Where does it end?"

His answer was a while in coming, and then, quiet. "You know where."

"Okay." She couldn't say the words aloud. "Part of it ends there. But what about after? I'm forty-three. I could wind up like Mother at sixty." She looked at Davis. "I think about that a lot. It's one of the little aftershocks of accepting what Grace has. So maybe I have eighteen good years left. Don't I want to make the most of them? Or, suppose I stay healthy. I could be working for thirty more years. *Thirty* more years," she echoed, then paused, thought, felt the big question crowding in. "Is this what I want to do with the rest of my life?"

She took a quick breath. "I can't come close to an answer. I swear, I don't know who I am. Who *I* am. Okay, I'm Grace's daughter and Sophie's mother. But who am *I*? Who can I be? I want to be The Confidante—but I don't, because The Confidante is Grace, and I run a poor second. But if I don't write the column, *The Confidante* goes down the drain. I can't let that happen, because *The Confidante* is part of everything I've always been. But everything I've always been isn't everything I've always wanted."

"What is?"

"Privacy. Quiet. Family. Family—that's what I'm losing here, Davis. First Grace. Now Sophie."

"Why Sophie?"

"Because I'm neglecting her to take care of Grace. I'm messing up *everything*."

"You're too hard on yourself, Frannie. Grace is sick. Anyone with half a heart would give her extra attention. Sophie knows that."

"But where do I draw the line? Where does extra attention end and absurdity begin? When do I cave in and hire extra help? Once that happens, once there are new people running around the house, once word gets out about Grace's illness, nothing will ever be the same. We've been so close, the three of us, so tight. We've kept so many things in our neat little circle. Now the decisions I have to make will break that circle apart. I don't want to do it, but how can I not? And *what am I* once the circle is broken?"

He listened patiently, his responses more often in the form of light touches than words. He didn't have the answers any more than she did, but he seemed to recognize her need to vent all that was festering inside.

In time, the catharsis quieted her. She thought to return

home to Sophie, then vetoed the thought. She wanted to be with Davis a little longer, just a little longer.

They moved to the shower, then to the kitchen and shared the pizza that Davis took from the freezer and baked. Francine felt startlingly content. Her hair was damp and waving loosely above her shoulders, her face was naked, her body clothed in Davis's shirt. She was relaxed—absurd given the circumstances that had brought her here, but in voicing her fears, she had unloaded a weight. Nothing had changed at home, still, she felt lighter of heart. If anyone had criticized her for what she was doing just then, she would have put her middle finger to good use.

She deserved this break, had earned it with sweat and tears, and she refused to dilute it with guilt. The pleasure was too high—a devastatingly appealing Davis, with his hair wet, his chest bare, and his sweatpants frankly advertising his sex as he moved with primal fluidity. As gentle as he was when they talked, his body was rousingly male. He made Francine feel daring.

Grace would never understand. She would never be off sleeping with a man while her closest of kin was ill. She would never run from her problems or, worse, pour her woes on an outsider. She was strong and self-contained. She was *good*.

At least, she had always been good before.

"Want to hear something sad?" Francine asked Davis. "Mother has developed a thing for Father Jim."

Davis swallowed hard on a mouthful of pizza. "Grace? A thing?"

"It's sweet, actually. He's over almost every night. She flirts with him, touches his arm, gazes at him with large, adoring eyes. He's an angel about it. Holds her hand. Draws his chair close to hers. It's especially bizarre on those nights when he's wearing his collar. Do you think he's dying inside?"

Davis pondered that. "No. I think he loves Grace."

"After the Father, the Son, and the Holy Ghost."

"Right. He won't do anything untoward."

"It's not him I'm worried about," Francine remarked. Alzheimer's patients often had surges of sexuality that created problems. Davis had told her that himself.

"Well, if she does try anything," he said now, "Jim will be able to handle it."

Francine had a thought. Since it verged on the blasphemous, she whispered, "Do you think he's ever done it?"

"Done what?" Davis whispered back, lips twitching.

She flicked a finger against his arm.

"I don't know," he whispered.

"What do you *think*?"

"I think it's none of our business."

Francine spoke in full voice. "*I* think that if what your dad said about him is true, he has. I think he was a ladies' man before he became a priest."

"He would have entered the seminary when he was eighteen. That wouldn't have given him much time."

She looked him in the eye. "How old were you when you lost your virginity?" She could have sworn he blushed. "How old?"

"Fourteen," he said.

Intrigued, she hushed her voice again. "How?"

His eyes held hers. "The normal way."

"You know what I mean. Tell me. I want to know."

He sat back in his chair. His cheeks retained that faint burned tint, stunning against the amber of his hair. "She was the sister of a friend. She was twenty."

Francine gasped. "An older woman. Surely she wasn't a virgin."

"Surely not."

"I'll bet she'd had her eye on you for a while." Francine could see it. She imagined him as virile as all get out at fourteen, a randy teenager with hormones as wild as his spirit. "If Father Jim was like you, he'd have had four years. Hearts have been broken in less time than that. I wonder why he became a priest."

"His family was fanatically religious," Davis said. "He was the oldest son. He grew up being told that he would take his vows, but he fought it for all he was worth. Then a close friend died of alcohol poisoning. Jim blamed himself. He was seventeen. It was the turning point of his life."

It struck Francine only then how little she knew about Jim O'Neill. "Did he tell you this?"

Davis nodded. "When I was having so much trouble of my own. The message was that different choices could be made and different roads taken. I kept arguing that it was too late. He said that was the coward's way out. He said that if I was really tough, I'd learn from my mistakes and let them make me a better person. The implication was that he'd done that. Or tried to. He looked stricken when he was talking, like he still blames himself for his friend's death."

"Grace often hears from people who are haunted by the past. It seems pretty common. Maybe she's haunted herself. Something has to explain the hallucinations she has."

"AD explains it."

"Do hallucinations relate to real things?"

"Real fears. Not necessarily factual occurrences."

"So she may be imagining that her family will yell at her because she was always afraid that they would." She shuddered. "Or maybe they did. In either case, how did she turn out so normal? How did she turn out so *good*?" The question reawakened her insecurities. "I can't be another Grace. I just don't have it in me. I can follow in her footsteps, but only to a point. So is the effort worth it? If I can't do it the way she did, am I better not trying at all? Will I ruin what's left? Should I quit while I'm ahead?"

"You love *The Confidante*."

"But I'm not Grace."

"So make *The Confidante* you. Decide what you like and don't like. Keep the first, change the last."

"I don't like the pressure of writing five Grace-perfect columns a week."

"So cut down to three. Or do five Francine-perfect ones."

She smiled at the phrase. Not that she was sure she could do any Francine-perfect ones. "The hard part is changing what worked so well for so long. How do I do that without the whole world guessing that something's up with Grace?"

"Maybe it's time."

"Grace won't have it."

"At some point," Davis said with care, "you may have to override her to do what's best for you."

"But that'll be so final. Once word is out, it can't be taken back. Once changes are made, the past is done."

"Life is like that."

Something about the intensity of his eyes tipped her off to the direction of his thoughts. She rose, went to the window, ran her fingers over the unfinished wood frame. "We can't go back to how we were, can we?"

"Do we want to?"

"It's safer."

"But a hell of a lot less fun."

She watched his reflection rise and approach. It was every bit as smooth as the man in the flesh.

He folded his arms under her breasts and told the Francine in the glass, "You turn me on. Have from the first. Didn't you feel it?"

"No. You were the bogeyman bringing bad news. I hated you."

"So when did you feel it?"

Maybe subconsciously she had felt it that first time. She remembered her heart pounding. It always did when he was close. But consciously? "The night you drove up when I was running with Legs. You looked like a trucker."

"Truckers turn you on?"

"Not truckers. Rebels. There you were, looking more than a little irreverent sitting up there with your muscles bulging out of your shirt."

"My muscles don't bulge."

Something else was. She felt it against her backside. Nestling against him, she slipped her arms behind, under the band of his sweats and down his bare flanks.

"I'm all wrong for you," she breathed. Her hands moved over the shower-soft hair on his thighs.

He stroked her breasts through the shirt. "Doesn't feel it right now."

No. It didn't. She loved strong thighs. She loved lean hips. She loved the soft spot her fingers found at his groin, and the way his breathing quickened when she touched him there. Still. "You need a woman who has nothing to do with her life but pamper you."

"I've never been pampered," he said roughly. "I'd hate it." He pulled up her shirt.

Her eyes were glued to the glass, to the reflection of her

nakedness, to the shape her breasts took under his touch.
His hands were very male against her skin. Above the buzz
inside her, she said, "You need a woman who can give you a
slew of babies to fill up this house."

"One or two would be plenty. I'm not greedy."

She found his penis. It was gloriously large. "You would
make very—beautiful—babies." If only she were younger. If
only she were freer. She wasn't either, still, she wanted him.

Fast as a wink, in a moment's naughtiness, she whispered,
"Gotta go," and slipped out of his arms.

He caught her before she reached the hall and pinned her
to the doorjamb. "Not so fast," he growled, pressing against
her until her legs had nowhere to go but open. His eyes glit-
tered. He was a devastating mix of broad shoulders, hard
tapering body, and aroused male flesh, with a touch of danger thrown in.

The danger sparked excitement, which was what she
wanted, what wiped all else from her mind.

"Gotta go," she repeated, but her arms were around his
neck. She held on when he boosted her higher. Her legs
found his waist.

He moved his sweats only enough to free himself, and,
while those dark, dangerous, glittering eyes held hers, he
entered her. Then he held perfectly still.

"You don't tease me and walk off, Francine."

"So I see," she whispered.

"I'm not sure you do."

"I do," she insisted. "Ahhh!" He had withdrawn and thrust
back in. She was on fire.

"Still want to leave?"

"God, no," she cried, laughing against his mouth. "Do
that again, Davis."

He did, then ground out, "You're incredible. No pretense at all."

"You just—feel—so—good."

He thrust again, harder, then harder yet, and kept it up until she came totally apart. When he finally let himself go, she came again.

It was an eon before she stopped gasping, before he stopped panting, before he slowly lowered her to the ground, and then she felt a sharp little pain. She put a hand to the spot.

Davis replaced it with his own.

"Ouch! There!"

He turned her around, swore, then laughed. Taking her hand, he led her to the bedroom, put her facedown on the bed, and efficiently removed a splinter.

"It was probably the only one there," Francine said, lying on her back once again. "Trust me to find it."

He was on an elbow over her. "There are others. This place needs work."

"Can I help?" she asked on impulse. She had no free time at all. Still, the thought held appeal. It was something Grace wouldn't do in a million years.

"Any time you want. Sand or screw—take your pick."

"You have a dirty mouth."

"Which you love. Confess."

"I do."

"And anyway, either one is therapeutic. When you need an escape, be my guest."

She sobered and sighed. "I may take you up on that. I sense hard times ahead."

"You'll do fine."

"There you go again. The Eternal Optimist."

"You're a strong woman."

She sputtered out a doubtful laugh. "I've leaned on my mother all my life."

"You don't give yourself enough credit. Deep down inside, you're your own person."

"Sexually maybe, here and now, but at home? All these years I've been indistinguishable from my family. We're talking a major identity crisis."

He gave a confident little headshake. "Everyone goes through identity crises. You have a leg up because you have solid grounding. Your family gave you that. It means that wherever you're headed, you come from a position of strength. You're predisposed to succeed."

"Me? I have a history of botching things up."

He grinned crookedly. "Not botching things up. Just making things a little harder than they have to be. But you get where you're going. You'll do good, Frannie. Trust me. I may have spent a lifetime being drawn to the wrong women, but every damn one of them has succeeded. Remember that, if you're feeling down. I don't fuck losers."

Twelve

The weight of a relationship, like the baton in a relay race, is carried at a given moment by the runner with the greatest strength.

—GRACE DORIAN, from *The Confidante*

Sophie was swathed in a voluminous sweat suit and an afghan, watching *St. Elmo's Fire* for the umpteenth time, when Father Jim peered around the door of her den.

"Got a minute?"

She paused the VCR. A minute for Father Jim? Always. He perked her up.

Boy, could she use it now.

He drew a box from behind him. "I brought you something. Actually brought it yesterday, only you weren't here, and I wanted to deliver it in person."

In the madness of her birthday, she had forgotten about Father Jim's gift. Now she felt a swell of warmth. "You are something else. You never miss one."

"Of course not. You're my favorite girl."

So it seemed. As a child, Sophie had accepted each present with innocent glee. In later years, she had alternately felt special that she was so chosen, guilt-ridden by the money he spent, and touched by the thought that went into each gift. Each one was appropriate for the time and place in her life, each was personally given.

As a child, she had torn into each with abandon. Now, she removed the ribbon with care to keep it intact, then eased off the wrapping, and gently removed a box. It gave nothing away. She slipped off the top. Inside, buried in a nest of tissue, was the sweetest teddy bear she had ever seen. It had light brown, close-cropped curly fur, long limbs, chocolate eyes, and a plaid neck ribbon. Rather than being round, fuzzy, and perfect as modern bears were, it was old-fashioned, wise, and one of a kind.

She hugged it with one arm and opened the other to Jim. "I love it. Thank you."

"You may be twenty-four," he said, settling beside her on the sofa, "but that doesn't mean there aren't times when hugging a bear feels better than anything else."

"Sure feels good now."

"Actually, I bought it a month ago."

"That was intuitive. The Man Upstairs must have tipped you off."

"How are you feeling?"

"Physically fine," she said, but her tone held discouragement.

"Want to talk about what happened?"

"Last night?" She sighed. "I was angry. I wanted to have fun. So I said, screw diabetes, this is my birthday, I'm going to do what I want." She hugged the bear tighter. "Backfired, huh?"

"What was Gus saying through all this?"

"Not much. I was pretty insistent."

"Did he express any qualms?"

"No." Lest he blame Gus for what had happened, she said, "We weren't doing anything out of the ordinary. It was just me, messing up with food and drink."

Father Jim didn't look convinced. "He had some responsibility, too. He should have seen you had food. I'm not pleased with him."

"Is he being fired?"

"No. But he's being closely watched. I had hoped that getting him out of Tyne Valley and bringing him here would set him on the right course. I don't think it has."

Sophie couldn't say anything to put him at ease. When he wasn't with her, Gus spent most of his free time with the lost souls at the local bar. He had introduced her to them several times, which was several times too many. Drawing Gus into her own circle was risqué enough to be exciting, but the reverse wasn't true.

"What about the drinking?" Father Jim asked.

Sophie shrugged. "He does it sometimes."

"Do you ever have to be the one to drive home?"

She hesitated, then confessed, "Sometimes."

Father Jim frowned at his hands. It was a minute before he said, "I worry about you with him, not just about times like the other night. When I suggested that Grace hire him, I didn't anticipate that he'd go after you."

"He didn't," Sophie said honestly. "I went after him."

"Why? What's the appeal?"

She arched an amused brow.

"This isn't funny, Sophie," he insisted, sounding hurt and so genuinely worried that the reproach lost its sting. "I want more in life for you than Gus. He can't give you what you need."

"And what's that?" she asked in a higher voice that told of her deepest angst. "I can't seem to figure it out for myself."

Father Jim's focus immediately shifted, just as Sophie had known it would, had hoped it would. She needed to talk.

"You're feeling lost?" he asked.

"Confused. I mean, I'm here. I have a gorgeous home and a cool job. But I'm antsy."

He smiled. "That's what the bear's for, to remind you that you're young. Being antsy is okay. You've been confined lately."

"The problem," Sophie said, focusing her thoughts, "is that the confinement will only get worse. With Grace sick, I can't leave."

"Do you want to?"

"One part of me does."

"To do what?"

"I don't know. Something different. Something new. If I keep on the way I am now, my future will be more of the same. It's pretty sick, to be settled into life at the age of twenty-four."

"It doesn't have to be that way."

"It does, for now." She snorted. "I used to think it was important for me to be here to protect my mother from Grace. Suddenly it's important for me to be here because Grace isn't. Mom can't do everything alone. All of Grace's stuff has been dumped on her back. I can't just walk off and leave her with my stuff, too. Besides, *The Confidante* has always been a family thing. It's hard to break the tradition. Mom needs that tradition. Maybe I do, too. One thing's for sure, I can't just turn my back on it. So, do I stay or go? I'm damned if I do and damned if I don't."

Father Jim shook his head. "You are not damned, Sophie. Quite the contrary. You're blessed."

"With what?" Sophie asked, needing a boost.

"You're blessed with intelligence and looks and good breeding. You're blessed with good health—even if you don't think so sometimes, but by comparison to many others, you are. You're blessed with a family that loves you, and with financial security, and with the ultimate freedom to do what you want. You're also blessed with a sense of respect for the accomplishments of your grandmother, and that drives you crazy, I know. You rebel against it whenever you can. But if you didn't respect *The Confidante*, you wouldn't stay here one minute. And then there's compassion. You're blessed with that, too. You feel for your mother, and you feel for Grace. All of that is what's keeping you here. You're a very special young woman, Sophie."

"So what do I *do*?" she cried. It was fine to be all the things Father Jim said, but that didn't ease the restlessness she felt.

He took her hand. "You hang in there. You give your mother and grandmother the support they need, because this is a rough time for them, but you keep reminding yourself that things will get better."

"Not for Grace."

"Yes, for Grace. Right now she knows what's happening to her. In time she won't. Our job is to make her as comfortable as we can for as long as her awareness remains. Give it time, Sophie. Little by little things will come clear. Your family is experiencing a trauma. Think of the person who loses a limb. There's the initial shock and pain, then the healing, and that involves adaptation, reeducation, and change. Your life won't always be like this. There will be shifts as new insights come, but you will have input, more and more, because your mother needs you for that. So you'll be able to direct the changes and help shape them. Look at it as a challenge. You, Sophie Dorian, are in a prime position to personally mold *The Confidante*. Quite honestly, I'm impressed."

Put like that, Sophie was, too.

A tiny squeeze of her shoulder brought Grace awake. She was disoriented until she saw Jim's face. Then she smiled.

"Time for bed," he said.

She assumed it was, though she didn't remember anything of the earlier evening. She was getting used to that, and to taking things on faith. If Jim said it was time for bed, it was.

She brought his hand to her cheek. "This is nice."

"Dozing on the sofa?"

"Waking up to you."

He kissed her hand with a sweetness that brought tears.

"Oh, Jim."

"Yes, m'dear?"

"Fate hasn't treated us kindly."

He studied her hand, stroked her fingers with his thumb. "No life is perfect. We've succeeded in so much else."

"But do you ever think . . . ever wish . . ."

He touched her lips. "Shhhh."

"Do you?" she whispered.

He nodded.

"I dream about it," she said. "I dream about us together. Will we be one day?"

"Yes, we will."

"And you'll love me then?"

"Very much."

"Even after . . . after . . ."

"Shhhh."

"This is my punishment, all these years later."

"No. It's simply God's will."

"But if not for punishment, why?"

"To give the rest of us a chance to show you our love."

She clutched his hand close. "I'm frightened."

"I'm here."

"What if I repulse you?"

"You could never do that."

"Not knowingly." She closed her eyes on her tears, and repeated more softly, ". . . knowingly." She slowly opened her eyes. "If you were anything else, I'd end it before the worst."

"But I'm not, and you won't," he commanded. "You won't do that to me, or to Francine or Sophie."

"Such a burden."

He stroked her hair. "We love you. Love is about taking care of people. You've done it to us all these years. Now it's our turn."

At that moment, Grace detested the concept of love. She found it painfully binding. She found it merciless. Love made her illness all the harder to accept. It made the leaving devastating.

Francine was home by eleven. She was physically spent—limbs weak, muscles aching—but feeling sinfully buoyant, stronger than she had in days. Slipping into a neck-to-ankle nightgown that hid all the rosy spots left by Davis's stubble, she went to Sophie's room.

Though the light was on, the night owl was asleep.

As Francine watched her from the door, the horror of the night before flashed back. They had already talked some about what had happened, but some wasn't enough. Sophie blamed her carelessness on anger. That anger had to be addressed. Likewise, Francine's selfishness. She wanted Sophie with her, but Sophie more likely needed to be with her friends in the city.

Sophie stirred, opened her eyes, stretched. "Hi," she whispered. "When did you get home?"

"A little while ago." She went to the bed and sank down. Her eye fell on a fuzzy something at the edge of the comforter. When she gave it a tug, an ear emerged. "What's this?"

Sophie pulled out an adorable teddy bear. "My gift from Father Jim. It's a reminder that we're never as grown-up as we think."

"That is the sweetest thing." Dryly, Francine said, "Bless him, he's always on target. How do you feel?"

"Fine. My levels have been steady all day."

"Emotionally. Are you miserable and not wanting to tell me?"

"I'd tell you," Sophie said. "Really. I'm not miserable. By the way, Father Jim said I was right making you go out." Her eyes searched Francine's face. "You look better. What did you do?"

Francine fought a blush. "Oh, drove around. Stopped here and there." One part of her, the part that had had the most *incredible* evening and felt giddy each time she remembered, wanted to tell her best friend, Sophie, every last, lewd detail. The other part, the more sensible part, couldn't do it. Francine had no idea where her relationship with Davis was going, *if* it was going. One-night stands weren't good examples to set for daughters.

"I just freed up my mind," Francine said without lying. "Put a little distance between me and everything that's been crowding in. I've been too close to it. Unable to put things in perspective."

"Can you now?"

Francine nodded. Though the details of the future were sketchy, she felt a new hope. "We're making changes. Repeats of last night won't do. There is more to life than the past. We don't have to be chained to this house."

Sophie looked hesitant. "What about Grace?"

Francine knew just what she was thinking. The nightmare of yesterday's outing with Grace was a preview of what was to come. But if they limited themselves to her shrinking world, they would go mad.

So, resigned but determined, she said, "There may be times when we need a break from Grace. I can't be a full-time caretaker, not with all else she's piled on my plate. I haven't been able to do anything well," which was, in Francine's book, a greater insult to Grace than taking time off. "We're hiring help."

Sophie's eyes went wide. "We are?"

"For starters, we need someone to be with Grace when we're not."

"Will she let you hire someone like that?"

"If we call her an executive assistant, she will. We're also hiring someone to help with *The Confidante*. Whoever it is may even be able to help Grace with her book."

"How do we find the right person?"

Francine conjured up the image of Robin Duffy. She was a writer. She knew *The Confidante*, knew Grace. But Robin was trouble, so she said, "Amanda will help us find someone. She has contacts in the publishing world. Besides, I think it's time she knows the truth."

Sophie's eyes went even wider. "Grace told us not to."

Francine gave her a poke. "Hey. Where's the rebel?"

"Being upstaged. I've never seen you disobey her before."

"I'm not disobeying her. Well, not maliciously. If I were

as good as she is—was—and could handle everything on my own, keeping secrets would be fine. But the calls are coming fast and furious, and I just can't deal with them on top of everything else. If we don't do something, the whole world will know. Amanda will be our buffer. If there's any hope of keeping Grace's condition secret a little longer, she's it."

Sophie looked amazed. "When you make decisions, you really do it. All this from driving around one night?"

Francine was nearly as amazed. Something had happened at Davis's house. Then again, maybe it had happened at the hospital the night before. She had reached the point where practical considerations superceded both her fear of Grace and her fear of failure.

Not that she had the details worked out. She was doing that as she spoke. Call it impulsive, but hell, she *was* impulsive, not at all like Grace, whose every move was thought-out and well planned. But Grace wasn't the one trying to single-handedly manage as large an enterprise as her career had become.

With that realization—stunning, as realizations went—came a sense of triumph and a grin. "Other than the very early days, when The Confidante was tiny, Grace *never* single-handedly managed her career. She's had help, first me, then you. So if she's out of it, we need a third. Right?"

"Right."

"I'll call Amanda in the morning and meet with her ASAP."

"What do we tell Grace?"

Francine gave it a moment's thought. Feeling a boldness that may or may not have had to do with the evening she'd spent with a guy from Tyne Valley, she said, "Only as much as won't upset her. If the goal is to keep The Confidante up and running, the end justifies the means." Not to mention the fact that if Francine was into sinning—selfishness, impulsiveness, *sleeping with the enemy*, for God's sake—one more little sin wouldn't hurt.

Francine had taken to looking in on Grace at night. She often needed a reminder that it was time to sleep. She also often needed the reassurance that the sitting room was empty.

Francine didn't even make it as far as the sitting room this night. Grace was pacing the floor in the hall beyond it. At first glance, she looked elegant in her white dressing gown, with her skin properly moisturized and her hair neatly brushed. At second glance, her distress spoiled the image.

When she spotted Francine, she stopped her pacing, pressed her lips together, and clutched her hands to her middle.

Francine guessed the problem. "They're in there again?"

Grace nodded but didn't speak. Francine knew that her fear was caused as much by her family's presence as by her awareness that she was hallucinating it.

"Have you been to bed at all?" Francine asked.

"No. Jim was here late. I took a long soak and went to the kitchen for breakfast. They were here when I got back. I went to the office and tried to work, but I had no idea what to write."

"No wonder. It's very late."

"I just don't know what to tell and what not to."

Patiently, because the discussion wasn't a new one, Francine said, "Tell your life story. That's what an autobiography is. Write what you're comfortable writing."

"I'm not comfortable writing any of it."

"Are you saying you don't want to do the book at all?" That *was* new, and would certainly solve one of Francine's problems. She was nowhere near as bound to the project as Grace was.

"I *do* want to do it. But I can't very well tell the world about my childhood." She cocked her head and held up a hand. "Do you hear them?"

Francine glanced toward the sitting room. "Are they talking?"

"*So loud.*"

"What are they saying?"

Grace whispered a disconcerted, "That I'm always causing trouble. But that's not true. We were unruly sometimes. But not always."

Francine couldn't imagine Grace ever being unruly.

Grace was listening, frowning. "Well, if we drank, it was only because the whole town was doing it. Good God, there was nothing else to do. And I was *not* the instigator. *I* was never arrested. Wolf was, and Scutch. Johnny and I, never."

Drank? Arrested? Francine was mystified. "Mother, what are you talking about?"

"Not me. *They're* the ones doing the talking. I'd never talk about what happened. We made a pact. We swore we'd never tell."

"Who swore?"

"All right, I was irresponsible. But they were worse. They sent us out of the house hungry. They sent us out without proper clothes. They didn't bother to send us to school— couldn't have cared less until the truant officer came, and then they said *we* refused to go, which wasn't true. So who are they to tell me I drank too much? Who are they to call me a slut? I made good, didn't I?"

"Mother," Francine said softly, grasping her arm in an attempt to draw her back to reality. "You're not making sense."

"That's what they'll say if I write these things. So I can't. I can't write this book."

Francine grappled with the choices. Either Grace was dreaming up nonexistent childhood horrors, or she had been lying for years.

But Grace didn't lie.

"I think," she proposed gently, ingeniously, she thought, "that you're taking things from the letters you've received all these years and confusing them with your own life. You were introspective and shy. You weren't a troublemaker. You didn't drink, and you certainly weren't a slut."

Grace folded her arms on her chest. "Tell *them* that."

"Okay." Francine opened the sitting-room door and announced, "Grace doesn't cause trouble, or drink, or sleep around. So you're all wrong. And if you don't believe me," she tacked on, "ask the hundreds of thousands of people all over the world who hang on her every word." She looked back at Grace and whispered, "Okay?"

Grace nodded. Then her expression grew sheepish. "You think I'm foolish."

"No," Francine said sadly. "I know you hear them. But they're gone now. You must be tired." Slipping an arm around Grace's waist, she guided her toward the bedroom. She was aware of the nervous way Grace looked around the sitting room, but she kept her on course. "Can I get you anything?"

"No. I'm fine." Grace draped her dressing gown on the chair beside the bed and, wearing a silk nightgown that made her look fragile, slipped into bed. She lay back on the pillows and frowned up at Francine. "Where were you before?"

Francine took her hand. "I went out. I needed air."

"I work you too hard." Her eyes held a touch of humor, but it vanished in a blink. "I worry." Her deeper meaning was clear.

"Don't, Mother. We'll do fine."

"I worry. This shouldn't be."

Francine shook her head in agreement.

Grace took a breath, started to speak, stopped.

"What?" Francine coaxed, just as Grace had so many times over the years when she wanted Francine to talk.

Grace looked lost in thought for another long minute. Then, in the softest, most apologetic voice, she said, "There's still the problem, you know. If I can't write the truth, what can I write?"

Francine had no qualms about the central body of the book. There were anecdotes aplenty on *The Confidante*. No, her worry had always been that Grace's childhood had been too boring to make for exciting reading. It struck her that Grace might share that worry, hence be creating embellishments.

In the next breath it struck her that there might be more to Grace's childhood than she had ever let on.

She ruled out the possibility. But it came rushing right back. Wolf. Scutch. Johnny. The thought of a story untold both shocked and intrigued. If any small part of Grace's hallucinations were reality-based—if she hadn't been the quiet little mouse but a wild child, if she had a larger family, if some of that family still lived—the ramifications would be stunning.

Thirteen

When the wind picks up, I close the door to keep my child from the chill. When someone threatens her, I spread my strength around her like a woolen cloak.
—GRACE DORIAN, from *The Confidante*

Francine and Sophie met Amanda the next afternoon at a tony little restaurant in lower Manhattan. The urgency was Francine's. She didn't want to lose her resolve.

Amanda was understandably shaken by the news of Grace's illness, though not entirely surprised. She had known something was up, what with the recent scuttlebutt in New York, and though the official word from the Dorians had been that things were fine, she had worked with Grace long enough—and found the woman's prolonged silence odd enough—to suspect otherwise.

The good news was that she was comfortable with Francine writing *The Confidante*.

The bad news was that Katia Sloane was wondering if Grace's book would ever be done.

Francine wondered it herself. She couldn't write the book. She didn't know where to begin—and that, with regard to style. Content was even more iffy in the light of Grace's hallucinations.

Francine wanted to categorically deny them, but the disconcerting fact was that she knew little more about Grace's pre-Dorian years than the rest of the world did. As Grace had always told it, she had been a quiet child from a quiet family in a quiet town flooded into oblivion. There were neither living relatives nor little family anecdotes, though Lord knew Francine had begged for both over the years. For all intents and purposes, Grace's life had begun when she had met John.

If her hallucinations were to be believed, that might not be entirely true. Francine felt a dire need to learn about those early years before Grace lost them for good.

"Have you asked Jim about it?" Davis asked. He was on his back, on the quilt that they had thrown down in front of the fire when the idea of making love on bare flagstone had paled.

Francine was draped over his side, feeling safe enough, replete enough, to share the dilemma. "Dozens of times. He's no help."

"Is it that he doesn't know?"

"I guess." She palmed his ribs. His skin was damp, warmed by the fire, musky from sex. "Not that he says, 'I don't know.'"

"What does he say?"

"Either that Grace doesn't like talking about it, that I should ask her myself, or that it doesn't really matter. I'm not sure he'd tell me even if he knew. He'd consider it privileged information." She shifted to slide her ear to his heart and hummed out a satisfied sigh. "This is my favorite thing in the world." For all the years that she'd fantasized about being with someone as unabashedly male as Davis, not one of her fantasies had included a heartbeat. "Maybe it's guilt, that heartbeat," she remarked. "Did Father Jim tell *you* something?"

"No, ma'am."

"Did Grace, when you were taking her history?"

"It was her medical history I was taking. I asked if there had been any instances of senile dementia in her family. She denied it."

For all the times Francine had wished to know her mother's family, what she wanted now wasn't so much a source as a resource. "If only there were someone I could ask, but they're dead, and I wouldn't know where to *start* looking for people she knew growing up. They scattered when the town died."

It had always seemed a crime to her, flooding land that held people's pasts. She would have liked to see where Grace was born, where she grew up, all the little haunts she had called her own in seventeen years there.

She gazed across Davis's chest toward the fire. "She could direct us, but she won't. I tried again earlier. Maybe she didn't understand the question. Maybe her mind chose that moment to detour. Only, looking back, there's a consistency to it. She doesn't want to talk about those years. I wonder why?"

The question was only one of many that haunted Francine. Others had to do with letting the cat out of the bag. Now that Amanda knew the truth, it was official. The torch had been passed. The Confidante had shifted a generation. Francine's skills were about to be put to a very formal, very crucial test.

It was the state competition revisited. Her bow was

rosined, her fingers limber, her stomach knotted. Now to play.

She took a deep breath to loosen the knot. It helped when she moved her hand over Davis's skin, across his waist to the scar at his belly, then on. She tipped up her face. "I don't want to think about this. Distract me."

His eyes were dark and naughty. "How could I possibly do that?"

He caught an audible breath when she ran the heel of her hand over his erection, and when she began to knead the heaviness beneath it, he was quickly inspired.

Francine loved that about Davis. He was quick to rise, quick to match her need, quick to take control and push her higher when she thought she might die of satiation. As distractions went, he was the best.

The fire was fading to embers before he finally separated himself from her and tossed another several logs on the grate. When he returned to the blanket, he folded his legs and drew her sideways into his lap.

She settled in with a long-shuddering breath. "It's shameless, how I use you."

"It's a two-way street."

"Bad day?"

"Yeah."

"What?"

It was a minute before he said, "I lost a patient."

"Of what?"

"He had Parkinson's. But that wasn't what killed him."

"What was?"

"An overdose of pills. Pills I prescribed to help him sleep. He saved them up."

She searched his troubled face. "Oh, Davis. I'm sorry."

"So'm I."

"You can't blame yourself."

"Easy to say."

"Did he give any hints?"

"None. His family is as stunned as I am."

Francine tried to imagine what it would be like to deal with life and death issues every day. She wasn't sure she could. Compared to what Davis did, writing an advice column was tame stuff. "It must be hard, keeping an emotional distance."

"Mmm."

She stroked his throat, ran the vee of her hand over his Adam's apple, lightly, again and again.

In time he released a breath. "But death is only one part of what I do. There's healing, too. That's cool."

"I'll bet you get more involved with patients than some doctors do." He was reckless that way, caring.

"I sure got involved with you," he said with a recklessly caring, crooked smile.

"I'm not a patient. But, boy, am I needy." Knowing that she had to be getting back home, she asked in a softer, more urgent voice, "So what do I do about Grace?"

"You let me work on Jim. He may let his guard down with me. I'm just a thug from the old hometown."

Francine made a dry sound. "Just a thug. Uh-huh. But I'd be aiding and abetting if I let you try to weasel secrets from him. We'd both be risking eternal damnation."

"Which neither of us believes in."

"He's a *priest*, Davis. Besides, I love him. I can't use him. My conscience won't let me. Grace remembers her childhood. She just chooses not to talk about it."

"Then keep trying. Reason with her. Ask specific questions. You may catch her at a weak moment."

"What if she blows up?"

"Has she done that lately?"

"Not since you medicated her. She's calmer. Still can't remember what day of the week it is. But she is calmer when she forgets."

"Well. That's something."

Francine supposed that it was.

Sophie was having a manicure when Robin Duffy walked into the nail shop and did a double take. "Great minds think alike. I heard Lucy's manicure was the best for miles. I'm your two-thirty," she told Lucy. "I'm a little early. I'll just sit here and relax until it's time." She hung her coat on the rack, settled on the sofa by the manicurist's station, and smiled at Sophie. "Do you come here often?"

Sophie had been in a fine mood until Robin had come in, but no more. She didn't like phonies. Robin wasn't there co-incidentally. She wanted information.

Looking her in the eye, she said, "I come here every week. I assumed you knew that."

Robin smiled. "No." She picked up *People*, flipped through several pages, then set it down and feigned genuine concern. "How's Grace? I haven't seen her around. I heard she was sick."

"Actually," the devil in Sophie said, "she's visiting friends in Antibes. That's off-the-record, of course." It would serve Robin right to go after a red herring.

"Is Francine with her?"

"No. Francine's home working."

"Poor Francine. I'd love to be in Antibes." She thumbed through the magazine again. Sophie was putting bets on which question would come next when Robin said, "How long will Grace be gone?"

"Not long. She has work to do."

Robin nodded. She made a show of reading until Sophie's nails were done and they switched places.

Sophie would have left the shop right then if she'd had anywhere to go. But it was a raw, drizzly day, not ideal for a stroll, and Gus wouldn't be back for another fifteen minutes. So she picked up the magazine that Robin had discarded and began flipping through it.

Robin said, "I've been trying to get a fix on the little town where Grace was born. For an article on women who've made it big from small-town roots. Do you know its name?"

Sophie wouldn't have said if she did. "No. It's long gone."

"So I've been told. Flooded. Only I can't get a fix on a town in Maine that was sacrificed for a dam during the years Grace said. You'd think it would have made the news."

"I'm sure it did, maybe just not the news you're checking."

"I've checked most everything. But without the name of the town, I can't get local news, and if I can't find mention anywhere else of a town that drowned, I can't find the name."

"That is a problem," Sophie said, and turned a page, but the devil inside her was still at work. "You wouldn't be trying to upstage Grace, would you?"

"Upstage her?"

"She'll be telling all in her autobiography."

"Will she?"

Something about the way she asked made Sophie say, "Why wouldn't she?"

"The details of her early life may be embarrassing."

"Embarrassing?" Grace's life? "You have to be kidding."

"Have you ever met her parents?"

"They died long before I was born."

"Are you sure?"

"Of course, I'm sure. If not, I'd have met them. Grace wouldn't hide her granddaughter from her parents."

"What if it was the other way around? What if she was hiding her parents from her granddaughter?"

"Why in the world would she do that?"

"Shame. Her roots are very lower class."

Sophie rose and reached for her coat as the only appropriate protest. She resented Robin's inference and her intrusion on what should have been an hour's relaxation.

After easing her hands into the sleeves of the coat, she adjusted the collar and searched the street for Gus.

"No denial?" Robin asked from behind her.

"Not worth the effort," Sophie said without turning. "You have no idea what you're talking about. Here's my ride." And right on time, for once. "Thanks, Lucy. I'll see you next week."

She left without a word to Robin. But she slipped into the backseat of the car.

"Yo," Gus protested in his deep, whiskey voice. "Why back there?"

"Because I'm being watched. Let's get moving."

He drove down the street, turned the corner, and pulled over.

Robin waited for him to get out and do whatever it was he'd pulled over to do. When all he did was look at her in the rearview mirror, she said, "What's wrong?"

"I need you up here."

She had a sudden flash of what he needed her for and felt a stab of annoyance. "Sorry, Gus. I'm not in the mood."

"Rough manicure?"

"Gus."

"You make me feel like the chauffeur."

"You are the chauffeur."

His eyes held hers in the mirror.

She sighed. "Just drive, Gus."

He put his foot to the floor and sped down the street. "You're still pissed about your birthday. You been strange since that night. You blame me."

"Did I say that?" She blamed herself, not him.

"Maybe not you, but everyone else. Your mother, Jim O'Neill, even Davis Marcoux."

Davis? Sophie knew of the Tyne Valley connection, but she guessed Davis to be in his early forties to Gus's late twenties, which made them not exactly contemporaries. "How well do you know Davis?"

"Not well. But he knows my family. He figures he can put his two bits in, now that he's a hotshot doctor. He told me to wise up. The old lady said something along that line, too."

Sophie's annoyance flared. "Do you have to call her the old lady? She's my grandmother."

That quieted him, but only for the space of several more blocks. "Never bothered you before. You are pissed."

She considered that. "Now that you mention it, yes, I'm pissed. It wouldn't have killed you to keep an eye on me, y'know."

"I was your date, not your keeper."

Sophie remembered Grace's request that she be married to a good, responsible man who would take care of her. The married part was still wrong, but the rest—even the taking care of part—didn't sound as bad now as it had then. What had happened to her that night could have been lethal.

She tried to remember whether, in the handful of times they had been together since then, Gus had either expressed concern over what had happened or had apologized. "Didn't that whole thing scare you, even a little?"

"Yeah. I nearly lost my job."

Which told her just what she meant to him. Not that she'd had any illusions. Still. "You're a bastard," she muttered as he turned onto the drive. The instant the car pulled up to the door, she was out and on her way up the stairs.

He caught her elbow at the top. "What about tonight?"

"What about it?"

"You comin' over?"

She gave him a slow once-over that lingered at his crotch before focusing on the elbow he held. "If I need it." She wrenched the elbow free.

"Bitch."

She burst inside, slammed the door behind her, and strode toward the office, pushing Gus from her mind. She wanted to tell Francine about Robin Duffy.

But Francine was out, which only annoyed Sophie more. They had agreed that one of them would stay with Grace until they hired someone new—and that annoyed Sophie even *more*. Despite every rational impulse that said caution was right, Sophie resented the idea of coddling Grace. It smacked of the same kind of manipulation at which Grace was so skilled.

She was about to take refuge in her own end of the house when her eye passed Grace's office. The door was open. Grace was standing before the window, her shoulders slumped, her head bowed. The pose was so uncharacteristic that Sophie's anger faded. "Hi, Gram."

Grace looked up. Her face lit for one second and dimmed in the next. Her eyes returned to her hands. "Marny was babysitting me. It was a waste. I sent her back to her office."

She didn't sound manipulative. She sounded defeated.

But defeat was something foreign to Grace, or always had been until now.

Sophie's anger fizzled more. She didn't know what to say to this different Grace. Then she realized that Grace's hands were busy. Curious, she approached. "What are you doing?"

She was weaving a piece of string through her fingers. "Cat's cradle. We used to play. Only I can't remember the whole thing. I can only get here." She dropped her pinkies and the string went straight. "I wish I could do the rest." She shook the string out. "You need four hands for some parts." She laced the string around her fingers again. "My sisters and I used to see who could do it the fastest." Using the fingers of each hand in turn, she manipulated the string. One pattern gave way to the next.

Lightly, Sophie said, "You don't talk about your sisters much."

Grace looked up. "Sisters?"

"You just said you used to play this with your sisters."

"My friends. I played with my friends."

Sophie dropped her coat on a chair. "Tell me about them, then. What were their names?"

Grace was studying her fingers, frowning again. "The usual. There were Roses, and Marys, and Rosemarys. It's no good." She dropped a hand. "It's gone." The string dangled at her side. She sighed and looked out the window. "I can't work. I'm waiting for your mother to get home."

"Where is she?"

"Getting ceramic tile."

Sophie knew nothing about plans for redecoration—unless Francine was finally replacing the carpet that Legs had made such a mess of in her walk-in closet. But with ceramic tile?

"She said for a friend. I don't remember who." Grace sank

into a chair, stared out the window, and sighed. "Spring is too far off."

The discouragement in her voice said she was wondering if she would make it that long. Sophie waved aside her doubts. "It'll be here before you know it."

"We aren't even into the holidays."

"But they'll be fun. The Dorians do *great* holidays."

"They'll be different this year."

"Maybe better. We don't need whole gangs of people coming. All they do is eat our food, spill our wine, and pee on the toilet seat in the powder room. So this year we'll go the intimate route." The intimate route wasn't as dynamic as the party route, but it minimized the potential for disaster. It was also appropriate. No one knew how Grace would be in another year. This might be her last lucid holiday season. Their time with her was to be savored.

"Just us," Grace said.

"Just us," Sophie confirmed.

"And Jim."

"Of course."

"And maybe Robert."

Sophie was silent. Robert seemed to have withered away.

"And for you?" Grace asked. "I want you married."

Sophie felt a twinge of irritation. The old, controlling Grace had a way of bringing it out. "That may not be possible."

"Why not?"

"Because I haven't found anyone to love."

"Forget love. I didn't love your grandfather."

Sophie was startled. "You didn't?"

"Not at first. He offered safety. Love came later."

"That's incredible. I always pictured a storybook romance."

Grace shook her head. "Not necessary for me. Not necessary for you."

"But times have changed, Gram. I don't need a husband. I don't want one just for kicks. Back then, people married for security. Now they don't."

"Yes, they do. They just call it love now."

"Grampa already had security. What was in the marriage for him?"

Grace was pensive for a long minute. Then, looking confused, she said, "Someone called just before you got home."

"Oh-ho, no," Sophie teased. "Don't change the subject. What was in it for Grampa? I'll bet *he* was wildly in love."

Grace frowned. "She said her name, but I can't remember it."

Sophie had spent many an hour as a child oohing and aahing with Francine over Grace's wedding pictures. "You were a beautiful bride. I'll bet he thought you were the most refreshing thing to hit town."

"Fawn? No. Was it Lily?" Grace made a sound of frustration. "She was from the paper. She said that."

Sophie grew still. "What? Who said that?"

"The woman who called."

"What paper?"

Grace pursed her lips. She looked mystified.

Sophie had a chilling thought. "It wasn't Robin, was it?"

Grace lit up. "Yes. I think it was."

Sophie was incredulous. "But how did she get through to you? Marny should have taken the call, and if not Marny, Margaret." That was the chain they had set up to assure that the wrong people didn't reach Grace. "How did you *answer* the phone, for God's sake?" She *never* got it right.

Grace raised her chin. "I've been answering phones all my life."

Sophie didn't waste time arguing. She had to know how much damage was done. "What did Robin say?"

"Oh, the usual."

"What's the usual?"

"Just polite little—what's the word?" She gestured. "Polite little grab bag."

"Grab bag?"

"Gab bag. You *know*. Polite little—little gibgab."

"Chitchat?"

"Chitchat."

"Did she ask about your book?"

Grace crossed to the credenza.

Sophie followed. "What did you tell her, Gram?"

Opening a low door, Grace drew out a familiar vase.

"You didn't agree to meet with her, did you?"

Holding the vase in the curve of her elbow, Grace reached inside and produced a tiny box of raisins. "Eat this. You haven't had anything in a while, and it's that time of day."

For a split second, Sophie was a preteen again. Back then, the vase stood on the corner of Grace's desk and was filled with the kinds of goodies that active young diabetics munched on late in the day when their blood-sugar levels tended to fall.

"I can't believe you still have this," she mused.

Grace pressed the box into her hand. "Eat it. For me."

Sophie's throat grew tight. *Eat it. For me.* It was the old refrain that they had joked about for years. Grace wasn't joking now, though. She didn't seem to remember the joking, or the sheer number of times she had said those very same four words. They were spoken in total innocence now, straight from mind and heart, with the kind of caring that had too often been overshadowed by the pressures of work and adulthood.

It hit Sophie then, as it hadn't with quite as much poignance before, that Grace's world was shrinking. The past was coming to the fore, folding up on the future. Grammie was failing.

Smiling through her tears, she dutifully opened the box and slipped several raisins into her mouth. They were as hard as rocks, very, very stale. Still, she swallowed those first few and reached for more.

Fourteen

Genius may be a thing of awe, but the better part of brilliance is good common sense.
—Grace Dorian, from *The Confidante*

Francine hadn't taken two steps into the house when Sophie accosted her. "Big trouble, Mom. Robin Duffy showed up at Lucy's and started asking questions, so I told her Grace was in Europe. She must have picked up the phone the minute I left the shop, and somehow she got through to Grace, so she knows I lied about Grace being away, and I have *no idea* what Grace told her. Then Grace mentioned her *sisters* to me, but when I asked her, she denied it. Something's weird."

Weird was one word for it, Francine thought. Frightening was another.

"So, did Grace have sisters, or didn't she?" Sophie asked.

"She did not," Francine answered, then hedged. "Unless they died early, like her brother," she reasoned aloud. "But why would she talk of his dying and not theirs? No, there can't have been any sisters."

"Unless Grace is lying."

A short time before, Francine would have categorically denied the possibility. Now she simply said, "Unless Grace is lying."

"We have to find out if she is," Sophie whispered.

Francine agreed, though not without qualms. Grace had always been the embodiment of goodness, a loving and attentive mother, a successful career woman. She didn't simply preach compassion, she lived it in her columns, her sponsorship of charity events, the generosity of her giving. To suggest that she was a liar seemed blasphemous.

"We should start by warning her about Robin," Sophie went on. "She needs to be shaken up. If she knows what's at stake, she may come clean. By the way, she said you were shopping for ceramic tile. Was she dreaming it up?"

For a split second, Francine considered saying yes. Most anything could be blamed on Grace's disintegrating mind. But it wasn't the truth, and the truth mattered, particularly now. Lightly, she said, "She wasn't dreaming it up."

"Ceramic tile for what?"

"Davis Marcoux's kitchen floor."

Sophie smiled curiously. "*Whose* kitchen floor?"

Francine was nonchalant. "The good doctor's. He is overwhelmed choosing things like that, so I offered to help."

The curious smile lingered. "You hated having to decorate your own rooms."

"It's easier doing it for someone else. Less at stake. He has to live with it, I don't." Francine glanced toward Grace's office and a more immediate problem than Davis. "Is she in there now?"

"Oh yes. Waiting for you. Will you confront her?"

Francine couldn't think of any other choice. "We have to know what's going on."

She felt a pang when she found Grace at her desk, half swallowed by the chair and looking lost. This was a shadow of the Grace she had known all her life, a faint echo of the strong, focused, driving force. This Grace was an older woman.

Older, sadder eyes brightened when she saw Francine. "You're back. I was worried you'd gone on vacation."

"Without telling you?" Francine chided, smiling despite the catch near her heart. "I wouldn't do that. You knew where I was."

"But you were gone forever."

"Only a couple of hours." She drew up a chair. "Sophie said you talked with Robin Duffy. What did she say?"

"Robin Duffy?"

"She writes for the *Telegram*."

Grace frowned. "Did she call? Yes, someone did. But we didn't talk long. She asked how I was. I said I was fine."

"Anything else?"

Grace frowned, pondered, shook her head.

"It's important," Francine urged.

"Was I *supposed* to say something?"

"You weren't supposed to talk with the woman, period. I'm afraid you might have said something about your childhood. That's what Robin is digging into."

"But why?" Grace asked.

Francine remembered the letter Robin had sent her. "She fancies herself a specialist on The Confidante. No doubt she's looking for something that no one else has printed. No one else has printed any details of your childhood. No one knows them, not even me. You have to tell me, Mom, tell me anything about your childhood that Robin might find worth printing."

"There's nothing," Grace said.

"I want to believe that," Francine begged. "I do, but you keep saying things that make me wonder."

Grace set her jaw. "There's nothing."

"No sisters? No secrets?"

"Nothing."

"Are you sure? I have to know what I'm dealing with. I can't keep *The Confidante* going, can't write your book, unless I know the facts."

Grace pressed her lips together.

"You had sisters, didn't you," Francine said with a sudden soft conviction. She felt the newness of it, the excitement, the anxiety. "Did something terrible happen? Was there an illness? A betrayal? A *scandal*?" If there had been deep pain involved, she could understand why Grace might have blotted it out.

Grace frowned.

"Please tell me."

Grace shook her head.

"Does that mean there isn't anything to tell, or there is but you won't?"

"I can't," Grace said, and closed her eyes.

"Can't because it's so bad? Nothing's that bad, Mom. But a reporter like Robin Duffy may make it bad if we don't beat her to the punch. You tell me I'm not on top of things. Well, I'm trying to be now. I'm trying to save *The Confidante*. I'm trying to save your book. I'm trying to save the only history I've ever known." And, damn it, she was scared. "Is there *anything* you can tell me?"

Grace began to rock, slowly, quietly.

Francine waited for her to speak, but the rocking went on, and when Grace finally opened her eyes, it was to gaze out, through the window, across the rolling lawn, toward the river. Her expression said that she was miles away. Francine had no idea where.

Grace had always loved this view. Did it follow that the view reminded her of some small childhood pleasure?

Maybe yes, maybe no.

Did it follow that if Grace had sisters, they were still alive?

Maybe yes, maybe no.

Did it follow that if Grace had lied about these few things, she had lied about others, too?

Maybe yes, maybe no.

Francine felt suddenly helpless, as though the whole of life was getting away from her and she was just letting it go. She was being typically Francine, a pale imitation of the Grace who would have taken the bull by the horns.

How to take that bull by the horns?

The better part of brilliance was common sense, Grace always said, but there was only one bit of common sense that Francine could think of just then. She searched for another, couldn't find it, searched more, came up blank.

How to take that bull by the horns?

Driven by the need to act and, yes, raw instinct, she returned to her office and sifted through the In box until she found the letter Robin Duffy had sent her three months before.

Less than two hours later, Francine entered the small café in the center of town. Determined to be Grace-punctual, she was five minutes early. She had barely settled in at a small corner table when Robin came through the door.

Crossing the short space, she slipped into a chair. Her

leather satchel hit the floor with a thunk that bespoke the lethal tools of her trade. Breathless, she flattened a hand on her chest.

"I hope I haven't kept you waiting. After you called, I raced home for the car, which wasn't there, of course, since my son forgot that he was supposed to take his sister to her math tutor and was off with his friends, so I had to track him down, get him home, get her delivered, and get gas, because needless to say the car was running on fumes . . ." She ran out of breath.

Francine couldn't have asked for a better icebreaker. A winded Robin was less ominous. "I haven't been here more than a minute or two," she said with a smile. "We're both early. My excuse is being Grace Dorian's daughter. What's yours?"

Robin unwound her scarf. "Mine is being the daughter of Grace's disciple. The rest of the world might run late, but I'd die first, punctuality is so ingrained." She opened her coat and, looking relieved to be finally still, sat back in her chair.

"I appreciate your coming on such short notice."

"It doesn't seem like short notice to me. I've been waiting to talk with you for months. Is this an interview?"

"No. Is something running in the satchel?"

Robin reached into the bag, pulled out a tape recorder, and set it on the table. The tape was still.

"Thank you," Francine said, and saw the waitress approach. "Would you like anything?" she asked Robin.

Robin ordered coffee, black.

Francine ordered the same and watched the waitress leave. When she turned back to Robin, she saw a wariness that mirrored her own. "You're probably wondering why I asked for this meeting."

"I assume it has to do with my seeing Sophie today."

"Only indirectly. Your name has cropped up too often in the last few years to let one day stand out. You've been something of a thorn."

Robin actually looked embarrassed. "It's the job. The day of gentlemanly journalism is gone. A reporter has to be tough to survive. There are times when I hate it, but I don't have much choice. I'm a single mother. I have to write the story that sells if I want my kids to go to college."

Francine couldn't fault her motive. "How old is the sister of the seventeen-year-old son who dents cars?"

"Fourteen. She spits nails."

Francine laughed. "I remember those days. It does get better."

"When?" Robin asked so earnestly that Francine laughed again.

"Another few years. Certainly by the time she goes to college. Absence-makes-the-heart-grow-fonder kind of thing."

"I'm not sure I'll make it."

Francine had said the very same thing, as had more of her friends than she could count. It was a mother thing to say. She and Robin at least had that in common. "Are you at the *Telegram* full-time?"

"I freelance for several magazines, but the *Telegram* is my steady."

"Are you tied to it contractually?"

Cautiously now, Robin said, "No. Why?"

Francine studied her. She was an attractive woman—petite, sandy-haired, and blue-jeaned—with a nice smile, a skilled pen, and an admitted fascination with The Confidante. *My dream is to be the one most informed reporter on matters to do with Grace. I'm not sure whether I want this for my mother, or for myself, but in any case my history with* The Confidante *makes me the perfect candidate,* she had written in her letter. If the better part of brilliance was truly common sense, hiring her would be brilliant indeed.

"I'm looking for a ghost writer."

Robin's eyes went wide. "For Grace's book?"

Francine nodded. "Neither Grace nor I know anything about book writing. We've tried, but there's still *The Confidante* to put out every week. We need help."

"Are you offering me the job?"

"I'm thinking about it."

"I'm stunned," Robin said, sounding it.

"Why? You're a writer. You know Grace better than most."

"But we've had our differences, Grace and I, you and I."

"That's because we've been coming from opposite sides. If we were working together, those differences might cease to exist."

"I'm *stunned*," Robin repeated, then sucked in a sudden breath and said an accusatory, "You want to shut me up!"

"Excuse me?"

"That's it, isn't it?" She looked smug. "I'm hitting too close to home. Sophie told you about the town that wasn't dammed. Know something else? There isn't a record of the birth of a Grace Laver anywhere in Maine on or near the date she names. I've pored through records. I've had friends pore through records. So either her name isn't Laver, or she wasn't born in Maine. Who is she?"

Francine wished she knew. It was all she could do not to look as bewildered as she felt, and the bewilderment went deep. Grace's history was hers, too. Everything she didn't know had to do with her own heritage.

She gathered herself over the strong coffee that material-ized before her, one sip, a second, then set the cup down. "What else have you learned?"

"Not much," Robin said, "but I'm working on it. Grace is interesting—forthright here, enigmatic there. When I inter-viewed her the summer before last, I sensed that she didn't want to talk about anything that happened before she met her husband. The more I research those early years, the more enigmatic she becomes. We're talking dead ends here."

Francine knew it. Boy, did she ever. And the worst of it was that she had Grace at her fingertips, loaded with an-swers, refusing to divulge a one.

Robin went on, more earnest now. "Maybe it is an obses-sion with me. Grace was the model I was raised to admire, raised to imitate, only I could never do things like she did. For years I suffered trying to meet her standards. Well, those standards are beginning to look arbitrary, like Grace created them when she created *The Confidante*. There are too many questions, Francine."

"I *know*," Francine blurted out, because everything Robin had told her, she had told herself a thousand times. She fan-cied that Robin understood. So, if she was tipping her hand too early, tough. She was shooting straight from the hip.

"Come work for us," she said. "You'll have an office at the house, equal billing on the cover of the book, an expense ac-count for research. We'll pay you much more than the paper does. And you'll have free access to Grace."

Robin looked about to gape. Then she swallowed hard. "You *are* serious."

"Totally. It would solve problems for both of us. You need to write about Grace, I need someone to do it. You need money, I need help." She also needed someone who knew how to dig, and Robin was an expert at that. Hiring her *was* brilliant. How better to control the woman, to prevent her from hurting Grace, than to have her on the payroll? Make the enemy your own, Grace always said. It made sense.

"How much freedom would I have?"

"As much as you need to write a fair book."

"How do you define 'fair'?"

Francine gave it a moment's thought. Then she said, "We want this book to be a success. Grace sees it as the defining work on her life, the single most important, most lasting thing she'll ever do, but she won't stoop to sensationalism to boost sales."

"Are we talking pablum, then?" Robin asked. "Because I won't be part of a whitewash. I won't write a rehash of all the other interviews that have been done. Anything I do has to be honest."

"There are different levels of honesty," Francine argued. "Your piece after Grace's car accident was technically honest, but not inferentially so. You could have written that piece just as honestly, but more kindly. It's the kind honesty, the gentle honesty, that we want for Grace's book. To print something that disparages her image will be self-defeating."

"To you. Not to me. Knock sensationalism all you want, but it sells books."

"If that's your bottom line, we're wasting our time." Francine started to rise.

Robin reached for her arm. "Wait. Sensationalism isn't my first priority. I have standards." She withdrew her hand and wrapped it around her coffee cup. "If I work for you, I'd have to take a leave from the paper. There might not be a place for me to go back to."

"You might not need it. You'll have better options. Besides, we'll give you an advance, plus royalties, so you'll have money coming in for years." Amanda could draw up the agreement. Far better to share the take than not have any take at all, which would be the case if the book never got written. Not that the Dorians needed the money. But Robin Duffy did.

Francine guessed she was thinking just that, because she grew conciliatory. "One of the worst things about the paper was being tethered by an editor. Will Grace do that?"

"Grace won't stifle you, if that's what you mean." Grace in her present condition wasn't stifling anyone, not that Francine was telling Robin that just yet. It was information of the most privileged, most dangerous, sort. "You'll have the same freedom that I have, or that Grace has herself. Any decisions about what to include in the book will be joint ones."

"Are there questionable things, beyond what I've already found?"

Quietly, trusting Robin even when one part of her said she shouldn't, Francine said, "I don't know. Grace has never talked much about her childhood."

"How far is she into the book?"

"She has notes. She isn't sure how to organize them," which was putting it mildly. "That's why we need someone like you."

"Why isn't she here? If this book means so much to her, I'd think she would be. Is she sick?"

"She's back home working."

"Why did Sophie say she was in Antibes?"

"Because you annoyed her. She figured you thought she was young enough and naive enough to inadvertently say something she shouldn't. Sophie's sharp. Don't underestimate her."

"Does she know we're meeting?"

"Yes." It wasn't the truth, but what the hell.

"Make the enemy your own kind of thing?"

That, too, Francine thought with a smile. "You're up on your Graceisms."

"I was *raised* on Graceisms."

Francine glimpsed a kindred soul. It struck her that she might actually like working with Robin. "Poor you. Poor *us*." She shook her head in amazement. "You really are the best choice for the job."

"But will I survive?"

"Survive working with Grace? Yes, you'll survive." Grace wouldn't, though that had nothing to do with writing the book. "Look at it this way. If you're thinking of your kids, working with us will involve less risk for greater reward than anything else you can do."

"What if I say no?"

"We'll hire someone else. But you're our first choice."

Robin turned the coffee cup in her hands. "Even in spite of some of the things I've written about Grace?"

"That makes the pairing more interesting. I admire your persistence. Like I said before, you've been a thorn."

"In ten years as a reporter, I haven't done anything worth Pulitzer contention."

"True. But you have something none of the others do. You have a personal investment in this. You grew up with Grace. Just like me."

Robin didn't know whether it was fate, luck, or sheer persistence that had dropped the chance of a lifetime in her lap, but she was beside herself with glee. What a difference a day made. What a *world* of difference a day made.

What would writing Grace's biography mean to her? It meant regular hours, for starters, which meant spending more time with the kids. It meant focusing in depth on a single topic rather than cursorily juggling many. It meant money, which meant repairs on the car, a better apartment, maybe even a small house, *after* college tuition. It meant exposure, which meant a future of opportunities bigger and better than anything the *Telegram* had to offer.

Strange, she hadn't thought beyond the *Telegram*. Then again, not strange at all. The god-awful high standards she had been held to—that had caused an estrangement from her parents, eaten at her marriage until it fell apart, and jeopardized her relationship with her children many times—those standards set her up to fail. So she had learned to keep her sights low and do what she did as well as she could. Now, finally, at last, it had paid off.

Her mother would have *died* if she'd known.

And her father? She hadn't talked with him since her mother had died. Robin wondered if he cared what she was doing. She wondered if he would see the irony of it. Her brother had, but her brother saw things as she did. Grace's standards had beaten her down, now Grace would lift her up.

She didn't say anything to the kids, to her friends, to anyone at the *Telegram*. She wasn't burning her bridges until a written agreement arrived—which it did, two days later—and then she was ecstatic. The terms were fair. *Better* than fair. By teaming up with Grace, Robin stood to make twice what she would on her own—three times—*four* times. The contract even offered a signing bonus.

There was that clause, of course. As a precondition of setting foot in the Dorian home, she had to agree that anything she saw or learned about Grace or her family, other than that which appeared in the book, would remain confidential. There wouldn't be any kiss-and-tell sales to the tabloids, any follow-up books of castoffs from the first, any magazine articles on life with the Dorians.

In the course of delirious imaginings, Robin had envisioned Grace's book as the first of several lucrative publications with her name attached. Those would be out of the question, if she signed the agreement.

But the clause raised other possibilities—namely, that there were secrets galore behind the Dorians' walls. Grace Dorian might never mess her hair, chip her nail polish, or lose her temper. But if there were other things—and if Robin was privy to them, and if she could convince Grace that the world would love her in spite of her flaws, which it probably wouldn't, because people were fickle that way, but what the hell—things might work out just fine.

There were more ways than one to skin a cat, Grace always wrote. Robin was staking her future on it.

Fifteen

Like truth, the sun may be obscured by clouds, eclipsed by the moon, or relegated to the back side of the earth, but it always rises to shine again.
—GRACE DORIAN, on *Donahue*

Grace felt safest at home, where things were familiar, even labeled now to remind her of what was where. In strange places she risked making the kind of humiliating mistakes she had spent a lifetime avoiding.

Since the backyard, too, was safe, she went walking with Francine. The air was crisp, the evergreens laced with ice, the lawn pristine. Bundled in heavy clothing, she was safe from the cold and the wet.

She admired snow—the purity of it, the way it buried those things killed by the cold, the bright continuity it gave the rolling span from the house to the wooded riverbank. She looked for bird tracks and found them, saw a sweet little gray thing scamper toward a tree and up, its bushy tail twitching behind it. She tried to remember what it was called, then lost the thought.

As a precaution, she hooked her elbow through Francine's as they strolled. She lost her balance sometimes, got confused about which way was up and found herself on the floor. Fortunately, when it had happened, no one had been around to witness the indignity of it.

"Mother?"

"Yes, sweetheart?"

"Can we talk about your book?"

"On such a beautiful day?" Talking about the book made her feel itchy and achy. She needed to concentrate, that was all. A few good hours, and the book would be done.

"We're fooling ourselves," Francine said. "We can't do it alone."

"My goodness. Think of the glass."

"Half full, not half empty. Now think of the proof of the pudding. It isn't there, Mom. The book isn't one third done, or even one quarter. We need a ghostwriter. I've hired Robin Duffy."

Grace had heard that name before, but she didn't know where. "Do I know Robin Duffy?"

"She writes for the *Telegram*. Her mother was a die-hard fan of yours. Robin was raised on your columns."

"Have I met her?"

"She did an interview the summer before last. You liked it."

Grace suddenly remembered something different. "She was the one who wrote that *awful* article after my automobile accident."

"Yes, well, that was a problem with communication," Francine rushed to say. "It may have been my fault as much as anyone else's, but the point is that there won't be any communication problem if she's on our side. Amanda thinks it's a great idea. So does Katia."

Robin Duffy had written an awful article after her automobile accident. Robin Duffy was out to get her. So were Amanda and Katia.

"*I* don't think it's a great idea," Grace said. Pulling her arm free, she set off downstream. She hadn't gone more than five paces when she tripped on a tree root concealed by the snow. Francine caught her and steadied her.

Grace kicked at the root. Everyone, everything, seemed against her at times. Even a tree root. It was a—a—they were *ganging up* against her.

She allowed herself to be steered back toward the house and safer ground. "I don't want someone else writing my book."

"You're still writing it. Someone else is helping. That's all."

"It's my book."

"It's no book if it doesn't get written."

Grace glared at Francine. "That note of voice is uncalled for. What's gotten into you? Do you enjoy tearing me to threads? Do you *like* belittling me?"

Francine denied it, of course. "I'm simply trying to make sure that the book gets published. Katia's begging for the manuscript."

"I need time, not a helper. My gracious, you'd think I was a child. I can dress myself. I don't need a personal dresser."

"Of course not—"

"Then why have you hired one?" Grace couldn't remember the woman's name, but she had bad feelings about her already.

"Jane Domenic isn't a personal dresser. She'll be your assistant."

"You're my assistant. She's a babysitter." Grace wasn't being taken for a fool. She had read things. She knew this was coming. It was the most humiliating twist yet.

"Jane Domenic is no babysitter. She's spent the last twelve years as executive secretary and eighty-hour-a-week girl Friday to a Wall Street CEO. She's qualified to do anything. You'll have first dibs on her, but she'll be able to help Sophie and me, too."

"I can do quite well myself, thank you."

Francine sighed. "Please, Mom. You begged me to help you write your book. You admitted you couldn't do it alone."

Grace didn't remember doing that at all. She certainly would never have begged. "*You* help me, then. Not some outsider."

"But I don't know diddly-squat about writing a book," Francine cried, "and even if I did, you won't give me the information I need!"

"My fault. Always my fault." She tugged at her arm, but Francine held fast.

"Okay. If you're uncomfortable with them, we can skip those early years and write a witty little book mixing excerpts from your columns with the story of your life starting when you met Daddy."

Grace froze. "Don't bring your father into this. He has nothing to do with it. He was nowhere *near* here when *The Confidante* was born."

"He was here. I was here. I saw him here."

Grace was horrified. She had worked *so hard* to erase the past. And she had. Hadn't she?

"Are you trying to trick me?" she asked, because she was sure *she* hadn't said a word.

At least, she thought she hadn't.

But some things she couldn't remember. There were large voids where lists of events should be. Yesterday, for instance. She couldn't remember what she had done. She might have worked, then had her hair done, then gone shopping. She might have even met with Amanda. Or had they met the day before? No. She'd had lunch with Mary, then. Hadn't she?

Francine said, "I'm meeting Robin at the café in town tomorrow morning. After that, I'll bring her back here to meet you."

"Robin?" Grace asked. She assumed Robin was a new friend. Francine always introduced her new friends to Grace, always wanted Grace's approval. Such a good girl.

"Robin Duffy," Francine said. "The woman who'll be writing your book."

But, but that was no friend. "Oh no. She's not meeting me. And she isn't writing my book. She'll take everything I say and twist it around until it comes out slate."

"Slate?"

"Slate. You know, dirty."

"I won't let her do that."

"You won't be able to stop it. I know how recorders work. They get breath of something and don't give up until—until—" Her mind went blank. She gestured away the missing thoughts. All that was left was a premonition. "No good."

"I'll be watching her," Francine insisted. "Nothing will be done without your approval. She won't be able to hurt you. I *promise.*"

The premonition was a big, dark cloud. "She'll hurt me."

"She can't."

The cloud darkened, lowered. Grace wanted to push it up and away, but it was too large, too heavy. She wailed in frustration. "It's no good, I tell you, no good." She tugged at

her arm, fighting Francine's resistance, until she was free.
Then she took off, but her shoes couldn't get a grip on the
slippery stuff. She hit the ground with another wail.

Francine was quickly kneeling down, helping her sit.
"Good God, Mom. Are you hurt?"

Grace cradled her knee. It felt odd. "I think it twisted."

Francine probed the knee. "Nothing is sticking up at odd
angles. Does this hurt?"

"Oh, dear. Look at my trousers. They're all wet."

"Only the knees, where you fell." Francine brushed at the
snow. "Can you stand?"

"I'm not a cripple," Grace muttered, though she let Francine help her up. After adjusting her gloves, she straightened
her shoulders and started off, then felt a pang in her knee.

"Hurts?" Francine asked.

"A little. Strange, but I must have twisted it. I wasn't
aware of doing anything. I think I'm just getting old."

"Sixty-one is not old," Francine said.

This little knee ache was probably only a touch of arthri-
tis, but it reminded Grace of things to be done. She wouldn't
be around forever. No one was.

Sad. So sad, she thought. The house looked beautiful, all
damp and fresh, with snow caught at its eaves and corners,
glistening under the sun. Spring would be here soon. Then
flowers.

Grace loved flowers, loved the spray of colors that bor-
dered the patio. She would give a party in April, when things
were in bloom. The invitations would have hand-painted
borders. She had seen some like that once. They were lovely.

A summer party. Definitely.

* * *

Francine was relieved when Davis stopped by on his way home from work. She needed his magic. It had been a trying afternoon.

Grace was stretched gracefully on the den sofa, listening to Mozart. She roused enough when he came in to protest that she was perfectly fine and didn't need a doctor at all, though she winced when he examined her knee.

"Nothing's broken," he told Francine in the hall moments later. "If either the pain or the swelling increase, we can get it x-rayed, but there's no point in dragging her to the hospital yet. That would only upset her."

Francine knew that all too well. Even regularly scheduled appointments with Davis rendered Grace out of sorts and hard to handle. Staying put was just fine with Francine. She was just now beginning to relax.

Davis walked beside her, glancing down at her every few steps. She remembered the night, seven months before, when he had first come to the house. She had been furious then, threatened, actually, but aware of him, and the awareness had grown more vivid with time. The pounding of her heart told her so. Unfortunately it didn't tell her what to do with him now that business was done.

"Keep an eye on Grace," he said in a tone that was professional enough not to give her a clue. "She may forget the knee is hurt and give it more weight than it can bear. Should I get a Special to sit with her for the night?"

The idea was heavenly, but not to be. "Grace wouldn't appreciate a night nurse. She gets angry when I mention hiring extra help. That was what the explosion was about this afternoon." He already knew about Jane Domenic. Now she told him about Robin.

He gasped. "You hired the enemy?"

She poked him in the ribs with her elbow.

Chuckling, he drew her close. "It's a clever move."

His praise tickled a little spot inside. "Either clever or remarkably dumb," she said. "Robin could still stab us in the back."

"She won't risk a lawsuit, with kids to protect. Besides, if what she says is true, Grace is part of who she is."

"Part of who she resents. She's like me, Davis. She's had to live under the shadow of The Divine. Let's pray that she has more positive feelings than negative. I've been sweating about this book for months. I can't tell you how nice it'll be to have the help."

They had reached the front foyer. Davis cocked his chin toward the opposite hall and asked in a throatier voice, "What's down there?"

"Dining room. Kitchen."

"Then what?"

She smiled. "Three guesses."

He took her hand and set off.

Laughing, she tried to slow him. "Whoa. Wait. What is it you want, Dr. Marcoux?"

"Three guesses."

"Can't do," she cried, still laughing. "Not now."

When he stopped short, she plowed into him, then found herself pressed to Grace's elegantly flocked wall. He anchored her hands at the back of his thighs and leaned into her.

His mouth was a breath above hers. "I've never seen your bedroom," he murmured.

"I know."

"I want to see it."

She shook her head.

"Why not?"

"You'll spook Legs."

"She knows me now. Try again."

"It's messy."

"Can't be worse than my place."

Francine looked from his mouth to his eyes and, suddenly more serious, said, "I need the separation, Davis. What we have—what we do—it puts me in another world. Everything here is under the shadow of Grace and her illness. Especially given how we met, I want our relationship separate from that."

"You escape at my place. You could escape here, too. The key isn't where you are but who you're with."

"Maybe soon. Not yet."

He moved against her and made a sound that said she felt good. The feeling was mutual. Never mind that the mystique was gone, that she knew exactly what was under his clothes, had touched and tasted it all. Neither the novelty nor the attraction had worn off. She loved his scent, loved the body heat that set it off, loved the promise of that heat. When he came near, her insides shook.

He took her mouth in a kiss that evolved from whisper to caress to ravishment with hunger's rise, and she gave herself up to the pleasure of it, taking the little escape as it came.

Then a throat cleared loudly. "Excuse me? Uh, I'm sorry. Am I interrupting something?"

Francine was slow in registering the voice's ownership. By the time she did, the damage was done.

Her tongue slipped slowly from Davis's. Their mouths separated. Taking a shaky breath, she put her forehead to his chin. "Sophie."

"I was just walking down the hall, and here you were," Sophie said in a perky way. "What a surprise."

"Sophie," Francine said with more force.

"Shopping for ceramic tiles, huh?"

"*Sophie.*"

"We did pick great ones," Davis said, though his voice sounded strained. Francine knew why. It was the same reason why he didn't move away. "They're Italian," he said. "Fourteen-inch squares. Kinda tan, kinda brick colored. Warm looking."

"I'll bet," Sophie said.

Francine glanced sideways. Another child happening upon her mother in a man's arms would have fled in embarrassment. But Sophie was perfectly at ease, with a shoulder to the wall not three feet from where they stood. And she wasn't leaving. "Is this something new?"

"You could say that," Francine said.

"Something I should worry about?"

"Not yet."

"Oh. Well, still, I have one warning."

"Warning?"

"You folks are used to the seventies make-love-not-war kind of thing, but we don't do that anymore, because this is the AIDS generation. Yes, I know it's hard to believe that people like you might be susceptible to AIDS, but you can never be sure, so what I want to say is that if you absolutely, positively, can't abstain, you have to be *sure* to use condoms, and not just any old kind—"

Francine had slipped from under Davis to stopper Sophie's mouth with a hand and start her down the hall. "You're too smart, little girl."

From the corner of her mouth, Sophie whispered, "Dr. Marcoux?"

"What's wrong with Dr. Marcoux?" Francine whispered back.

"You *hated* him."

"No. I hated what he was saying. There's a difference."

"Have you slept with him?"

"What kind of question is that?"

"The kind you'd ask me."

Francine was about to point out the difference in their ages when she stopped short. Grace stood at the place where hall met foyer. Her look was thunderous. Without a word, she turned and set off at a limp back toward the den.

Francine was trying to decide how much she'd seen, guessing from the storm that it was more than enough, wondering whether to confront and confess or deny, when Sophie said, "You see to Davis. I'll see to Grace."

Davis had reached the foyer by the time she was gone. By that time, Francine was feeling stormy herself. "*That*," she said, "is why I didn't want to show you my bedroom."

"If you'd shown it to me, *that* wouldn't have happened."

"You're missing the point. Grace isn't ready for this."

"For what? Your kissing her doctor? I thought we settled that issue. Our relationship is totally outside the professional. So what's the problem?"

"Grace. She has fixed ideas. She isn't used to my kissing men in the hall. It would have been better if she'd had a chance to get used to seeing us together. She'd have been better prepared."

"Why the need? You're a grown woman."

"Who cares deeply for her mother," Francine said beseechingly, "who, P.S., is having a hard time. Let me talk with her, Davis."

"Let *me* talk with her."

"And say what? That her daughter turns you on? That she's the most fun you've had in bed in years?"

"How about that I love you?"

Francine rolled her eyes. "You won't say that because it isn't true, because I *am not* your future. I told you that at the start." She framed his neck with her hands, thumbs smoothing the roughness at his jaw. "Go home now, Davis. I'll call you later. Please?"

He looked like he wanted to argue—looked dark and heroic—and in that instant, Francine felt half in love with *him*.

In the next instant, she flattened her fingertips on his mouth, whispered, "Later," and left him to see himself out while she went after Grace.

Grace was in the den, no longer lulled, though symphonic sounds filled the room. She was sitting straight, her lips pursed as Sophie spoke.

Francine couldn't catch what Sophie was saying. The talk stopped the instant she appeared.

"Well, that was a surprise," Grace said with such acuity that something as numbing as Alzheimer's disease might never have existed. Francine tried to be casual. "He's a nice man."

"Does Robert know about him?"

"I doubt it. Robert doesn't know the details of my life. He has no reason to know them."

"He does if you want to marry him."

It was time, Francine thought. A Grace as lucid as this could be realistic. "Oh, Mom, you're the only one who wants me to marry him. I don't. He doesn't. It isn't in the books. There are no sparks."

From the corner of her eye, Francine saw Sophie thrust a

fist in the air and mouth a vivid "Yessss." She might have shot her a grin had not Grace looked so dismayed.

"So you have sparks with my doctor, but I'd wager to guess, that's all. Wasn't that the problem with your marriage?"

Ahh, the memory, Francine mused dryly. "Davis and Lee are as different as night and day. Lee was from the same mold as every other fine young gentleman I'd ever met at the country club. Davis is no fine young country-club gent."

"That's why it won't work. He's too different."

"I'm not expecting anything to work. He kissed me. Period." It wasn't a lie, exactly. Kissing was all they had done in the hall.

"I saw much more," Grace insisted. "Much more. It isn't right, doing that in broad daylight. Just *think* who might have come by. And with children nearby. Good Lord."

Children? Francine shuddered to think what Grace was thinking or remembering or imagining. "And if I did want something to work with Davis, would that be so bad? He's a good man, a skilled doctor."

"He comes from nothing," Grace said.

"And that matters? You've written column after column about the importance of love over money. What would change if he had a trust fund back home?"

"If not for Jim, he'd be in the gutter."

"Maybe yes, maybe no. But he isn't in the gutter. He's a well-respected doctor. How can you fault that?"

"He's from *Tyne Valley*," Grace cried as though that explained everything.

But it certainly didn't to Francine. "So's Father Jim. Does that make him less of a man?"

"Father Jim"—Grace's voice softened—"is a wonderful man."

"Yes. From Tyne Valley. So's Davis Marcoux."

"Not the same. Don't see Davis Marcoux."

"Mother," Francine said with a disbelieving laugh, "you're not making sense."

"I don't make sense. I don't make sense. That's all I hear. I *do* make sense, only you don't like what I say. Davis Marcoux isn't my friend. He isn't yours. He's bad luck."

"Mother!"

"I don't want him in this house."

"I'm sorry to hear that," Francine said, goaded now. "I was planning to invite him for Thanksgiving dinner."

"If you do, I won't come."

Francine sighed. "Come on, Mom. That's foolish."

But Grace looked determined. "I won't come."

"Look," Francine coaxed more gently, "let's not argue. For all I know, he won't *want* to come for Thanksgiving dinner."

"He'll be collecting evidence against me. He'll be watching me and reporting back. I can't have it." Looking close to tears, she bowed her head. "Not like this. It isn't right. Isn't good to see."

Francine was instantly contrite. When Grace dissolved like this, tearful, head bowed, painfully aware of her illness and the shrinking person it caused, there was little to say by way of consolation. So she wrapped an arm around her and held her, then said a quiet, "If Davis is here, it'll be as a friend."

"Just us, you said."

"But he's all alone."

"He'll be watching me."

"He'll be watching television. He loves football."

Grace drew back, sent Francine her most disapproving look, and rose. "I don't want him in this house. Now. I'm going to work. I can't afford to sit around. I have a column to write."

*   *   *

Robin Duffy arrived at the café at five before nine the next morning. She thought Francine looked harried when she rushed in a minute later, slid into a chair, and said without pause, "You're probably wondering why I wanted to meet here before we went to the house." She caught the waitress. "Coffee, hot and strong, strawberries, and a scone. Robin?"

Robin had indeed wondered why they were meeting there. While she didn't think it was for the sole purpose of having breakfast, she ordered the same as Francine, minus the scone. She'd had breakfast with the kids for a change. Not that another round would have hurt. Nervous energy would burn off what she ate.

"There are things you need to know before you see Grace," Francine went on.

"Ahhh," Robin couldn't resist, "here it comes."

"I couldn't tell you everything until you were safely on our side."

"I figured that. So I've been imagining what secrets might be coming. I've dreamed up some good ones."

"Like?"

"Like Grace died five years ago and has been kept alive and active through experimental artificial means, only those means have developed a virus, so she's temporarily sidelined while the technocrats find a cure."

Francine took the coffee the waitress delivered, smiled, shook her head. "Sorry."

"Then I fall back on my original theories. Drugs, alcohol, or illness."

"Illness," Francine said without guile. "She has Alzheimer's disease."

Robin froze, coffee cup in hand, heart mid-beat. Alzheimer's disease. *Alzheimer's* disease. She had imagined cancer. She had imagined heart disease, or a stroke, or something physically debilitating, like MS or Parkinson's disease. She had never imagined Alzheimer's.

"She's known about it for a while," Francine said. "I learned last April."

Robin didn't have to add two and two. "The automobile accident."

"She didn't know how to stop the car. It was as simple as that. When I saw you in the hospital that night, I had just been told the diagnosis. I was in denial then, and for three months afterward."

No need for elaborate calculations there, either. "Until Chicago in July."

Francine shot her a rueful look. "You do catch on."

But catching on was a far cry from grasping the extent of the tragedy. "I never guessed Alzheimer's. It isn't the kind of thing one associates with Grace Dorian."

"No kidding," Francine remarked.

"Is she bad?"

"That depends on how you define bad. Is she the even-tempered, intuitive, all-knowing, reliable leader who single-handedly wrote *The Confidante*? No. She can't write, can't put the words together, can't create the way she once could. But she still functions, still communicates. There are times when she's so rational you begin to second-guess the diagnosis. Then she flips out."

"Flips out?" Robin asked, wondering exactly how hard her job was going to be.

"Oh, she isn't violent. She just changes the subject, starts talking nonsense, or grows silent and lost. She's also paranoid sometimes. For instance, she's convinced you're joining us to screw her. I told her about the agreement you signed. I'm not sure she trusts it. In any case," Francine said sheepishly, "she may be a little difficult at first."

Robin had an awful suspicion. "When did she find out you hired me?"

Guiltily now, Francine said, "Last night. Look, I don't think it'll be terrible. You'll just have to work a little harder to gain her confidence. The more she sees you around the office, the more she'll accept your presence. Besides, she forgets. If you're gentle with her, if you make progress on her book, if you praise her for all the help she's giving you, she'll take personal credit for hiring you. And it isn't like you'll be doing all the work. She does have notes, reams of them. Like I said, they just have to be organized. And she can talk. She can answer questions. She remembers most everything about *The Confidante*'s beginnings. Distant events survive, recent ones just—" she flicked a hand—"vanish."

"What about her childhood?" Robin asked. It certainly fell into the category of distant events. "That's where I've been running into contradictions."

"Her childhood," Francine repeated.

"The truth," Robin urged, feeling a stab of annoyance. "You owe me, Francine. It might have been nice if I'd had all the facts before I signed my life away."

"There's an escape clause in the agreement. I had the lawyer include it for just this reason. If you want out, say so. The secrecy clause holds, but you'd be free in every other sense."

"I'd be free in *no* sense," Robin argued, thinking of the excitement, the honor, the triumph she had felt, and the disappointment she would feel if she refused the job now. "More than anything else, I've wanted to write about Grace."

"To debunk the myth."

"To tell the whole story as no one else ever has. There is nothing illegal, immoral, or ill-bred about Alzheimer's disease. That won't debunk any myth. The truth of her identity might. Tell me about her childhood."

Francine seemed to struggle for the briefest minute before raising her eyes and confessing with utter frankness, "What I said the other day is true. I don't know any more than you do. Less, actually. The contradictions you've found have come from research. Mine come from Grace, inadvertently on her part, which makes their factuality questionable. She has hallucinations. The scene is always the same. Her family is in the next room—parents, brother, and sisters."

"I thought she only had a brother."

Francine slid her an I-thought-so-too look.

The waitress deposited two bowls of strawberries and one scone. Robin picked at her strawberries and tried to digest what Francine had said. "Do any of them have first names?" she asked.

"Her parents are Thomas and Sara. Her brother is Hal."

"What about the sisters?"

"I've never wanted to give them enough credence to ask."

"I could do searches on Thomas, Sara, and Hal. Especially Hal. We could pinpoint the year he died. There should be a death record somewhere." She paused. "Unless he didn't die at all."

"He had to. That part of the story has never changed. Not once. Grace has consistently said that he died of whooping cough at the age of five." She put a hand to her chest. "Can you *imagine* if it isn't true? Can you imagine my having an uncle out there? Aunts, cousins?"

Robin's excitement rose. This was her book. *The Grace Dorian the World Never Knew.*

"The problem," Francine said, "is that Grace denies all but her original story. And that story may be true. Hallucinations aren't necessarily accurate."

"I'm an expert snoop. I'll get at the truth."

"We don't have much time."

"When is the manuscript due?"

"That isn't the problem. The problem is Grace's mind. We need to get whatever is there out, before it folds."

Thoughts gone, pasts erased, personalities wiped clean. Robin would have been inhuman not to feel for Grace. More, even, she felt for Francine. Watching a parent slowly but systematically lose her most treasured faculties had to be devastating.

Gently, she asked, "How long does she have?"

Francine shrugged. "Weeks, months, years—who knows. That's why I wanted you to start right away." She pursed her lips for an instant. "So. Are you with us?"

Robin didn't have to give it a second thought. She wasn't turning her back on the chance of a lifetime. "I'm with you, for better or worse." She frowned. "Now why did I say that? Why do we always go back to marriage as the standard for relationships?"

"Because society sees it that way. How long have you been divorced?"

"Six years."

"Was it amicable?"

"As amicable as any divorce can be. He's a thinker, I'm a doer. Our personalities went in opposite directions. He has the kids on holidays and vacations, since they have to be

with me while they're in school. It really isn't fair. He gets the fun times." By way of explanation for grousing, she added, "The holidays are nearly here. Everything closes down, life comes to a standstill. For a doer like me, that's hard. With the kids gone, it's doubly hard. I never know what to do with myself."

"Join us," Francine offered. "We're staying home this year, just family. It'll be low-key."

Robin was taken aback by the offer. "Are you serious?"

"That you're invited? Very serious."

When nothing about Francine's expression suggested otherwise, she shook her head in amazement. "My mother would have died and gone to heaven well *before* her time if she'd known any of this—her daughter working with Grace Dorian, her daughter spending *Thanksgiving* with Grace Dorian. Un-believable."

Francine seemed pleased. "You'll come then?"

Robin wanted to. Her brother was with his significant other in San Francisco, and it beat twiddling her thumbs. Besides, she liked Francine, had from the first. She was looser than Grace, less intimidating, more approachable. "Your mother might not approve."

"Well. That is true. But I invited her doctor, and she doesn't approve of that. Maybe we can sell her on the idea that you're his date. Nah. She'd never buy it."

"Why not? Is he awful?"

"No. He's great. But she caught me kissing him yesterday and was livid. She wouldn't be fooled for a minute if I tried to pass him off as yours." Francine took a bite of her scone. "This could be an interesting Thanksgiving."

"Interesting beats lonely."

"Lonely? That, too, for us. We're used to being with a crowd—happy hour at the club, dinner for two dozen back

home. Grace may not be a happy camper, period. So come.
The more she's exposed to you, the sooner she'll open up.
And anyway, I invited you, I want you to come. Hell, it's my
Thanksgiving, too."

Put in the context of rebellion against none other than
Grace Dorian, Robin couldn't refuse.

Sixteen

Men are solitary creatures, women communal. For a man, keeping a secret is an act of pride. For a woman, it is sheer desperation.

—GRACE DORIAN, from *The Confidante*

Grace knew it was Thanksgiving—not because her calendar said so, since the grid work was more confusing than not, nor because Francine reminded her, since she lost reminders quickly, nor because the stores were selling the chocolate turkeys she loved, since she hadn't been to a store in months. She knew it was Thanksgiving because of the smells. They brought back years of Thanksgivings held in this house with John and a host of friends.

The friends would be missing this year. At times she understood why, and felt the pain of the passage. Other times there was only the sense of loss and its questions: What's missing? Where are they? Why aren't they here?

But the questions were fleeting, as was so much else in her mind. Once, her life had been a continuous train of events. Now it was broken into moments. Events occurred disjointedly. She had lost the connectors to give them order.

So she was left with a potpourri of emotions, strewn haphazardly in a cornucopia shaped by the scents of roast turkey, mulled apple cider, and fresh-from-the-oven mince pie.

There was embarrassment when she appeared in the kitchen in her loveliest black gown, only to have Margaret guide her back to her room to change into something simpler for breakfast. Oh, yes, Grace explained away the mistake by saying that she had simply wanted to try on the black dress to make sure it fit, but the mistake set her off wrong. She was shaky all morning, not quite sure of what to do with herself, when to dress or go downstairs or take her place at the head of the table. Her sense of time had been steadily eroding. She couldn't seem to get a grasp on what was when.

To make matters worse, Jim wasn't there.

"It's too early for Jim," Francine explained. "It's only ten. He's celebrating mass."

Grace waited a while longer. When still he didn't come, she began to fear that he had forgotten their plans.

"Father Jim forget you?" Francine teased. "He'd *never* do that. It's barely eleven. He's probably still at church, and from there he's heading to the hospital to visit sick parishioners. He'll be here as soon as he's done."

Grace waited a while longer. It struck her that maybe he'd forgotten.

"He hasn't, Mom," Francine insisted. "He promised he'd be here by two. That's still an hour off. Don't worry. He'll come."

Robin Duffy was the one who came, creating immediate strain for Grace. Yes, Robin was in their employ now; still,

Grace felt on display. Robin was watching her, even slightly in awe. Grace knew the look, knew the deference. Robin was a fan. She was also a reporter. It wouldn't do for Grace to make mistakes.

All the more so when Davis Marcoux walked in. He watched her with a different kind of eye—too medical, too evaluative, too knowing on *too* many scores—just waiting for slipups.

Playing it safe, she sat quietly, smiled, and responded to comments directed at her. Much as she had done years before, standing at the entrance to the Palm Court, taking her lead from the elegant ladies there, so now she followed Francine. When Francine took a caviar canapé from the tray Margaret passed, so did Grace. When Francine wrapped her cocktail napkin neatly around the tiny stick that had come with the shrimp, so did Grace.

Francine had grown into a commendable hostess. Grace didn't know when it had happened, but it was reassuring.

Little else was, most noticeably Father Jim's absence. Grace kept trying to read her watch. When she couldn't, she shot worried looks at Francine.

"He's coming," Francine assured her time and again.

But Grace didn't know where he was. She wondered if he had taken sick. Or lost his way. Or—worst of all—been swept back into the—into the—the place where priests went to study and pray, never to be seen again. If that happened, she would die. No questions asked, she would do it. Somehow. The future was bleak enough. Facing it without Jim was unthinkable.

Then he arrived, as tall and straight and passionate as ever. When he took her hand, she felt the first relief she had in days.

Given her druthers, she would have held his hand through

the entire afternoon. That was forbidden, of course. But he was there, with his reassuring smile.

Francine's smile was a comfort, too. She knew when to lead their guests into the dining room, knew where each should sit, knew which utensil to use first. Following her lead, Grace did fine for a time. Then her mind began to trip over questions.

Why wasn't Robert there? If there was any hope for Francine and him, he should have joined them for the holiday.

Why was Davis Marcoux there? Was his presence precautionary, in case she lost herself completely?

And why was Sophie looking so sad? Was she ill? Or worried about something? That worried Grace. She wanted for Sophie all the peace, happiness, and success in the world.

Grace left the table several times during the meal—to use the powder room, she explained in her most genteel manner—but nature's call was the least of it. There were moments when she simply couldn't sit still, when the restlessness was overpowering, when sharp stabs of emotion tweaked her up and about.

One minute it was greed, the wanting of things for an eternity that wouldn't be. Another it was anger, or sadness, or fear. The holiday did it. How often she had advised readers that the first holidays without loved ones were the hardest—and yes, she had felt it after John died, the break in tradition, but this was different. The only thing changing after John's death had been his presence. Here . . . now . . . everything.

That might have explained the peril she felt, the sense of things beginning to rot, the urgency. Some Alzheimer's sufferers stayed at plateaus for years, some even long enough to die of natural causes. Grace knew that she wouldn't. She could see a daily worsening, could chart the steady

diminution of her abilities even *with* the steady diminution of her abilities.

Eating was a perfect example. At first she had trouble
remembering whether, in fact, she had eaten a meal. Then
she had trouble deciding *what* to eat, all the more so when
there were multiple choices. Then she found herself forget-
ting that waffles liked syrup and bagels cream cheese. There
were instances when she salted her eggs twice, even three
times, and God only knew what else she did that she didn't
remember, and now this. A festive Thanksgiving table set
with more silver, more china, more extra little doohickeys
than she knew what to do with.

Once, she had known. Once, she had taught readers the
function of each and every one of those doohickeys. Now,
she was reduced to imitating others. She was back at the
Plaza, a nobody, on the outside looking in.

Dessert had just been served when Grace felt her eyes fill
with tears. She didn't know why. Worse, she didn't know
what she should do. So she just sat there with tears streaking
her cheeks.

Jim took her hand, but it was Sophie who touched her
shoulder and said, "I can't eat this stuff, anyway. Take a walk
with me, Gram?"

Infinitely grateful, Grace followed her out of the dining
room to the front-hall closet. "Where are we going?" she
asked when Sophie handed her the silver lynx that had been
John's last gift to her.

"For a walk. Where are your boots?" She retrieved them
from the floor of the closet and helped Grace into them.

Grace held her shoulder for balance. "It wasn't so long ago
that I did this for you. Then you started in with, 'I can do it
myself, Grammie.' Four years old, and quite the independent
one."

"It was a matter of pride," Sophie said, slipping into her own coat. "I wanted to be as grown-up as you and Mom."

That thought seemed important. Grace tried to hold it as they let themselves out of the house, but she was distracted when Legs escaped and flew past.

"Goodness."

"It's okay, Gram. She just wants to run."

"I don't like that dog."

"Why not?"

Grace was about to say something about cowering—her first and lasting impression of the beast—when she was caught up in the purpling that dusk brought to the grounds of the estate. It was beautiful—no, more than that—the word eluded her—but she did love this light. It simplified things, brought out basic forms. Basic forms were Divine.

Such was she now, less man-made, more basic. How she had prided herself on her acquired knowledge and the power it brought. Perhaps that had been her sin to be so punished, not the other. Did God love her more as she was reduced to His basics?

What was the expression? Pride goeth before the fall? Where had she heard that?

"Did *you* say it?" she asked, slipping her arm through Sophie's as they started slowly down the drive.

"Say what?"

"Something about pride?"

"I said that I took pride in being as independent as you."

Grace smiled. It was what she'd been trying to remember. "You take after me that way. Independent. Even as a child."

"Were you?"

"I never did what my parents told me to do."

"Were they strict?"

"Mostly, they were—" she searched for the word and,

when she found it, blessed the cold night air for clearing her head, "angry. Angry people. They didn't have much. My father felt—" again she searched, but the word didn't come, so she talked around it— "he felt like he wasn't much because he couldn't earn money. He felt it most when he looked at my mother. So he took it out on her."

"Beat her?"

"Goodness, no. There are other ways to be cruel."

They walked in silence. Then, because she felt safe holding to Sophie in the cocooning dusk, Grace reminisced. "He didn't talk much. When he did, he was usually drunk. He didn't say nice things. My mother got back at him by yelling at us."

"What did you do?"

"Oh, stayed out whole nights with my friends."

"Did you really?" Sophie asked, sounding delighted.

"We danced. We smoked. We drank."

"Gram. I'm shocked."

Grace gave her a nudge. "You are not."

"I *am*. I can't picture you smoking. Or *drinking*."

Grace took a deep breath. The reminiscing was suddenly less fun. "Yes, well, that can be tragic."

"Something happened, didn't it?"

Grace knew enough to realize she was skating on thin ice. "*You*," she said, scrambling to safety, "went into insulin shock."

"Not to me. What happened to *you*?"

"Why didn't you make sure you had food in your stomach?"

"Gram."

"You didn't look very happy at the table just now."

"And they say short-term memory is the first to go," Sophie teased. "Shows how much *they* know."

They walked on.

"It's an interesting thing, this disease," Grace said at last. "I have fewer thoughts. But the ones I have are important. I worry. About your mother. About you."

"Don't. You have enough else to worry about."

"What else? Nothing's as important as you."

Sophie's hold on her tightened. They kept walking, down the drive, away from the house, deeper into the night.

"What's wrong?" Grace asked after a time.

Sophie barked out a half laugh. "Today? Or every day?"

"Today." Grace saw a pale flash streak through the dark. She clung to Sophie. "What's that?"

"Legs."

"What?"

"Francine's dog. She won't hurt you."

Grace thought of another time, another dog. It had been a vicious thing, foaming at the mouth from the end of a chain on the Gruber brothers' front lawn. Walking—not running—past it in the dead of night had been the supreme test of courage. She and Johnny had done it together. They couldn't have been older than six.

"That dog had *killed*," Grace told Sophie lest she not understand the significance of what they'd done.

"Legs? No way. Legs would hide in a closet before she'd hurt a fly."

"That was what Johnny said, but only to make me feel better."

"Grampa never knew Legs."

Grace wasn't sure what she meant. John had nothing to do with the dog on the chain. Did he? Confused, she simply said, "Goodness."

They reached the end of the drive, made a wide turn, and started back. The house was an ornament, looking more gay than Grace felt.

"Things are changing," Sophie said. "It's hard."

Grace thought of her muffin. "You love change. You love adventure. I'm more rigid than you. You rebel against me."

"Maybe."

"You could hurt yourself."

"The thing is, you can take care all you want, and then something like this happens, and all the good care is worth shit—excuse me, Gram, but that says it best."

"Goodness" was all Grace could think to say, because she couldn't quite follow the thoughts, and then the dog began trotting along beside them. She couldn't quite see if it was foaming at the mouth.

"Look at you," Sophie said. "You've followed the rules—*more* than followed them—done everything right, and here you are."

"Here I am." Walking through the night again. Trying to ignore her fears again.

"Want to know a secret?" Sophie said in the kind of secret voice best friends used with each other. "I mean, I never thought I'd be admitting this to you, but if I could be anywhere in the world right now, I'd be here with you and Mom, celebrating Thanksgiving the way we always used to celebrate it." She paused. "Then I'd take off tomorrow and go do something wild."

In the spirit of the secret, Grace whispered an excited, "Wild?"

"Like motorcycle across the country. Or move to Paris and spend afternoons in little cafés talking literature. Or sign on with the CIA as a corporate spy."

Grace had a quick vision. "You and I could escape, go somewhere new, take new names, get new jobs." When Sophie didn't jump at the offer, she said, "I did it once. I could do it again." She thought about that as they walked on.

"Maybe," Sophie said gently. "We'll think about it."

Grace was thinking about it a short time later when they reached the house. When Sophie opened the door, a dog streaked right past them and inside. Grace jumped. "Goodness! What—get that dog *out*."

"It's only Legs, Gram. She's fine."

"Do you have any *idea* what filth these dogs carry? They're in every trash can in every alley." She stopped and darted nervous looks first around the front porch, then the foyer inside. Her mother was there. She was *sure* of it. That had been her voice just then.

But Francine was coming toward them with a smile on her face. "Here you are. We just finished. How was your walk?"

Grace left the answer to Sophie while other hands helped her off with her coat and her boots. She was concentrating on assisting those other hands when she looked up and caught her breath. There, coming toward her with a woman she didn't know, was a younger man.

Her voice was a wisp of air. "Johnny?"

"That's Davis," Jim said, slipping a comforting arm around her. "With Robin. We're going to play Trivial Pursuit in the den. You're my partner. No one knows arts and literature like you do."

Davis? Of course. How could she have made the mistake? Johnny was much younger. Still, there had been something about him that reminded her of Tyne Valley.

Francine mourned Grace that Thanksgiving Day. She mourned the woman who had been full of life and laughter, the one who had been competent and optimistic and energetic.

She mourned the woman who had made Dorian holidays
something unique. She mourned her mother, who had given
her life, love, and livelihood.

Grace had a dream that night. She was back in the barn with
the guys, with the friendly taunts and Scutch's stolen whiskey, and the bad, bad feeling she sometimes got when things
were getting out of hand. Sparrow was sitting on one side of
her, Johnny on the other, laughing as they passed the bottle
back and forth, and she took her share. There was no better
way to block out the bad.

Wolf circled around and slid down close behind her in a
way that left no doubt how the drink affected him.

"Leave her be," Johnny said.

"Christ, she feels good." He slid closer, thighs flanking
her hips.

"Leave her be," Johnny warned.

"Y'oughtta share. You ain't th'only one with needs."

"Get away from her, Wolf," Johnny threatened.

"Or what?"

The words hung in the air only as long as it took Johnny
to haul back and give Wolf a mighty shove. He landed on the
matted straw a distance away and didn't move. Didn't move.
Didn't move.

Grace awoke with a start. She was shivering, sweating,
panting, needing Wolf to get up off that ground, because
Johnny might have been the tool, but she was the cause, and
the bad, bad feeling was real—

She scrambled out of bed, opened the bedroom door, and
looked furtively around the sitting room. Thanks be to God,
it was empty. She dashed through, ran down the hall and the

stairs, and went all the way to the kitchen. For a minute she stood flattened to the door with a hand to her chest. Slowly her pulse steadied.

A kettle stood on the stove. Not knowing what else to do but make tea, she turned on the gas. Then she drew a chair back to the wall and sat down within full view of each entrance to the room.

She looked at the clock. She looked around the room, at her hands, at the clock again. She studied the back door. She listened for sounds from the hall.

She waited. She wasn't sure what for. But waiting seemed right.

Then something told her to move. Eyes alert, back to the wall, she left the kitchen and sidled down the hall, through the foyer, to her office. Once inside, she shut the door with a sigh of relief and sank into a chair. This room reassured her more than the others. It was filled with the trappings of a strong, powerful Grace. She looked slowly around, began to slowly relax.

Then the night exploded in sound and she bolted up.

There was an instant's total paralysis, a cross of panic and paranoia. Acting on instinct, she rushed from the office.

"Fire! Fire!" she yelled when she reached the foyer, because it seemed the thing to do. Then she followed faint ribbons of haze to the kitchen. Through the thicker haze there, she saw someone cooking.

"Goodness!" she cried loudly, to be heard over the noise. "Goodness! What are you *doing*?"

"Trying," shouted Francine, who was actually at the sink running water, "to stop this kettle from smoking."

"Were you making tea? At this hour? Goodness!" She covered her ears. "That *noise*!"

Even as she said it, she saw Sophie at the keypad by the

back door. The noise ended. Francine turned off the faucet, dropped the kettle in the sink, and opened the window. Sophie started the fan.

Neither of them said much, other than Francine's soft, "Come back to bed, Mom." But Grace had the sinking feeling that she had done something wrong.

Let loose in Grace's office, Robin was the proverbial kid in a candy store. There were books, diaries, and files. There were photographs of Grace with famous people, and fan letters from others. There were reams of notes that Grace had made under the guise of starting her book. There were also reams of reminders—who people were, how things worked, what was supposed to happen when—written and rewritten in sad testament to Grace's failing faith in herself.

Robin pored through everything in the days between Thanksgiving and Christmas. Sometimes she worked alone, either at Grace's desk or with papers spread over her own in a smaller office down the hall. Often she worked with Francine or Sophie.

They accepted her with startling ease, given past differences, usually finding more in common than not as they talked about Grace, about *The Confidante* past and present, about family dynamics. Often the talk grew personal.

Robin never made notes during those talks, simply listened and absorbed. In her wildest dreams, she couldn't have wished for as clear and revealing a glimpse of the Dorians.

Working with Grace was the challenge. Polite, even formal, she was good for only an hour at a stretch—and that, sitting poised and calm one minute, moving impatiently the next—before she tired of talk and left the room. She did have stories to tell about *The Confidante*, but she couldn't come up with them on her own. Robin had to find hints of them in notes and ask her, and then the talk lingered for days as Grace's attention ebbed and flowed.

They were wonderful stories—interesting, amusing, touching. Robin couldn't deny a respect for Grace's accomplishments. Nor could she deny a sympathy for her plight. The Grace she saw was the antithesis of the Grace she had resented—which didn't mean the resentment was gone, just that it was sometimes hard to sustain.

It was particularly true given the changes that working for Grace brought to Robin's life. Gone was the fevered pace that had driven her husband wild, the rush to try everything in an attempt to excel at something, the compulsion to do for and with the kids to assuage the guilt of her absence. Suddenly, now there was order, a defined workday around which to organize the rest of her life. There was flexibility when one of the kids needed her, and quality time with them even when they didn't. Writing Grace's book was the first prolonged activity she had done in years. She actually had time to *breeeeathe*.

All that, and psychological satisfaction. In being singled out from the crowd to chronicle Grace Dorian's life, she was succeeding—thanks to Grace—in ways that—because of Grace—she hadn't succeeded before.

She hadn't learned anything shocking yet. But Grace's early years remained to be plumbed.

One morning shortly before Christmas, Francine handed her a list. "Mother mentions these names. They're childhood friends. Does she mention any of them in her notes?"

Robin scanned the list. None of the names rang a bell. "What does she say about them?"

"Not much. When I ask her, she clams up. I thought you

might try slipping something in when you're talking with her. Subtly. Very subtly. She may open up."

"She may up and walk out."

"Nah. She likes you. She feels that you know *The Confidante*."

Robin was inordinately pleased. "Did she say that?"

"Uh-huh. So. What do you think? Do we have the makings of a book?"

"Oh, we do, and I've only been through two thirds of what's here, but there's catchy material. Like the man who hit Grace with an alienation of affection suit after she advised his wife to question late-night meetings, extended business trips, and odd credit card charges. Or, conversely, the wife who cited Grace as 'the other woman' when her husband divorced her because she couldn't match up to Grace. Then there's the couple who clipped every column of a sexual nature and made a scrapbook for teaching their daughter the facts of life. My mother did something like that."

"Made a *scrapbook*?"

"No. Just handed me the columns as they came. She didn't teach me about sex, herself. Like it was too bad to be discussed. Either too bad, or too good. I never did find out which. I never quite got up the courage to ask."

"I know how *that* is," Francine said. "Funny, we think we're different from our parents, that we can talk about anything. But we can't to them. They set the tone. Certainly about sex. Want to know my opinion? I think they did it plenty."

"Not my mother," Robin said with conviction.

"How do you know what she did while you and your brother were at school?"

"I don't. Still." Robin thought about it, shook her head. The image wouldn't fly.

"What was your dad like?"

"Henpecked. Docile, obedient. The only time he raised his voice was in defense of my mother when my brother or I dared speak out, he was that loyal."

"It's a good thing he died before she did. He might have been lost without her."

"Oh, he's still alive."

"I'm sorry. I thought—"

"It's all right. I haven't seen him since she died. She and I had unfinished business. Neither he nor I care to touch it."

"Sad," Francine said.

Robin thought so, too, with something of a new insight that had come of late. Illness was chipping away at Grace, making her less and less of the person she had been, taking her farther from Francine and Sophie each day—while Robin just let her healthy, lucid father go.

She supposed she should call him. But he hadn't worried about *her* emotional well-being, not even when she was getting divorced. She didn't know why she should worry about *him*.

Well, she did know why. But she wasn't sure she was forgiving enough to do it.

"Anyway," she said with a sigh, "what about John Dorian? Was he a toucher?"

"Only with Grace. He was kind and warm and sweet to the rest of us, but not touchy-feely."

"What was his family like?"

"Stiff, from what Grace said. She softened him up."

"They're all dead, I take it."

"Actually, there are still brothers and sisters. He was the oldest, so he inherited the farm, so to speak. The others scattered. There were hard feelings. He wouldn't talk about them."

"Feelings, or family?"

"Either. I always asked. I was desperate for relatives on his side, since there weren't any on Grace's. At least—" she hesitated, looking at Robin with something akin to a cry for help—"there didn't *seem* to be any on Grace's."

Robin felt a stirring inside. If Grace wouldn't talk, there had to be others who would. *The Real Grace Dorian.* It was her ticket to fame. "I don't have access to her personal files, but you do. There has to be a birth certificate somewhere. Is there a safe-deposit box?"

"Yes. Her lawyer has the key. But he would never give it to me without permission from her. Not while she's still at all lucid."

Robin took another tack. "What about a close friend? Someone she confides in? Jim O'Neill?"

"He is her best friend, all right. Loyal as the day is long. But forget it. He won't betray her."

"How long have they known each other?"

"For as long as I can remember."

"Would you mind if I talk with him?"

"No. But he won't tell you anything."

"What about trying to contact your father's siblings?"

"Could be hard. Last I heard, they were strewn along the West Coast. I've asked Grace about them, but she has nothing to say. Dorian isn't an unusual name. I wouldn't know where to begin."

"Weren't they at his funeral?"

Francine slowly shook her head. "I'd have called them if Grace hadn't been so upset. But she was vehement. She didn't want them there. When it was time to clean out Dad's office, she did the packing herself. If there were papers to do with his family, they're with the rest in the file room, safely sealed." She paused. "I never had a reason to break the seal. Or the courage."

Robin was thinking that Grace was probably past the point of noticing when Francine said a soft, "I could do it now, I suppose. There may be an address book. It'd give us a place to start."

Francine found the address book that night, but she didn't immediately tell Robin. Something held her back.

"I keep asking myself what it is," she told Davis. She hadn't planned on telling him, either, but there was something about the intimacy of priming bathroom walls in the aftermath of sharing a hot shower in the aftermath of sex. What was on her mind was on her tongue.

She was on her knees, working her brush along the baseboard in the even strokes Davis had taught. "I always hated that we had no relationship with his siblings. These are my aunts and uncles. I met them once, purely by accident. I was with Dad in New York. We said hello, then they parted ways, and that was that."

"What caused the rift?"

"Jealousy, greed, the usual things that tear families apart. Dad was the oldest. The others couldn't abide by his inheriting the house and the mill. I don't even know that the four are still alive. But there must be cousins, too. I've always wanted cousins." She sat back on her heels. "So why am I guarding that address book like it's Pandora's box?"

"Because it may be," Davis said, typically blunt. "Have you looked inside? Are the addresses there?"

"Yes. But they're old. They may be dead ends."

"All four? Not likely. You'll connect with one of them. Are you making the calls?"

"Robin would do it in a minute, she's that eager. But it's

my job, don't you think? If they hang up in my face—" her greatest fear—"Robin can take over." She put brush to wood distractedly.

Davis set his brush across the top of the can and sat on the floor. "What's the worst that can happen?"

"If not a hang-up?" Francine was back on her heels again. "A diatribe against John, then against Grace, then against me." She shot him a droll look. "It's the old fear of rejection."

He shifted until they were side by side. "Anyone who rejects you isn't worth shit." He took the brush from her hand and set it aside.

"Yeah, well," she smiled, "you're biased."

Slipping a large hand around her thigh, he tugged her closer. In a softer voice, eyes touching her mouth, he said, "I'll miss you over Christmas."

"You will not. You're going home."

"There's no one in Tyne Valley like you. Who'll I love?"

"Love someone else, and we're through."

"Ahh. Ultimatums. What a turn-on."

"Davis."

"Are you sure you won't come home with me?"

"I can't go north if I'm going south."

"The trip's on, then?"

Francine nodded. "I got confirmation today. We have a private jet to St. Bart's, a private villa, private beach, private cook. With a little luck we'll forget it's the holiday."

"What does Grace say?"

"Only that she wishes Jim could come. He can't, of course, not at Christmas. But everything else about the trip will be controlled so that nothing can go wrong." She studied his face. The features were as rough-hewn as ever, but gentler now, so very close, and concerned. "Can they?"

"They shouldn't. Grace may be uneasy for the first day, but after that, in a private space with no strangers around, she'll be fine. The change of scenery will be good for you and Sophie."

"It's just that Thanksgiving was so hard. To have some things stay the same and others not . . ." It had been hell, wearing a smile when she wanted to cry. She wasn't repeating the torment. "I'd rather do something entirely different. We'll stay down there through New Year's and come back refreshed. How's that for optimism?"

"Not bad," he said, and whispered a kiss on her lips, one on her cheek, one on her chin.

She opened her mouth to catch his at the next pass, but he stayed just out of reach. So she closed her eyes and simply enjoyed the anticipation.

It struck her then that pouring her heart out to Davis didn't have to do with the intimacy of the bathroom, but with Davis himself. He was knowledgeable and accessible, brainy and brawny, caring and fun. And he talked dirty in bed.

She liked that a lot.

Seventeen

I am an optimist. I dream by day and sleep by night.
—Francine Dorian, from *The Confidante*

Back in New York after ten days on St. Bart's, Sophie knew she looked good. She wore layers of white, added one by one as the plane winged north, until she was bundled like a snow bunny, but rested and tanned. Not even the cold air that hit her when she left the shelter of the terminal to find Gus could dampen her spirits. She saw him and waved, then ran back for Francine and Grace. When they were tucked inside the car, she went to the trunk, where Gus was stowing their bags, and gave him a quick hug. "How've you been?"

He didn't smile. "Not as good as you." He leaned into the trunk to rearrange things. His voice came back, accusatory. "You've been on the beach."

She wondered where he had thought she would be, spending ten days on a Caribbean island. "Beach, pool—the weather was perfect. It's a great place."

"I'll bet."

"How was the Valley?" she asked, hoping to lighten him up. He had spent Christmas back home.

"Beats me," he said. "I stayed drunk."

"Gus, you didn't."

He shot her a look before straightening. "I told you I would, if you left me alone."

"Oh, no, don't blame it on me," she said, but he was slamming the trunk and opening the back door in proper chauffeur mode.

Sophie wasn't being dragged down from her Caribbean high. With a smirk, she walked past him, opened the front door, and slid in. She turned so that she would be facing him, draped an arm over the seat back, and said to the two behind, "Should I turn up the heat?"

Grace looked uncertain in her disoriented way.

Francine looked amused behind the huge aviators she had worn through most of the trip. "It's warm enough, thank you."

"Looking forward to getting home, Gram?"

Grace didn't answer. She was frowning at the window.

"Gram?"

Gus pulled out into the traffic. "Did you enjoy your vacation, Ms. Dorian?" he asked the rearview mirror.

"She did," Francine answered for Grace. "We all did."

Sophie certainly had. She hadn't suffered any of Thanksgiving's sadness, any painful flashbacks to past holiday celebrations. The setting had been too different for comparison.

"So," Gus asked in a private little rumble, "what else d'ya do beside sit in the sun?"

"Walked the beach. Gram liked that. It was isolated, peaceful."

"Sounds boring as hell."

"It was very romantic." She couldn't resist the dig. He deserved it, trying to rain on her parade. "There were little shops and cafés, open places to sit and talk with people."

"*She* talked with people?" he murmured with a dubious glance at the mirror.

"Several times." Grace had had her moments as a sweet social thing. "She was fine, as long as we stayed close."

"Boring as hell," Gus muttered.

"It wasn't boring at all. It was nice being with her that way. Besides," Sophie goaded, "I got out at night. Mom and I took turns staying with Grace. There was dancing at a little place on the water. It was *very* romantic."

His profile hardened.

Satisfied, she turned full face to the windshield and ignored him. He wasn't killing *her* good spirits when they had been so long in coming. For years, family had been a mixed blessing to her, a source of both pride and oppression. Incredible, perhaps cruel to say, but the oppression was lifting.

How to explain it? Yes, she missed those parts of the old Grace she loved, but she sure didn't miss the parts she hated. Times were changing. St. Bart's had shown her that the new wasn't necessarily worse.

"You met someone, didn't you," Gus grumbled a while later.

She looked at him in surprise. "What makes you say that?"

"You're smug."

"I'm just sitting here thinking. I had a nice vacation. I'm feeling good about it."

"Who is he?"

Sophie eased back against the door for a longer view of Gus. He wasn't much taller than she, but he had a broad chest, lean hips, and strong hands. He was well made, and terribly insecure.

Was it her life's mission to stroke his ego? No way, José.

"He's French, actually," she answered. "Blond hair, very tall. He's a businessman. Flies around in his corporate jet."

"Did you sleep with him?"

Sophie glanced back, caught Francine's aviator eye, and winked. "I'm not answering that question. My mother is listening to this conversation." Francine knew there hadn't been any Frenchman. But Sophie wasn't telling Gus.

He didn't speak to her again until they arrived home, until the car had been unloaded and the appropriate luggage divvied up. Sophie was in her den, listening to the messages on her answering machine, when he set her bags in the bedroom and leaned against the doorjamb.

"You gonna tell me?" he asked.

She didn't play dumb. "Relax. I didn't *sleep* with him."

"But you wanted to, didn't you."

"I honestly wasn't thinking about it."

Gus gave her a moment's glittering stare, then made a sputtering sound, straightened, and strode toward the door. "If you weren't thinking about it, baby, he didn't have it."

"Whoa," she called, stopping him. "What's that supposed to mean? Wake up and smell the roses, Gus. Sex isn't everything."

He stood stock-still with his back to her. "Could'a fooled me, the way you go for it. If there's more to life, you wouldn't know."

"Not with *you*," she shot back. "That's for sure."

Slowly he turned. She could have sworn she saw a glint of hurt on his face, before anger masked it. "You complaining?"

She thought about that for a minute. Gus wasn't her

future, had never even been in the running. Not in *her* mind, at least. If he had other ideas, it was time—hadn't Francine said it a while back?—time she set him straight.

The question, as her defiance faded, was how to do it without causing more hurt. She cared for him on some level, felt compassion, physical attraction, maybe even loyalty.

"Where are you going?" she asked.

He made a show of looking front, back, to the side. "I don't look to be goin' anywhere."

"In life. What do you want?"

"Ah, Christ." He pulled his cap off and ran a hand through his hair. "What kind of question's that?"

"A valid one. Don't you ever ask it?"

"Not if I can help it."

"Maybe you should."

"Yeah? Why?"

"Because you don't have a goal. People need goals."

"What's yours?"

"Staying healthy. Being successful at work."

He snorted. "Like you really need more money."

"Not for the money. For the self-respect. Where's yours?"

He looked her straight in the eye. "Mine is down at Grady's."

"A bar. That's great."

"Don't knock it. It keeps me happy."

"No. It keeps you drunk. There's a difference."

"Could've fooled me."

"Well," she said with a long inhalation, "maybe that's where we part ways."

"Are you telling me to get lost?"

"I'm telling you to *think*. Getting plastered doesn't solve anything. It doesn't get you ahead in this world."

"And what will?" he asked pointedly. "I'm no scholar. The only reason I got a high school diploma was because the principal had the hots for me. Shocked? Don't be. It happens all the time."

"You slept with the *principal*?"

"Slept? Not likely. We did it on the desk in her office. I got the diploma but not much else—no brains, no money, no luck. So where am I supposed to go? What do *you* think I should want in life?"

Sophie could have spouted off her other friends' goals, but Gus wasn't like them. "It's what you want, not me. You have to be the one to decide. But you can't do it if you're drunk all the time."

He pursed his lips. Insolent eyes traveled down her body, lingering at her breasts, then her crotch, before rising again. He drew himself up and stuck the cap on his head. "Is that all, ma'am?"

"Gus—" she protested, wanting him to listen and hear, but he had turned and was on his way.

"I'm on duty," he called. "Want to talk more, come to my place tonight. We'll talk after."

"You're back!" Davis said.

Francine started smiling. "Uh-huh. About an hour ago."

"You sound pleased. Is that because the trip was great, or because you're relieved to be home?"

"Both. We had a great time, but it's good to be home." And very good to hear his voice. She hadn't realized she had missed it so, until then. "Happy New Year."

"Same to you. How's Grace?"

"Right now? In her glory. Father Jim just arrived. She did well, Davis. We took your advice and stayed close to the villa for the first few days. Then we started taking her out for an hour or two, just walking through the shops. As long as one of us was beside her, she was fine. And no," she said before he could, "I'm not kidding myself into thinking she's improving. We're improving in handling her. That's all."

"Good girl. Did you get any rest?"

"Actually, yes. Sophie and I took turns sitting with her, and she liked the cook, so we even got out alone together."

"Are you tanned?"

"Respectably so."

"All over?"

Francine's smile turned coy. She said not a word.

"I know about these French islands," Davis said. "Topless, at the very least."

"We had our own private beach."

"Nude. Shit. What are you doing now?"

Innocently, she said, "Unpacking."

"Can I come over? I want to show you something."

"You got a tattoo." She ribbed him about it a lot, said that a man with his past *had* to have a tattoo.

"No. A horse. Do you ride?"

A horse? "Uh, I have. But not for years."

"Put on jeans. And dress warm."

"Davis, it's the middle of winter!"

"That's the best time. See you soon."

"Davis? Davis!" She heard a dial tone, looked at the phone, hung up.

A horse?

With barely a glance at the mess on her bed, she pulled jeans, a turtleneck, and a heavy sweater from the dresser. She tugged on wool socks and looked out the window. The light was fading fast.

A horse? In the middle of winter? In the *dark*?

Airborne earlier, she had had blue moments thinking of the reality that awaited at home, but there was nothing blue about this image. It was bright red.

She twisted into the sweater, studied herself in the mirror, thought she looked fat. So she hauled it off and put on a less bulky one. Then she joined Grace and Father Jim in the parlor.

"Do you know anything about Davis and a horse?" she asked Jim.

He grinned. "Only that he used to muck out stalls for local farmers as punishment for a multitude of sins. So he's got a horse of his own now, does he?"

Francine didn't actually know that. "Maybe it's borrowed. He's coming over."

"He doesn't need to see me," Grace protested, holding tight to Jim's hand. "I'm perfectly well."

Ever so gently, he stroked her cheek. "Better than well. Your mother looks wonderful, Francine. Something about the islands agreed with her. You've been in the sun, Grace."

Grace blushed. "I was careful. A lady doesn't tan, you know. But the sun was divine. I couldn't resist coming out from under that parasol every once in a while."

Francine savored the image. It was right out of a picture book. Actually, it was right out of any one of several little art stores they had visited on St. Bart's. Seurat, she believed.

The doorbell rang. She was halfway into the hall when she realized that Grace hadn't complained about her seeing Davis. Self-absorbed, as AD sufferers often were, she only feared he was coming to see *her*.

Nonetheless grateful not to be made to feel guilty, Francine opened the door. One look at him, and her insides seemed to fall away. She put a hand to her chest and stepped back.

"Hi ya," Davis said, grinning. "All set?"

His cheeks were red, his breath white, his scarf neon green, all that, plus a Stetson, a long leather duster, and boots, and the whole of him dusted with snow. Before she could tell him how spectacular he looked, he tugged up the hem of his jeans to show off intricately tooled boots. "These are the real thing. Aren't they wild?"

"Where did you *find* them?"

"Took some looking." He turned and went down the steps. There, tethered to Grace's very proper, very dignified, very polished brass lamppost, was the horse. Horse, post, everything in sight was covered with a fine dusting of the snow that continued to fall.

Davis took something from behind the saddle. By the time he had returned to the door he was holding open a leather duster to match his. Entranced, Francine slid in one arm, then the other. He fastened the buttons from behind, slipped his arms around her waist, and buried his face in her neck. The kiss he put there was loud, wet, and cold. His mouth remained when the kiss was done, warmth galore and humor in his voice.

"Got a hat for you on the saddle horn, but you need your own boots. Sorry. Wool socks alone won't cut it."

Francine didn't rush to leave him. Being in his arms felt like being home, only a different home it was from the one she had known all her life. This one was carefree and unstructured, even slightly naughty. It promised the unexpected.

She layered her arms over his and said to his cold cheek, "We're really going riding? Now? Where'd you get the horse? You didn't ride over here all the way from your place. Did you? How *could* you? It's ten minutes in a car. That has to be thirty, no, *forty* minutes on a horse. At *least*. I have to warn

you, Davis, the last time I went riding, I fell head over heels
into a tomato patch and broke my coccyx. Have you forgotten who you're dealing with?"

He was laughing against her neck. "Nope. But I'm doing
the riding. All you have to do is hold on. Trust me to keep
you safe?"

"Yes."

"Then go get some boots. And mittens, and a scarf. I'll
answer your questions once we're aboard."

The horse was his, all right. It was from Tyne Valley. He had
bought it several years before from a friend of his sister's
who needed the money. It wasn't a purebred, or even a
pretty horse, though Francine would have been hard-pressed
to notice minor things like that when the whole of the picture was so provocative. The horse was large and gentle, and
it could run when prodded. Mostly, it trotted along at a
comfortable pace.

Francine sat snug behind Davis with her arms hugging his
waist. Once the house disappeared, the only light came
from the faint blue of the snow, the only noise from its whispering fall and the muffled beat of the horse's hooves on the
blanketed shoulder of the road.

Davis guided the horse easily, the tug of a rein here, the
nudge of a knee there. She might have known he would be
good at this, too. Being fallible, she found it infuriating. Being female, she found it exquisitely appealing.

They went down the road a bit before taking a path into
the woods. Francine wanted to ask him dozens of things—
about the horse, about his visit to the Valley, about that
multitude of sins Father Jim mentioned—but she didn't
voice one. She was too engrossed in the beauty of the winter

woods, the rhythm of the horse, the slip of her thighs against Davis's flanks, the warmth of his back.

He pulled up when they reached the river. She put her cheek to the side of his shoulder, so that she, too, could see. The river was frozen, snow-covered, save for patchy trickles that sang softly through the night.

Loath to impose her voice on that melody, she didn't speak. Davis must have felt the same, because for the longest time he just sat there holding her hands on his middle. Then he tugged one gently. "Come on in front."

Game for most anything, though not without the occasional gasp and squeal, she let herself be guided—an arm around him, then a leg, then her torso and hips—until she faced him in the saddle. He slipped a hand under her bottom, drawing her onto what little lap he had with his legs straddling the horse. By the time she was settled to his satisfaction, it wasn't such a little lap, a fact that she acknowledged with a feline smile.

"Warm enough?" he asked, tipping her hat back so that he could see her easily.

She slipped her arms around his waist. "On your horse? Always."

He grinned.

"So," she said, "where do you keep it, when you're not taking it out for me?"

"Excuse me?" he asked with barely suppressed mirth.

"Your *horse*," she specified primly.

"My horse. Uh, it's a she, by the way. I'm stabling her at Paley's. The place she was staying in the Valley is on the market. I figured it was only a matter of time before I'd have to come get her, and since I was already up there, and since I knew Paley had space down here, I just rented a trailer and did it."

"How was your family, or shouldn't I ask?"

He sobered fast. "You can ask. They're the same. Older and shabbier, just like the town. I've got a new grandnephew."

"*Grand*nephew. You're not old enough to have a *grand* anything."

He gave her a lopsided grin. "Oh, I am. So are you."

"No. I'm too young, too."

"Sophie's not too young to have a child."

"She is. Times have changed."

He sighed. "Not in Tyne Valley. They fall farther behind with each kid, still they have them, and who are we to say they shouldn't? But things are bleak up there."

"How's your dad?"

"Failing. Emphysema, cirrhosis of the liver, probably a dozen other things, but he won't see a doctor, won't even let me treat him. I leave pills. He throws them out."

"I'm sorry. That must be frustrating."

"He's a stubborn old goat," Davis muttered in a way that said it was frustrating indeed. "I took them all out to a charming old inn for Christmas dinner. They loved it. Beyond that, well, there isn't a whole hell of a lot to say, once we get done with catching up on who's where, doing what. I keep thinking they'll ask about my work, but they never do. I guess it's so far away from their world that they don't know where to begin. Either that, or they're just not interested. Anyway, we didn't have much time to talk. I headed back here the day after Christmas."

"But I thought you were staying the week!" Francine cried. She felt terrible, having lounged so indulgently in the sun while he was alone in the cold.

He grimaced. "Too awkward. They don't know what to do with me, any more'n I know what to do with them."

She raised her arms to his neck. "I'm sorry. Being with family means the world to me. I wish you had that, too."

"Maybe some day," he said lightly, and gave her a squeeze. "I missed you. Gimme a kiss." He ducked his head and took a deep one. Tugging off his gloves, he pushed his hands into her coat, under her arms, up to her shoulders. Caressing them, he kissed her again.

Francine felt the same bottoming-out, belly-deep shock she always felt when he kissed her. It swept her up and took her away, wiped her mind clean of all else but Davis, made her hungry, no, *starved* for totality.

His voice was uneven when he raised his head. "Damn, you do that good. You get me going, Frannie."

"Doesn't take much," she breathed. Her insides ached. She moved against him to ease it.

He grunted. "Do that again."

But that would have been cruel, given the limitations of the setting. "Maybe I'd better not."

"Do it again," he commanded as he caught her chin in his hand, then her lips with his mouth. When his tongue thrust inside it, he had his wish. Quite helplessly, she arched against him.

He grinned against her mouth. "Missed me, too, did you?"

"No, I did not." Served him right, goading her. "I didn't think about this once."

"Not once?"

"Well, maybe once." She found his belt and released the buckle.

"What are you doing?"

"Warming up." She slipped her hands inside jeans and briefs. His flesh was hot enough to satisfy her every wish.

"Oooh, baby. You do *that* good."

"Pure survival," she remarked, but there was an element of desperation in it. She wanted more than groping on horseback. "It's snowing, Davis."

He made a wanting sound and stilled her hands. Then, with a shaky breath, he removed them and repaired his clothes. He turned her to face front, gently reined the horse around, and headed home.

At the lamppost again, he slipped to the ground and helped her down, so that they stood middle to middle. "I made a New Year's resolution."

"Tell me."

"I'm gonna sleep with you someday soon."

She tried not to smile. "Haven't you done that?"

"Nope. Never woke up beside you. Not in the morning, but that's what I want."

"I look awful in the morning."

"So do I. That's not the point."

She knew it wasn't. But she didn't know what to say. Spending the night with Davis—not just making love, but spending the whole night with him and waking up to slow kisses, coffee, the morning paper—that was something else. It was serious. Maybe too much so.

"Anyway," he eased the anticipation by saying, "there's no rush. In the meantime, want to go to a hockey game?"

That was a novel thought. "I've never been to one. Are we talking Madison Square Garden?"

"No. The Hotchkiss School. Docs versus jocks."

"*You're* playing?" she asked excitedly. "Which are you, doc or jock?"

"Doc."

"But you played hockey in college."

He grinned his crooked grin. "The jocks don't know that. As far as they're concerned, I score goals by accident."

"That's dishonest."

"Yup. Dishonesty's good for the soul, sometimes. And for the wallet. Loser pays for dinner. You're invited for that, too. The game's this Sunday at two. I'd have to pick you up by one. Can you get someone to stay with Grace?"

Francine couldn't help but think of life's little reversals. Once upon a time, she had asked Grace to stay with Sophie. Now, she asked Sophie to stay with Grace.

Sophie had planned to meet friends in the city on Saturday morning and return on Sunday. She assured Francine that she could be back by one.

That settled, Francine agonized over what to wear. After poring through her closet three times, trying on and rejecting outfit after outfit, turning on a televised game to see what people *did* wear watching hockey, she decided she needed something new.

Friday night she went shopping. Sophie, who had witnessed the drama in her closet, all but kicked her out of the house. She had no plans herself, she said. She wanted to be fresh for the next day with her friends, she said. She would be with Grace before and after Father Jim, she said.

So Francine went.

Eighteen

Take a lesson from dance. In a well-choreographed piece, the strategically timed back step is as critical as those steps that move the dancer ahead.
—GRACE DORIAN, from *The Confidante*

Sophie had dinner with Grace, just the two of them sitting at right angles to each other at one end of the long dining-room table. She would have preferred a more casual dinner in the kitchen, where slips like salad dressing ladled on baked potatoes and sole eaten with a spoon weren't so blatant. But dinner was a ritual. Until the day Grace forgot that, it would be served in the dining room.

Not so long ago, Sophie would have resented this rigidity, but it was hard to sustain resentment now. Not so long ago, she would have loved Grace's gaffes, but the joy of the fray was gone. Where once Grace had controlled and directed the dinner discussion, now Sophie scrambled to keep the conversation flowing so that Grace would be as comfortable as possible. It was sad, always sad, the forgotten words, the wandering mind, the new quirks. At these times, Sophie found herself wanting the old Grace back.

Grace wandered away from the table even before her precious fruit tart was served. She needed to freshen up, she said, needed to get ready for Father Jim's arrival. Sophie was able to convince her that her blue evening gown was too dressy and finally sold her on a simpler skirt and blouse—though not before Grace accused her of trying to sabotage her relationship with Jim.

Sad, always sad. This wasn't the Grace she knew.

She was relieved when Father Jim arrived. He kissed Grace's cheek and folded her arm firmly in his.

Back in the south wing, Sophie changed into spandex. She checked her sugar levels, spent twenty minutes on the StairMaster, twenty on the treadmill, did another check. After mopping her face and neck, she collapsed in a chair and picked up the phone.

She was still talking an hour and a half later when Gus appeared at the door. He was wearing torn jeans and a black jacket. His hair was disheveled, his expression dark. His hands were balled in his pockets.

Sensing trouble, she ended her conversation. "What's up?" she asked him.

"Where you been?"

She gave him a curious look. "Did we have plans?"

"I been waiting for you all fuckin' week."

He had been drinking. She could see it, hear it, a telltale recklessness, a vague wildness. "Gus," she warned.

He advanced on her, hitching his chin toward the phone. "Who was that?"

"Samantha."

"Was it the guy from last week?"

"I said, it was Samantha. And before her, Julie, and Kate."

"Sure." He stood over her, seeming implacable. "Who was it?"

"Gus," she protested, trying to laugh, but uncomfortable now. "What is your *problem*?"

He answered by looking her up and down. By the time his eyes returned to her face, they were darker than ever. He bent over her, hands on the arms of her chair. "My problem's my dick. It needs a workout."

"Gus." She sighed and looked away.

"Gus, what? Gus, I want it? Gus, I need it? Gus, give it to me quick?"

"Gus, not now!" she fired back, meeting his eyes in warning.

He shot her a livid look. Before she could grasp his intent, he hauled her from the chair and dragged her toward the bedroom, muttering, "'Gus, not now' my foot. You'll get it now, baby, you'll get it good."

Furious, Sophie pulled back for all she was worth, but he was stronger. "Cut it out, Gus! You're drunk. You don't want this."

"Been wantin' it all week," he growled, throwing her on the bed, following her down to pin her there with an arm across her throat. She clawed at the arm and tried to buck him off, but he simply immobilized one of her legs and used the kicking of the other to his advantage in peeling down her pants.

"Get off me!" she cried, suddenly frightened. She and Gus had played rough together, but this wasn't playing. There was nothing fun about the hands that tore at her clothes, nothing arousing about the body holding hers down with brute force. Try as she might, she couldn't squirm free. "Stop! Christ, Gus, *stop*!"

He was breathing hard, not from exertion but arousal, fully atop her now with his jacket open to bare his chest and his pants opening fast.

"Get *off* me," she gasped. "Get off me, *get off me.*" She pushed and pushed to no avail, scratched him until he yelped, but, he only came back more brutally, yanking up her top, then ramming into her.

She screamed once, and again, as terrified by the pain as by helplessness and fear, but the hammering of his hips didn't cease. He was grunting with the force of each thrust, going faster and harder.

"*No-ooo!*" she yelled, "*no-ooo!*" but with decreasing force when the arm at her throat tightened, and then she was clutching at that arm, struggling for air, fighting suffocation along with the ripping inside and the awful, awful realization that, with little more than the twist of his arm, Gus had the power to end her life, and *she couldn't stop him.*

She was in a raw panic, feeling dizzy, even drifting in and out of consciousness when a voice that wasn't Gus's penetrated.

"What the bloody devil—"

Gus was bodily hauled off her.

"*What the bloody devil do you think you're doing—*"

Gulping horribly for air, she rolled to the side, coiled into a tight ball, and covered her head against the angry sounds that came from behind her, and then she was crying, hearing even less, gasping still, while she pressed her thighs together against the pain and tried to make herself invisible, impenetrable, invulnerable. When it didn't work, she scrunched up even tighter.

Then the comforter was being wrapped around her, and Father Jim was crooning a shaken, "It's all right now, sweetheart, he's gone, he won't hurt you again." He stroked her hair. "You're safe, shhhhh, you're safe now, shhhhh, he's gone, there now, there now."

She couldn't stop gasping, couldn't stop crying. With infinite care, he gathered her up and held her, comforter and all, in his arms. He continued his soft crooning, and incredibly, when a male voice and male hands should have frightened her more, she felt safe. Father Jim was Father Jim, always kind, her guardian angel. His voice was achingly gentle, his holding of her a balm, not a bond.

"I had no idea he'd do that, no idea, or I'd never have let him step foot in this house," he swore.

She wept more softly now. "Not your fault."

"I knew he had a drinking problem. And I knew he was involved with you. I should've known the combination would mean trouble."

Her tears yielded to low, hiccoughing sounds. "*My* involvement. *My* fault. I taunted him, then avoided him. He wanted revenge."

"Holy Mother, he took it. Are you hurt, child?"

"*Yes.*" She started crying again.

He held her quietly for another little while. "I think we should go to the hospital."

"No!" Hospitals meant strange, cold, probing hands where she hurt most. She wasn't going there. The only place she was going was somewhere to lick her wounds and hide. But where? "What if he comes again?" she cried. "He can walk right in here, he has a key, he has keys to everything."

"We'll change the locks in the morning. I fired him, Sophie. He won't be back. But I want you to see a doctor. There are things they do in—in cases like this."

It was a minute before Sophie realized what he meant. Then she shook her head, long, sure movements back and forth. "No. No doctor. No police."

"He raped you."

Back and forth, sure movements. "I won't press charges."

"He was *strangling* you. That's attempted *murder.*"

"I can't."

"He has to be punished. He had no right—"

"I *can't,*" she wailed, and began to weep again. How to explain that beyond the fear and the pain, that beyond the anger, was guilt, and that beyond the guilt was, even now, something gentler? She and Gus had been lovers for many months. He might be disturbed and lost, he might drink too much, but he wasn't evil.

"Jim?" came Grace's call, distant at first, then closer. "Jim? Jim, where are you? Ahhh, *here* you are. But—what are you doing? Who's that—what—Claire?" Her voice rose. "What is going on? What terrible, terrible, terrible, terrible? Johnny? Johnny! What are you on this bed? Goodness. Goodness."

"It's all right, Grace," Jim said. "Sophie's just had an upset."

Grace's voice jumped even higher. "I should have known! It was just a—a—just time! I *should* have, should have known!"

"Grace, please. Why don't you go back into the other room—"

"And leave you—her?" she cried. "I'll—no—no! Who? Who *is* that? Goodness, goodness! Johnny! You *know* who she is—"

"Who who is?" Francine's voice joined in, clearer as she entered the room. "Why are you shouting, Grace? Jim? What happened?" There was a pause, then a frightened, "Sophie?"

"Claire, Claire, Claire," Grace was crying.

"Sophie's had an upset," Jim told Francine. "If you can come take her, I'll take Grace."

It was only when he started to shift her into Francine's

arms, when Francine was whisper close, that he told her what had happened. Francine gasped, whimpered, clutched Sophie to her as Jim led a belligerent Grace from the room.

"I'm okay," Sophie murmured from the comforter's folds.

Francine held her convulsively tight. "My God. *Rape*."

"He was drunk."

"That doesn't excuse it! It's okay, baby, okay, you'll be fine." She rocked her. "What happened? Did it happen *here*? Don't talk about it if you don't want to."

Sophie was still, not because she didn't want to talk but because she was too busy absorbing the safety that Francine's arms conveyed.

After a time, Francine asked a soft, "Did he hit you?"

"No. Just held me down. Cut off my air." The memory made her shiver. "I thought he was going to kill me."

Francine chafed her back through the comforter. After another while, she said, "Are you bleeding?"

"I don't know."

"I'm taking you to the hospital."

"No! I'm not going there!"

"Then Davis. I'll get Davis here."

"No!"

"I shouldn't have gone out. If I'd been here, this wouldn't have happened. But I wanted new jeans, stupid new jeans—"

"It would've happened anyway," Sophie cried, "if not tonight, another night. It was coming. I should have seen it."

Francine's arms tightened. Incredibly, she started to cry.

"Don't, Mom."

"I can't help it." She sniffled and said brokenly, "I want you to see a doctor."

But all Sophie wanted was a hot bath. *When* she felt like moving, which she didn't yet. For one thing, she was cold, shivering with each flashback to the terror of imminent death. For another, she was afraid to unwrap the comforter, afraid to look at the damage, afraid that pieces of herself would spill out onto the bed. Her body had moved from painful to sore—throat, chest, thighs, and between—but she didn't trust movement not to stir up more pain.

"If you take a bath," Francine coaxed, "you'll wash the evidence away. Even if you don't press charges, if the hospital has a record of what happened, it'll help keep him away from you. This was not your fault, Sophie."

"I taunted him."

"Taunting does not justify rape. You did nothing to deserve what he did." She hugged Sophie tighter, rocked faster. "How do you feel now?"

"Shaky."

"Do you need a shot?"

"No."

"Are you sure?"

Sophie knew that emotional upset could cause hyperglycemia, but she felt none of the symptoms—no fever, no nausea, no thirst. If anything, shakiness was a sign of *low* blood sugar. She was convinced hers was due to terror alone.

"Let me get you a drink," Francine said, and Sophie didn't have the heart to stop her. She knew not to hope for anything potent. Orange juice was what she expected; orange juice was what she got. She sipped it slowly.

"Better?" Francine asked when she was done, taking the glass from her, then finger-combing the hair back from her face.

Sophie nodded. One intact arm was out of the comforter. She needed to see if the rest was intact, needed to wash it clean and make it her own again. "I'd like a bath now."

"Are you sure?"

She was very sure. She wasn't pressing charges, wasn't

making something public out of a private ordeal, wasn't reliving one single minute more than she had to of what had happened that night.

"It'd be different if I didn't know him," she tried to explain, "but this was Gus. He wasn't really trying to kill me. He was just angry and stinking drunk—" She gave a single sob. No, he hadn't been trying to kill her, but he might have done it anyway, and then she'd have been dead, and he'd have been a murderer, and God knew what the punishment would have been for that. "A nightmare. *Nightmare*. Okay, so he's a bastard. But now he's out of a job, fired, gone. He's losing his housing and his income. What'll he do?"

"You feel *sorry* for him?"

She tried to decide. "I feel—something."

"Not love," Francine declared.

"No. Not love. Maybe empathy. We were both a little lost. And familiarity. We were lovers. He could be surly, but he never lifted a hand before. I liked parts of Gus."

"Not me. I could kill him."

Sophie actually smiled. "You're my mother. That's what you're supposed to want to do."

"You, too, after what he did. Where's my rabid rebel?"

She sighed, suddenly tired. "Turning realist. If I go to the hospital, if they get their evidence and call the police, and if one person leaks something to the press—can you see the headlines? Can you hear the phone calls? Tabloids all over the country—'Dorian Granddaughter Raped by Chauffeur.' Then, once they've sniffed around a little—'Dorian Rape Caps Passionate Love Affair with Chauffeur.'"

It wasn't worth it. Sophie had never been one to capitalize on the Dorian name. Grace had been the only audience she had craved. She had never asked for media attention, had never sought the limelight. To be thrust into it in this way would be more cruel a violation than the other.

Yes, she was angry—and frightened by her powerlessness—and stunned by the realization that her control of her life was limited. She was also sad. Her relationship with Gus had been doomed from the start, but she hadn't thought it would end quite this way. So there was that loss. But more. The loss of innocence. Gone was a sense of immunity. Gone was the illusion that she could thumb her nose at whatever she wanted and get away scot-free. She was responsible for her actions. Just like the rest of the world.

While Sophie took a bath, Francine stripped the bed, neatened everything in sight, and tried not to think of the purpling bruises on Sophie's body.

"How is she?" Father Jim asked from the door.

Francine leaned wearily against the bedpost. "She'll live. How's Grace?"

"Calmer."

"Jim, who is Claire?"

"Claire?"

"When I got home, I heard Grace yelling. She mentioned Claire, and Johnny. Johnny's my father, though I never, ever, heard anyone call him that before. Claire is a new one. Do you know a Claire?"

Jim shrugged, pursed his lips into a grimace, shook his head. "Have you asked Grace?"

"Not yet." She had been hoping to avoid it by picking Father Jim's brain. "She doesn't respond well to questions about the past. I don't like upsetting her. It's weird, though."

"What is?"

"Johnny. You knew my father. He wasn't a Johnny. Maybe it was Grace's pet name for him. Still, you'd think it would have slipped out at least once while I was around." Francine tried to express what was bothering her without feeling traitorous, but there was no help for it. "I keep thinking she's talking about someone else."

"Why?"

"The context. Okay, once she mistook Davis for Johnny. That could have been innocent—a younger man, a younger John Dorian—even though they don't look much alike. Usually she mentions Johnny in the same breath as her parents."

Father Jim looked lost. He arched a brow, shook his head.

Francine's maternal antennae, aimed toward the bathroom, picked up the occasional splash of water, but it was a peaceful sound. So she asked, "When did you first meet Grace?"

"I moved here shortly after she did. She was a regular churchgoer in those days."

"And you two talked a lot?"

"She was always a fascinating woman."

"Did she ever talk about her family?"

"Francine—"

"I know." She held up a hand. "Confidentiality and all. But she says strange things, and other things just don't add up. There are too many questions. I'm starting to wonder who I am."

"You're your parents' child."

"But what before that? I don't know a single relative. Is that incredible?"

Father Jim shrugged. "Not so, in this day and age."

"But sad. Very sad. So maybe Claire is my aunt, even though when I ask Grace for the names of her sisters, she denies having any. So maybe Johnny is—was—I don't know—

a relative, a friend, a *boy*friend. Why won't she talk about him? Why won't she talk about *any* of it?"

"We have talked about that, she and I. When she married your father, she started a new life. The other is over and done."

"Fine, but why can't she *talk* about it?"

"Those early years were troubled."

The door on the past opened a crack. It was the first such admission Francine had heard. "Troubled how?"

He made that pursing grimace again, as though he'd already said more than he wanted to.

But Francine wanted the door open wider. "It's my heritage, Jim, who I am," she pleaded. "It's everything that made Grace who *she* is—no, don't deny it. People don't just turn around one day and become someone else, without any touch of the past. Even if Grace hadn't written words to that effect so often, it's common sense. Who her people are is who *I* am. If I don't find out soon, I never will."

She waited, pleaded silently, finally sighed. Jim was either a faithful servant of God or a faithful servant of Grace, she didn't know which—and then Sophie called from the bathroom, and the point became moot. Much as she needed to know where she'd come from, Sophie was where she was going.

Reluctant to sleep in her bedroom, much less alone, until the locks were changed, Sophie slept with Francine that night. Even then she had nightmares. Twice she bolted up in a sweat. Twice Francine talked her back to sleep.

Feeling tired, sore, and not at all adventurous, she canceled out on her friends in New York, and spent Saturday at home.

Like Grace, she felt a need for familiar walls and trusted faces. Though their reasons differed, security was their goal.

Father Jim helped with that. He personally supervised the changing of the locks, personally talked with Marny about her brother's fate, personally saw to it that Gus was packed and gone.

Margaret helped, too. She cleaned Sophie's suite top to bottom, washed everything she could wash, ran to the store for sheets and a comforter to replace the others, made everything smell and look and feel soft and new.

Still, Sophie was edgy. The scene with Gus remained too raw, the pain, the fear, the sense of powerlessness too new. As a diabetic, she had been taught that she could control her fate. Gus had taught her differently.

She found herself gravitating to wherever Grace was. Strange, but not. Grace was the backbone of the family. Grace would talk with her, would absolve her of guilt, would assure her that wounds would heal, terror fade, control return. Grace had the answers.

But she didn't. Oh, she held Sophie's hand. She asked how she was feeling. She stroked her hair and smiled in the loving way she had when she wasn't being Grace Dorian, The Confidante, but she made no reference, however indirect, to what she had seen or said.

Sophie and Father Jim? In any other situation, it would have been laughable. Now it was sad, even scary to think how far off the mark Grace's mind could wander. Grace had always been constant. Now she wasn't, and Sophie felt the loss.

Constancy was what she needed now—constancy, security, companionship. Without quite realizing that she was dreading it, she was relieved when Francine told her that she

wasn't staying alone in the house with Grace on Sunday afternoon after all, but was coming with Davis and her.

Jane Domenic was more than willing to sit with Grace, and
while Grace wasn't quite as willing in return, Francine put
Sophie's needs first. When Davis pulled up at one, she hus-
tled Sophie out to his truck.

"This is silly," Sophie protested.

"Not silly at all."

"You don't need me along."

Francine had an arm through hers, propelling her on. "I
do, too."

"I'll be in the way."

"In the way of what? He's playing hockey, then we're having dinner with his friends." She stopped just shy of the
truck, took Sophie's face in her hands, and said, "I don't
come without ties. If Davis doesn't know that, he'd better
learn. Love me, love my daughter. Right?" She turned Sophie toward the opening passenger's door, and pushed her
up and in. She took the window for herself. When she leaned
forward to smile at Davis across Sophie, her stomach did a
set of little somersaults. "Hi."

"Hi, yourself."

"This wasn't my idea," Sophie put in quickly.

"I figured that," Davis said. "No gorgeous young thing in
her right mind would voluntarily give up her Sunday afternoon to watch a group of has-beens trying to recapture their
long-lost youth."

Sophie gave him a dubious look. "Long-lost youth?"

"I used to be able to skate all night without getting winded.
Now? Forget it. Same with having eyes in the back of my
head. I used to instinctively know what was happening

everywhere, now I just don't have that . . . that *gestalt*, know what I mean? And as for my knees . . ." He made a sputtering sound.

"What's wrong with your knees?" Sophie asked.

"They give out. All I ask is that you don't laugh. This could be embarrassing." He looked at Francine. "Maybe neither of you should come."

"We're coming," Sophie said.

"You sure? We're talkin' marginal slapstick, here."

"I could use a laugh."

"I asked you *not* to laugh."

Lips pressed together, Sophie raised her right hand.

Davis looked at Francine. She pressed her fingertips to her mouth to hide the humor there, and echoed Sophie's vow by somberly shaking her head.

As it happened, they laughed aplenty, though not at Davis's expense. The game was serious, but not, the rivalry fierce, but not. The spectators, all friends or relatives of the skaters, cheered for whoever spiced up the game. Steals brought hoots, fights brought shouts, goals brought the bleachers to its collective feet.

Francine and Sophie started the afternoon huddled together, but the enthusiasm of the others was infectious. Sophie caught on first, jumping up with the rest, yelling with the rest, then sitting down, looking at Francine, and saying, "That felt good."

Francine found that it did. In no time, she and Sophie were just another two of the crazies in the stands, having every bit as much fun cheering, razzing, and goading the skaters as the skaters were having themselves.

Davis was, of course, the best one on the ice. He sped along with an economy of movement, put stick to puck in a way that had his opponents twisting and turning, glided gracefully across the ice with his arms in the air when he scored.

"His knees give out, huh?" Sophie remarked one minute, then flew out of her seat the next to add her own raucous shout to the others when a fight broke out.

Fights were the highlight of the game. There was a grand show of shoving, arm waving, and shouting on the ice, followed several times by the emptying of the stands, but laughter dominated even these peacemaking efforts. The laughter carried over into the dinner that followed, which was held at a family-style restaurant that didn't mind if the largest of its diners smelled vaguely ripe. There were toasts. There were jokes. There were cold beer and lighthearted jibes.

Francine and Sophie shared a table with Davis, one of his teammates and his wife, and the wife's brother and sister. The teammate, an old medical school pal of Davis's, practiced internal medicine in western Massachusetts. His wife practiced law with her sister, who was six years younger. The brother, who was younger still, was the black sheep of the family. He was an artist.

"Did you hear what he was saying?" Sophie asked Francine that evening after they had returned home, put Grace to bed, tucked themselves face-to-face under Sophie's new comforter, and turned out the light. Her voice was a whisper in the dark. "He does illustration work for the Audubon Society. That supports him while he works on pure art. He's had shows. His work is in galleries in New York and San Francisco. I'll bet he's good."

"I'll bet," Francine said. She wasn't about to overreact, lest Sophie think she was pushing. But the artist—Douglas—seemed a gentle, laid-back, easygoing sort.

"He asked me out."

"Did he?"

"To dinner. I told him I didn't know."

"Why don't you?"

"You know."

Francine touched her hair. Grateful for the opening, she said, "There's no rush. Meet him for dinner in a month or two, or never, if he doesn't interest you enough. But don't go gun-shy on me, Sophie. Don't isolate yourself from the world. Not every man is like Gus."

"I know. But what happened was scary. I never saw it coming. What if I don't see it another time?"

"You will. You'll know what to look for—drinking, frustration, anger. You won't put yourself in a vulnerable position."

"Maybe if Douglas was ugly. Or *bo*-ring—"

"You'd be miserable. You like interesting people. Because *you're* interesting. You have spunk. Don't lose that, Sophie."

"I like Davis, by the way. Do you?"

Francine smiled. "Uh-huh."

"Are things still hot and heavy between you two?"

"Who said hot and heavy?"

"No one said. I saw."

"What did you see?" Francine asked, trying to minimize the kiss in the hall.

"I saw his tongue."

"*Jesus*, Sophie. You're not supposed to look for things like that when you stumble on people kissing."

"Well, I saw. So, is it serious?"

"How would I know? I haven't been seeing him for long."

"I think it is. I saw how you were looking at him. There was feeling."

Feeling? Oh, yes. Particularly that afternoon. Davis had been perfect with Sophie, offering the right amounts of attention and fun to take her mind off Gus without belaboring the point. He had been perfect with Francine, too, warm, close, sexy.

She decided that he skated the way he made love, a little rough, a little smooth, bold but expert.

"Would you marry him?" Sophie asked.

"No. He wants babies."

"Do you love him?"

"I like him."

"A lot?"

"Uh, yes. But I'm not right for him. I'm too old."

"Too old for what?"

"Babies."

"You're not too old, not that that matters—"

"It does." Particularly knowing that Grace's fate might be hers one day.

"What matters is you and him."

"But he wants kids."

"You could have kids."

"If I were in a pediatrician's waiting room, they'd think I was the grandmother." And if she acted it and worse when her baby was a teen?

"There are lots of new moms your age. You could have two babies, even three, if you wanted."

"One a year. Can't you just see it?"

"It's not like you wouldn't have help."

"I'm not having babies for someone else to raise."

"That's not what I mean, and you know it. Wouldn't you like to have Davis's babies?"

Francine opened her mouth to say that she wasn't having *any* babies, but the words didn't come. Having Davis's babies was a tempting thought.

So was taking calcium supplements to prevent osteoporosis—and putting super-rejuvenating cream on her aging neck—and pulling out gray hairs—and taking an organic potion that a holistic someone or other was peddling as a preventative against Alzheimer's disease.

"I wouldn't mind," Sophie said. "If you wanted to marry him, I mean."

"Grace would. He's from Tyne Valley."

"So's Father Jim, but to look at Grace with him, you'd think they were lovers."

"Sophie."

"Really. Think they ever were?"

"No."

"She waits all day for him to come. Doesn't that tell you something?"

"It tells me she adores him. That doesn't mean they were lovers."

"Do you think she had a lover before Grampa?"

"She always said that the greatest wedding gift a woman could give her husband was her virginity." Then again . . . "She also said that she was born Grace Laver in a tiny Maine town that was flooded into oblivion. I don't know what to think anymore."

"It kind of affects how we think of ourselves," Sophie said with a yawn.

Francine yawned back. "Um-hmm." She thought about that for a time, and was about to label it an understatement when she realized that Sophie was asleep.

Nineteen

We can never fully shake the past. Long after its sun has set, yesterday shadows today and tomorrow.
—GRACE DORIAN, speaking before the National Association for the Enhancement of Mental Health

Francine ran into dead ends in her attempt to contact John Dorian's siblings. Two of the numbers in the address book were out of service, the third was answered by someone who claimed not to be related to *that* Dorian, the fourth hung up on her when she identified herself—whereupon she handed the address book over to Robin.

Robin couldn't have been happier. She was sure she could get more from an unwilling subject than Francine. As a non-Dorian, she could be more innocent and tougher.

On the premise that more might be learned face-to-face, and with Francine hesitant to leave Grace alone, Robin flew to the West Coast herself. After landing in Sacramento, she

rented a car, and drove to the address given in John's book—
one of the out-of-service phone numbers—for his youngest
brother, Milton. The house was of moderate size, well kept,
nicely landscaped. Its door was opened by a young woman
who claimed to have bought the house after Milton Dorian
died. To her knowledge, he had always lived alone.

"Who did you deal with during the sale?"

"Just realtors and lawyers."

"No family?"

"None that I knew of."

Robin got the name of the realtor, through whom she
could track down the lawyer if need be and learn if Milton
had children. But a contemporary of Milton's would know
more about Grace. So the next morning she went on to San
Jose in search of Millicent Dorian Bluett.

Her house was much like the other, moderate in size,
well kept, nicely landscaped. Even the Georgian style was
similar. It was a minute before Robin realized that both bore
a resemblance to the larger, stone-fronted family home on
the Housatonic.

A tall woman answered the door. Robin was looking for a
resemblance to the John she had seen in pictures when the
woman demanded, "Yes?"

Robin smiled. "Millicent Bluett?"

"Who are you?"

"My name is Robin Duffy. I'm a writer. I'm working on a
biography of Grace Dorian—"

"When you called on the phone, you were her daughter,"
Millicent accused. "I told you then, and I tell you now, I am
not related to Grace Dorian."

"To her husband—"

"I am not related," the woman said, and shut the door in
Robin's face. Seconds later, it opened again. "And don't come

by pretending to be someone else. I don't know who you really are, or what you want, but you won't get it from me."

The door shut and stayed shut. Robin waited five minutes before daring to ring the bell again. She suspected the woman had been watching from a window, because the door wasn't half open when a strident "I told you to leave!" came through.

"One question," Robin said at her quickest, humblest. "If you aren't the right Dorian, maybe you know the right one. I'm trying to learn about Grace Dorian before her marriage—"

The door slammed shut.

Robin stopped talking. Closed doors didn't give information. Neither did stern old ladies with dug-in heels.

But there were more ways than one to skin a cat. Right, Grace?

Leaving Millicent's house, Robin sought out the nearest mom-and-pop restaurant. Its name was Over Easy, and it was small but bustling. She went inside, took a seat at the counter, and ordered coffee. The waitress had three conversations going at once.

Robin drank her coffee. When the woman made to refill it, she covered the cup with her hand. "You seem to know everyone," she remarked with a glance at the other patrons.

"I should. I've been working here thirty-two years. Most everyone living within twenty miles has stopped in at some point."

"I'm looking for relatives of Grace Dorian."

"Grace Dorian?"

"*The Confidante.*"

"*I know The Confidante.*" She pulled a paper from under the counter and rustled through it. "She's right here. I read her all the time. I don't always agree with her, mind you, especially lately. She's getting too modern." She leaned forward and whispered, "Actually suggested that young people could *take care* of themselves—if you know what I mean—instead of having sex. We'd *never* teach that to our kids. Who did you say you were?"

"I'm a writer. There's a Dorian who lives about three blocks from here. I was told she was a relative."

"A Dorian? Here? Gee, I never knew that. What's her name?"

Strike one, Robin thought. Within minutes, she was back on the street, wondering why she had imagined that a woman as snooty as Millicent Dorian Bluett would frequent a place like Over Easy.

On the other hand, even snooty people needed hardware. Crossing the street, she entered the hardware store and asked for the owner.

"You're talking to him," said a man with HARRY on his shirt.

She smiled. "Harry. Hi." She held out her hand. "I'm Robin Duffy. I'm doing a piece on Grace Dorian, you know, *The Confidante*?"

"I do. The wife reads her columns."

"I'm looking for long-lost relatives of hers. I understand there's a Dorian here in town."

"Millie. But she's no relation. I know. I asked. The wife made me. She does the billing and saw the name. That was years ago."

"No relation at all?"

"No, and she doesn't appreciate being asked. I've a feeling people hound her about it. She must be fed up."

Either fed up or defensive, Robin thought. With a silently mocking "Steee-rike two," she thanked Harry and returned to her car. She drove another two blocks and was feeling discouraged when she slammed on the brakes, stopped the car, slowly backed up.

THE TURNED LEAF read a small wooden shingle hanging in front of an unimposing ranch house. Books filled the windows nearest the garage. An OPEN sign stood in the corner of one.

Robin pulled into the driveway and found the nearest door. A bell tinkled. The air inside was stuffy.

"Hello. Can I help you?" asked an elderly woman from her perch on a stool behind the counter.

Robin heard seasonal music, smelled years of old books, saw rocking chairs among the shelves, and decided that if Millicent Dorian frequented anything in town, it was this.

"You sure can," she said. "I've come all the way from New York trying to track down relatives of Grace Dorian. Do you know who Grace Dorian is?"

"Yes," the woman said flatly.

"Do you know who Millicent Bluett is?"

"I've known Millie for years."

Thank God, Robin thought. "Have you ever talked with her about her sister-in-law?"

"I have. They were very close. She was crushed when the poor thing died."

"Died? Not Grace."

"Lynette. I never met her myself, their living up north and all, but Millie used to visit them every year. Alfred is gone now, too, rest his soul. That was her brother. Alfred."

Robin knew about Alfred. He was the next-oldest brother to John. "What about John?"

"John who?"

"John Dorian. Another brother. Did she ever talk about him?"

"No."

"He was married to Grace. Did Millicent ever talk about Grace?"

"Not to me."

"But you knew they were related?"

"No. I didn't."

Robin headed back to the dugout. If Millicent was related to Alfred, she was related to John, but if she wouldn't talk and her friends wouldn't talk, and if Alfred and Milton were both dead, there was only one hope left.

Janet Dorian Kerns.

Robin returned her rental car and flew to Seattle, but it wasn't until late the next afternoon that she tracked the woman down through three moves to progressively smaller homes. Janet looked startlingly like Millicent. Robin prayed she had a looser tongue.

After introducing herself, she said, "I'm here on behalf of Francine Dorian. She's searching for relatives. Her father died three years ago. His name was John."

Janet regarded her in silence.

"Your name was listed in John's address book. I take it you're his sister."

Janet didn't blink.

"I'm actually working with Francine—and with Grace, her mother—on a book. We're trying to piece together Grace's early years."

"Someone called me on the phone," Janet charged.

"That would have been Francine. You hung up."

"John is no brother of mine."

Robin held her breath. It might be as close to an admission as she would get. Then again . . . "I understand there was a rift."

"You don't know the half."

"I hear it had something to do with Grace."

"Who told you that?"

"It isn't true?"

Janet seemed to catch herself. She drew herself up straighter and tipped up her chin. "No matter."

"But it does," Robin urged, afraid of losing the thread after coming so close. "This is just the kind of thing that Grace's fans want to know."

Janet's eyes hardened. "I don't air my dirty laundry in public."

"Oh, I wouldn't do that," Robin backpedaled, "but anything you tell me will give me a better understanding of Grace. It'll help me write a more honest book. Was the rift because of Grace?"

"Why ask me? Why not ask Grace?"

"Because Grace has trouble talking about it." It wasn't a lie. "It's an emotional thing."

"Well, I don't know why it would be," Janet said, puffing up a shoulder. "She didn't know us. She moved in, and we were gone."

"John made you leave?"

Again Janet caught herself. This time, she stepped back from the door. As quickly, Robin stepped forward. "No, no, Mrs. Kerns. Don't shut me out. You're the first one I've found. Please. I've come all this way."

That actually riled her up. "I didn't tell you to. I made it clear I didn't want to talk when I hung up the phone on that girl."

"Francine's your niece."

"She is not."

"Did John cut you off?" It would explain the denials, an eye for an eye.

"John didn't have to cut us off. He was the oldest son. He got everything." That admission seemed the opening of a floodgate. "He might have shared if he'd wanted, but he didn't, and once he married, we were no longer welcome. We were living right there. He asked us to leave. Not that we wanted to stay. Not with that woman. She wrapped him right around her little finger, and that was that. It was interesting that she made something of herself, while he closed the sawmill and lost the family money in risky investments— or so the story *we* heard went. We never believed it. He was just hiding his assets so we couldn't take him to court. You see, when John died, the inheritance was to go to his heir, only he didn't have an heir."

"He did. Francine."

Janet didn't respond to that at first. She was silent for so long that Robin was beginning to fear that in interrupting the monologue, she had stemmed the flow.

Then, with deliberately spoken words and a look of disdain, Janet said, "When John Dorian was young, he fell under his horse during a polo game. The accident left him sterile."

Sterile. Robin's mind started to whirl. Sterile meant that Francine wasn't biologically John's. It meant that Grace had been with another man prior to the marriage, *more* than reason enough to hide her past.

And Francine didn't know.

Robin tried to grasp the implications of it. She was still trying as she flew home, but something was dampening what should have been a triumphant mood. One part of her felt she had stumbled onto something so personal that she was intruding where she had no business being.

"What?" Francine asked in disbelief.

Robin hesitated, then repeated, quietly and with a regret that gave credence to the word, "Sterile."

Francine's stomach started to churn. "Maybe after I was born. That would explain why Grace never had other children, though not why I wasn't told. Janet was either lying, or confused."

"She said there was a polo accident when he was young."

"He didn't play polo."

"Not as a boy?"

Francine couldn't answer that. All she knew was that he had never played as an adult, and that he wasn't sterile. If he had been, he couldn't have fathered her. "Janet is up to no good. Scratch the possibility of sterility."

She couldn't stop thinking about it, though, couldn't stop thinking about John and certain things she had always taken at face value. Like his lack of demonstrativeness toward her. Like his acceptance of Grace, Francine, and Sophie as a threesome that often excluded him. Like his complacency about his own family's disinterest in Francine, and about Sophie's diabetes, which couldn't be traced to an earlier generation.

Innocent facts, each one, but looking different in a different light.

Francine dug out her parents' marriage certificate to see if they had lied to her about the date. They hadn't. She had been born nine months after they were married. No fault there.

But the issue of sterility was a snake, slithering around, feeding off odd doubts and an imaginative mind.

She found herself watching Grace when Grace didn't know she was there, wondering if it *was* possible somehow. Grace's wedding pictures proclaimed her a beautiful bride. Even without the elegant lace gown, even without the elaborate headpiece, the pearls at her throat, the diamond on her finger, she would have been a beauty. Had she been dressed in *rags*, men would have taken notice.

Maybe they had. Maybe the notice had been mutual. Maybe one thing had led to another and Grace had found herself pregnant. Maybe she hadn't known it when she'd come to New York. She and John had met the first week and been married within the month. Maybe there had been a reason for the rush. Maybe the marriage certificate had been altered. Maybe Grace had carried Francine for *ten* months. Maybe John hadn't even known Francine wasn't his.

But he would have known. So would Grace.

John was dead. Grace was working her way in that direction.

If Francine had been going through an identity crisis with the shift in power at home, this made things worse.

At wit's end one afternoon, tired of grappling alone with her doubts, Francine went looking for Grace. She found her in her bedroom, standing over what seemed to be the entire contents of her closet.

"What are you doing?" she asked as gently as she could.

Grace pushed a dress here, a suit there. "Cleaning. I always clean." Twice a year, like clockwork, she weeded unwanted clothes from her closet.

"But you did this last month."

"I don't think so."

Sad fingers squeezed Francine's heart. "Here. I'll help you get these back in the closet. If you take much more away, you won't have anything left to wear." The fact that she didn't need these clothes, that most were inappropriate to her shrinking life, didn't matter. Grace's closet had always been as elegant as the woman herself.

"Pretty," Grace said, taking a red wool suit from the pile and holding it against herself. "Pretty. I wore this in Dallas.

I should give it to that nice woman—you know, in town—you know, that *store* . . ."

Francine couldn't imagine which one, but Davis had encouraged her to be specific about things. "Concreteness" was the word he used for what Grace needed as she ceased to be able to find thoughts on her own. So Francine said, "The dress store?" because it was the first thing to come to mind. Grace barely knew the woman who owned it, had never actually shopped in the store, and Francine doubted the woman would want Grace's hand-me-downs anyway. But that wasn't the point. The point was giving Grace a word, a person, a thing.

Sure enough, Grace brightened. "The dress store. You'll give this to her?"

"I will."

Francine set the red suit aside and started replacing the other clothes in the closet. She wasn't sure this was the best time to mention sterility. Grace wasn't at her best. But then, she wasn't often, and time was short.

With a deep breath and the hope of getting the truth by taking Grace off guard, she said, "Mom? Remember I told you that Robin was going to California? Well, she met Janet Dorian." When there was no reaction, she added, "Dad's sister?" Nothing. "Janet said something that doesn't make any sense at all, but you're the only one who can refute it. She said Dad was sterile."

Grace looked bewilderedly at the clothes on the bed.

"Did you hear me, Mom?"

She looked up. "What was it you said?"

"Janet said Dad was sterile. Was he?"

"Why did she?"

"I don't know. Revenge, maybe. It's a preposterous idea. I mean," Francine forced a laugh, "he's the only father I've ever known."

"I don't think so."

"You don't think what?"

"I don't think so," Grace repeated, as though that answered everything.

"You don't think he was sterile? It isn't something you'd think. It's something you'd know."

"I don't *think* so," Grace insisted.

Francine tried to stay calm. A yes or a no, that was all she wanted to hear. She didn't need details, didn't need grand recollections or explanations. She wasn't asking anything of Grace that Grace couldn't give. A yes or a no. That was all.

"I always asked why you never had other children," she said in something of a pleading tone. "You wouldn't have been able to, if Dad was sterile. If he was sterile, you wouldn't have been able to have *me*, which means that someone else is my biological father. I'm forty-three years old. I have a right to know."

"Holy Mary—"

"*No. Not* immaculate conception," Francine cried. Her stomach was knotting. "Look, Dad is dead, so your telling me can't hurt him. I certainly won't think less of him— actually, *more*, realizing what he did all those years for another man's child. And I won't think less of you. Hell, I was pregnant with Sophie when I married Lee—wouldn't *that* be a kick," she diverted helplessly, bitterly, "after I felt *so guilty* disappointing you." That was only *one* of the things she would regard differently if her parentage were a fraud.

Grace covered her ears and shook her head.

Francine took her hands back down and said an urgent, "Please, Mom. I need to know."

Grace was breathing rapidly. "I don't think so," she whispered.

"It's my genes, my heritage. The same with Sophie."

"I don't think so."

Francine held her hands tighter. "*Tell* me. Was Dad sterile? I'll find out anyway. I'm not letting this go until I know for sure one way or the other. If you tell me, I won't have to look elsewhere. It'll be more *secret*, if you tell me."

Grace pressed her lips together.

"What's *so awful*?" Francine cried. "So you were pregnant when you met him. So *what*? *I* don't care. I just want the truth. Who was my father? You have to *tell* me."

"I don't think so."

"Mother!"

Her shout had barely bounced off the walls when Grace puckered up and began to cry. There was nothing ladylike about the way she did it, nothing genteel or adult. It was the uncontrolled, uncaring dissolution of a child who was confused beyond bearing, and it broke Francine's heart.

Grace hadn't known what was happening. Clothes were strewn all over her bed, but she didn't recall putting them there. She might have done it. Or someone else, though she didn't know why. All she knew was that there were too many people running around the house, and that there was a mess in here.

Things weren't in their proper places. She didn't know if she could straighten it all up.

Take this business about John. She didn't know why Francine had mentioned it or who had told her, but there was suddenly such a buzzing in her head that she couldn't hear anything of what John said except fragments.

"All right—don't care—like my own . . ." So calm, so

reassuring. Even relieved, because he had had secrets, too. But the secrets were between them. They had agreed on it. They had *sworn*.

Fragments. She heard things, felt things, thought things. But they came and went with little order.

And now something was coming undone, and she didn't know what to do about it. She was supposed to know. She would have a year ago, maybe even a week ago. People came to her for answers all the time. But she didn't have them now. She didn't have anything now. So many years. So much work. Nothing.

Overwhelmed by it all, not having control over *anything*, she started to cry. She hated the awful sounds she made, hated the wetness on her face, but she couldn't stop what was happening, and that made it all the worse.

Suddenly, arms encircled her. They held warmth and caring and gentleness. They held love and forgiveness. Her mother? No, not her. Still, motherly they were. She gave herself up to their comfort, and things were better.

Francine found Father Jim in the small subbasement classroom of his church. The air held its share of the January chill, conducted through the fieldstone of which the entire church was built, but the room wasn't gloomy. Father Jim prevented it. He was a warming presence—his eyes, his voice, his smile.

He was teaching the catechism to a class full of children, each seated in his or her own way at small wooden desks. Francine remembered being one of those children. Father Jim—a full-headed Father Jim—had been new to the parish. Much as Francine had hated the restraint of the classroom and the roteness of the catechism, she had loved Father Jim.

Nearly forty years had gone, along with much of Father Jim's hair, but the catechism was the same, as was the children's love for their teacher.

Francine waited just outside the classroom, leaning against the stone wall, impatient but not so, with the soothing of Father Jim's voice. In time the children ran out, and she slipped in.

He looked up at her in alarm, one arm suspended, the other filled with books. "Francine? Is Grace all right?"

"She is." The crying had stopped, and been forgotten with a move to the solarium. "I'm not." She smiled thinly. "It's the old skeletons-in-the-closet thing again." The smile went. "Do you know anything about my father being sterile?"

Father Jim grew pale. He set down the books and stood his fingers on the desk. "Who said he was?"

"His sister. As far as she's concerned, I'm not her niece. Grace wouldn't confirm it or deny it, and then she started to cry." The memory of that brought tears to Francine's eyes. "It was awful, awful. I couldn't push her after that. So I'm pushing you. You knew my father. Did he ever mention a problem?"

Father Jim was reflective. "No."

"Did Grace?"

"That would have been private, between your parents—"

"—and God, and since you're God's servant, you'd have known."

"Not necessarily. Not unless the situation was creating problems for them that they couldn't deal with."

Francine loved Jim. She trusted him. But he was protecting Grace again. "Why can't you give me a direct answer? All I want is yes or no. Was John Dorian sterile, or was he not?"

"I can't tell you that."

"Can't? Or won't." Tears welled up. "This isn't just an incidental little thing. It has to do with my parentage. I'd call that major. But no one will tell me the truth. It isn't fair, Jim."

Everything about Jim softened then. He came to her, put a gentle arm around her shoulders, said in that soothing voice of his, "Why is it so important, Frannie? Regardless of what that truth is, John was your father. He loved you, cared for you, gave you everything any young girl could have wanted."

"He did," she conceded, "only I'm not a young girl anymore, and I'm tired of being given the runaround. It's true, isn't it? He was sterile."

Father Jim shook his head, not in denial but in sadness.

Francine wrenched free and started off. "There are other ways to find out."

"Frannie—"

She wheeled back. "I will find out. If you and Grace want to play games, go ahead. I'm done."

Francine debated asking Davis to sneak a look at John's medical files. Sterility would have been noted in his records, and he had records aplenty in the last years of his life. But asking Davis would have compromised him. She couldn't do that until she had exhausted every other outlet.

Paul Hartman was not only Grace's, but John's, internist, sometime golf partner, and frequent party guest. He was the one who had initially referred Grace to Davis, and continued to visit her often. He never left without reminding Francine to promise to call if he could be of help.

She therefore had no qualms about phoning him at home that night, asking to see him, and rapping his heavy brass door knocker twenty minutes later. She let him lead her into a leather-clad library, but remained bundled up and standing. She refused his offer of brandy.

"Something has come up, Paul. I need the truth. You treated my father for—how many years?"

"I've been practicing here for thirty years," he said without pause. "John was one of my first patients."

"Was he sterile?"

Paul recoiled. "Sterile. Where'd that come from?"

"His sister. And I think it's true. It answers some questions. Unfortunately, it raises others. Was he?"

"Now, Francine," Paul chided, "you know I can't divulge private information."

"He was," she decided.

"I didn't say that."

"But no one's denying it. You're all doing the same thing, turning the question back on me, avoiding a direct answer. If it weren't true, someone would have said, 'No, he was *not* sterile.' Why shouldn't I know? What *harm* would it do at this late date? John is dead, and Grace has bigger things to conceal than a premarital love affair. But there isn't much bigger a thing for me. I'm the product of that affair. We're talking about my parentage."

Paul scratched the back of his head, smoothed down the hair there, took a deep breath, gave her a beseeching look.

"Please, Paul?" Her voice trembled. "I don't know where else to turn. John is dead. Grace is fading fast. I don't have any relatives to ask, because I don't *know* any relatives, so once Grace is gone, there's *nothing.*"

He looked torn.

She clutched his arm. "If John is not my biological father, I could find out who is, and once I do that, I'd have a key to who Grace is. That's the bottom line here, Paul. Grace won't talk, I don't know how much is deliberate and how much isn't, but if I can find that key, I may be able to unlock things before she's gone."

She kept her eyes on his, kept waiting. She gave his arm a small tug. "Please?"

His shoulders slumped. "You're tough."

"I'm desperate. Was John Dorian my father?"

He hesitated for a final minute before saying a reluctant, "I never asked him directly, but I assume not. He was sterile. When I asked how, he mentioned an accident. When I asked when, he said many years before. I remember his eyes when he told me, warning me not to ask anything else, so I didn't. It never came up again."

Francine let out a long, shaky breath. She sank into a chair and put her head in her hands. She accepted Paul's of-fer of a brandy this time, because she needed something to prop her up and hold her together. Half an hour. That was all she figured she needed to reach Davis.

He met her at the door, hauled her out of the cold, and lis-tened to her tale. Then he took her in his arms and held her while she trembled and cried and was as weak as she wanted to be, without making her feel weak at all. He made her feel honest, made her feel justified in every one of her worries. And when she had aired them all and grown tired of words, when she sought forgetfulness, he made love to her with such caring that she was in tears by its end.

His passion was a song, flowing across, beside, under her, catching her up, raising her high. Whether it was his hands on her back lifting her, or his mouth suckling along the rim of her breast, or the slide of his rangy torso, or the abrasion

of hair-spattered limbs over parts of her that were smoother and smaller, he lit her up.

And it wasn't just sexual. She had had just sexual with Lee. This was different. It was filled with soul.

When he made love to her, there was an element of wonder, first in his eyes, then in the rest of him. He made her feel sacred no matter where or how they loved, and they tried most everything they could, as long, as hard, as deep as possible. Always his body cradled her, his hands adored her. Always he made her feel perfect.

She was in love with him, of course. Foolish to kid herself and deny it. She loved the way he looked, felt, thought. She loved the fun they had and the heat they shared. She loved the way she could lean on him without toppling them both to the ground.

She loved the way he would thread his fingers into her hair, caress her face with his eyes, and whisper, "I love you," when the rush of orgasmic pleasure finally allowed for breath. And she loved the way he didn't demand an answer, the way he understood that with her present in such transition, she couldn't deal with the future.

Someday soon. But not yet.

Francine never came out and asked him to snoop, but three days after she told him that John was sterile, Davis gave her a copy of the ancient hospital report that credited John's sterility to a riding accident that had occurred when he was nineteen.

Twenty

As complex as life sometimes seems, its greatest mysteries are as simple as a baby's cry, a lover's touch, or the smile of a friend.

—GRACE DORIAN, from *The Confidante*

"Where to from here?" Robin asked.

Francine had been asking herself the same question nonstop. The answer was always another question: *Who am I?*

She was Sophie's mother, more needed now than ever before. She was Davis's lover, more needy now than ever before. She was Grace's daughter, though Grace no longer called her by name.

Was she The Confidante? She was managing to satisfy Tony with five columns a week, though she was getting flak for not touring. Actually, Grace was getting flak for not touring. The inquiries kept coming. They were getting harder to refuse.

Grace would have had her appearing in public, but that wasn't what Francine wanted to do with her life. Forget her fear of public speaking. She simply preferred to be home with the people she loved.

Was Grace disappointed in her? Probably. So a little more wouldn't hurt.

"We find out who my father is," she told Robin, and shot Sophie a dry look. "Sounds easy enough." They all knew it wasn't. Without a starting point for Grace, there was no starting point for Grace's lover. But there was one small New England town with which Grace was associated. "Let's start with Tyne Valley."

"Grace isn't from the Valley," Sophie argued. "She hates the Valley. Father Jim's the reason she sends money there every year."

"The question," Robin said as she poured refills of coffee around the kitchen table, "is whether there might be another reason."

"Davis was under the impression that Grace came from the Valley," Francine said. "He was stunned when I said she wasn't."

"Well, I can check it out easily enough," Sophie declared. "There should be birth records, school records, old newspapers. If we can't access them from here, I'll go there." Her face suddenly clouded.

"Gus won't be there," Francine assured her softly. "He's in Chicago. Davis's friend confirmed it." And she thought it would be good for Sophie to get away. Since her run-in with Gus, she had been largely homebound, communicating with her friends by phone. It remained to be seen whether she would chicken out of this trip—not that Francine was letting her go alone. She would send Robin along.

"Do we work with the name Laver?" Robin asked.

"We have no other choice for now. While you're doing that, I'll contact Joseph Crosby. He's the parish priest who administers Grace's grants. Father Jim directs, Father Crosby doles out."

"Why not just ask Father Jim?" This, from Sophie.

"Because he won't talk. He thinks he's protecting Grace."

"What if Father Crosby feels the same?"

Francine had considered the possibility. "I may be able to catch him off guard. It's February, right? Our accountant is organizing Grace's tax information, right? I'll tell Father Crosby that we need a breakdown of the outlets to which Grace's money has gone."

"You'd lie to a priest?" Sophie said, not quite serious, not quite not.

Francine gave her a dead-on look. "Blame it on Father Jim. Blame it on Grace. Blame it on John Dorian." The hurt that was never far from the surface seeped out. "An awful lot of people haven't told *us* the truth. Somehow, a small lie seems justified, given that it's a greater truth we seek."

There was no record of a Grace Laver having grown up in Tyne Valley. "We went through everything," Sophie reported upon their return. "I found three other Graces in five years' worth of high school yearbooks, but the town moderator, who took over the job from his father thirty-eight years ago, accounted for all three. He hadn't ever heard of a Laver. Grace Dorian, yes. *The Confidante*, yes. Grace Laver, no."

"What about Thomas, Sara, and Hal?"

Sophie shook her head. "There's a slew of families squeezed into the poorest part of town. According to Father Crosby, no one knows all their names, they just come and go, men here one day and gone the next, children running around ragged, dying early in those days."

"Davis's father?"

"No help there."

"Drunk?"

"Uh-huh."

Francine knew how that upset Davis. It was one reason why she had turned down his offer to take her to Tyne Valley himself.

"Father Jim, meanwhile, is beloved," Robin put in. "He's a local hero. Everyone in town knows who he is. A few remembered the old days. Apparently he was wild, before the church tamed him."

Davis had told Francine as much. Now she wondered if there was more to the tale. "A friend of his died just before he joined the seminary. Can you learn more about that?"

"Easy," Robin said. "The people I talked with were wonderfully innocent. When I said I was writing a book on Grace, they offered to help in any way they could. I have names and numbers."

"They're apt to be more reticent when you call back," Francine warned, "especially if someone gets to them first." Somewhere there was a father who had gone forty-three years as an unknown and might not want that changed. Not for the first time since she had learned the truth about John did she resent this faceless man.

She turned to Sophie. "What was it like?"

"The Valley? It's surrounded by mountains, like you'd expect. Sleepy. Picturesque." She frowned. "Y'know how Grace can buy Margaret a new coat that doesn't quite fit? That's what the center of Tyne Valley is like. Everything is newly painted and repaired, but it's like blusher on a dog."

"The people there are tired," Robin said more kindly,

"even the young ones. Life isn't easy. So Grace's money is appreciated. Father Crosby had nothing but praise for her."

"He denied that Grace came from there," Sophie put in.

Francine had asked him the same question and had been trying to rationalize it ever since. "He came to town well after Grace would have left. He may not know the truth. As for the money, it goes into a church fund for use at Father Crosby's discretion—someone needs help after a house fire or in a medical emergency, someone else exhausts unemployment benefits and needs tiding over until a job comes through. There are annual bequests to the Beautification Committee and the Gold Star mothers, a biggie to the library, another biggie to a home for battered women."

"Battered women." Sophie mused. "Interesting. Spousal abuse is a recurrent theme in Grace's columns."

"Which could mean," Francine took the obvious step, "that she was abused, or her mother was abused, or her sisters, if she had sisters, but we're nowhere without a name." To Sophie, curious if tentative, she said, "Did you . . . feel anything there?"

"Like a genetic link? No. You'd be more apt to feel it than me. But if Grace *was* from there, wouldn't someone make the connection?"

"Years have passed since she left. People might have forgotten what she looked like then. They've probably only seen recent pictures of her. Clothes and makeup can turn a person's looks around, and if no one's looking for a connection—"

"How could they *not*, what with the amount she gives?"

"We didn't," Francine answered. Place blame where blame is due, Grace always said. "We simply assumed she gave that money because of Father Jim." It kept coming back to him. "He's the key," she said with conviction. Unfortunately, her annoyance with him only went so far. Still, always, he was a man of the cloth and a friend. She couldn't stab him in the back.

"Let me see what I can learn," Robin said. Her voice was quiet. Her eyes said she understood Francine's dilemma.

Francine was infinitely grateful.

Davis altered Grace's medication in the hope of slowing down the disease, but Francine saw little change. Lucidity became distraction with no warning at all. Grace could be focusing in on a discussion, responding rationally, if in the short, simple sentences she had taken to, when she would veer off in another direction. The transition was sometimes so smooth that Francine was sure it was intentional. Grace either digressed, or made a pretense of digressing, when Francine broached touchy topics.

And broach touchy topics she did. Though she was torn—hating herself for upsetting Grace, wanting to please her still—as long as there was rational information left in Grace's mind, she had to try to ferret it out.

The touchiest of topics were Francine's parentage, Grace's real name, and Tyne Valley. Grace was either upset into babbling confusion at their mention or was as wily as a fox in evading their discussion. Francine made no headway at all.

"It's like she's sifting through my fingers," Francine tried to explain to Davis. "I catch the parts of her that I already know, but the rest goes right on through and away. I get so close sometimes. I'm *sure* she's about to say something, then she changes her mind. It's uncanny. She's lost awareness about so much, but not that. She won't tell secrets."

"Stay close," Davis suggested. "Alert Jane and Margaret to what you want to hear. Keep Grace's mind active. Go through old pictures. Something may inadvertently come out."

Francine tried that. She got references to Thomas and Sara, to Hal, to Grace's sisters, though they never had names. She got references to Johnny, and to the guys in the barn—to Scutch and Sparrow—and to Wolf, who wouldn't get up, wouldn't get up—it was always repeated twice and in anguish. But she never got last names, never got enough to give the incident a time or a place. It could have occurred when Grace was six, or ten, or sixteen.

Then Robin returned from a second trip to Tyne Valley with more information on Father Jim. "He and his friends weren't lawbreakers, per se. They camped out in vacant homes, borrowed cars from their parents without asking, took liquor from hidden stashes they stumbled upon. They weren't into guns or violence."

"But one of them died."

"His name was William Duey. He 'drunk himself to death' was how the paper put it, and the people who remembered it said the same thing. No one knew the details, other than that he'd been drinking with his friends. The paper didn't list their names. It was a pretty straightforward obituary. I'm not even sure the police knew who all was there," she checked her notebook, "but people who were around at the time mentioned Spencer Heast, Francis Stark, Rosellen McQuillan, and, of course, James O'Neill. Father Jim was the one who got the doctor out there. Everyone had left by then but the girl."

"Rosellen McQuillan," Francine said, trying out the name.

"She was James O'Neill's longtime steady. She left town when Jim entered the seminary."

Francine wondered if Grace could have been Rosellen McQuillan, but quickly rejected the idea. It might have been a possibility if there had been a Scutch, a Sparrow, or a Wolf among the list of Father Jim's friends—and maybe there were, if their nicknames were given. But, if so, what about Johnny. *He* had been Grace's boyfriend, back in that barn with Wolf. And Wolf hadn't 'drunk himself to death.' He had fallen and hit his head.

Without a great stretch of the imagination, the surface details just didn't match.

Grace was asleep on the sofa. Father Jim pulled the afghan to her chin, tucked it under her shoulder, touched her cheek.

From the chessboard, Francine watched. She refocused on the board when Father Jim returned to his seat, and made a pretense of concentrating.

Then, tired of being in the dark, of hitting brick walls, of being a coward, she raised her eyes. "Are you in love with Grace?"

Jim arched a quick brow before returning to the board. "I'm a priest."

"You're here once a day, often twice. It's like your second home."

"I have good taste, don't you think?"

"What I think," Francine said, "is that you treat Grace with such exquisite gentleness that it's either love, or lunacy. You're not a lunatic, Jim. Devout, certainly. Cagey, perhaps. But not mad."

"Thank you. I take that as a compliment."

Since he wasn't answering her question, she tried another.

"If you hadn't become a priest, would you have married Grace?"

"Grace was already married."

"If you'd met her before that. Say, in Tyne Valley."

The only reaction she got, if she could call it that, was the twitch of a finger abutting the chessboard.

So she went on. "We've been trying to piece together possible backgrounds for Grace. One theory is that she was born in Tyne Valley—not as Grace, not even as Laver, we've researched those and ruled them out. So maybe she was someone like Rosellen McQuillan."

He did look up then. "How did you learn about Rosellen?" He answered the question himself. "Robin and Sophie."

"Seems you were quite the rogue."

He cleared his throat. "I was young. I was fighting what my parents demanded."

"How long were you with Rosellen?"

His eyes softened at the memory. "Forever, it seemed. We played together as children. By the time we started school, we were nearly inseparable." A small smile tugged at his mouth. "Oh, I spent the requisite time with the guys, and she with the girls, but the rest of the time, it was just us two. Even in a crowd. We were soulmates. We knew what the other was thinking without having to speak." He sighed, laced his fingers on the table, studied them. "She was a more integral part of my growing-up years than any other single figure. We experienced adolescence together, puberty together. We went to each other with the most intimate things, things we couldn't take to our parents."

"Why not?"

"My family was too religious. I was their priest-elect. Carnal matters—" He shook his head, a vehement no.

"And her family?"

"Too mean. So we loved each other. That made the rest easier to take."

"But you left."

He looked bereft. "Yes."

"Are you sorry?" she asked, then immediately chided herself for the whimsy. Of course, he wasn't sorry. He loved God and the church. The greater his sacrifice, the greater the proof of that love.

She was stunned when he whispered, "Sometimes." His eyes touched hers for an instant, then lowered again.

"You still love her."

"A love like that never dies."

"Where is she now?"

He pursed his lips and studied his hands. When he raised his eyes, they brimmed with tears.

Francine couldn't ask anything else.

Annie Diehl called with a talk-show invitation for Grace and wasn't pleased when Francine refused. Tony called soon after to ask what Grace had against talk shows, and wasn't pleased when Francine said she had tired of that life. George called soon after that to ask why in the world they were paying a publicist if Grace wouldn't accept her bookings.

Amanda called to apologize for not being more of a buffer. "They're getting impatient," she warned. "They know something's wrong with her and want to know what it is. We may have to tell them soon."

"Not yet," Francine said. Grace had been vehement. Francine wanted to honor her wishes for as long as was humanly possible.

Less than a day later, Robin drew up a chair and picked up on a variation of the theme. "I have the body of this book outlined and ready to write. It could be done in a month. The start and the finish are something else. Okay, we're still working on the start. But the finish? Do we talk about AD? We're scheduled for Christmas publication. Going public with something like this in the midst of the season of goodwill would guarantee the book's success."

"I'm sure," Francine remarked. "We'd make headlines— TV, newspapers, magazines. Grace would hate it."

Robin regarded her silently.

"I know, I know," she breathed. "She may not know, but what if she does? What if it's the *last* thing she knows? I'll feel like a traitor. I'll have let her down worse than I ever did before. Can I live with that for the rest of my life?"

That night, Francine went shopping with Davis. He had a house to furnish, and since she had helped finish floors, walls, and windows, it followed that she would help with this.

They wandered from one elegant room display to the next. Most were too formal for Francine. "But don't listen to me," she cautioned. "I have lousy taste."

"Who told you that?"

"Grace, who has impeccable taste."

"She did her own decorating?"

"With a decorator doing the legwork. The house was photographed for *Architectural Digest* last year."

"Fine. Good. But I don't want *my* house as prissy as that. I want mine warm, inviting, and fun."

He took her hand and led her back through the rooms, pointing to a sofa in one, a chair in another, a desk in a third, an armoire in a fourth, with little thought to typical pairings. Francine loved what he picked out.

"These things don't match," she said. "Grace wouldn't approve."

"I'm not worried about Grace. I'm worried about you." He tucked her hand in his jacket pocket, drawing her whisper close as they walked.

She wasn't sure she wanted to hear his follow-up. So she said, "I *am* worried about Grace. People are wanting to see her. How much longer can we hide the fact that she's sick?"

Davis didn't say anything, simply kept her tight to his side and walked on. He stopped at a Mediterranean den display. The colors were bold, the flavor pungent.

"I'd buy that rug," he said. Then, "Why do you still want to hide it?"

"Because Grace wants to."

"Does she? Or do you?"

The question took Francine by surprise. She hadn't turned it around that way. But she couldn't turn it back. "Me. It's me."

"Are you embarrassed that she's sick?"

"Lord, no. I'm just not ready for people to know that she isn't doing the work. And that I am," which was the crux of it.

"Another person would be telling the whole *world* she was doing the work," Davis said, leaving the Mediterranean room. "You should be proud. You're doing it without Grace, and you're doing it *well*."

"I don't know about that."

"Have you had complaints?"

"No."

"Doesn't that tell you something?"

"I don't know. What does it tell you?"

"You *know*."

She grinned. "Yes, but I like hearing you say it. That's why I spend time with you, Davis. You're good for my ego."

They were at a safari display that touted a four-poster bed draped in gauze. While the accessories spoke of adventure, the bed was pure whimsy.

"Marry me, Frannie."

She caught her breath and stared.

He grinned. "Cat got your tongue?"

"No. I mean, not the cat. I'm shocked."

"Don't know why you should be." He dropped an arm around her shoulders and led her from the room. "I keep saying I love you."

"In the heat of passion."

"So? There's chemistry enough between us to keep you coming back for more. I don't need to promise love for that. Still, I say it. Doesn't *that* tell you anything?"

She rolled her head to the side so that her cheek lay on his wrist. "Oh, Davis."

"What, oh, Davis."

"We've been through this before."

"I have never asked you to marry me before."

"But I've told you that I'm wrong for you. I can't give you what you need."

"Seems to me you're already doing it."

"Babies. I'm too old."

"Yeah?" he said, inhaling deeply. "Well, maybe you're not. Why don't we try?"

Her gaze flew to his face. The devil signs were all there—the scar, the dark eyes, the mussed hair, the beard shadow—but the mouth was straight, no crooked grin in sight. "You're serious."

"You bet."

"'Try'?"

"Do it without a rubber."

Francine caught the curious looks of two young women nearby. "It's all right," she said as they passed. "I'll make him get tested. Better safe than sorry."

But she wasn't thinking about safety. She was thinking about the endless work a baby entailed, the drooling, the diapers, the crying, the gurgles, the hugging, the playing, the joy . . .

"I will be tested, if you want," Davis said.

She snickered. "Seems to me we negated the issue the first time we made love. You didn't use anything then."

"It was the first time I hadn't in years."

"Well, it was the first time I *had* in years, so we're safe."

They entered a kitchen. It was early American, bright in color, totally homespun. "I'll take those pots," Davis said.

"The pots aren't for sale, only the table and chairs, but you already have a table and chairs."

"Are those brass?"

"They're not *selling* the pots."

"I like this kitchen. It feels homey."

Francine thought of where he had come from and all he hadn't had as a child. She had thought it before, and she thought it now, what a wonderful father he would make.

"So, what do you think?" he asked in an offhand way that she knew wasn't offhand at all.

"I think there are some big worries."

"Like what?"

"AD. What if I get it? Is it fair to have a child now, knowing I may be sick by the time it graduates from high school?"

"You could die in five years of something totally different, but you can't not live because of that fear. Think of all you could give a child in the meanwhile."

"But my life is in turmoil."

"What turmoil? Your mother's sick, so you've taken over the business, but you're doing fine. You're in control."

"But to take on a baby—"

"You wouldn't be doing it alone. You'd be doing it with me. I'd do my share. And if you didn't get pregnant—"

"I'd be heartsick. I'd never forgive myself, because you want it so much."

"I want you more."

"You say that now, but in ten years if there wasn't a child, you'd have second thoughts."

"We could have fertility treatments, in vitro fertilization, artificial insemination, or we could adopt, but all that's beside the point. Do you love me?"

She sighed. "A lot."

"Do you want a baby?"

"I *love* babies."

"Do you want mine?"

She took the deepest, most wanting breath, and suddenly every worry in the world seemed petty. "Do I ever."

He grinned. Then he took her hand and set off at a clip.

"But you haven't *bought* anything, Davis," she protested as they sailed through room after room.

"Oh yeah, I did."

The bed was dressed in yellow, the pillows in dark green and white. Both yielded to sheets of the whitest percale, softened and scented. An antique highboy watched, as did oils of the hunt and a bouquet of lavender, and if the brass scrollwork behind their heads spelled a message, they didn't get it.

The inn was elegant and high-priced, the room vacant only because it was midweek. Davis had allowed Francine one phone call en route, to give Sophie his beeper number. They had no spare clothes. None were needed. By mutual consent, they slept little.

Grace was frightened. Something was missing, but she didn't know what it was. She sat on the edge of the bed, trying to ignore the voices in the sitting room, and waited for help, but it didn't come.

The voices rose. She slid from the bed to the chair, then backed up to the wall. From there, she snaked out a hand and grabbed the telephone.

"Where are you?" she cried in a furtive whisper, but all she heard in return was a droning hum.

She dropped the hand piece, hugged her middle, and looked outside, but she couldn't see a thing in the dark.

Something was missing. Words, thoughts, comfort.

Silently, stealthily, she moved along the wall to the door. They were out there, all right, but she had no choice. She couldn't stay here all alone all night.

Inching the door open, she peered out. She watched them closely, picked a moment when they were lost in argument with each other, then slipped through the crack and made a dash for the door at the other end of the sitting room. Her bare feet didn't make a sound, but they must have heard the swish of her nightgown, because their heads flew around. She fled into the hall and slammed the door, pulling it tight to make sure the latch caught.

Oh, were they mad. She could hear them shrieking. Fearful that this time they would come after her, she ran off down the hall. Something was missing. Someone.

She had to find help, but she didn't know which way, there were no signs, no markers. So she ran a few steps, flattened herself to the wall, ran a few more steps. She darted into one room, but there was no one there, no comfort. She darted into another room. It was worse. Pitch-black.

Everything was like that, if not pitch-black, then shadowy. Dark forms loomed in corners, taking her breath, sending her running on with one eye over her shoulder. They were after her, she heard their angry chatter. She had to keep going, had to find the one who could make her feel safe.

She turned in at another room, then another adjoining it, so sure that this was where help should be that she closed the door and sealed herself in. She turned to find a small lamp burning on a table, and looked around in hopeful expectancy, only to see—she gasped and plastered herself to the wall in terror—a dog!

She was done for! She couldn't possibly get past it this time! It was too close, too large, too mad!

Whimpering, she pressed a hand to her chest to still the wild throb of her heart. She thought of opening the door and escaping. But *they* were out there, loud and clear, and, besides, the dog would tear her limb from limb if she so much as tried to leave. Chained dogs, filthy dogs, foaming-at-the-mouth dogs were chained for good reason, her mother always said.

That this dog wasn't chained made it all the more frightening.

But—it wasn't chained. Nor was it foaming at the mouth. It didn't even look dirty, and she would certainly be able to see if it was, because its hair was very short. This dog wasn't at all monstrous. It was thin and oddly shaped. It wasn't crouching. It didn't look like it was ready to attack.

Strange, but it was making the same kind of whimpering noise she was. She wondered if it was afraid of them, too.

"Good dog," she said in a wobbly voice. "Good dog. Good

dog." Because her legs felt wobbly, too, she slid down the wall to the floor.

The dog ducked its head. Eyes on her, it took a step forward. She gasped. It stopped and whimpered.

"Good dog, good dog, good dog," she whispered.

It shook its short tail and ducked its head again.

She didn't think it looked scary that way. She thought it looked sad. Maybe even lonely.

This time when it started forward, she held her breath. She didn't think it was going to hurt her, and, anyway, she couldn't go anywhere. Still, she tucked everything loose away—hands, elbows, knees, toes.

At her movements, the dog stopped and waited. She stayed as flat to the wall as she could. It crept forward. When it was inches away, it sat down. Its head was level with hers.

"Good dog, good dog."

She had to let it know that she wasn't the enemy, that it was *them* out there, squalling. So she held out a shaky hand. The dog sniffed it. At the first touch of its tongue, she whipped her hand back to her chest. The dog simply watched. It wasn't panting, wasn't showing its teeth. And it *wasn't* dirty, she saw that close-up now. Nor, despite what her mother always, always, said, did it smell.

As she watched, torn between bemusement and horror, it stretched right out on the floor by the bulge of her nightgown that marked her feet, and put its muzzle on its paws. Every few seconds it looked up at her.

The fist at her chest slowly opened. She lowered a tentative hand and touched its head, thinking, good dog, good dog. The head felt bony, but smooth and silky. And warm.

The dog made a sound. Not a whimper this time, but something sweet. She rubbed the top of its head. When it didn't snarl or move away, she rubbed it more.

It was a *nice* dog. It felt good, all silky and smooth. It seemed to like what she was doing. Her mother was wrong here, too.

Slowly she began to relax. The warmth of the beast soothed her. It made her feel less alone, almost content in the silent night.

Only then, thinking about that silence, did she realize that the noise outside the door was gone. She listened. It was true. Either they had given up on finding her and left, or they had been too frightened of the dog to stay.

As her tension ebbed and her limbs slackened, her feet slipped from beneath the nightgown. Moments later the dog covered them with its chin, making them warm.

Twenty-One

Painful memories are like knots on a piece of pine. Though sanded and smoothed, they never quite disappear, and for good cause. They add character to the finished work.
—GRACE DORIAN, from *The Confidante*

Robin tapped away at her computer long into the night. She was so engrossed in her work that she didn't hear a thing until a voice touched her ear. "Mom?"

She whirled around. "Megan! Megan. You frightened me." She glanced at the clock. It was nearly one. "What are you doing up so late?"

"I had to go to the bathroom." Her voice was groggy, her eyes squinted against the light. She looked defenseless for a change. "How's the book?"

Robin pressed Save. She had no desire to lose what she had just written. It was good stuff. "Movin' right along."

"Do you like it?"

"Oh, yeah."

"When'll it be done?"

"With a little luck? May."

"In time for Brad's graduation. Then what?"

"Professionally? I don't know. I haven't thought that far."

Megan was leaning against her arm, by way of the arm of the chair. She looked very young with her face bare, her hair sticking up, and her huge T-shirt hiding newly formed curves. Robin loved the innocent little girl she had been. She wasn't wild about the bitchy teenager who was always bickering with her brother, but a woman was growing inside there. Robin wanted the kind of relationship with that woman that Francine had with Sophie, even that Grace had with Francine. Differences and all, they were close. So maybe Grace had done something right.

"Any suggestions?" she asked Megan.

Megan gave a one-shouldered shrug. "You'll be making lots of money. Maybe you could take a couple of months off."

"Over the summer?"

"In the fall. Once Brad's gone. I've never had you alone. He did, before I was born. I want my turn."

Robin was startled to think of Brad being so grown as to pack up and go off to college. Where had the time gone? She had raced her way through his life.

Not that his absence wouldn't bring a certain peace to the household, and yes, time with Megan. "I like that idea," she said, slipping an arm around her daughter's waist.

"Me, too. Let ol' Brad bug someone else. Wow. It'll be weird."

"I think you'll miss him."

"I will not."

"Who'll you fight with?"

"I don't know." Then, a sheepish half smile. "Maybe we can fight on the phone."

"So I'll have to work to pay the phone bill."

"But you'll have all this *other* money that'll keep coming in from the book. Are you gonna do talk shows and stuff?"

"Maybe. Publicity boosts sales."

"Do you want to write more books?"

"I might. What do you think?"

She sucked her lip. "I think I like you better writing books than being gone all the time for the paper. I like you writing *The Confidante*."

Life was certainly easier now, Robin reflected. Even aside from sensible hours and financial stability, there was that little thrill she felt each time she turned into the Dorian estate, each time she entered Grace's office like she belonged, each time she talked with Grace. In her debilitated state, the woman was human. She was likable. Though she generated but a shadow of the charisma she once had, it wouldn't let go. The Confidante was apt to live forever.

"I don't write *The Confidante*," Robin said. "Francine does."

"She's your friend."

"She's my boss."

"You go out to lunch together. You go shopping together. Francine might do most of the column herself, but you help. That's what you talk about most when you come home."

"Do I really?"

Megan nodded.

Too vividly Robin remembered her mother talking about *The Confidante* every night. The last thing she wanted was history repeating itself. "Is it awful?"

"No. I *like* it. It's wild to read the paper and know that my own mother had a hand in it."

"What about all the other articles I've written?"

"Those were articles. This is *The Confidante*. My friends read it all the time. I tell them that I hear about columns before the paper does. They are so jealous. You're a celebrity. I wouldn't mind if you kept on doing it."

It struck Robin that she wouldn't mind either. Not that it was likely. She was only part of *The Confidante* because she was writing Grace's book—and she was doing a damn good job, if she did say so herself. Her mother would have been proud. Then again, probably not. She would find something to fault. She was never satisfied for long. Perfection was the only way to go.

Her mother should only see Grace now. No perfection there. Between Francine, Sophie, and Robin, and Jane, Marny, and Margaret, and, of course, Jim O'Neill, she was rarely alone. But she was. The talk could surround her, could go right over her head, while she was miles away in her own non-world, looking lonesome, frightened, or lost. At times like those, Robin actually felt for her.

Not enough, though, for her to forget her goals. They were foremost on her mind when she arrived at work the next morning. Grace was having breakfast in the kitchen. When Robin joined her, Margaret went off to make beds.

"How are you this morning?"

"Fine," Grace said brightly. She knew Robin now, though she didn't always remember her name. "How are you?"

"Fine, too. But I was up late trying to get the facts straight for this book. I still can't find the town where you were born. What was its name?"

Grace frowned.

"The town where you were born," Robin prompted gently.

"That was a long time ago."

"Was it in New Hampshire?"

"We don't go north."

"Because you don't want to go back there?"

Grace considered that. "Goodness" was all she said.

So Robin tried a different angle. "Did you know Margaret in Tyne Valley?" When Grace gave her a curious look that could have meant a dozen things, she tried, "Are your parents still there?"

"Oh, my parents are dead."

"Your sisters?"

"Sisters?"

"Your brother?" When Grace looked confused, she said, "Hal."

"But Hal died."

"What about Johnny? Is he still in Tyne Valley?"

"Why is he there?"

"Maybe he lives there."

"Johnny? Goodness, no."

"Where does he live?"

Grace looked worried. "Why are you asking?"

Robin sat straighter. "I'm trying to write your biography, but I don't have those early facts."

"Why do you keep *asking*?"

More softly—since Grace looked like she might cry, which, to her own chagrin, made Robin feel awful—she said, "Because your readers want to know about where you grew up and what you did there."

"I say nothing."

"But if you want them to buy your book—"

"Nothing," Grace cried, and stood up.

"I don't even know what your name was then," Robin said, but Grace just walked through the door and was gone.

Always a hugger, Grace had grown even hungrier for physical contact. She liked to be stroked, liked to be held. Even the smallest touch seemed to calm her.

So Francine sank down hug-close on the piano bench and picked out accompanying notes.

"There's a long, long trail a winding . . ." Grace sang in a soft soprano.

Francine stumbled a time or two, laughed, caught up.

". . . where the nightingale is singing," Grace went on, leaning into her, swaying, "and the white moon beams . . ." She continued to sing, Francine continued to play, they swayed together right through to the end. ". . . 'til the day when I'll be going down that long, long trail with you."

Francine would have started to bawl if she had dwelled on the words, but Grace was eminently pleased. "Very nice. You're a good player."

"Thank you. You're a good singer. That's a lovely song."

"It was popular when I was little."

"But you weren't Grace then."

Grace smiled at her strangely. "What?"

"What was your name when you were young?"

"When I was young?"

"I don't think it was Grace. It may have been Doris. Or Kathleen."

Grace said nothing.

"Am I warm?" Francine teased.

"Where were you?"

"When?"

Grace waved her free hand over her shoulder.

"Last night?" Francine asked, and for once didn't even *think* of hedging. Rarely did five minutes pass without her thinking of Davis and what they were trying to do. She was in love. She wanted Grace's approval. It might be too much to ask. But she couldn't stop trying.

"I was with Davis," she said.

"Davis?"

"Marcoux."

"Every night. It's every night. You're not home anymore. Always running out. I don't know where you go. But it's no good."

The words were so absurd, the voice such an abrupt turn-around from the sweet singer Grace had been moments before, that Francine had a thought. "Is that what your mother used to say?"

"Every night. And you're with him. I know you are."

"Who is he?"

"Why, why, you said his name."

"Not my guy. Your guy. Who was he?"

Grace glanced at the door. Her face grew hopeful. "Is Jim here?"

"He won't be here for a while. But think, Grace. Not about Father Jim. About your boyfriend before that."

Grace thought. And thought. Sweetly, almost coyly, she said, "Your father was my boyfriend."

"What was his name?"

"You tell me," Grace said.

"Johnny."

"John."

"Before John Dorian. Johnny. Johnny who?"

Grace looked confused.

Francine rubbed her arm, wrist to shoulder, lightly, lovingly. "It's important, Mom. I want family. If I have relatives out there, I need to know."

"His family didn't like me. Did I tell you that? They said I was nothing. They left when I came."

That sounded like the Dorians. "Why did they think you were nothing?"

"No money." She smiled gamely. "I sure showed them."

Francine couldn't help but chuckle. "You sure did. What about the other family? Is there family in Tyne Valley?"

Grace's smile waned. She grunted.

"I need a starting point. What was your name?"

"Don't ask me that. I'm tired of it." She started to rise, but Francine clutched her arm.

"Have I ever met any of your family?"

"Don't ask me that. You're trying to confuse me." She made a mournful sound and shook her head. Sitting back down on the piano bench, she cast a fearful glance at the door. "They're after me, you know. I've had calls from the President and the Vice-President. They tell me that I'm being protected, but I know how these plots work. There's always someone who breaks through the guardrails. It's a big, big, big conspiracy. From Dallas."

"No, no, Mom, there's no conspiracy."

Grace remained unsure for another minute. "No?"

"No. It's just me. Francine. Your daughter. Wanting to know more about where I come from." Because I may be having another baby. *Another baby. Incredible.* "I need to know, Mom."

Grace put a hand to her chest. "Goodness. I don't."

"Someone in the family tree had diabetes. Do you know who?"

Grace considered that. "Doesn't—doesn't—?" She pointed toward the other room.

"Sophie, yes, but someone in an earlier generation must have, also. Maybe one of your sisters?"

Grace tugged at her arm. "I have to go."

"Where?"

She plucked, plucked, plucked at her blouse. "This—this

thing isn't good. I thought it was. But I haven't been shopping. I need to change clothes."

When she rose this time, Francine let her go.

"Okay, Grace," Robin said. "Let's brainstorm." It was worth a shot. Nothing else seemed to be working. "I'll say a nickname, you say the real name to match. Give me the first one you think of."

Grace sat back in her desk chair and folded her hands in her lap. "Why?"

"You may remember something if we do it this way."

She grew worried. "I'm not good at remembering. I used to be. Not now. I can't do my work. There's *so much*."

"That's why I'm here," Robin reassured her. "I'm helping you get it done." But time was growing short. She couldn't include anything in the book that hadn't been confirmed, but she hadn't yet found a snitch in Tyne Valley, and Grace was right about her memory. It was bad and getting worse. "When I say 'Sparrow,' what's the first thing that comes to mind?"

"Why is everyone asking questions?"

"I'm your biographer. It's my job to ask questions. Who is Sparrow?"

"I know Sparrow."

"What's his real name?"

Grace scowled. "I don't know. We just called him that."

"What did his parents call him?"

"His parents? Goodness."

"What were *their* names?"

Grace waved the question aside.

"Scutch, then," Robin tried.

Grace tensed. "How do you know Scutch?"

"I don't, but you say the name a lot."

"I do?" She pondered that.

"Scutch was another friend. What was his real name?"

"Do I talk about Scutch?"

"What was his family name?"

"I shouldn't do that," she murmured to herself.

"What about Wolf?"

Grace's head came up fast. "I didn't say anything. *Nothing*."

"I know," Robin soothed, "but if you had a friend called Wolf, what would his real name be?"

Grace turned in her chair until she was facing its arm. "I didn't say it." She shook her head, swallowed. "Not me."

Robin touched her shoulder. It felt frail. "No one's accusing you, Grace. I'm asking. That's all."

Grace drew into herself. "Did I say it? I don't remember. No. I did not. I *did not!*"

Robin wanted to believe she was being deliberately evasive, but she wasn't sure at all. Grace looked haunted, as though the secrets she kept were as painful for her as for everyone else.

Suddenly, badgering her smacked of prodding a wounded bird with a stick. "Would you like some tea?" Robin invited.

Grace remained huddled sideways in the chair.

Robin added to the lure. "Hot tea, maybe with a scone? Margaret was putting a batch in the oven. I'll run and get you one, if you'd like. Tea and a scone, Grace?"

Grace drew in a long, shaky breath. She gave Robin a hopeful look. Wanting, helplessly, to comfort her, Robin set off for the kitchen.

Robin's mother had gone quickly, six months after her diagnosis and then of a heart attack rather than what would have been a slow-growing cancer. Robin had seen her once at the very start of those six months, a perfunctory visit that had been as shallow as the best of their recent discussions. Robin hadn't taken her to a single doctor's appointment, bought her a single nightgown, or cooked her a single dinner. Suddenly she was gone, and it was too late.

In the person of Grace, Robin sensed she was being given a second chance to prove herself. As the days passed, she thought less about making headlines and more about writing the very best book she could.

Grace turned her face to the sun. Once upon a time, she would have worried about its effects on her hair and her skin, but she had forgotten all that. She was responding now to sensation alone.

Francine stretched out on an adjacent lounge chair. Had it been May, the warmth under the solarium glass would have had them opening windows and turning on the fan. But this was early March. The world beyond the glass was crystalline following a night of freezing rain. The sun was a sparkly joy.

Knowing a good thing, Legs had followed them in and now lay in the sun at the foot of Grace's chaise, where she wouldn't be seen unless Grace sat forward and looked. Even then, it wouldn't be a trauma. Grace seemed to have forgotten her fear of the dog.

"Comfy?" Francine asked.

Grace didn't answer, but she looked content.

"I've been going over the list of organizations you give money to. The Tyne Valley Beautification Committee is one. I didn't think you'd ever seen the place." She waited, but Grace seemed unaware that a response was in order. So she asked directly, "Have you ever seen Tyne Valley?"

"We don't go north. I don't like the cold."

"You also give money to the Gold Star mothers. Did you know boys who died in the war?"

"The war?"

"The Korean War."

Grace would have been in high school when it was fought. Even if she had never graduated—a stunning possibility, Francine realized—she would have known boys who had died.

She shuddered, but remained quiet, eyes closed, face to the sun.

"Did you have friends who died in the Korean War?" Francine repeated.

"I don't know what happened after I left."

"After you left where?"

"High school."

"What high school?"

"We used to wonder what would happen."

"To whom?"

"Everyone. Then I left." She shrugged, as though that was that.

Francine shifted gears. "You give money each year to the Tyne Valley Public Library."

"A library is good. I used to go." She shrugged again.

"Where was the library you went to?"

"Why, in town."

"Where in town? Do you remember what was beside it?" There was a grocery store on one side of the library in Tyne Valley, Sophie said, but if Grace named something else that was distinctive, they might track it to another town.

"We used the side door."

"Where was the side door? I mean, what was beside it?"

Grace shot her a "What are you *talking* about?" look.

The expression was so sane and Francine's need so strong, that she shifted to the chaise and took Grace's shoulders. "Tell me, Mom," she pleaded, lest the moment's lucidity end, "where was that library?"

Grace looked startled.

"Please. Where was it?"

Nothing.

"You know. I *know* you know. Where were you born? New Hampshire? Vermont? Canada?" Francine gave her a tiny shake. "It's right there in your head."

"No," Grace said.

"It *is*. Same with your name. That would be the last thing to go. Your. Name. You can't have forgotten it."

"Grace."

"Before Grace. Think. Think about the man you loved, the one you loved enough to carry his baby and let another man raise it as his own. Who was he? *Who was my father?*"

Grace drew in her chin. "Don't get mad. I never did anything to you."

"You held out. All these years, you led me to believe something that isn't true." And now there was Davis and a possible baby between them. Francine was thinking about genes in ways that she hadn't before Sophie.

"Don't tell them," Grace said.

"Tell *me*, and I won't *have* to tell them."

"We were supposed to be home. If they knew—if they knew—"

Francine gentled her fingers. "If they knew, what would they do?"

"Ohh-ho, Lord," Grace cried. "Don't ask."

"What would they do?"

"Yell. Hit. Cook. Clean. Run. Run. *Leave*."

"Is that what you did? You left, when they hit you?"

Whatever was in Grace's mind vanished. "What?" she asked with nothing more than simple curiosity.

"Did you leave home because someone hit you?"

Grace didn't answer. Even her curiosity was fading.

"Is that why you fund the home for battered women?"

"Battered women. Write them, for me."

"Write *who*?" Francine cried.

"My column. People don't know what to do. Did I answer that letter?"

Francine had no idea what letter she meant, and doubted Grace did either. The words seemed more reflex than anything and were accompanied by a blank gaze. The moment's lucidity was gone.

"Yes. I think you did," Francine answered sadly.

"That's good," Grace said, and humming, returned her head to the chaise and closed her eyes.

Prior to then, Francine had seen Grace as her adversary, the knowing hoarder of information that she craved. In her desire to get it, she had given only passing thought to its contents. Now, for the first time, she wondered if Grace was a victim.

Haunted by the image, she spent longer than ever wading through the new courier pack that arrived from New York.

"Dear Grace," one woman wrote, "Six months ago I met a man who seemed like the answer to my prayers. He was handsome and had a good job. He said he loved me. He even paid for a big wedding. Then he changed. He started complaining about everything I did. The other night he didn't like the dinner I made so he slapped me . . ."

"Dear Grace," another wrote, "My boyfriend got laid off last month and is taking it out on me. He kicks me whenever he walks past me. When I tell him not to, he says he's just kicking the chair 'cause he's angry. But it's my legs that're all black and blue. He says if I ever tell he'll do more than kick . . ."

"Dear Grace," a third wrote, "I'm running out of excuses. I've fallen down stairs and walked into walls and slipped in the shower so many times that the doctors are asking questions. You know what I'm saying? But if I leave my husband, I lose everything. He's the one with the career. The credit cards, the cars, and the house are in his name. I had a drug problem a couple of years ago, and I've been clean ever since, but he'll say I'm not. He holds the power."

Write them, for me, Grace had said. So Francine did.

> *You aren't alone. Violence against women has reached epidemic proportions. Every fifteen seconds, say FBI statistics, a woman is beaten by the man in her life. She neither asks for it nor deserves it. Nor do any of you.*
>
> *While violence against women is about power, your being abused doesn't mean that you have no power at all. You do. You have the power to leave. You may not want to. You may be afraid, or embarrassed, or too proud. You may be in love with your man. But is love worth the pain and degradation of what he does to you?*
>
> *There are many reasons for why a man batters a woman. They usually go deeper than the frustrations of a lost job or a meal he doesn't like. But violence is wrong. He needs counseling. If he refuses, suggest that you see a counselor together. If he still refuses, see a lawyer. File a report with the police. Get a restraining order from the court.*
>
> *Whatever you do, act now. One beating should*

alert you to your man's potential. Don't wait for
the second beating. Remember another statistic:
Nearly one third of all female homicide victims are
killed by husbands or boyfriends.

Check your local phone book for Battered
Women shelters and hotlines. I have listed several
below. Use them. Please.

Francine liked the column. It was bolder than others
she'd written, but she was feeling bolder. She kept thinking
about what Davis had said about her doing things well. His
confidence gave her confidence. She couldn't pick a better
cause to use it on.

It was the lead-off column the following week. Francine read
it to Grace first thing in the morning, when she was freshest
and most apt to absorb it. She listened and nodded, but said,
"That sounds good," in a way that suggested she hadn't absorbed it at all.

"We've never been as direct," Francine said, "but this re-
flects the present day in tone and content. Battered women
should get out. Don't you think?"

Grace nodded.

"I mean," Francine added on the chance that she didn't
think so at all, "I know it's easier said than done sometimes,
especially when there are children, but it is one way to stop
the battering."

Grace nodded again.

"Like your leaving home," Francine said, then, fearing she
might distract Grace from the immediate issue, which was
winning her praise, added, "Tony loved it."

Grace smiled. Francine had the awful feeling that she

didn't remember who Tony was but was too embarrassed to ask. Even after losing so much of herself, she still had the occasional wherewithal to hide the extent of the loss.

Francine sighed. "I want you to be proud of what I'm doing."

Grace nodded.

"Are you?"

Grace frowned. "What?"

Francine sighed again, gave Grace a hug, and went off to work, telling herself that the column was super, that *The Confidante* was on the cutting edge, and that Grace would certainly have approved had she been herself.

Then Tony called, in a snit.

Twenty-Two

It is fine to equate courage with grand schemes and lofty ideals. More frequently, it is the by-product of recklessness and wishful thinking.

—GRACE DORIAN, appearing on *Oprah*

"She's done it this time," Tony declared. "She's been edging away from the center for months, but now she's gone too far. The phones are ringing off the hook. Proponents of the nuclear family are upset. One instance of lost temper, and the woman should leave? What kind of advice is that?"

"Sound advice," Francine stated, though a knot was forming in the pit of her stomach. "Those letters weren't about lost tempers. They were about beatings. A man who hits once will hit again unless he gets the message that hitting is wrong."

"So tell him. No need to walk *out* on him."

"For God's sake, Tony, do you think these women haven't

tried telling? Do you think cowering in a corner trying to ward off blows isn't saying something? But it doesn't register. Men like that need to be shocked."

"Oh, they'll be shocked, all right. They'll be shocked into doing worse. That's what the statistics show, y'know."

Francine did, and it frightened her, but she wasn't backing down.

Tony raced on. "Do you have any idea what would happen if every woman who was ever hit went to a shelter? The shelters would burst."

"That's right, and the people who deny that there's much of a problem would have to admit that there is."

"Yeah, well, in the meantime, those people have threatened a boycott of the papers that run *The Confidante*."

Francine laughed. "Cute."

"I'm serious. A boycott."

She didn't laugh this time. "Because of *one column*?"

"That one column has hit the stands just when the extremists are wanting a vehicle. As volatile issues go, vilifying husbands is right up there with abortion. No matter that other people have said the same thing Grace did, she has an audience that those others don't. Her popularity will be used against her—against *us*. We don't like boycotts, Francine. I doubt her other affiliates do either."

Francine had a sudden vision of the work that she'd been so proud of destroying *The Confidante*. She was trying to grasp the horror of that when Tony whined, "Didn't it occur to Grace that something like this might happen? Her audience is middle America. They want moderate solutions to things, not militant ones. Christ, if I didn't know better, I'd think *you* wrote this. Where the hell is she, anyway? I haven't talked with her in months. If she refuses to leave that castle of hers, it's no wonder she's out of the mainstream."

"*She* isn't out of the mainstream," a riled Francine shot back. "If she was, there wouldn't be any uproar. What scares those extremists is that so many women will agree with her column. And let's *talk* about that nuclear family they love. What good is it, if the wives are battered? What good is it, if the children are witness to hatred and disrespect and bloodshed?"

"You're missing the boat, darlin'," Tony said in a smarmy way. "The nuclear family isn't my concern. This newspaper is. We're in business to make a profit. If we're boycotted, there is no profit."

"So what do you suggest?" Francine challenged.

"A little humility, maybe."

"Grace should apologize for saying the right thing? *Think* about it, Tony. If the nuclear family is held together by fear, it isn't worth diddly."

"Eloquent. Is that your view, or Grace's?"

"Mine," Francine said without apology, "and I'm in a position to influence Grace on this, so it's good that you know where I stand. We're not backing down, Tony. We're not printing a retraction. Someone has to stand up to bullies. I'm proud that *The Confidante* did."

"And when it loses its forum?"

"It won't lose its forum. Let's be real here."

"O-kay," he said with a loud sigh. "Tell me what *you* think Grace should do."

"Off the top of my head? Take on the opposition. I think we should dedicate an entire *week* of columns to the issue of battered women. Let the bad guys threaten a boycott. Let them do it on the evening news. Let them do it *tonight*." She grinned, on a roll. "The sooner the better, the louder the better. Letters will start pouring in from our readers. Let's print what they say."

"What if they disagree with Grace?"

"We've printed many letters disagreeing with Grace."

"Will Grace admit she was wrong?"

"Is that necessary?"

"If we lose sales, it may be."

Francine suddenly realized something. "You said you liked this column. You went out of your way to tell me that—or was it all feel-good baloney?"

"You sounded down. I tried to cheer you."

"Pu-lease." He had macho instincts with the timing of a toad. At least he wasn't asking her out anymore. She couldn't imagine being with Tony, much less having *his* child.

Davis was something else.

"You don't seem to understand what's at stake if business plummets," Tony went on. "We could both lose our jobs."

"Not me. I don't have that worry."

"Wise up, sweetcakes. If we drop your column, where do you think you'll be?"

"At the *Telegram*," Francine said calmly. "And at all the other papers that will jump to run Grace Dorian's column not so much in spite of, but *because* of a boycott. Boycotts generate millions of dollars worth of free publicity. Just think. *The Confidante* will make newscasts all over the country. *Time, Newsweek, People*—the possibilities are endless. The *Telegram* is dying to have us. Shall I give them a call?"

"Good God, no. George would have my head."

"Then back us up, Tony. Because I'm telling you, if you don't support us on this, we'll quite happily get up and walk."

"You told him that?" a worried Amanda asked over the speakerphone to an audience of Francine, Sophie, and Robin.

"I did," Francine said. She had the nervous stomach to prove it, but she wasn't backing down. "Grace was loyal to Tony and George when the paper changed ownership and was shaky. Now it's payback time. Besides, Tony is panicking needlessly. The calls he got were probably from anonymous members of an anonymous group that wouldn't know how to organize a boycott if it tried. We're talking the fringe here."

"The fringe can make a hell of a lot of noise," Amanda warned. "That's what makes them scary."

"And *because* they're scary, we have to stand up to them."

"With caution."

"There's no place for caution when it comes to abuse."

"I didn't realize you felt so strongly."

Francine hadn't either. But the column had practically written itself. "Maybe it was talking with Grace, or learning that she funds a shelter in Tyne Valley—" Or looking at Sophie, who had been abused. Or thinking of having another child, who might be vulnerable years hence. "I'd like to do what I told Tony. Let's defy anyone who dares boycott our papers. Let's run a week of letters from Grace's readers. What do you think?" she asked Sophie.

"Perfect," was what Sophie thought without any hesitation at all.

"Robin?"

Robin grinned. "Pretty exciting. The concept of letting the abused speak for themselves is brilliant. What they have to say, and the fact that they can say it, will take the steam out of a boycott. Not to mention that, selfishly speaking, the more notoriety Grace gets now, the better her book will sell."

"Amanda?"

There was a pause. Francine held her breath. Amanda

was their link to the commercial world. Her support was a must.

Amanda sighed. "I guess I have to agree with all of the above. Besides, the column is already in print. To waffle after the fact won't speak well for the thought that goes into its preparation."

Francine felt a moment's guilt. It was basically her thought, her preparation, her lack of anticipation of a problem, thank you, Grace. "Do you think a boycott will materialize?"

"Someone might try. But I doubt it'll work. Let's hope I'm right."

The story made the early news, the late news, the entertainment shows, and the morning papers. By noon the next day, a boycott had been called against those newspapers that carried *The Confidante*, and the Dorians' phone was going wild. Grace was in demand. Reporters wanted her, talk shows wanted her, friends wanted her.

Francine had painted herself into a corner.

Again Amanda's voice came from the speakerphone. "You have no choice, Francine. The media world wants Grace, but Grace can't appear. You'll have to do it."

Francine's stomach was twisting. "You know I can't."

"No, I don't. Okay, so you're nervous. But you're an articulate spokesperson, particularly on this issue. I heard you myself."

"They want Grace, not me."

"They can't have Grace. So what do we tell them?"

Francine scrambled for viable excuses. "That Grace is sick. That she can't travel. Hell, we tell them that The Confidante speaks through her columns, period."

Robin said, "That would be fine if Grace hadn't always been so visible. But if no one appears on her behalf, the questions will be rife, and if that happens, the controversy could shift from wife beating to Grace."

"Won't it happen anyway if I suddenly appear in Grace's stead?"

"Not if you face the questions head-on. Point out that *The Confidante* has been a joint effort for years, and say that Grace is simply sitting this one out. People expect Grace because they've never had an alternative. Give them one, and they'll be fine."

Sophie came to Francine's side. "They're right, Mom. You may hate the public side of the business, but right now it'd be worse to sit home. It'd be seen as cowardice. Or indifference. It'd be like shooting ourselves in the foot."

So it was three against one.

Then four against one. Only Davis's arguments went deeper. "Remember we talked about doing *The Confidante* your own way? Well, you're almost there. You're putting your own stamp on things in ways you wouldn't have thought you were able to a few months ago, but that's only because you never had the chance. So here's your chance to do something even bigger."

"But I don't *want* to be a celebrity," Francine pleaded. Some things had become very clear in recent weeks. She wanted a quiet life—yes, to write *The Confidante*, but, more, to be a wife and, oh yes, a mother.

She was due for her period soon.

Absurd thought.

At her age, even if she *did* conceive, it would take a while. Hadn't she and Davis done it without a condom the very first time? And she hadn't conceived.

He took her face in his hands. "I don't want you to be a celebrity, either. But if you do this, you'll prove that you *can*, and once you have, you won't ever have to again. The transition will be complete. *The Confidante* will be yours. You can do whatever you want with it then—keep it the same, change it around, ban any and all public appearances. But you can't let it die now. It's too much a part of your raison d'être."

Looking at him then, totally lost in his love, she would have believed anything he said. "What if I throw up on Larry King's desk?"

He laughed and hugged her tight. "You've come to the right man, little lady. I have just what you need."

Just what she needed was a mild stomach settler, and while it didn't do much for a thudding heart or sweaty hands, it did keep her from the ultimate embarrassment. That was some comfort. She had plenty else to keep her on edge. She worried that she would trip over a wire and fall on her face, or look at the wrong camera, or forget the host's name. She worried that she would look unappealing, jerky, not at all Gracelike. She worried that she would say something stupid, that people would laugh at her, that she would embarrass *The Confidante* and negate all that she was trying to prove.

She worried for the fate of *The Confidante* should a boycott take hold.

She worried that Grace would wander away from the house, or not understand where she was, or forget her while she was gone.

She worried that Grace would forget *everything*, leaving no hope at all of learning certain truths.

She worried that she would get her period.

Sophie was a godsend, her escort-cum-cheerleader on the road. "You were incredible, Mom," she said after the first show, and, "Awesome," after the second, and, "I don't care *what* you say about your wrists shaking, you looked totally *calm*," after the third.

It got easier with each one, not that Francine was ever comfortable before or dying to see tapes after, but she found that she could handle most any question posed. Project confidence, Grace always said, and it worked. She appeared as The Confidante, hence she was The Confidante. Having decided not to even try to look like Grace, she looked more bohemian than proper, with her waving hair and her untailored clothes, but there were few comparisons made.

That actually bothered Francine. She didn't understand how people could forget so quickly, any more than she understood how Grace's friends, most of whom now knew about her illness, could stay away. Yet the flow of visitors had slowed to a trickle. The queen was dead; long live the queen.

Those thoughts added to her fire. Once she got going in defense of *The Confidante*, she was passionate. With interviews as often as not centering on *The Confidante*'s place in American life, rather than the narrower issue of domestic violence, she was in her element. Borrowing Robin's analysis, she suggested that the letters *The Confidante* received each week reflected the mood of the people. She read those letters, she said. She *knew* how much *The Confidante* meant to its readers. The concept of outside forces trying to manipulate the column was an insult to its millions of fans.

She was always most eloquent after getting updates on the boycott, which was taking the form of flyers handed out at newsstands, and picket lines strategically placed for media attention. Newspaper sales had taken a slight dip, Tony delighted in telling her when she checked. Only at her prodding did he admit that the dip was *very* slight, possibly related to the late-winter storms that were keeping some commuters home, and doubtful to hurt the paper's general health.

By week's end, Francine was eager to be home. Robin had been sorting the letters New York sent, but she wanted a hand in deciding which ones to print. So there was that to face. And Grace, who hadn't dealt well with the telephone, had been more agitated than usual, more paranoid. And Davis, who didn't yet know that her period was late. By just a day. Still.

"You are really very good at this," Sophie remarked shortly before they landed at La Guardia. "Are you sure you don't want to do it again?"

"Not on your life," Francine declared. "I'll be thrilled to become reclusive. You do understand," she added only half in jest, "that what I did, I did for you."

"You did not."

"I did. I had to show you that a woman *can* do even things she thinks she can't."

"Meaning?"

"If I can swallow sheer terror and go public, you can go on a date." She ignored the warning look Sophie shot her. "You can't hide forever." Much as she loved having Sophie around, twenty-four-year-olds didn't belong with their mothers.

"I'm not hiding," Sophie insisted. "I see my friends."

"Only girls."

"I meet guys, too. There's Jamie the chef and Alex the brother of my friend Julie's roommate. Now, there's Barry the producer and Dave the soundman. And there's Douglas. We talk on the phone a lot. I'm just not rushing to go out."

"Because of Gus?"

Sophie hesitated, then moved her head in a way that said it probably was.

With feeling, Francine said, "If it weren't for the fact that I want him staying far away from here, I'd call his employer and get him fired."

Sophie snorted. "He deserves it, the bastard."

"But he is far away. And you're older and wiser. Really. If I can trust myself to tackle a talk show, you can trust yourself to tackle a date."

"I will. In a little while."

Grace didn't know about the boycott. Francine hadn't dared tell her—hadn't known if she would understand and, if so, how she would react. A critical Grace would have made her more nervous. So, prior to leaving, she had simply said she was doing a publicity tour, which should have pleased Grace but, in essence, evoked no response at all.

Don't expect too much, every book on Alzheimer's said. Still, as the week progressed and her confidence rose, Francine hoped. Surely Grace had watched one of the television spots. Surely she would be impressed.

Francine was nervous when the house came into sight. She remembered other separations and reunions, the chest-tightening she had always felt as a child, the relief at having her mother home again. Her relief now was mixed with apprehension.

Grace was in the kitchen. She looked up in alarm when they appeared and said a high, tremulous, "Goodness. You're here. But you're too early. I'm not ready."

Francine thought she had been fully prepared; still, she was shocked to find this older, frailer, and more simpleminded

Grace rather than the one in her memories, the one she wanted.

Smiling through unbidden tears, she gave her a hug. "I *missed* you, Mom." She held her back. "You look pretty. Very domestic." Francine hadn't seen her wearing an apron in years. "What are you doing?"

"Making dinner. There's quite a crowd coming. You're too early."

Did she recognize them? Hard to say. At least she hadn't backed up to the wall and called them spies.

"Oh, but you can keep right on cooking," Francine assured her. "Our plane just got in. Sophie and I couldn't wait to see you."

"How are you, Gram?" Sophie asked, giving Grace a squeeze. "What are you making?"

"Something—hmmm," Grace seemed to sample the words, "something nice."

"It's veal à la Russe," Margaret said, "with new potatoes and broccoli. Have you eaten?"

"Not for hours," Francine said, though she wasn't particularly hungry, what with her stomach jumpy. "And then, nothing like veal à la Russe." She touched Grace's cheek. "The interview in L.A. went well. It's being run nationally later tonight. Will you watch with us?"

Grace frowned. "We have quite a crowd coming for dinner. At least a hundred. Maybe three. I don't know how long they'll stay." She was looking at Francine, seeming confused. Suddenly, her face crumbled. She sounded heartbroken. "Where were you? I was looking all over. I couldn't find you anywhere."

Francine took her in her arms, frightened by how fragile she felt. It was a minute before she could speak. "We were doing all the things you wanted us to do—talk shows and print interviews. You would have been proud of me. I didn't stumble once."

"You weren't here," Grace whimpered. "I didn't know where you'd gone. I was worried that someone had taken you away. Kidnapped you."

"Oh, no. That wouldn't have happened. That's why I took Sophie with me. She was my bodyguard."

"I have one, too," Grace said. "A dog."

Francine held her back and gave her a skeptical look. That was when she saw Legs on the other side of the table.

"She doesn't leave your mother's side," Margaret said. "She keeps the conspirators away. She even keeps the bad dreams away. Grace takes her outside for walks, don't you, Grace? The fresh air is good for them both."

Francine had wanted Grace's approval of a dozen other things, a dozen more important, more immediate things. Still, she felt an odd little joy in this.

"Well?" Davis asked. He had come straight from the hospital, walked in the front door, taken Francine's hand, and strode down the hall to the bedroom he had never seen before.

She was being pressed sinfully flat to the closed door now, too pleased to see him, too excited to feel him, too anticipatory herself to pretend not to know what he meant. "One day. It might not mean a thing. It could be the trauma of travel."

Davis grinned his cocky, crooked grin. "It means something."

"I'm always late when I'm tense."

He slipped a hand between them. "You're not just late."

"One day, Davis. That's *nothing.*"

His grin grew. "Hot damn."

"Davis," she protested, though it was hard, what with his hand low on her belly, "you aren't listening. I wouldn't have even *said* anything if you hadn't asked. You'll get your hopes up, and my hopes up, and then we'll be let down."

Davis slowly shook his head, his grin now the smuggest of smirks.

And, of course, Francine wanted to think he was right, so she laughed in delight: "You're an arrogant beast. What do I ever see in you?"

"Beastiality," he said, and hungrily caught her mouth.

Francine was two days late, then three days late. She didn't tell anyone but Davis, and then she continued to point out the dozen other possible causes. When he pressed her to run a home test, she held off. She was worried that it might read negative.

The Confidante was a consuming diversion. Of the thousands of letters that had arrived, two thirds supported Francine's stand, half of the remaining disagreed, and the rest asked advice on variations of the theme. Working with Sophie and Robin, she selected a representative sample of the pros and cons for print the following week.

While the media attention died down, those intent on enforcing the boycott kept at it. Two of the smaller affiliates dropped *The Confidante*, causing a brief media blip. The other affiliates continued to monitor their sales.

If Grace was aware of any threat to *The Confidante*, she didn't let on. Once a cover-to-cover newspaper reader, she did little more now than make a show of studying the front page when she came to the kitchen for breakfast. She was able to read individual words, but put them in a group, sandwiched between other groups, and she was lost. So Francine read to her—from the newspaper, from magazines, from books. She didn't read her anything about the boycott.

Time crept.

Francine went through moments of intense self-doubt, alternately convinced that she had ruined *The Confidante*, that Grace's book would be a dud, that she wasn't pregnant at all, that Davis wouldn't want her in spite of what he had said, since, apparently, her very own father hadn't wanted her.

Then George called to say that sales had begun to climb, and Amanda called to say that *The Confidante* was being picked up by four new papers, and the picketers dispersed and the pamphleteers went home.

Francine deferred all other doubts. Where *The Confidante* was concerned, this was her hour of glory.

Triumphant, she ran to Grace and told her the story start to finish, keeping her focused by holding her hands and her gaze. "We won, Mom!" she cried in conclusion, and waited for Grace to offer praise or a smile.

Neither came.

Francine gave her hands a little shake. "We *won*," she repeated, more urgent now. Grace *had* to understand. "Not only did we *not* lose popularity, but we gained accounts. *The Confidante* is stronger than ever. Aren't you *pleased*?"

Grace looked unsure for a minute. Then she nodded.

"*Think* of it, Mother," Francine kept on, wanting a sign so badly. "I wasn't sure I could do *any* of it. Remember, when you asked me to take over? I was *terrified*. But we did it. We came in *first*."

Grace sat through a silence, then said, "That's very nice."

"Did you follow my story?"

"Yes."

"Are you proud of me?"

"Yes."

Francine wanted to cry.

During those few days, it had been easy to ignore the unanswered questions about Grace's life. Suddenly, with the crisis over and the distractions gone, the unanswered questions loomed.

Grace offered nothing more than vague wisps of thought. She remained the same—which was, never the same. She could be calm or agitated, talkative or silent, trusting or paranoid. Davis changed her medication in the hopes of stabilizing her, but the disease was relentless.

"Why is she deteriorating so *fast?*" Francine asked him after easing Grace through a difficult bout of paranoia.

"It hits every victim differently," he explained, frustrated, too. "This is simply how it's hitting Grace."

Time was running out. Francine had to know what Grace was hiding, not so much for the book now but for herself. She begged Grace, but Grace couldn't give. She begged Father Jim, but Father Jim wouldn't give.

Another trip to Tyne Valley was called for. She knew she should make it herself, since she was the one with the most at stake. But she was afraid of what she might find. So she put it off.

Then Davis learned that his father had died.

Without the slightest hesitation—because Davis was the man she loved and his father had made him, and because she knew that despite the distance between the two men, Davis mourned, and because Davis's father was the grandfather of the child she might be carrying and she needed to pay her respects to him and to those others who might be hers by either blood or marriage—Francine packed her bags.

Twenty-Three

As with most virtues, honesty is relative. At the short end is the woman who confesses to wearing reading glasses, at the far end the one who admits that her diamonds are on loan.
—GRACE DORIAN, from an interview in *Mirabella*

Tyne Valley, just as Francine had pictured it, was quaint upon desolate. Though it was mid-afternoon, the main street was deserted.

"Gas station, general store, auto parts place," Davis narrated. "That's the Town Hall. Town Meeting's held there, usually the second Sunday of March."

"One day?"

"Not much to discuss. Main purpose is to give people something to do besides dig themselves out of the mud. There's a garage down that street. Cars breaking down is a given. That, and mud in March, and the Town Meeting. There's the library."

It was a sweet white house several hundred feet past the grocery store, and it did have a door on its far side. Francine wondered if that was the door Grace had stolen in and out of when she hadn't wanted to be seen.

"I'll show you the school," Davis said.

Francine touched his arm. "It can wait, if you'd rather see your dad."

"I'm not ready."

She slid closer. He tucked his hand around her thigh and shot her a smile, but it was feeble as smiles went, particularly his. She covered his hand with hers.

He showed her the schools where he'd raised hell—elementary school, junior high school, even, though it was a distance away, the regional high school. Then he circled back to town and stopped in front of the church, but made no move to leave the truck. His gaze went to the adjacent cemetery. It was a minute before Francine saw the two men digging far in the back.

Davis made a pained sound.

She drew his hand to her throat. "Is that where your mom is?"

He nodded.

She hadn't lost a parent young and could barely begin to imagine what he was feeling with regard to his mother. And now his father.

Francine remembered John's burial and the gut-wrenching feeling that came from seeing that dirt, that hole, that swallowing up for all eternity. With a chill, she realized that she would be going through it with Grace sooner than she wanted—Grace, who should have lived forever, or close to it, because she was good.

But she hadn't always been.

"There's something about parents," Davis murmured. "Something about losing them." He hitched his chin. "Putting them there."

The tremor in his voice had Francine fighting for composure. Pushing aside thoughts of Grace, she said, "You did everything you could for him."

"It wasn't enough. He lived a sad life. He died a sad death."

Duncan Marcoux had been alone, found stiff after a long, cold night. Davis had told her that more than once. It haunted him.

"You tried," she said softly.

"I left town."

"And in so doing, helped hundreds and hundreds of people."

"But not him."

"You made him proud."

Davis made a disparaging sound. "He barely knew what I did."

"He knew you were a doctor."

"But he didn't know what I *did*. Not really."

"He didn't need to, to be proud."

"He never said a word."

"That doesn't mean the feeling wasn't there. Don't you think he bragged about you to his drinking buddies?"

"Yeah. When he was drunk."

"So, he wasn't vocal when he was sober, but he had to be proud. You made it through college, medical school, and years of specialty training. You've built a practice and a house. You've helped so many people live such better lives. He would have been proud, Davis."

Davis took her hand to his mouth and held it there while he watched the men work as if it was his responsibility, as

Duncan's son, to supervise. After a time, he put the truck into gear.

He drove all the way back through town and out the other end, down a mud road to the quarry where the town kids swam in summer. They parked there for a bit, then he drove her up a winding mountain road to the lookout at its top. Closing their coats against the March wind, they climbed out.

The view was lovely, all gray-green with the occasional burnt orange roof or red barn, still winter shabby but not without charm. Francine tracked surrounding villages by the white steeples rising like pins from a map.

"Feel anything?" Davis asked.

She looked at him in surprise. She had thought he would be too consumed by his own thoughts to be thinking hers. But she should have known better. He was a remarkably sensitive man. That was just one of the things she loved about him.

"I like the town," she said. "It's small and sweet and quiet. The greenery is striking, and it isn't even spring. Do I feel like I've been here in another life? No."

"You haven't met people yet. The whole town turns out for wakes and burials. Kind of like Town Meeting. Better'n mud." They were having the wake for Davis's father that night, burying him the next morning. "Maybe someone will recognize something in you, or know something that might help."

"Maybe," she said, and slipped her hand into his pocket.

When Sophie turned fourteen, Grace had given her a slim, gilt-edged book of poems. She knew most of them by heart, even now, a decade later, still took solace in their lilting rhythms and poignant thoughts. Hoping Grace would, too, she had taken the book from its sacred place and tried reading her favorites aloud.

But Grace was upset. She sat, she stood. She walked around the solarium, returned to the chaise, and sat down, only to stand again a minute later.

Sophie closed the book. "What's wrong, Gram?"

Grace laced and unlaced her fingers, knit and unknit her brow.

Sophie glanced at the window. "If it weren't raining, we could take a walk. Want to take a drive instead? Just down the street and around? I'll go slow."

"I can't go that far." Grace looked at the window, looked back. "Where is she?"

It was the fourth time Grace had asked in less than an hour. Once, Sophie would have chided her, but this Grace was ill. "Francine is in Tyne Valley with Davis. His father died."

"His father?"

"Duncan Marcoux."

"Duncan Marcoux," Grace repeated. She rocked back and forth, hands knotted. "I don't think it's safe. Someone may have her."

"Francine?"

"Why isn't she here?"

Still patient, still confident in an attempt to make Grace confident, Sophie said, "Because Davis's father died. She's in Tyne Valley for the funeral. She told you she was going. She'll be calling later."

Grace rocked a little more, knotted her hands a little more. She glanced worriedly at the door. In a fearful voice, she said, "People all over the country are after me. I don't think I'm well hidden. I need someplace where they won't be able to find me."

Sophie put an arm around her. "You're fine, Gram. You're with me. I'll keep you safe. Come on. Let's walk around the house."

"Where's—um—the other girl?"

"Jane had a dentist's appointment. She left an hour ago."

"Not Jane," Grace said, visibly frustrated as she tried to recall the name she wanted.

"Robin?" Sophie asked.

"Robin's right here," Robin said, walking in. "You," she said to Sophie with a twinkle in her eye, "have a caller."

Sophie was instantly wary. "Who?"

"Douglas."

With a look of raw fear, Grace clutched her arm. "Goodness. Goodness. Where's my dog? I need my dog. My dog will keep me safe if they attack. Dog?" She looked on the far side of the chaise, then, frantically, around the room. *"Dog?"*

Legs was under the chaise, directly beneath her. Sophie pointed and waited until Grace had looked herself. "She's on the lookout, Gram. She'll take care of you."

Not quite sure that she wanted to see Douglas, Sophie went down the hall. He was in the front foyer, wearing jeans, an anorak, and a light sheen of rain.

"I know you didn't invite me," he began before she could speak, "but I had to drive through on my way to Greenwich, so I thought I'd stop and see if you were in."

He looked damp, mellow, and harmless.

She leaned against the newel post at the base of the stairway, folded her arms, and dared a small smile. "I'm in. What's in Greenwich?"

"A gallery interested in a show. I have some of my stuff in a minivan out front. Want to take a look?"

"Come see my etchings kind of thing?"

He slipped his hands into his pockets. "Purely innocent.

This is, at least. Not all my thoughts are. I keep asking you out. You say you aren't seeing anyone else. Is it me?"

"No."

"Then what?"

Sophie liked Doug. If he was the black sheep of his family, he was a gentle one, long on hair, long on legs, long on tolerance. The same creative strain that made him an artist made him worth talking with for hours on end, which was what they had done often of late. She was thinking she might like more.

Sliding down the newel post to the second stair, she wrapped her arms around her knees. "The last time I was with a guy I was raped."

His eyes opened wide.

"We'd been together for a while," she said. "I wanted to cool it. He didn't."

"Christ, Sophie, I'm sorry."

"So I'm feeling a little . . . gun-shy is the word my mother uses. I guess it's accurate."

"You haven't dated since?"

She shook her head. "It happened two days before I met you." She sputtered a laugh. "Good thing, maybe. Otherwise, you might have hated me on sight. I have a perverse side—y'know, do things just because someone tells me not to. Funny how certain experiences tone you down fast. So, anyway," she said, feeling self-conscious, even weak, shaking her hair back to suggest indifference though she felt none, "I am bruised, as they say. I'm not sure you want to date me."

"I want to date you," he said without missing a beat. "Besides, you don't sound bruised. You sound pretty straight. Have you been in therapy?"

"Lord, no. Dorians don't do things like that."

"Why not?"

"Because they don't *look* good. Actually, that's not true. Well, it is, but it's not the main reason. We don't see psychiatrists, or join support groups, because we have each other. This is a strong household of women." Minus one now, she realized, but still strong. Yes, strong, in spite of everything.

"That's slightly intimidating."

"Not for a strong man. And I don't mean strong physically."

"I know you don't," he said with just the right measure of strength.

"I'm also diabetic."

He gave her a blank look. "Is that supposed to scare me off?"

She shrugged. "It means I have to be careful when I do things. It's a drag."

"So's all of life, if you want to look at it that way. I don't."

He was still by the door, still with his hands in his pockets. Grace would have had her throat for not inviting him in, Sophie thought, then thought again. The Grace in the other room now would be sitting beside her on the stair, wondering if Doug had an Uzi under his anorak.

There wasn't any Uzi. Sophie trusted him.

She had trusted Gus, too.

But Gus had been all brawn—work, play, everything in between. He hadn't known about feelings, or hopes and fears, or true sensation. He functioned with his body alone.

Doug functioned with body, mind, and soul. She knew. She had popped into a gallery in New York and taken a look at his work. Not that she would tell him that, yet. A little insecurity did the male ego worlds of good.

But if his work showed sensitivity, and his telephone

persona showed sensitivity, and his remaining at the door rather than crowding her showed sensitivity, he might just be worth a cautious shot.

So, rocking a little on her butt, hands still cinching her knees, she said, "Want to come in?"

Davis drove around town for another hour, stopping occasionally to point something out, tell a story, or sit in silence. One of those silent stops was at his father's house. He didn't leave the truck, just looked.

The house was small and less shabby than others on the strip. Francine imagined that Davis had paid someone to paint it so it was painted, that he had paid someone to fix the steps so they were fixed, that he had paid someone to plant grass so grass grew, and grew, and grew. Even winter dead, it had a bushy look.

Francine wondered why Davis's sisters hadn't had it mowed. She wondered other things, too, but sensed Davis's need for quiet. So she communicated her caring by simply holding his hand.

"He wouldn't move," was all Davis said as he shifted into gear and drove off.

They went to his sisters' houses then, one diagonally across from the other, neither more than a block from Duncan's. Both women were rangy. Francine guessed that they had been handsome once. Now, they had the same bleak, overgrown look as their father's lawn.

She met husbands, children, grandchildren, and friends. She saw the same and more at the funeral home that evening. There, too, she saw Duncan Marcoux. "Done up nice" was the prevailing opinion.

"Damn right," Davis muttered under his breath when

they heard it still another time. "He never looked that kind in his whole stinkin' life. It's the ghost of his potential you see. The real thing died an early whiskey death."

Francine saw the physical resemblance at once. Whereas his sisters captured a feature here or there, Davis captured it all. A larger, kinder version of the man laid out in his Sunday best in the casket, Davis was definitely his father's son.

That alone might have been reason enough for him to grieve, but Francine knew there was more. He grieved for that potential—for jobs never held long, a better life never realized, intelligence lost. He grieved for the relationship he had never had with his father, and the comforts he had offered that had been rebuffed. He grieved for his mother as he hadn't had the maturity to do when he'd been young.

Francine knew all this from the words he murmured, from the way he kept her hand in his through the evening, and, later, the way he fell asleep with his head tucked to her breast.

It struck her that she could be perfectly content doing nothing more than holding him just so when he was in need.

It also struck her that there might be something to be said for fertility treatments, or artificial insemination, or surrogate motherhood, or even adoption if she wasn't pregnant.

It struck her that she ought to find out if she was.

But that thought took a backseat to the emotion of the next day's funeral. Afterward, Davis had food enough brought in to his father's favorite bar to feed the whole town, and the whole town came. The weightiness of wake and funeral gave way to something almost celebratory, with Davis in its midst smiling, shaking hands, even laughing with an old friend or two.

Francine's thoughts turned inward. She willed the room

to be a Ouija board and her eyes the hands that would move and move and move and stop on a person who bore her genes. But they didn't.

She chatted with Father Joseph Crosby, with the town moderator and his wife, with the town librarian and dozens of others who thanked her profusely for her mother's generosity, but when it came to asking questions, she was tongue-tied. How did one suggest to a total stranger that one's own mother, now a prominent woman, might have come from their town and had a secret lover, to boot? Such an intimate thing. It would have been a betrayal of Grace.

So she was feeling blue, as though an opportunity had been lost, by the time the luncheon broke up. When Davis asked if she would mind a final stop at the cemetery before they headed home, she was almost relieved to burrow back in his grief.

She stayed at the graveyard gate while Davis walked back, affording him those last few moments of privacy. The diggers, who had joined the rest of the town at the bar before returning to finish the job, were just leaving. Davis shook their hands, slipped his in his topcoat pockets, and stood, a dark, distant figure, with his back to Francine.

One of the diggers passed by her with a finger to the bill of his cap. The other stopped. He was beanpole tall and angular, red-cheeked from the cold, and in his sixties judging from the bristle of gray hair escaping from his cap and the wrinkles fanning his eyes.

"I'd give you my hand, Ms. Dorian, but it's a bit dirty," he said. "The name's Jeb George. I'm the undertaker."

Of course. She had seen him at the wake, and again at the funeral. He had been formally dressed both times, with a pinched manner to match. Now, wearing baggy wool pants and a plaid hunter's jacket, he seemed more at ease.

"I never did like the ceremony part of the business," he said, reading her mind, "but it was all my daddy had to hand down, and all I had to keep my wife and kids fed, and when you get something, anything, in a town like this, you take it. Tough part is burying people you know." He shot a glance in Davis's direction. "Take Duncan Marcoux. We were buddies as kids. Then he started drinking, and he didn't have much time for buddies."

Francine remembered Davis saying that Duncan and Father Jim had been pals. She pulled her coat tighter at the throat and held on. "Then you knew Jim O'Neill?"

"Sure did," Jeb said. "Boy, were we sorry to see him join up after all that, but he's done more for us by leaving than he ever could around here. He got us your mother. She's helped bury many a local who couldn't afford much. My thanks to her, and to you."

"It's our pleasure." She took a breath. "So you knew Father Jim." She kept it light. "Then you must have known Rosellen McQuillan."

"Couldn't know one without the other. They were together all the time. She left when he did. Couldn't have stayed here without him. He was the only thing kept her sane."

"Where did she go?"

He pondered, shrugged. "No one ever heard from her again."

"Not even her family?"

Jeb George made a disdainful sound.

"How many of them were there?"

"McQuillans?" He raised his eyes to count. "Five. No six. But the boy died young. It might have been a blessed thing, that death, compared with what he'd'a had living under Thomas McQuillan."

Francine barely breathed. "Is the boy buried here?"

"Sure is." He gestured her into the graveyard and led her back almost to the place where Davis still stood. "Got a new stone a while back. It was one of the first things Father Jim asked be done with the money he brought. He wanted it for Rosellen."

It was a simple stone, smooth on its face, rough all around. It stood with three others. One belonged to Hal's father, Thomas. The second belonged to his mother, Sara. The third belonged to his sister, though Francine couldn't make out the name through her tears.

She held her chest and managed a broken, "Who was Johnny?"

"Johnny?" Jeb George grinned. "Why, Johnny's Jim. He's James John O'Neill, just like his daddy was. Since everyone called the daddy Jim, we called Jim Johnny. Sounds confusing, but it makes perfect sense."

Oh, yes. Perfect sense. And so simply learned. No battles, no long interrogations. Just the right questions asked, the right connections made.

Francine pressed gloved fingers to her upper lip to keep from sobbing.

Robin was showing Grace the manuscript pages that were complete, telling her how she had organized the chapters on *The Confidante*, reading portions that she liked.

Grace seemed to know that she was supposed to be listening, but Robin doubted that she absorbed much. She would look at the pages and nod, then glance worriedly at either the window or Legs.

"Francine will be back tonight," Robin tried to assure her. "No need to worry. She's safe and sound. You talked with her this morning. Do you remember that?"

"I think so," Grace said.

"She said she'd be here for dinner. She wouldn't lie to you. You've raised her on honesty."

"Honesty before."

Robin smirked. "Honesty before dignity. That was what you always said. That was what *my* mother always said, because you said it." She sat back in her chair. "It still stuns me sometimes, being here with you. You were a fixture at our dinner table all those years, so perfect, so out of reach."

Grace frowned. "Out of reach?"

"You were all my mother ever talked about. She thought you were brilliant. She read us your columns over dinner, then told us how they applied to our lives. I remember one. It was the prettiest thing in the world. 'Life is a garden,' you wrote. 'Seeds sown and tended will grow.' Whoa," she breathed voluminously, "did my mother ever get mileage from *that*. As far as she was concerned, it explained why we were lousy kids. Forget tending our seeds—we weren't *sowing* them properly. We didn't have the basics, couldn't add right or read right or write right, so of *course* we didn't get A's. Then we couldn't study right. Then we couldn't dress right. Then we couldn't *speak* right. So how could we even *think* of growing?"

Grace was staring at her in alarm. Robin stopped talking, took a calming breath.

More quietly, she said, "My mother took things to extremes, but we didn't understand that. We were young. We had no way of defending ourselves. She would take what you said, interpret it to her liking, and drill it into us over and over again." She made a frustrated sound. "It's been more than twenty years since some of it, but I still get upset."

Grace rose and went to the window. Robin watched her for several minutes, then joined her there.

"The thing is," she said, needing to make the point, "it's fine to say that seeds sown and tended will grow, but what if there's no rain? What if there's a sudden frost, or a blight? What if the seeds aren't good to begin with? Does the person who sows and tends have control over that?"

There was a silence, then a low "No" from Grace.

"Could I help it if I lost out on a plum summer job because my major competition was the state senator's daughter? Was it my fault that my hair was curly and just wouldn't *do* what Dorothy Hamill's did?"

Another silence, another low "No."

"Could I help it if my husband's childhood sweetheart showed up newly divorced, with her sights on him? Could my brother help it if he lacked the small motor control to make his handwriting neat?"

"No."

"So what it boils down to is that 'life is a garden' is sweet and rosy and optimistic, but not realistic. So is it fair to push it down people's throats?"

"No."

"Then why *do* you?"

"I don't mean to."

"You talk of flexibility, but there's always a fixed message. If it isn't 'Rise Above,' it's 'Invest in Life,' or 'Every Cloud Has a Silver Lining,' or 'Sugar Wins Hearts.' Take that last one. Sometimes it works, sometimes it doesn't. If you're dealing with a hardhearted son of a bitch, you can use a *ton* of sugar, and it won't do a thing."

"I know."

"And then there's 'Strength Is the Show That Must Go On.' Well, it's surely clever. But the fact is, damn it, that we're human."

"Yes."

"No human can be strong all the time. Or we can be strong, but not strong enough to do what has to be done. Or we can be *totally* strong and still not be able to make the show go on. So it's *bullshit*."

"I'm sorry."

"And then you attach love to it." Robin barreled on so that her mother could hear it once, at least once, before dying on her so fast. "You expect the world from us—you expect more than *you've* ever given—and then when you don't get it, you resort to little digs and jabs and put-downs. Oh, they're subtle, but they come out in place of expressions of love so that in the end I don't know whether you love me or not—"

"I do," Grace cried. "I always did, I always did, I *always* did, only I wanted more for you, more for you than I made."

Robin stared at her. She took a shuddering breath and swallowed hard. It was a minute before she realized what she'd done.

Feeling embarrassed, but oddly relieved and somehow aware that an apology had been given, then humbled in its wake and stunned to see this different side of the old Grace, a side that said she was human, too, she threw her arms around her and held her tightly.

They were both trembling. Grace was making soft weeping sounds, saying she was sorry—or perhaps Robin was saying it, she was certainly thinking it but suspected that Grace might be the more honest of them, after all—until after a bit Grace broke free and ran from the room.

Francine stayed at her grandparents' graves long after Jeb George left. Davis kept a supporting arm around her, but after an initial blurting out of what she had learned, she couldn't speak. She could only stand there shaking. When she began to shake from the cold as well, he put her in the truck and started driving again, much as he had the day before but for her benefit this time.

He showed her the house where the McQuillans had lived. It wasn't far from his father's and was in worse shape, though it had been years since a McQuillan had lived there.

He showed her the house where Jim O'Neill had grown up, where his parents had died, one soon after the other, and the houses where Jim's brothers and sisters still lived. He asked if she wanted to meet them. She did. But she had to meet Jim as her father first. So she shook her head no.

He parked for a time outside the library Grace had used, then cruised through town pointing out those of his father's oldest haunts that might have been hers, too.

"Was your dad Wolf, Scutch, or Sparrow?" she asked, thinking that it would be ironic to the point of cruelty if Duncan Marcoux had been a player in Grace's hallucinations.

But Davis said, "No. He was running with a tougher crowd by the time he was sixteen. Maybe Jim blamed himself for losing Duncan, too. Maybe that was why he took me on. I don't know."

Francine didn't either.

But then, she didn't know much about what made Jim O'Neill tick. She had no idea how a man could see his own daughter day after day, year after year, without letting on. Even when she asked. Even when she *begged*.

Francine remembered the story of Father Jim's love for Rosellen. She remembered crying for his loss, for all he'd given up. But he hadn't given up all. He'd had the best of both worlds. And he hadn't had the decency to tell her.

"I actually thought of it and ruled it out," she said at a

random moment. "I decided that it was just too much to think that a man so honorable as to aspire to be a priest wouldn't have married the girl he impregnated."

A bit later she said, "It explains so much—giving birthday gifts to Sophie, playing chess with me, coming to the house in a heartbeat when anything went wrong, especially once John died." She caught in a breath. "I wonder if John knew?"

"You'll have to ask," Davis said, idling the truck on the shoulder of the road. "It's nearly five. You told Grace you'd be home for supper."

Francine shook her head. "I'm not ready." Her eyes filled when she turned them on him. "Why couldn't she tell me? There were times when I thought she wasn't saying because my father was a murderer, or something. But Father Jim? Did she think I couldn't keep a secret? Didn't he know I'd keep wondering, keep asking? *What were they thinking?*"

Davis's beeper sounded. He took it from the dashboard and studied the number on its head. Then he drove to a gas station less than a minute down the road and used the phone booth by its side. When he came out, his face was drawn.

He climbed into the truck and started off before saying, "Grace wandered away. They can't find her. We have to head back."

Twenty-Four

Winning matters far less in the overall scheme of things than who brings you roses when you don't.
—FRANCINE DORIAN, from *The Confidante*

Grace hitched her legs in close and hugged the brick wall. She knew where she was. She always came here when she was homesick, or scared, or tired of being someone she wasn't. But she didn't remember climbing up. And she didn't think she could get down. Everything beneath her was black.

But she was safe. They wouldn't find her here.

If only it weren't so cold.

She tucked in her face. Her breath was warm and felt good.

What had happened? She had been warm enough before, talking with—talking with—what *was* her name? She had been talking with—talking with—that girl, and had started to cry because that girl was onto her. That girl *knew*.

They were coming. She knew they were. They had been closing in for days. Now they were coming to take her away.

She peered into the dark and saw nothing. "Where's my dog?" she asked the night. Her dog was supposed to protect her. But she had lost it. "*Dog? Where are you?*"

She listened, but she didn't hear the dog. What she heard were musical sounds, trickles and bubbles and rushes, and she was suddenly in another place, sitting on the ground with her back to weathered clapboard, sheltered from the rain by the eaves as she watched water spurt from the rusty down-spout at the corner of the roof.

But that was a bolder sound. This was gentle, soothing, even musical. Because she liked music, she let herself listen and be lulled. Smiling, she closed her eyes.

If only she wasn't shaking like this. Was it time for tea?

She heard a sound. Lifting her head, she looked around in fear. Where was she? How had she gotten here? Why couldn't she *see*?

Something hurt—her foot, she thought—so she unfolded her leg and extended it, only to have it hit air. She recoiled fast and shrank against the wall.

Then she listened to the music again. She did like music. She heard the tinkle of piano scales, felt her fingers pressing the notes, but only when no one was home. No one should know that she knew so little. No one should know how bad she really was.

The drive was filled with cars and the house ablaze with light when Francine and Davis arrived. They ran inside to find a worried group.

"We've searched the house top to bottom," Sophie said.

"We've searched the grounds. We've searched the garage and the cottage. It's raining again, and it's cold." She looked frantic.

"What happened?" Francine asked.

"I was with her," said an equally frantic Robin. "I was telling her about my mother, and it got emotional—but she was lucid, more so than she's been in a while. She was hearing me and answering me. Then she broke away and went into the other room. I gave her a minute to collect herself, but when I went looking, she wasn't there. I checked the other offices, and the solarium, and the parlor."

"We thought she might have taken Legs out," Sophie picked up, "so we ran along the drive to the road, but we couldn't find them. We figured they might have gone with Jane to the bakery, but by the time we tracked her down, she was on her way home without Grace. By then we were *all* looking, and then Father Jim came."

Francine felt a hammer hit her chest. She looked across the room, along a path cut through the men who had come to search, at Father Jim, and for a minute she couldn't think of anything but what she had learned.

He seemed to know. Quietly he came toward her, and between his look and her thoughts, the intimacy was so strong that she took a step back. He held up an unsure hand, then touched her shoulder.

"We have to find her," he said in a voice that lacked its usual calm.

Francine swallowed. Yes, finding Grace was the first priority.

"Hubbell is taking half of the men to search the road," he said. "The other half are going to the river."

Francine shuddered at the thought of black water, rushing cold this time of year. "Where is Legs?"

"She must be with Gram," Sophie said. "They've been gone *four hours*, Mom." It seemed like an accusation.

No one had to explain the significance of the time, least of all Francine, who was trying to stay calm but entertaining the worst of thoughts.

Davis put a comforting hand on her neck. "AD patients may be unpredictable, but caretakers have found certain things to be true. The last memories to go are the oldest. Sing them 'Jingle Bells' and they'll think of Christmas. Give them fresh-from-the-oven cookies and they'll think of Mother. They retain childhood fears. Same with comforts. What comforted Grace when she was upset?"

Francine didn't have to think hard. Comforting Grace had been a major part of her life of late. "Gardening. Music."

"What else?"

"A bath."

"Any kind of water," Father Jim said. "When she was young, she loved the rain. She'd sit for hours under an eave near the downspout, mesmerized by the flow."

Sophie stirred. "She used to take me to the river when I was upset. We'd walk along the banks to the old sawmill and climb up behind the waterwheel—" She stopped, looked from face to face, said an apprehensive, "She wouldn't have. It's too slippery, too wet, too dark."

But it seemed the most obvious place to Francine. Taking one of the lanterns that stood on the table, she ran out the back door and across the lawn toward the river. The rain was a fine mist, made slick by the cold. She hadn't gone far when she slipped and landed hard on the ground, on her seat.

"God *damn* it," she cried, trying to scramble up, slipping again, more annoyed with clumsiness than anything else.

But Davis was all over her in concern. "Are you okay?"

"Help me up."

"Maybe you should go back to the house."

"That's my mother out there."

"It's our child in here."

She caught her breath. Then she took his face and whispered a fierce, "I wouldn't hurt it for anything in the world, Davis Marcoux. I'm fine, really I am, but the longer I sit here, the wetter I get."

He helped her up. By then the others had neared, so they set off again. As they approached the river, north of the line of lights that marked the other searchers, the noise of the water rose. They ran on toward the sawmill, calling for Grace all the while, but their voices were swept downstream on the current.

Legs came bounding from the water's edge. Francine knelt and tried to catch her snaking form, but she wouldn't be held. She ran in circles, darted up and back, looked positively ecstatic.

"What is she *doing?*" Sophie cried. "She's supposed to lead us to Grace!"

But Legs wasn't a bloodhound. She continued to gambol, running ahead only when they set off again for the sawmill's bent black shadow. The path around it was strewn with tree roots and rocks, so rough that Francine had no idea how Grace had crossed it. But she must have. The alternative was unthinkable. If she had gone into the water, cold as it was, surging as it was, she was surely dead.

"*Grace! Grace!*"

Legs was barking somewhere ahead.

Davis, who carried the largest flashlight, trained its beam on the waterwheel. Francine huddled against his side for a moment's warmth.

Sophie huddled against his other side. "There's only one spot to sit. Up in the corner—put the light there—no—behind the wheel—farther back—*there*."

"I see her!" Father Jim said, and ran toward the narrow strip of land between the mill and the water. Legs was already there, racing back and forth.

Sophie went after Jim. "I'm going up. He's too big."

Francine caught her. "You're not going up. You'll slip."

"I'm the best one. I'm the smallest, thinnest, lightest. Besides, I'm the only one wearing combat boots."

Combat boots. Sweet. Sophie would have traction. It occurred to Francine that one of the searchers downstream might be a climber, but there wasn't time to find out. Grace was perched precariously on slippery stone, in a raw drizzle, pitifully clothed.

Francine's hand shook as she aimed her lantern at the brick steps behind the wheel. Every other lantern was aimed there, too, with the exception of Jim's. He was standing directly beneath the spot where Grace was, using his lantern to light himself.

"It's me, Grace," he called. "It's Jim. Sophie is coming up to get you. Don't move yet. Wait for her. She'll help you, so you don't fall."

If Grace answered, her voice was either too feeble or the rush of the river too loud for them to hear.

Francine had a horrid thought. Terrified, she shone her light on Grace. She looked tiny, all huddled and wet and cold, but she did lift an arm to shield her eyes from the glare. She was alive.

Francine quickly retrained her light on Sophie and held her breath. She imagined Sophie slipping halfway up, or reaching Grace and both of them slipping and falling twenty-odd feet to the ground.

Davis came up against her back. She welcomed the support. "I never knew she took Sophie here," she cried. "Sophie never said a word. I'm going to wring Grace's *neck*."

"No, you won't."

"I will so. How did she get up there in the first place? She's sixty-two!"

"And in perfect physical health. It's an AD dilemma, reconciling a fit body with a failing mind."

Sophie moved slowly up the wall, hand over hand, in the lanterns' light wet and shiny against the wet and shiny gray stone. When she reached the top, she leveled off onto a narrow ledge, sliding slowly along it until she reached Grace.

Francine waited for them to start the slide back together. She could see Sophie talking, could see the movement of her head, of an arm. "What's wrong?" she yelled up.

It was a minute before Sophie yelled down, "She won't come! She doesn't trust who's here."

Francine tried to do what Davis had done, to think about what would make Grace feel most comfortable. Fewer people would do it. So she turned to those watching fearfully from the side. "Margaret, go back to the house. Jane, drive along the road and tell the men we've found her. Marny, alert the men downriver, but don't let them come close with their lights."

She approached the sawmill wall. Voice trembling, heart pounding, she called, "Mom? It's Francine! Everyone's gone but us. There's Davis and Robin. And Father Jim."

"No one's going to hurt you," Jim called in a voice that trembled nearly as much as Francine's. He moved even closer to the wall. "All we want is to take you home to warm up."

They waited tensely while Sophie repeated their words.

"She's still scared," Sophie called down.

"Legs is here! She'll protect you! She can't climb the wall, and she wants you down!" Francine held her breath for an instant, then added, "Please, Mom? I *need* you. And now Sophie's up there. If you don't come down soon, she'll get sick. You don't want Sophie to get sick. You've worked so hard to keep her well."

Jim was nearly flush to the wall, stretched to his full height, arms extended as though to snatch Grace to safety with only a few more inches. "You can't stay there forever, Gracie. You must be tired and hungry and cold. Please come down so I can warm you up."

"He's right, Mom," Francine tried, feeling weak and wet, struggling now to be heard over the water. "He's waiting for you. He's waited so long. You can be with him now, but you'll have to let Sophie help you down."

"I'm not going anywhere," Jim threatened, "not *budging* until you come down, so the longer you stay there, the colder I'll get." His voice gentled, pleaded, "But how can I warm you up if I'm cold? Please, Rosie? For me?"

Francine heard a gasp from behind her and knew it was Robin, but the words she wanted to hear—what Sophie was saying, what Grace was saying—were lost to the water's rush.

"Rosie?" Jim begged. "I want you with me, Rosie. Please come down, so I can carry you home."

"My God," Robin breathed, so close by Francine's side that, without taking her eyes from the two on the ledge, Francine easily grabbed her hand and held it tightly.

Her heart hammered. She saw Sophie slip an arm around Grace's shoulder, saw her talking, nodding, gesturing, saw Sophie glance to the side and move one booted foot in that direction. Slowly, slowly, the pair edged out of the corner and along the short stretch to the steps.

"Oh God," Francine breathed.

"They'll make it," Davis said. He took the flashlight from her because it was shaking so much, and held it steady on the pair.

"Oh God."

"Come on. Come on." This, like a prayer, from Robin.

Sophie descended the narrow bricks on her knees, manipulating Grace on her bottom, one step behind, while Legs barked and jumped, and the four on the ground moved along the wall beneath them. Her foothold slipped once, raising a collective gasp, but she steadied herself and continued down. By the time they were three feet off the ground, they were surrounded. Davis threw his coat around Grace, but when he made to lift her, Jim was there first.

"She's mine," he said, and scooped her into his arms.

No one suggested taking Grace to the hospital, where she would be more upset than not. Davis examined her and saw little wrong that a bath, hot tea, and warm bedclothes wouldn't cure. When all that had been done, and Father Jim made no move to leave her side, Francine left them alone.

She was sitting in a corner of the den's sofa with her knees to her chest, the whole of her wrapped in an afghan and her eyes on the chessboard when he appeared.

He leaned against the door frame with his hands in his pockets. "She's asleep. Robin took over the watch since Sophie's sleeping, too."

Francine nodded. She swallowed. So this was her father, this James John O'Neill. Her father. Who had taught her to play chess and had been her partner ever since. Who had taught her to be truthful in the eyes of God but hadn't been so himself.

Back in Davis's truck in Tyne Valley, she had been furious at him, but the past few hours had blunted that, leaving residues of bitterness along with an awful, awful hurt.

"So it's out," she said, "after all this time, all the begging and pleading. Want to know who told me? Jeb George."

Jim grimaced a smile. "Good ol' Jeb. Never were no fleas on him."

"I wish I could say the same about you." She tugged the afghan tighter. "Would it have been so hard to tell me yourself?"

"Yes."

"*Why?*"

"Because I promised Grace I wouldn't."

"Then it's *her* fault?"

"No. It's my fault. My fault, starting way back in the Valley. I left her to enter the seminary. If I hadn't done that, I'd have known she was pregnant and married her myself, and there would never have been any secret to keep. But by the time I learned it, she was already married."

"Why didn't she tell you?"

"She didn't know it herself. Not when I left. Not when she left. She didn't learn it until after she'd met John, and he was thrilled with the situation, for reasons that you understand."

Oh, yes, Francine understood that part. What she didn't understand was the subterfuge that had started then and continued even when John died, even when she learned of his sterility, even when she begged Father Jim for answers.

"So even when she learned she was pregnant, she didn't tell you?"

"She wrote me letters, but she never mailed a one."

"Why *not?*"

His gaze drifted to the floor. "She figured I had God and

she had John and that was the way it was meant to be. I guess there was an element of self-flagellation, too. We'd all been drinking that night in the Valley. I fought with one of the guys. Turned out he died of alcohol poisoning, but we were goading him on. We felt responsible. We thought being separated was our punishment." He looked up then. "Turns out we both led meaningful lives, and I got to be near you anyway."

It was neat and pretty. All's well that ends well, Grace might have said, but Francine wasn't wrapping it up so fast. "When did you learn you were a father?"

"After you were born. She carried you well past her date, so that wouldn't have given it away, but one look was all it took. You have my grandmother's face."

That raised a dozen other questions—about his grandmother, about his parents and siblings, about Grace's lost sister, about Claire, whoever she was—but for later. For now Francine's interest was more narrow, between her father, her mother, and her. "How did you feel when you found out?"

He studied his feet, thought for a minute, finally nodded. "Cheated. I knew I had no right, but I felt it. I felt like I'd lost Rosie and I'd lost you, and I knew it was probably just punishment for things I'd done, still, I felt cheated. I considered leaving the seminary. But what would that have done? Grace was married. I knew I'd never want to be with another woman. It seemed better to dedicate my life to God."

That sounded very noble. But Francine had had it with false virtue. "So you got an assignment near Grace."

He gave her a wry smile. "Near, yet so far." He shot a look heavenward. "Another of His little tests. Give with one hand, take with the other. I could be close to Grace, close to you, but only to a point."

"You passed that point after John died."

He held up a defensive hand. "No. After Grace got sick."

"Which was," Francine accused, "conveniently after John died."

Jim straightened from the door and advanced, looking fierce. "There is nothing convenient about what Grace has. Do you think I wouldn't have done most anything to spare her this? Do you think I dreamed of *this*? No, Francine. I did not. My dreams were the kind of dreams we had when we were kids, when everything around us was so dismal that we made up a fantasy world." He didn't blink. "And they were carnal, those dreams. Can't deny that. Oh, they had no chance of being realized; still, I dreamed them because they were all that I had. I'd held her in my arms. I knew what it was like—" He broke off, looking stricken, and turned away. His voice was less steady when he said, "I've often wondered if Grace's disease isn't His way of punishing me for those dreams."

Francine swallowed. "You should have told me."

He turned only his head and caught her gaze, looking more human than she had ever seen him. "You think I didn't want to? You think it didn't kill me to be here as a visitor? You think I didn't want the joy of claiming you as my daughter and Sophie as my granddaughter, and having you know who *I* was? You think it was *easy* watching my good friend John living with the people I loved?" He took a laborious breath. His voice grew even more harsh. "Do you think it was easy for me to reconcile the vows I took with the thoughts I felt? To pray? To hear confession? To counsel parishioners? To feel like a *fraud*, standing up there so righteous in church, knowing what I knew about myself?"

Francine reacted without thinking. "You've been a good priest."

"Good Father, cap *F*. Lousy father, small *f*." Stiff-backed, he walked toward the window. "Irony there, eh? And with Grace, too. She chose the name deliberately, you know. It was right after our friend died, and I'd gone off to the church. She wanted to be nearer to God, too. So she called herself Grace, as in a divine influence operating here on earth."

"But her life was a *lie.*"

Jim came around fast. "No. She did her best with the hand she'd been dealt. She never betrayed her husband. And she never betrayed me."

"What about *me?*"

"She gave you everything she could."

"But she lied all those years."

"No. She didn't. She simply didn't tell the whole truth."

Francine waved a hand. "Forget the issue of my parentage. I'm talking about Grace, herself, alone—the Grace who had every answer and did everything right and made everyone else pale by comparison. She was goodness personified. She put herself up on a pedestal—"

"She didn't," he interrupted with a sudden powerful calm. "You did. Her perfection was in your mind far more than it was in hers."

Francine opened her mouth to argue, but the words wouldn't come.

"She was your mother," he said. "She loved you—you felt her love, you responded with sheer adulation. Children do that. They think their parents are perfect until something happens to shatter the image. Spouses can do it. Disagreements over life decisions can, or just physical distance. In this case, it was Grace's illness. Suddenly she was saying and doing things that showed fallibility."

"Do you know," Francine said, teary now, "how . . . how *inadequate* I've felt next to her all these years?"

"Maybe she should have praised you more. Maybe she

should have been more tolerant of your need for your own strengths. But try to understand. She came from a place where people amounted to nothing. She had seen it happen time and again. She wanted more for you than that—she wanted the *world* for you. I couldn't blame her. So did I. So do I."

They had come full circle. The issue was accepting Jim as her father. She loved him, always had, but there was this new discovery and the hurt it brought.

"I never lied to you," he said quietly. "I may not have told you the whole truth, but I never lied. That's something, what with all my other sins."

"What other sins?"

"Loving Grace like I do." He gave a great, long, relieved-to-be-saying-it sigh. "All these years. Loving Grace."

Robin felt an odd peace as she watched Grace sleep. She had called and talked with the kids, had told them what had happened, and had said she was spending the night. They had no problem with that. She wanted to think they understood what she was feeling, but she doubted they did. She hadn't shared enough with them.

She planned to remedy that. She wanted them to know about second chances, because, sure as day, that was what she'd been given. Not only was she writing what was going to be a beautiful book, but the job gave her an excuse to be here. Grace was going to need help. Robin would be pleased to give it.

Her eye fell on the bedside phone. She glanced at her watch, then at Grace. She lifted the receiver, put it back down, lifted it again and held it to her chest. Then she turned it faceup and punched out the numbers that, though unused for a long, long time, were far from forgotten.

On the other end of the line, the phone rang once, twice, three times. Then it was picked up, and the voice of an elderly gentleman, a docile and obedient man, said, "Hello?"

She didn't have to worry about waking Grace. Her voice was made whisper quiet by the emotion clogging her throat.

"Dad? It's me. Robin."

Jim didn't once ask Francine how much of the past she planned to reveal in Grace's biography. She suspected he saw it as another of God's little tests.

She knew what she would do. But she wanted to hear what Sophie and Robin would do. So she let her coffee cup sit on the kitchen table, warming her hands, and was quiet.

Sophie looked at her, then at Robin.

Robin looked at Sophie, then at Francine.

Sophie looked at Francine, too. "Well?"

"Well, what?" Francine asked.

"We have truths now. What do we do with them?"

"What do you want to do with them?"

"I don't know. I'm still in shock. Prim, proper Gram, carrying on a torrid love affair with Father Jim."

"He wasn't a priest then."

"But he was destined for it."

Robin sighed. "We should all have a love like that."

"Once, not long ago," Sophie said, "she told me that I should find a good man without worrying about love. That the love would come. Why would she say that after what she had with Father Jim?"

"She was thinking about the circumstances of her own life and the decisions she made," Francine tried to explain, as Jim had tried to explain to her. "She thought Jim was lost to her. So she did what she thought was best for her child.

Once the decision was made, she made the best of it. The glass was half full."

"Are you defending her choice?"

"No. Just explaining it. Personally, I think it's sad. I'd opt for love first."

Sophie shot Robin a droll look. "In case you haven't guessed . . ."

"Set a date yet?" Robin asked Francine.

Francine felt a little thrill. "This weekend. Want to come?"

"Just like that?"

"One o'clock Sunday, in the parlor, followed by brunch. I told Sophie that she could wear whatever her little heart desires. Same with you." She smiled. "I'd really like you there, Robin. You turned out good, for a foe. Besides," her smile turned a little wry, a little sad, "it'll be interesting. Grace is wearing white lace. The part of her that takes little detours to another time and place thinks she's marrying Jim."

"Oh dear," Robin said. "Is that because she's still resisting your being with Davis?"

Francine wished she knew. But the greatest certainty about Grace now was that nothing was certain. Hard as it was to accept, there would be no peace until she did.

Take last night. Armed with three weapons and a battalion of organized thoughts, she had sat at the piano with Grace, picking out light little tunes. A mellow Grace had sung along, rarely missing a word.

"Tell me why . . . the stars do shine . . . tell me why . . . the ivy twines . . ." Then, finally, ". . . that's why I love you."

Francine gave Grace a hug. "I love you, Mom."

"Of course you do."

"And Sophie. And Davis."

Grace didn't say anything.

Francine wasn't sure she heard. More bluntly, she said, "We're getting married, Davis and I."

Grace said, "You are married."

"No. Lee and I were divorced years ago."

She was confused. "This isn't Lee?"

"No. It's Davis. He's your doctor."

"But, why are you marrying him?"

"Because I love him." It was her first weapon, and should have scored a direct hit.

"But . . . but . . ."

"I won't be leaving you. I'll be here with you every day, and only ten minutes away at night."

Grace looked worried.

So Francine hit her with weapon number two. "Jim is pleased. He says he couldn't wish his daughter with a better man."

"He couldn't?"

"No. He gave Davis the ball, and Davis ran with it."

"What ball?"

Francine rephrased the thought. "He gave Davis an opportunity. Davis made the most of it. Jim respects him tremendously."

Grace seemed to ponder that. Growing suddenly dreamy, she said, "I wore white lace. It was a long, long dress with a . . . a . . . what's that thing in back called?"

"A train."

"A train. It was just beautiful."

"It was. I've seen pictures."

"You have?"

"Many times. We can look at them later, if you'd like. Sophie is going to take pictures of Davis and me. We want the quietest, sweetest wedding in the world. It's exciting, don't you think? Will you be happy for us?"

"I'm happy," was Grace's dutiful response.

"I want you to be happy and proud and excited, like we are."

Grace didn't look to be any of those things.

"Want to know the most exciting thing?" Francine said in a conspiratorial whisper and launched her third weapon, "We're going to have a baby." She waited for Grace to respond. "Isn't that *incredible?*"

"A baby?" Grace asked.

Francine nodded.

"I had a baby once," Grace said, and burst into tears.

"Mother, Mother," Francine cried, squeezing her, "what's wrong?"

"My baby's gone."

"I'm your baby. I'm all grown-up, that's all."

But Grace had been disconsolate.

"I think," Francine told Sophie and Robin now, "she may never give us her blessing, not in as many words."

"But you know that deep in her heart she approves," Sophie said.

Francine wanted to. Just as she had told Davis that a sober Duncan Marcoux would have been proud of him, she wanted to think that a healthy Grace would have been proud of her.

It struck her that what mattered even more was whether she was proud of herself. And she was.

"Yes, she would approve," she decided. "She would approve of *everything* we've done—which gets us back to the project at hand." She shot Robin an expectant look. "How much should we say?"

Robin said, "You tell me."

"No. I want your opinion."

"My opinion? Grace's story, told in its entirety, would be parked at the top of the best-seller lists for weeks." She took a fast breath. "But your parentage is your business. The world doesn't need to know Grace's birth name, or the name of the town she lived in or the man she loved. There's a wonderful story without it, vignettes of a young girl leaving an unforgiving life, going to the city, investing her life savings on dresses enough to play a part, then getting the leading role. It may be a typical rags-to-riches story, but it's a whole new view of Grace."

Francine tried to remember the reporter who had done her best to trip Grace up. That woman was gone. This one had come to care for Grace. And Francine had come to care for her.

Robin went on. "No one has ever known about the threadbare clothes and the rusty downspout, about the three fancy dresses, or the Plaza, or the club where she worked. No one has ever known about the sawmill as a sanctuary. These are charming stories, not demeaning at all. They give the woman depth."

"And AD?" Sophie asked.

Robin deferred to Francine with a look.

"AD," Francine said. Less than a year had passed since Grace's diagnosis had turned her life upside down, and the illness continued its downward spiral. Grace's night trek to the sawmill was only one instance. There would be others, and greater challenges, as she worsened.

But Francine could learn to live with the havoc. She could put it into the perspective of a life that had been more full than most. So there was this new appreciation, and there were memories to savor. And there was, still, the future. Having planted the seeds of an inner peace, she wanted to make the most of these last days, weeks, and months with Grace.

She loved Grace. Neither AD, nor truths discovered late, nor approval withheld for all eternity could change that.

With confidence, she said, "Grace asked us not to tell when she thought it would hurt her image. But *The Confidante* is secure. And the people who matter already know what she has. And saying something might just draw attention to the disease. If we're talking about divine influences operating here on earth, Grace would like that."

Epilogue

Love is a meeting of minds between imperfection and adoration.

—FRANCINE DORIAN, from *The Confidante*

Francine ran her hand up Davis's thigh. She loved the tawny hair there and the sinew beneath, loved the way his hips cupped her hips and his front hugged her back. She loved the way his mouth nuzzled her neck. She loved the strength of him and his heat and the redolence of sex that enveloped them in lieu of sheets.

She was in heaven, and why not, with the man she loved bracing her spine and the babe she adored at her breast?

A year had passed since her marriage, and an emotional one it had been. There had been highs with Davis and the baby, ups and downs with Sophie in her own search for self, and lows, mostly lows with Grace.

But Francine had survived and grown stronger. For the very first time, she knew who she was, what she wanted, where she was going. For every heartache there was a brighter joy, for every failure a greater success.

"Look at her," Davis whispered.

Francine couldn't look elsewhere. Cream-sweet cheeks, a nub of a nose, downy tufts of honey-colored hair, with the sound of suckling above it all—it was dream stuff.

"Ever seen anything so beautiful?" he asked.

She hadn't. Nor had she felt it, the tugging that started in her breast and worked inward. She had never nursed Sophie. Breast-feeding hadn't been the thing to do in the Dorian home, what with a baby nurse waiting to give the new mother her rest. But Francine was doing things differently this time around.

Her age played a role in that, a blessing in disguise. So did Davis.

"I never imagined this kind of peace," he said. "Do all new parents have this?"

"I didn't with Sophie. I loved her to bits right from the start, but I was too young to appreciate moments like this." For that reason alone, having Kyla was special. If the worst came to pass, and Francine took sick as Grace had, there would be these memories to hold to the last.

Davis sighed against her cheek. "I could stay here forever."

"Not today. We're due at the house in an hour. Do you think Grace will know?"

"That it's her birthday? She'll know it's someone's when the cake comes out. Hers? Probably not."

Francine wanted to disagree, but couldn't. Grace didn't know names, often didn't know faces. Increasingly she didn't know sensations and emotions. She spent her days in a variety of activities designed to keep her alert and active, but she was led through them, more a spectator than a participant, a rider on a train lurching slowly downhill. She had reached the point of needing round-the-clock nursing care though she barely knew it.

She was just sixty-three.

Attuned to the direction of her thoughts, Davis stroked her cheek. "You care for her well. She gets plenty of love and attention. That's what she needs the most now."

"Like Kyla," Francine said.

The baby opened her eyes. They were Davis's eyes, all dark and daring, but in every other regard she was delicate and feminine, a little Dorian lady through and through.

"Hello, sweet," Francine cooed. "Was that good? You're just a little dallier, taking so long. Are you enjoying yourself?"

Kyla gave a toothless grin.

Davis laughed his delight. Francine felt it, and her own, straight through to her heart.

He sat up, reached down for the baby, and, with a crinkle of disposable diaper, put her to his shoulder. Francine rolled over to watch them together. There were gentle hands bottom and back, a soothing voice, soon a burp, and then there was Davis, strolling buck naked across the room with his daughter tucked in the crook of his elbow, gone off in search of diversion while his daughter's mother showered and dressed.

Grace was in the solarium when they arrived. Francine saw her every day, but coming upon her at odd times like this she most noticed the change. It was in her skin, her expression, her carriage, a concavity that suggested a doll that had lost the stuffing that gave it form and personality. She looked far older than her years.

Jim was beside her, returning her teacup to its saucer, dabbing at her mouth with a small linen napkin, stroking her cheek in such a gentle way that Francine was touched to tears.

It was a minute before she gathered herself. Then she went forward, gave Grace a big kiss, and said brightly, "Hello, birthday girl."

"Look who's here, Grace," Jim said. "Francine's here. And look who's with her."

Grace was looking. Her eyes held Francine's without expression. As Francine neared, her eyes shifted to the baby.

"It's Kyla," Francine said, "come to wish her Gram a happy birthday." She knelt before Grace with Kyla propped on her knee and put her mouth to the baby's sweet ear. "Gram is sixty-three today. And who's that with her?" She caught Jim's eye and whispered, "That's your Grampa."

He sent her a chiding look—they had agreed that the baby would call him Father Jim until she was old enough to understand—but his eyes twinkled when Francine teased. And she did it often. There was something about having two grandparents—like having two parents—something rich and full.

Grace's eyes stayed on the baby.

Francine moved her closer. No matter that Grace saw Kyla nearly every day, she didn't remember. "Isn't she a beauty, Mom? Kyla, say happy birthday to Gram. Can you do that? 'Happy Birthday, Gram'?"

"Puuuh," Kyla said.

"And there we go," Francine concluded with a smile.

"She's precious," Jim said. "Where's her daddy?"

"Meeting Sophie at the train." Sophie had moved into the city the month before and was living with friends.

Grace didn't know from missing her. Francine did, but

she knew that Sophie needed this time. She was having fun with her friends. She was dating. She was working as an editorial assistant to Katia Sloane. They talked on the phone daily, so she still knew every twist and turn *The Confidante* took, and she knew that there was a place for her if she wanted to return.

Francine looked forward to the day she might. In the meanwhile, she had Robin, and, between them, *The Confidante* was a cinch.

"Exciting news," she said with singsong appeal. Balancing Kyla with one arm, she reached for Grace with the other. "Just in time for your birthday. We're publishing again. Collections of your columns this time, so there's no writing involved. Just organizing what's already been written. Isn't that great?"

Grace kept looking at Kyla, who was curiously fingering her teeny-weeny mint green party tights.

"These will be books," Francine tried again, "in libraries. Katia has been desperate for something else since your biography did so well. What do you think?"

Grace didn't take her eyes off Kyla.

"Well, *I* say you should be very proud," Francine decided. "This is your work, printed up and saved for eternity. Isn't that the nicest birthday gift ever?"

Grace moved her hand in Kyla's direction, tentatively at first, then more surely. She touched the tiny head, stroked the silken hair, and in the smallest, sweetest voice said, "A baby? I love babies." Raising her gaze to Francine's, she smiled.

There it was. Grace's smile. Warm and brief, but filled with love and pleasure and, so very simply, approval. Grace's smile, to be remembered forever.

Photo by Robert Clark

BARBARA DELINSKY, a lifelong New Englander, was a sociologist and photographer before she began to write. There are more than 30 million copies of her books in print. Readers can contact her c/o P.O. Box 812894, Wellesley, MA 02482-0026, or via the Web at www.barbaradelinsky.com.

Barbara Delinsky